"YOU LOVE ME," HE MURMURED

Alexandre's warm breath sent shivers through her. "Say it."

Tess opened her mouth, but the only sound that escaped was a soft moan. Through the layers of her clothing, she could feel the heat of his hands burning her.

"Say it, Tess. Admit it. You love me."

This was madness, but she was powerless to stop it. She reached up and pulled at the ends of his silk cravat, untying the knot. Both of them sank to their knees. Their movements were frantic, as clothes were stripped away.

She cried out his name, her hands tangling in his hair, pulling him closer. The words he wanted tumbled out between her soft cries. "I love you, I love you. Yes, I love you!"

Prelude to Heaven

⚜ Laura Lee Guhrke ⚜

HarperPaperbacks
A Division of HarperCollinsPublishers

This is a work of fiction. The characters, incidents, and dialogues are products of the author's imagination and are not to be construed as real. Any resemblance to actual events or persons, living or dead, is entirely coincidental.

HarperPaperbacks *A Division of* HarperCollins*Publishers*
10 East 53rd Street, New York, N.Y. 10022

Copyright © 1994 by Laura Lee Guhrke
All rights reserved. No part of this book may be used or reproduced in any manner whatsoever without written permission of the publisher, except in the case of brief quotations embodied in critical articles and reviews. For information address HarperCollins*Publishers*,
10 East 53rd Street, New York, N.Y. 10022.

Cover illustration by Pino Daeni

First printing: January 1994

Printed in the United States of America

HarperPaperbacks, HarperMonogram, and colophon are trademarks of HarperCollins*Publishers*

❖ 10 9 8 7 6 5 4 3 2 1

*To Elizabeth Guhrke, a heroine in the
classic tradition, a woman of
courageous heart and generous spirit.
I love you, Grandma.*

SPECIAL ACKNOWLEDGMENTS

This book could not have been written without the help of some very talented people who generously gave their time to answer my perplexing—and sometimes bizarre—questions.

William Patrick and Steve Acree, who willingly showed me the basic moves of fencing and gave me the left-handed fencer's "killer move."

Leslie Giallombardo, for her help with French phrases.

Stephan Hunt, D.V.M., a wonderful veterinarian, who showed me the old-fashioned way to mend a goose's broken wing.

Julie Day, whose beautiful paintings are known to many art-loving Boiseans, and who gave me tips on painting the head and figure.

Melinda McRae, whose help with research of the Regency period was invaluable.

The Thursday Night Gals, just for being there.

My heartfelt thanks to all of you. Or, as Alexandre would put it, *merci beaucoup!*

Part I

1

June 1818

Alexandre Dumond cursed softly as his left hand moved the brush across the canvas. He knew the rain was coming, but he wanted to capture the fury of the waves crashing against the rocks before the deluge began.

He dipped the brush into a blob of steel-gray on his palette and continued to paint. His black gaze moved rapidly from canvas to sea to canvas as a crack of thunder echoed in the hills behind him. The wind tore away his ribbon, but Alexandre tossed back his flying black hair with an impatient shake of his head and kept painting. Storms of such violence were rare along the Provence coast this time of year. Now. He had to get it on canvas now, before it was lost forever.

He painted with a kind of frenzy, obsessed by the vision before him. The need to paint had been coming on for days. Filled with restless energy, he had tramped through the hills, walked along the coast, and prowled through the nearby forests, searching for what he envisioned on the edge of his mind, not knowing what it was but certain he would know when he saw it. Until this afternoon, everything he saw had left him dissatisfied. Suddenly, he had sensed the sharpness in the breeze, the change in the sound of the sea, the smell of a storm. And he had known what his mind had been searching for.

He frowned at the canvas. Something was wrong with the cliff that jutted out to meet the waves. The angle was wrong. He applied touches of black to the shadows, gradually altering the perspective. *Voilà!* It was coming, he was getting it. Just a few moments more.

Without warning, the rain began, pouring from the sky like the tears of a thousand angels, soaking his rumpled white shirt and paint-spattered trousers. But he paid no heed. He kept painting, knowing the rain would not hurt the oils. He only needed a little more time to capture the storm's essence on canvas; he could finish the painting in his studio.

Another powerful gust of wind erupted, tumbling both easel and canvas to the ground. *"Sacré tonnerre!"* he cried. Too late. He threw aside the brush and watched in helpless agony as the rain poured over the canvas, which now lay face down in the mud.

The painting was ruined. His agony faded, leaving him bereft and empty. It was over. The obsession would return, but for now it was gone, washed away with the rain.

Alexandre wrapped the ruined painting in a ragged cloth, gathered his brushes and supplies, folded his easel, and carried them slowly home through the pouring rain. These were the moments he dreaded, these quiet times after the passion to paint had spent itself, when he could not drown out the echoes of other passions lost.

He could not forget. That was the problem, he supposed, as he began the steep climb toward Château Dumond. Many times he had sworn he would leave this place, and had gotten as far as the road once. But he could never do it. Leaving here would be leaving Anne-Marie, and that Alexandre was not prepared to do.

As he reached the top of the cliff, he paused. Ahead of him, the path wound through the overgrown garden to the empty château, and he almost expected to see her by the gate, waiting for him. But she wasn't there.

Sometimes, he heard her voice, soft and filled with teasing laughter. Sometimes, he even answered her. Sometimes, he could swear she walked beside him.

Three years. Three years had passed since her death, and still he could not let her go. She was dead. That was his fault. He was alone. That was his punishment.

Alexandre kicked open the decrepit gate and walked toward the château, oblivious to the rain washing over him. Realizing he hadn't eaten all day, he paused in the garden. He set down his ruined painting and supplies, then pulled a fistful of tarragon from among the weeds.

He had no idea what he was going to flavor with it. Potato soup, perhaps. He could cook a chicken, if he felt like chasing down one of the damn things, but he decided it wasn't worth the effort. Soup would be easier, and he liked the sweet, fresh taste of new potatoes. He ventured a few steps further into the garden in search of thyme, when a low moan stopped him.

"Mon Dieu," he whispered and froze. Certain his mind was playing tricks on him, he tried not to listen.

The moan came again and with it the guilt. Still clutching the tarragon, he slammed his hands over his ears to stop the sounds. Moans of pain just before death. He had heard those moans in his dreams many times. Was he now hearing them when he was awake as well? He couldn't bear it.

After a moment, he dropped his hands and waited, but he heard nothing except the falling rain. Relieved, he took another step forward and bent down to pull some thyme from the weeds.

Then he saw the girl. She was lying on her side several feet away, unconscious and unmoving, with one cheek in the mud. He froze again, staring at the tiny, tired face of a stranger. He straightened and moved closer, then knelt down beside her.

She was wearing men's clothing. His gaze flew back to her face, then traveled down the length of her body. The clothes were a man's but, rain-soaked, they clung to her in all the curving feminine places. In one hand, she clutched a half-eaten potato. The other hand was spread protectively over her rounded stomach.

She was pregnant.

Memories swamped him, and he swallowed hard, trying to keep the past at bay. He wanted to run. But he couldn't. He wanted to scream at God to stop tormenting him. But he didn't. He reached for the girl's limp wrist.

Her pulse was weak but steady, her breathing shallow but even. She felt hot to his touch, even with the dampness in the air. Lines of pain and weariness were carved in her pale, heart-shaped face. He gently turned her onto her back, put one arm beneath her knees and one behind her head, then lifted her from the weeds and mud as she let out another soft moan.

Even pregnant and soaking wet, she couldn't weigh more than eight stone. He carried her through the courtyard, also overgrown with weeds, and into his crumbling château. He ascended the back stairs to the kitchen, crossed the empty hall, then carried her up another flight of stairs into his bedchamber.

He could feel the heat of her fever through her wet clothes, and he began to panic. Sick women always made him panic. He laid her on his disheveled, unmade bed and desperately began to strip away clothing. Piece by piece, the sodden clothes were removed and tossed aside onto the dusty floor. A cursory glance confirmed that she was very thin and definitely pregnant.

He found a goose-down quilt somewhere amid Anne-Marie's stored-away wedding linens and an old nightshirt he never wore. He pulled the nightshirt over her shivering body. Then, after shaking out the quilt to remove the dust, he tucked its thick folds around her. Helpless to do more, he stared down at her unconscious form, so small in the huge bed, wondering who she was and what the hell he was going to do with her.

Her head moved restlessly on the pillow, and she cried out in her sleep. It was the frightened cry of a child.

He reached forward to brush back a short, wet curl that had fallen over her eyes. *"Pauvre petite,"* he murmured, running one finger down her hollow cheek, then let his hand drop. Abruptly, he turned and left the room.

The face of an angel hovered above her. A handsome, golden-haired angel, holding out his hand, offering marriage, taking her to heaven. But the hand always moved so quickly; in the wink of an eye, a tender touch became a vicious slap.

Her head rocked sideways from the force of the blow. The baby. She had to protect the baby. She sank to the floor, curling into a tight ball. She felt the kick in her kidneys, and her body twitched convulsively, but she did not cry out. She curled herself tighter, tighter, squeezing her eyes shut to stop the tears. But she could not stop the sounds of taunting rage above her.

The second kick in her kidneys forced a cry of pain from her lips. She knew she should say something, try to stop him. Tell him about the baby, her mind screamed. But she knew that wouldn't stop him. When he was in one of his rages, nothing would stop him.

The third kick was too much. She uncurled her body and began to squirm away, crawling across the polished parquet floor on her belly. She felt his hands seize her, hold her down, and she knew there was no escape from a nightmare where angels were really devils and heaven was only hell in disguise.

Alexandre watched her crawl across the bed in her delirium and managed to catch her before she fell off, pulling her away from the edge and turning her onto her back. Her arms flailed wildly, and her fist slammed against his cheek before he caught her wrists in his hands. He wrestled with her until she finally quieted, overcome by exhaustion.

He let go of her and turned away to dip a rag in a pail of cool water. Wringing it out, he placed the rag across her hot forehead, then sat down in the chair beside the bed. She immediately pulled the cloth from her face and threw it across the room. He didn't bother to retrieve it.

Through the night, he watched her. She shivered, rolled, and tossed in the bed. She cried out, tiny, terrified cries. Sometimes she spoke. He understood her mumbled English words, but the sentences had no meaning. Every time she threw aside the covers, he pulled them back over her. Several times during the night he tried to get her to drink some water, but she always pushed his hands away. Toward dawn, he finally drifted off to sleep to the distressed sounds of her unknown demons.

She couldn't escape him. She felt the shattering pain of another blow, and she screamed for help, but it was useless. The servants would never intervene. There was no one to help her, no one to defend her.

She saw Lucifer in his angel-blue eyes, and she knew that this time he was going to kill her. He would kill the baby, too.

The baby. She couldn't let him kill the baby. She

clawed, she kicked, she fought, but he was so strong. Her fists were such puny weapons. She managed to raise her knee between his legs, and when he doubled over in pain, releasing her, she saw her chance to run.

But there was nowhere to go. She saw him struggling to rise, and she darted past him. The gun. She had to get the gun.

She knew where it was. She could only pray that it was loaded. Yanking open the drawer of his dressing table, she grabbed the pearl-handled pistol and whirled around to find him standing in the doorway, watching her.

He looked so surprised. She lifted her chin, returning his astonishment with defiance.

His expression changed, softened. The devil was gone, and the angel was back. But she was not fooled. She raised her arm, cocked the pistol, and fired.

Something woke him. He sat up abruptly, wincing at the pain that shot through his neck. Chairs were not made for sleeping. The rain had stopped and bright morning sunlight flooded the room, causing him to blink.

He looked at the girl, watching as she raised one trembling arm toward the ceiling and listening as she began to whimper with fear. Suddenly, her arm fell limp to her side, and she quieted.

She was shivering violently now. He noticed that the covers had once again been tossed aside and now lay in a tangled heap at the foot of the bed. "Imbecile," he muttered—uncertain if the criticism was directed at her or himself—and rose. He pulled the covers over her and felt her forehead. She was still feverish.

He rubbed a hand over his stubbled jaw, wondering if perhaps he should fetch someone from the village, but he immediately discarded that idea. There was no doctor in Saint-Raphael. Only a midwife, and he doubted she would come with him in any case. No one else would come either. Most of the villagers thought him very odd. Many were afraid of him. Besides, it was a long walk down to the village, and he didn't want to leave her.

She stirred, rolling her head restlessly from side to side. Her short auburn hair was stringy and damp with sweat. Her face was ashen gray, and her skin felt like parchment to his touch. Her lips were dry and cracked. Though she was now sleeping quietly, her expression was far from serene. There were shadows of fear and lines of strain in her face. Alexandre didn't know when he had ever seen anything so vulnerable. He found himself staring down at her, wondering what journey had led this young, pregnant girl to his door, to collapse in his garden. Who was she?

He closed his eyes and turned impatiently away. He didn't want to know anything about her. He didn't want to care what happened to her. He wasn't fit to care about anybody. He couldn't even care about himself. But when he carried her muddy clothes downstairs to wash them in the kitchen, he found himself examining them closely for clues to her identity.

They were the clothes of an *aristo*, well-made and of fine materials, though they were now tattered and stained. There was no tailor's label on any of the garments, but they were of English style and workmanship. The boots of black leather had straw stuffed in the toes. The contents of her pockets revealed five francs, a soiled linen handkerchief, and a pistol.

It was sensible, he supposed, for a woman traveling alone to carry a pistol. He examined it curiously. It was expensive, pearl-handled, and empty. He put it in a drawer with the money and handkerchief.

He washed the mud from her clothes and hung them in the sun to dry. He walked out into the garden but could find nothing more that belonged to her. He brought in the supplies he had left among the weeds the evening before, throwing his ruined creation into a corner of the kitchen with a snort of disgust, then he went back into the garden with a basket to rummage among the weeds for herbs and vegetables.

He returned to the kitchen and started a pot of soup. He took a handful of leeks from the basket and reached for a knife. She was pregnant, but wore no wedding band. A young servant girl, perhaps, who had made a mistake and had run away, unable to face the shame. She had probably stolen the clothes and the pistol from her master, thinking they would give her some protection traveling on the road alone. He felt a stab of pity and wondered again why he should care.

He began slicing vegetables with a vengeance. He *didn't* care. He dumped potatoes, leeks, carrots, and herbs in a pot of water, concentrating on indifference. She would probably die, he told himself, adding garlic to the pot, and he refused to take responsibility for her death. He already had more than his share of that.

When the soup was bubbling over the fire, he went back upstairs, but she was still sleeping quietly. He took that opportunity to fetch water for a bath and a shave. Then he changed into a clean shirt and trousers and tied back his newly washed hair with a fresh ribbon. When the soup was ready, he took it to her. She was tossing again, slapping her hands in the air at imagined adversaries and crying out. He tried to spoon-feed her, but she refused to eat. He doubted she even knew he was there.

Wherever she ran, he followed. Everywhere she turned, he was there. Again and again she shot him, she saw him fall, she watched his blood spill across the floor. Still, he followed her. Hadn't she known she could never be free of him?

She felt his hands again, on her face, opening her mouth.
Forcing liquid down her throat. She spit it out, certain he
was trying to poison her. She pushed the hands away.

Alexandre stared down at the soup all over his shirt and
sighed. He dipped the spoon into the bowl and tried again.
Three times, she spit out the soup and pushed him away.
The first time, he was patient. The second time, he was frustrated. The third time, he was angry. *"Mille tonnerres!"* he
exploded, grasping her chin between his fingers and turning
her face toward him. "Do you want to starve to death?"

She stared at him with glassy, unseeing eyes. She
opened her mouth as if to answer, and he shoved in the
spoonful of soup. He forcibly closed her mouth with his
hands until she swallowed, ignoring the weak fists that
pounded him. But she didn't have the strength to fight.
Within moments, her clenched fists dropped wearily to
her sides. Between her delirious protests and pleadings,
he fed her spoonfuls of soup until the bowl was empty.

For three days, Alexandre poured soup and water
down her throat, bathed her sweat-soaked body with
lavender-water, and washed more sheets than he ever
had in his life. But she only seemed to worsen.

Her fever was higher than ever, and she was still delirious, muttering nonsense about angels in hell. Sometimes,
she would dream violent dreams, striking out at the air with
her fists. Other times, she would cower under the covers,
whimpering, but he had no idea what frightened her so.

He was afraid she would miscarry the babe. He was
certain she would die. He tried to resign himself to her
death, to accept the idea that he would be the one to
bury her. But each time he envisioned that possibility, he
shook it off and redoubled his efforts to save her. *Le bon*
Dieu had given him one more chance for redemption. By
saving her, he might save himself.

2

Tess opened her eyes to find herself in a strange room. She blinked rapidly as her eyes adjusted to the sunlight washing over her. Her head ached, and her body felt battered and weary. She moved one hand to her rounded stomach, reassuring herself that the baby was all right, as her gaze traveled slowly around the room. Where was she?

She took in the unfamiliar furnishings and white-washed walls, coming finally to the window on her left. A man stood there, looking out the window, his profile to her. He was drawing in a sketchbook that rested in the crook of his right arm. His shirt of white linen was torn and smeared with paint, and his dark trousers were tucked into black boots badly in need of polishing. His thick, ebony hair was unfashionably long and caught back in a queue.

Startled by the sight of him, she sat straight up in the bed, letting out a gasp at the sharp pain in her head.

The man turned around. Tess realized she was clad in only a nightshirt. A *man's* nightshirt. She couldn't remember changing her clothes. She felt her face flush as she frantically pulled the sheets up to her neck, wondering what had happened to her clothes. The man didn't seem to notice her discomfiture. He merely raised one black eyebrow at the sight of her awake and watching him. "*Bonjour*, mademoiselle."

Tess didn't reply. She scooted back against the pillows, clutching the sheets and feeling waves of panic within her. It took a moment for his words to sink in, then she glanced down at her ringless hand. Was he insulting her by calling her mademoiselle, when she was obviously pregnant? But there was no hint of mockery in his face or his voice. "Who are you?" she whispered in English.

"I am Alexandre Dumond," he answered her in the same language. "And you?"

Dumond? The name was familiar. She glanced at the sketchbook in his hand and the paint all over his shirt. Could he be Dumond, the French painter? Dumond's works were well known, even in London. "The artist?"

He gave her a small bow. "*Précisément.*"

She stared at him, vague recollections of whispered London gossip coming to mind. Dumond had once received an invitation from the Prince Regent to submit his works to the Royal Academy and had actually refused. It was rumored that he lived alone, an eccentric recluse hiding from the world at his villa in France.

His deep voice interrupted Tess's meandering thoughts. "How do you feel?"

She tightened her grip on the sheets defensively and did not answer but continued to stare at him, suspicious and wary. She watched him drop the sketchbook and charcoal on the table beside him, then stride toward her. He was a tall man and powerfully built. She pressed her back to the carved headboard behind her, willing herself not to show the fear she felt at his approach.

But when he stopped beside the bed and reached out with one hand to touch her, Tess could not prevent her cry of panic as she frantically slapped his hand away. "Don't touch me!"

A puzzled frown drew his dark brows together, and he sat down on the edge of the bed, ignoring her protests. He reached out again, catching her wrist in one hand before she could strike out at him again. His other hand reached toward her. Tess tried desperately to pull away, hating the strength, hating the feel of a man's hands. But all he did was gently press his palm to her forehead. His callused hand felt cool against her skin.

"The fever has broken," he said, letting his hand drop and releasing her wrist. "I'm relieved."

Tess fell back, exhausted from her brief struggle. She licked her dry lips nervously, wishing her head didn't ache and she could think clearly, wishing he would move away from her side. "Where am I? How did I get here?"

"I carried you, of course. You were in no condition to walk, mademoiselle. I found you in my garden."

"I didn't mean to trespass," she mumbled. "I didn't think anyone lived here."

His lips tightened slightly. "That is understandable, I suppose."

"How long have I been here?"

"Four days."

"Four?" Tess drew a deep breath. "I don't remember anything beyond being in the garden. I dreamed—" She stopped. She didn't want to remember her dreams.

"You have caused me a great deal of worry, mademoiselle. You have had a fever I feared was mortal. You were delirious."

She stiffened. "What did I say?"

"Nothing that made sense."

She watched him turn to the table beside the bed and ladle water from a pail into a cup. Then he held the cup out to her. When she didn't move to take it from him, he pressed it to her lips. "Drink it," he ordered.

Her whole body tensed, and she closed her eyes. The memory was there before she could stop it. Nigel, yanking her hair back and pressing a glass of hated port against her lips. "Drink it, Countess. Drink it. I know you love a glass of port." She could still feel the sticky red liquid running down her chin, mixing with tears, staining her dress.

"Drink the water, *chérie*," a husky voice murmured, snapping her back to the present. Her eyes flew open, and she found herself staring into eyes of intense black, not blue. Not Nigel. She swallowed as the stranger tilted the water into her mouth.

He set the half-empty cup aside and rose. "Are you hungry? I'll bring you some soup."

Tess did not relax her tense muscles until Alexandre Dumond had left the room. She rested her aching head against the headboard and clenched her hands into fists to stop the shaking. Nigel was dead, she told herself. He could never hurt her again. But she had killed him, and she was still afraid. So afraid.

She'd had three months to come to terms with what she had done. She had killed a man, the man she had once loved. She knew she should feel guilt and shame, but she didn't. Those feelings had passed. All she felt now was fear. And the need to survive.

When Alexandre brought the soup, he sat down on the edge of the bed and spooned the broth into her mouth as if she were a child. Tess didn't flinch or move away, even though she felt suffocated by his closeness, and she could hear her heart pounding in her breast. She kept her gaze fixed on his hand as it held the spoon and moved toward her, then away. Though it was quite a different hand, she half expected the sudden movement, the touch, the slap, and she waited, watching for it. But he continued his task slowly and methodically, never touching her at all, and soon Tess began to relax, weariness and hunger overcoming fear. When he had given her the last spoonful in the bowl, she dared to look at his face.

He was studying her, and when she met his thoughtful gaze, she studied him in return. His eyes were truly black, so black the pupils disappeared, and surrounded by thick, sooty lashes. His face was lean and brown, with tiny creases carved from the sun and time and something more. There were stories written on that face, hidden in those eyes. Tess found herself unable to look away.

Abruptly he stood up and the spell was broken. He retrieved his sketchbook from the table by the window and walked to the door. He paused in the doorway, glancing over his shoulder at her, and said in a quiet voice, "Sleep now, *mon enfant.*" Then he left the room, closing the door behind him.

She did sleep, deep and dreamless, waking only briefly to take more soup or water, then drifting off again. But when she woke to the sound of a cock crow two mornings later, she felt no sharp pain of headache and no sickening rush of dizziness as she sat up in the bed.

She glanced down at the round swell of her abdomen under the sheets and gently rubbed it with her hand. She wished the baby would turn or kick, but she felt no flutters of movement. She hoped her illness had done the child no harm.

To prevent herself from dwelling on that possibility, Tess reached for the ladle and poured herself a cup of water. Her mouth felt as if it were full of cotton. When she ran a hand through her hair, it felt sticky. She grimaced, knowing she must look as disheveled as she felt.

She wondered about her mysterious host. She had seen no one but him, and she wondered if anyone else even lived in this house.

She glanced down at the nightshirt she wore. If he did indeed live alone, then it must have been he who had—

The door opened and Alexandre entered the room, carrying a bowl and spoon. "*Bonjour,* mademoiselle. You appear to be feeling better."

This man must have seen her without her clothes. Mortified, Tess blushed to the roots of her hair and pulled the nightshirt together at her throat. She knew what artists were like. And he was French. She lowered her gaze to the bed covers, wishing she could hide beneath them.

But Alexandre didn't seem to notice her embarrassment. He came to her side and sat on the edge of the bed. Tess could not bring herself to meet his eyes. She kept her gaze fixed on the tiny, embroidered blue stitches of the white quilt.

"How are you feeling?" he asked.

She could not—*could not*—look at him. "Much better, thank you." She tightened her grip on the nightshirt.

As if he read her mind, Alexandre said in a quiet voice, "You were soaking wet, mademoiselle, and very ill." He thrust the bowl at her. "Eat."

He left without another word.

She had finished eating by the time he returned. He carried a washbasin in one hand. Draped over his arm were towels, a dress and several undergarments. In his other hand was a pair of women's shoes. He set the basin on the table by the window, then laid the clothes and towels at the foot of the bed. As he left the room, he looked over his shoulder at her and said, "Your clothes are in tatters and not fit to wear." As he looked at her, a small smile touched the corners of his mouth. "These will perhaps fit you better, *n'est-ce pas?* But, should you wish for your old clothes when you continue your journey, I have washed them for you."

Tess watched the door close behind him. Continue her journey? He sounded as if he wanted her to leave. *Perhaps I should go now,* she thought, panic overwhelming her again at the thought of being in this house, a man's house.

Yet, when she thought of leaving, she remembered the harrowing and exhausting days she'd spent crossing France on foot. During her three months of traveling, she'd slept in clean inns, then in dirty inns, and finally, when she'd run out of money, ditches. She'd accepted rides in wagons until one farmer discovered that she wasn't a man and tried to rape her. From then on, she had walked, walked until her feet blistered, and she couldn't take another step. She'd bought food when she could afford it, then stolen it when she couldn't. Now, she was at the southern coast with no money for passage to anywhere. Continue her journey? Where could she go?

Tess knew the answer was nowhere. She rose to examine the clothes he had brought her. They were fine, the clothes of a wealthy woman, but several years out of fashion. Though clean, they smelled musty, with a faint tinge of lemon verbena. She wondered who they belonged to.

She used the water in the basin, bathing as well as she could, then pulled on the linen chemise, petticoat, and silk stockings. The high-waisted dress of blue muslin accommodated her pregnancy easily but was much too long. Not for the first time, Tess wished she were taller. She knew she would have to be careful not to trip.

Her bedchamber was large, with walls of white-washed stone and carved oak furnishings. Hand-knotted wool rugs on the wooden floor provided bright spots of color. There were two doors leading out of the room.

One led into a corridor. The other, she quickly discovered, opened into a much smaller room, a wardrobe of some kind. It was empty, save for a few white shirts and black trousers hanging on hooks. This was apparently Monsieur Dumond's room.

Closing the door, she rested her hand on her rounded stomach and sighed. What was she going to do now? She had run as far as she could. She was five months into her pregnancy. For the baby's sake, she could not run anymore. She just hoped that she had run far enough to hide from the authorities.

She thought again of Alexandre Dumond. But she didn't trust any man, even one who seemed to be kind. Even if she trusted him, would he let her stay here until her baby came? He had taken her in and cared for her, but now that she was well again, would he toss her out? Would he expect some kind of payment to let her stay? Or worse, was he a man like Nigel? She shuddered, remembering how she had once thought Nigel to be kind.

Suddenly, without warning, the baby moved. It was only a tiny flutter, but it eased her worries somewhat. She patted her belly with her hand, knowing that it didn't matter if Monsieur Dumond were kind. As long as he didn't beat her, she knew there was no other choice but to remain here, if he would let her. She wrapped her arms around herself protectively. "I won't let anything happen to you, my baby," she said with fierce determination. "I swear it. I'll think of something."

She grasped a fold of muslin in her hand and wondered what woman had worn this dress. She thought of Monsieur Dumond's unkept garden, crumbling castle, and torn clothes. She wondered why he seemed to have no servants. She thought of the rumors surrounding him and wondered what secrets hid behind those enigmatic dark eyes.

Suddenly, she had an idea.

*   *   *

Alexandre leaned his back against the stone wall of the courtyard and stared at the weeds flourishing between the paving stones. In his mind's eye was a picture of violet eyes and a blue muslin dress and lavender in bloom. He closed his eyes and fought back, struggling until the image disappeared.

It was the dress. He should have given all her clothes away. But he had not been able to give away any of Anne-Marie's things. Her dresses still hung in the armoire of her bedchamber, her undergarments still lay in a careless jumble in her chest of drawers, her jewel case still sat on the bedside table covered with dust. It had been three years since Alexandre had been in her bedchamber, three years since she had died there. After the funeral, he had stepped out of that room and locked the door, never opening it again. Until today.

"Monsieur Dumond?"

Alexandre opened his eyes. There was the dress again, on the wrong woman. He straightened away from the wall, coming out of his reverie with difficulty, trying not to look at her. "You should be resting, mademoiselle," he said, fixing his eyes on the scraggly lavender bushes.

"Tess."

"Pardon?" He looked at her then. The dress hung on her thin frame, except around her swollen abdomen, and the hem swept the ground. There was a bit of color in her cheeks, though, and her eyes, dark green and huge, were clear as they met his.

"My name is Tess."

"Tess?" he repeated, waiting for more.

But she gave him no last name. She turned away and looked about her. "Your gardener should be dismissed." Over her shoulder, she cast him an inquiring glance.

She was probing for information that he had no intention of providing. "I will make a note of it."

She sighed and straightened her shoulders. Then she turned around again. "Monsieur, thank you for your help. I am grateful. Truly, I don't know what I would have done if you had not found me."

He shrugged but did not answer.

She went on, "I realize you know nothing about me. I am not—" She stopped, then started again. "I am, as you can see, in trouble."

If she hoped for chivalry, she was disappointed. He merely continued to watch her.

She said, "I'm concerned about my child. I don't know what to do."

"I would think the solution to your problem would be obvious, mademoiselle. Go home."

Her face went pale, and he caught a fleeting glimpse of the fear that had been so evident during her illness. She shook her head. "I can't."

"Why not?"

"I have no home," she answered in a low voice, ducking her head to hide her expression.

So that was the way of it? He had guessed as much. A harsh father who had thrown her out of the house, a dishonorable lover who had refused to marry her, and a family scandal. "What will you do, then?"

She met his gaze and took a deep breath. Instead of answering, she asked, "You live alone here, monsieur? No family? No servants?"

He stiffened and his eyes narrowed. He said nothing.

Tess continued, "I would be very grateful if you would allow me to stay here. I could keep house and—"

"No." The word was flat, unemotional, and final.

"I know how to run a household, monsieur."

"Perhaps," he acknowledged with a slight nod, "but I need no one to run my *household*." The last word was said in a mocking voice as he gestured to the overgrown courtyard. "I prefer it as it is."

The decision was made. She could see it in his eyes. Nonetheless, she persisted. "I could cook for you."

"I can cook for myself."

"Perhaps I could tend your garden?"

He glanced down pointedly at her swollen abdomen. "Not for long."

Heat stained her cheeks, but Tess didn't give up. "Well, I could mend your clothes, then." She gestured toward his torn shirt. "That's something you obviously can't do for yourself. And I can clean and keep house for you. I beg your pardon if this sounds rude, but you seem to need a housekeeper. And I need a place to stay."

He folded his arms across his chest and met her eyes. "You do not seem to understand, mademoiselle. I don't want you here."

Tess's whole body tensed at his words, and she felt a sickening knot of fear in the pit of her stomach. She made one last desperate attempt. "I won't cause you any trouble. Please, monsieur, please let me stay."

He stared at her long and hard. His shadowed eyes gave nothing away. When he spoke, his voice was harsh. "Why should I?"

"Because," she whispered, "I have nowhere else to go."

3

Martin Trevalyn drummed his nervous fingers against the leather case beside him and stared out the carriage window, oblivious to the rain-washed Sussex countryside. He wished there had been some way to postpone this meeting, but the earl had been adamant. And Martin knew better than anyone that Nigel Ridgeway was not a man to be gainsaid.

Martin was solicitor to the Earl of Aubry, handling the private legal affairs of the Ridgeway family, as had his father and grandfather before him. The private legal affair of the moment was one requiring both discretion and finesse, and Martin had both. He wished, however, that he had more time. But he sensed Lord Aubry was running out of patience.

The carriage turned down the tree-lined lane leading to Aubry Park. Martin removed his gold-framed spectacles and polished them with a linen handkerchief. Resting them once more on his broad nose, he pulled out his watch and was relieved to note that he would not be late. The earl was obsessed with punctuality. Martin put his watch back in his waistcoat pocket and pulled the leather case onto his lap. His fingers continued their agitated rat-a-tat as the carriage turned again, pulling into the drive.

Martin had been to Aubry Park, the earl's country estate, many times. But, as always, he paused a moment to admire its symmetrical beauty. Aubry Park was always stylish and elegant, with its long windows, marble columns, and classical sculpture. But now, in early summer, with the roses in bloom and the wide lawns lush and green, it was splendid indeed.

Martin gripped the handle of his leather case in one hand and alighted from the carriage. He ascended the wide flagstone steps, where he presented his card to the properly expressionless butler and was shown into Lord Aubry's immense library.

He studied the long wall of leather volumes with a wistful smile. A lover of books, Martin knew that the Earl of Aubry was not. Traditionally, the Ridgeway men had always hunted, drank, and gambled, sometimes to excess, and would no more have opened a book by the fireside than Martin would have gone fishing. Lord Aubry was no exception. Martin knew all the books had been acquired simply to furnish a "gentleman's library," and he doubted they had ever been opened.

He spared only the most cursory glance for the priceless paintings and artifacts, the exquisite rosewood tables, and the elegant carpets and draperies, but cast a covetous eye over the books as he crossed the long room to the massive desk and sat down in one of the brown leather chairs opposite it. He placed his leather case on the floor beside his chair and waited, knowing with a growing sense of dread that he would not wait long.

Within moments, the library doors opened. Martin rose, turning to watch the tall and lean Earl of Aubry stride toward him. Even Martin, whose knowledge of

society gossip was sadly lacking, knew that Nigel Ridgeway was purported to be one of the handsomest men in
England. Even he had heard that women were known to
swoon at one smile from Nigel Ridgeway's lips and that
his wife was the object of both admiration and envy by
every woman in the *ton*.

Martin watched the earl draw closer, and he continued to view the other man surreptitiously behind his
spectacles. The earl was, indeed, a magnificent-looking
man, with his waving golden hair, handsome chiseled
face, and strong lean body. Martin glanced down at his
own portly shape and gave an inaudible sigh, thinking of
his thinning hair and double chin. The most amazing
thing was that he felt no envy toward the other man. He
sensed a dangerous side to the earl, a subtle cruelty, and
knew he would not trade places with Lord Aubry, even
had he the power to do so. He felt a sudden twinge of
pity for Lady Aubry.

"Well?"

The voice of the earl slashed into his thoughts, and
Martin gave a start. Aubry was seated. Martin quickly
followed suit, settling himself in the chair again and
reaching for his case.

"Have you found her?"

Martin once again felt a tremor of nervousness run
through his body and tried to keep his hands from trembling as he opened his case and removed a sheaf of
papers. He began his carefully rehearsed reply. "These
things take time, Lord Aubry. It is very difficult—"

"You haven't found her," the earl concluded for him.
He leaned forward, placing clasped hands on the pol-
ished desk top. "Did I not make my wishes clear to you,
Trevalyn, three months ago?"

The question was voiced in a quiet, even tone, but
Martin felt his insides twist with apprehension. He
rushed into speech. "We have made progress, sir. Bow

Street runners have discovered that Lady Aubry pawned the emeralds at a jeweler on Bond Street. The jeweler identified her miniature and described the clothes she was wearing as those taken from your wardrobe. He thought, of course, that she was a lad."

"The fool," Aubry muttered. He looked up and gave the solicitor a piercing stare. "I trust the family emeralds were recovered?"

Martin removed the necklace and earrings from the case and placed them carefully on the desk, relieved that he had accomplished at least one of Lord Aubry's orders. "Yes, sir."

"I take it," the earl continued, "that the jeweler is now doing something more suited to his capabilities. Cleaning stables, perhaps?"

"Something like that," Martin answered, meeting the earl's eyes with difficulty. He had done what he'd known the earl would want him to do, but it had left a bad taste in his mouth.

"Surely you have more to tell me, Trevalyn?"

"Yes, sir." Martin turned a page on his lap and gave it a quick glance, then went on, "We have ascertained that a 'young man' answering to the description of Lady Aubry boarded the night ferry from Dover across the channel, on the evening of March 17, and landed at Calais the following morning."

"She's in France?" The earl made no movement, but Martin saw the anger and frustration seething beneath the surface. "Where?"

The solicitor coughed nervously. "We don't know that yet, sir. As I said, these things take time."

"How much more time will you need?" The earl's voice clearly conveyed his impatience and irritation. "You've had three months already."

"Yes, sir. But we had been working under the assumption that Lady Aubry was somewhere in England."

"The Season is nearly over. Speculation about my

wife's absence has been bandied about for weeks. To avoid further gossip, I was forced to cancel the remainder of my time in London." The earl's cold voice told Martin he was not at all pleased by the talk. "I want her found, Trevalyn."

"We are making every effort. I will be journeying to France shortly to continue the search. There are not many places for a woman traveling alone to hide, even if she is dressed as a man."

The earl nodded and rose to his feet, indicating that the interview was at an end. "Find her, Trevalyn. I can't pretend she is ill and staying with my mother in Northumberland forever. As I've told you before, I don't care what it costs. As long as you are discreet, I don't care how many men you have to hire or bribe. Find her. Your family has served mine well for many years. I would hate for that tradition to be broken."

Martin swallowed the lump of dread in his throat and closed his case. Rising to his feet, he turned and left. As the carriage rolled down the road toward London, Martin Trevalyn knew that if he did not find Lady Aubry soon, he'd be the one cleaning out stables.

Nigel paced across the Persian carpet of the library after the solicitor had gone, his anger growing with every step. He reached up to touch the scar that slashed across his temple, the one everyone thought he'd gotten in a riding accident. His physician knew a bullet wound when he saw one, but only Nigel and his valet knew how it had happened.

His eyes scanned the family portraits that hung above the recessed shelves of books. Scandal! No breath of scandal had ever touched the Ridgeway family. Nigel met the painted eyes of his father and vowed it never would. His explanations to the curious members of the *ton* were wearing thin. It was only because everyone was in Town for the Season that no one had yet discovered his wife was not in Northumberland. If he didn't find her soon, people might begin to suspect that she had actually left him.

His gaze moved from the portrait of his father to the pair of rapiers that hung above the fireplace, their points crossed over his family coat of arms. His ancestors had defended their honor with weapons of steel, but how could he fight the scandalous rumors of the *ton*? Wagging tongues could not be silenced at the point of a sword.

Nigel scowled. He would find Teresa, and when he did, he'd make sure that beautiful, conniving bitch never put his reputation at risk again.

He thought of Trevalyn blinking behind his gold-framed spectacles like a sleepy frog. "These things take time, Lord Aubry," he mocked the fat solicitor's tiny voice. How long could it take to find one stupid girl?

His gaze moved on to the portrait of his wife, which hung on the opposite side of the fireplace. He stared into her huge green eyes, studied her finely molded features, and the rage simmering beneath his surface calm erupted with sudden force. He seized the poker beside the fireplace and laid a vicious gash across his wife's heart, then another, then another. But the poker never touched her face. Not her beautiful face.

Alexandre walked with long, impatient strides along the beach, his thoughts tumbling over themselves ceaselessly, like the waves against the rocks. He had told her no, and he wasn't going to change his mind. That was the end of it. As soon as she was well enough to travel, he'd give her some money and send her on her way.

But her whispered words came back to him, floating on the sea breeze. *I have nowhere else to go.*

He stopped walking and sat down, resting his forearms on his bent knees. He stared at the sea, thinking of her. He thought of the way her hands rested protectively on her roundness, the way her eyes pleaded for understanding and help. She needed him.

He didn't want to be needed. Frustrated, he picked up a pebble and threw it into the sea. He didn't want the responsibility. He didn't want painful reminders of the past.

No, he would send her to the village. He'd find someone who would take her in. Some peasant family who had eight children and needed the money. Why should he be the one responsible for her?

Besides, a peasant woman with a brood of children would know how to care for a pregnant girl.

He lowered his head to rest in his hands. He certainly didn't know anything about that. He thought of Anne-Marie. He thought of her pain. Her death. His fault.

He couldn't take care of the girl. No, he would send her on her way. She had made the choice to run away from home. It was not his problem.

I have nowhere else to go.

Alexandre rose to his feet. He wasn't out here to contemplate the girl's future. He had to get food and painting supplies from the village. The girl could solve her own problems. He wasn't her father or her brother or her lover. He wasn't responsible for her. He didn't even know her.

Her voice echoed in his mind again and he cursed God for doing this to him. He cursed the girl for depending on him. He cursed Anne-Marie's memory for haunting him. But, most of all, he cursed himself for being alive when those he had loved were dead.

*   *   *

Tess wandered into another unused room of the castle. This was the dining room. As in all the other rooms, the furnishings were covered with dust, and cobwebs hung in the corners. She ran her finger over the heavy walnut dining table and idly stared at the grime on her finger, wondering how such a beautiful home could be allowed to fall into disrepair. Although built during the Middle Ages, it had been modified over the centuries and many amenities had been added. The furnishings spoke of wealth and excellent taste. The gardens and grounds had once been lovely. So why was everything in this shameful condition?

Perhaps Monsieur Dumond's family had lost their money during the upheaval of the Revolution. Perhaps painting didn't earn him much blunt. Perhaps he was poor and could not afford to maintain his home. That would explain many things, but nothing could explain the beautiful dress she wore that was several years out of fashion.

She tried to keep her mind on Monsieur Dumond, tried not to dwell on her own future, but soon her mind turned inevitably to her own problems. Monsieur Dumond had told her that she couldn't stay here, but she hadn't given up hope. She had to keep that. Hope was all she had.

She tried to reassure herself. He wouldn't just turn her out, would he? If he were the kind of man who would do that, he would never have taken her in to begin with. But what kind of man lived in a huge castle all alone? What kind of man shut himself off from the world and lived as a recluse?

Although puzzled as to why he lived this way, and concerned for her own safety, she was grateful for the isolation. If he let her stay here, no one was likely to find her. Ignorant of the law, Tess wasn't exactly sure whether the English authorities would follow her to France, but if they did, she was sure they would take her back to England to stand trial. She had no idea what the penalty was for killing your husband, but she knew her story of how it had happened would never be believed. No one in England, man or woman, would ever believe Nigel Ridgeway capable of beating his wife so severely that she shot him in self-defense. Besides, Tess reflected bitterly, it was perfectly acceptable and legal for a man to beat his wife. He only had to use a rod no thicker than his thumb.

And no one knew. Everyone in the *ton* believed that Lord and Lady Aubry had an idyllic marriage. If Lady Aubry was often "indisposed," well, there was nothing so extraordinary about that. The servants knew, of course, but they would never tell the truth. If they did, they would never find employment again because no one wanted servants who told family secrets. If the authorities were able to find her and take her back, she knew she would be accused of murder. She doubted her pregnancy would gain her any sympathy.

If she stayed here, what would happen? Would Monsieur Dumond expect her to become his mistress in exchange for a roof over her head? Would he humiliate her? Beat her?

Yet, if she left, what would become of her? She thought again of wandering alone on the roads. She thought of the very real possibility that she would have her baby in a ditch at the roadside.

Tess left the dining room, still pondering her problem. No, for the baby's sake, she had to find a way to convince Alexandre Dumond to let her stay with him, at least until her baby was born.

Her hope and her optimism began to return. He wasn't like Nigel, she told herself. No other man could be that cruel.

*   *   *

Alexandre sat in the tavern and drank his wine. The other tables were crowded, but his was not. He drank alone and did not speak to anyone. No one spoke to him. But the stares and low murmurs of disapproval made it clear he was not welcome.

Everyone in the village knew about Anne-Marie, of course. Some, he knew, pitied him, refusing to believe the worst. Others feared him, certain of his sin. Still others knew that he simply wanted to be left alone, and they respected his wishes.

Lise, the barmaid, paused at his table. She did not fall into any of the other categories. She wanted him. Some women, for reasons he could not fathom, found an aura of danger irresistible. She leaned forward to refill his glass, giving him a plain view of what she could offer him. His gaze traveled slowly from the outline of her breasts beneath the white muslin, past the lips that parted seductively, to the brown eyes watching him with more than passing interest. He shook his head slowly.

Her lips pouted and she reached out a hand to stroke his arm. He waited for the stirrings of desire. There were none. Gently, he grasped her wrist and removed her hand from his arm.

"Lise!" The sharp cry of the girl's stout *maman* rang out from the doorway of the kitchen.

With an indignant flick of her skirt, Lise moved away. "Celibate as a monk," she muttered.

At the next table, a man grabbed her skirt and gave it a playful tug. "I'm not," he told her, laughing.

She pushed his hand away. "Oh, leave me be, Gaspard," she snapped, slamming a bottle of wine in front of him and striding away toward the kitchen, her long black hair swinging behind her. Her mother followed, scolding the girl for even speaking to Alexandre. Her mother's disapproval of him, he concluded cynically, was probably part of his appeal.

He watched her go. He hadn't had a woman in a very long time, and Lise was a pretty girl. She could be his for the taking any time she could escape her mother's careful supervision. But she was right about him. Celibate as a monk. Over three years now. What the hell was he waiting for?

He leaned down and grabbed the sack at his feet. In it was the bread, butter, and olive oil he'd come into the village to get, as well as the packet of sable paintbrushes he had ordered from Marseilles. Swinging the sack over his shoulder, he tossed a few coins on the table. Eyes bored into his back as he moved toward the door. The men crowding around the doorway parted silently to let him through. No one spoke to him or smiled a farewell. He left the tavern and made the long, lonely trek back to his château.

By the time he reached home, it was dark. But the moon was out, lighting his way as he crossed the courtyard. In the distance, a wolf howled. An owl hooted softly. Somewhere nearby, a rat scurried through the weeds. The sound of his boot heels tapping against the flagstones mingled with the chirping of cicadas and the other sounds of the night. But when he climbed the back stairs and entered the kitchen, he found the château as dark and silent as a tomb.

"Mademoiselle?" he called, but there was no answer. Wondering where the girl might be, he set the sack on the worktable and lit a lamp. Then he left the kitchen to go in search of her. He went upstairs first, thinking she might have gone to bed, but she was not in her room.

As he descended the stairs, the thought crossed his mind that after his uncompromising answer of this morning, she might have left. The possibility of her out alone at night caused a frown of worry to crease his brow as he began to search the rooms on the first floor.

"Mademoiselle?" he called again, but only the echo of his own voice answered him.

She wasn't well enough yet to go anywhere, he told himself, crossing the armory and opening one of the double doors leading into the salon. But that room, too, was dark and silent.

Truly worried now, his mind conjuring up visions of her in any number of desperate situations, he continued to search the first floor. "Foolish girl," he muttered, turning to go down one of the hallways. "If she's gone off by herself . . ."

He paused, seeing the light at the end of the corridor. It spilled through the open doorway leading into the library. Alexandre quickened his steps and strode down the corridor, a combination of relief and irritation replacing the worry he had felt only moments before. "Mademoiselle, why didn't you answer when I . . ."

He stopped abruptly in the doorway. She was there, curled up on one end of the dusty leather sofa, sound asleep. An open book from the shelves behind her had fallen from her hand to the floor. Her other hand rested on her abdomen.

Alexandre set the lamp on the table beside the door and moved into the room, careful not to make a sound. He picked up the book from the floor and glanced at the title. She'd been reading Aristotle, in Greek. He frowned, his gaze moving from the book to the sleeping girl, then back to the book. What was a common English miss doing reading Greek philosophy? It appeared there was more to the petite mademoiselle than he'd first thought. He set the book on the table before returning his thoughtful gaze to her.

The light from the lamp beside her fell softly over her, but it could not soften the thin, shadowed planes of her face. It could not disguise her troubled, hunted look. It could not hide the fear that enveloped her like a black

cloak. Tenderness, a feeling he'd thought long dead in
his soul, stirred within him. No woman could look more
in need of protection and help than this thin, pregnant
girl.

He bent over her and slid one arm beneath her knees,
the other behind her head. With an exquisite gentleness,
he lifted her from the sofa, hoping not to wake her.

Her whole body stiffened, even in sleep. "No," she
mumbled, "Let me go."

"Shh . . ." he commanded softly, turning toward the
door, cradling her in his arms, enjoying the forgotten
luxury of human contact.

She was awake and struggling in an instant. "Put me
down," she gasped, pushing against his chest.

He should have complied, but he found he didn't
want to. "Stop twisting about, mademoiselle," he
ordered, carrying her to the door, where he paused.
"Pick up the lamp."

"Let me go." Her voice was low and tense. He heard
the fear behind it and his arms tightened protectively as
she began to struggle in earnest.

He ignored her protest. "Pick up the lamp."

She did as he bid her, holding the oil lamp in her
hand as he carried her down the corridor into the wide
entrance hall.

Her struggles had subsided, but he could feel her
trembling, hear her shaken breathing. "What are you
doing?" she whispered.

"My sofa is not for sleeping," he told her as he began
to ascend the stairs. "That is what beds are for. You,
mademoiselle, should be in one."

"This isn't necessary. I can walk. You needn't make
such an effort."

"You don't weigh enough for it to be an effort, mademoiselle," he answered. They were at the top of the stairs
now, and he turned toward his bedchamber, the one

she'd been sleeping in since her arrival. "I think I need to feed you better."

She did not answer, but she felt rigid in his arms. It wasn't until they were in the room that he set her down. Her feet had barely touched the floor before she jumped backwards, out of his reach. One small hand held the lamp and the other reached up to clutch at the collar of her dress. Her eyes watched him warily.

The realization struck him like a bolt of lightning. *Bon Dieu!* She was afraid of *him.* Just like the villagers. Perhaps she had heard the rumors. Perhaps she knew about Anne-Marie.

No, if she did, she would never have come here. But then, what was she afraid of? He wasn't going to attack her, if that was her fear. "Go to sleep, mademoiselle." He turned on his heel and left, walking down the corridor to the chamber he was now using.

As he lay in bed, moonlight washing over him, he watched the breeze tease the curtains at the open window and thought of her. He thought about the frightened cries she had uttered in her delirium whenever he touched her and how she had slapped his hands away. He thought about the way she jumped back whenever he came close. He thought about how her eyes watched him so suspiciously. He wondered for perhaps the hundredth time why she was so afraid. Could she somehow sense what he was, what he had done?

He knew she only stayed because she had no choice. He knew she was afraid of him. And he found himself wishing that she weren't.

4

When Tess came downstairs the next morning, Alexandre was gone. In the kitchen, she found a loaf of bread, a sausage, butter, and cheese set out on the table for her. Tucked beneath the bread was a note. Written in bold black letters were the words, "Eat. I will return at sunset. Dumond."

Tess set down the note, feeling relieved. She wouldn't have to spend the day looking over her shoulder, feeling tense and apprehensive at being alone with him in his house.

She sat down at the table and tore a piece of bread from the loaf. Smearing it with butter, she began to eat her breakfast, grateful that her months of morning sickness had passed. She also began once again to contemplate her problem. If Monsieur Dumond would not let her remain here, where would she go?

When she finished her breakfast, Tess still had no solution, but she had decided how to spend her day. She would take a walk in the grounds, then explore the rest of the château. Perhaps a solution would come to her. She wrapped the remaining food in clean cloths and put the bundles in the buttery. Brushing the crumbs from her skirt, Tess went off to explore, telling herself to be optimistic.

The château was perched high on a craggy cliff overlooking the Mediterranean Sea. On the landward side, the sloping hills to the left were covered with deserted, overgrown vineyards. The hills to the right led through forests of chestnut trees and pines, interspersed with meadows of wildflowers and lavender. Having passed the vineyards on her journey here, Tess did not go that way. Instead, she wandered around the grounds of the château itself.

The courtyard was bordered on two sides by the château. Along the other two sides ran crumbling stone walls, one of which had completely fallen down. She stepped through a huge gap in the other wall where an archway had once stood and took the first path, leading her past the garden to a group of outbuildings. The outbuildings were of stone and timber, with crumbling tile roofs. They were badly in need of repairs.

Opposite the outbuildings was a pasture, choked with weeds, where a goat stood grazing. The animal was tethered to a tree stump, for the fence surrounding the pasture was in very poor condition. The cross poles were falling down and there were many gaps where the goat could easily escape. The berry brambles that grew wild beside the pasture were a tangled mass of canes.

One of the outbuildings was a henhouse with a fenced pen. Although the fence wasn't falling down like the one that surrounded the nearby pasture, it looked about to. She noted the strip of linen handkerchief that held two pieces of the fence together and shook her head. If the fence fell, he'd lose all the chickens.

Tess continued to follow the path, past another pen, the barn, and the stables. The path continued on, winding down sharply to the sea, but Tess followed it no farther. It looked too steep, and she didn't want to stumble. She turned and headed down another path, which curved through overgrown rose gardens and potagers with unruly boxwood hedges. Once, this château had been a beautiful place. Now it seemed sad and lonely, a fitting home for the man who owned it.

After a midday meal of more bread and cheese and a short nap—she seemed to tire so easily—Tess explored the upper floors of the château itself. Two of the rooms on the second floor were locked. They were located side by side at the very end of a corridor. She stared at the oak panels of one door thoughtfully. None of the other rooms were locked. Why these two?

She continued her explorations. Those rooms she could enter were musty and undisturbed, and the dust and cobwebs seemed even thicker than down below.

It wasn't until midafternoon that Tess found Alexandre's studio, located at the very top of the only tower in the château. The room was huge, exactly square, with tall windows in all four directions. Tess paused at the top of the spiraling corner staircase and caught her breath. This was definitely a room for an artist. The windows let in the light, no matter what the time of day.

She walked slowly to the center of the room, stepping around tables littered with pots of paint, brushes, sketchbooks, and charcoal. Below the windows, sheet-covered canvases leaned against the walls of whitewashed stone, but not a single painting or sketch adorned the limited wall space. There was no need. The view was adornment enough.

Tess turned slowly in a circle, admiring the incredible views of sea, cliffs, vineyards, and distant village. She didn't know how long she stood there, but she couldn't seem to get enough of the landscape surrounding her.

Finally, she tore her eyes away from what lay outside to what lay within. Although far from tidy, this room seemed to be the only one in the château without a thick layer of dust, cobwebs, and neglect. In the far corner, by one of the windows facing the sea, was an easel holding a half-finished painting in oils. Tess walked over to study it.

A burning sea of orange and blue and black raged around the barely discernible white sails of ships engaged in battle. Columns of smoke and plumes of fire swirled upward into a gray sky. Though not complete, the painting conveyed clearly the pain and passion of war. Anger seemed to emanate from the canvas. Tess admired it, but she wasn't certain she liked it.

Still, she discovered that there were other paintings much more to her liking hidden beneath layers of linen sheeting. An airy landscape, all pinks and greens and blues. A still life of wine, cheese, and grapes that was so French, she smiled. A portrait of a woman in a blue dress.

Curious, Tess pulled it out from the paintings leaning against the wall to study it more clearly. A lovely girl, with milk-white skin and violet eyes and spun-gold hair stared back at her. There was so much laughter and joy in the girl's expression, so much life to her that Tess could almost imagine her breathing or opening her mouth to speak. Who was she?

Tess stepped back from the painting and glanced down at the blue muslin dress she wore, comparing it to the one in the portrait. No, it wasn't the same gown, but it was of a similar color and style and conveyed a similar taste in dress. She had wondered about the clothes Alexandre had given her and who they belonged to. Now she knew.

But who was this girl? A sister? A wife? And where was she now?

Suddenly feeling as if she had intruded on something very private, Tess wrapped the portrait back in its linen sheeting and returned it to its place among the others. Then she left the studio, hoping without knowing why that Alexandre would not be able to tell she had been there.

Wandering back downstairs, Tess realized it was still early afternoon, and she had no idea what to do with the rest of her day. The idea of reading did not appeal to her. She didn't want to do any more exploring.

Aimlessly, she wandered around, her steps bringing her back into the kitchen. Feeling she had come full circle, Tess sat down at the table and restlessly drummed her fingers against the wooden surface.

The house was so quiet. She had thought this morning that she would enjoy her day alone, but by midafternoon, she found herself wishing for the sound of another voice. Three months of solitary wandering and two days alone in this empty castle were enough. She wanted someone to talk to. Even a man, even Alexandre, might be better than no one.

She remembered the puzzled look on his face as she had backed away from him in fear the night before. She suddenly realized the meaning of that look. The evil intentions she had assumed had simply not occurred to him. Her fear seemed silly now. After he had carried her upstairs and set her down, he hadn't even touched her. Perhaps she had misjudged him.

She knew all men weren't like Nigel. Her father, a mild-mannered vicar, had never raised a hand to her mother. Alexandre hadn't raised a hand to her. She had to stop judging all men by her husband. Alexandre Dumond was *not* like Nigel, she told herself, hoping it was true.

Tess's gaze wandered restlessly around the kitchen. She didn't want to think of Nigel, she didn't want to remember. She wanted to do something, she wanted to be useful. Inactivity and solitude were becoming quite tiresome.

She noticed the dust balls that rested around the bottom of the stove. There were dirty dishes piled on the wooden counter. There were bottles of linseed and used paintbrushes scattered carelessly about. She sat up straight in her chair, suddenly considering her plan and Alexandre's refusal in a new light.

Suppose she just quietly began acting and working like a housekeeper. If she wanted to convince Alexandre that he needed one, wouldn't it be best to show him how useful she could be, show him how much nicer his life would be if his home were in order? She could start by tidying the kitchen.

Filled with new resolve, she began to search for a broom, rags, and a bucket. Room by room, she would clean this château and turn it into a home again. Alexandre would see that she was sincere and hardworking. She would earn her keep, prove that she could be useful. True, he had already said no to her plan, but Tess told herself not to be defeated by one refusal.

She knew there would be a great deal of work ahead. She also knew that her knowledge of domestic affairs ran more along the lines of supervising servants than doing the work herself, but that wasn't going to discourage her. After all, how hard could it be to clean, cook, and keep house for one man?

It was late afternoon when Alexandre returned to the château. He walked past the garden and up the stairs. Setting his sketchbook and a pail full of spider crabs and seawater on the worktable, he moved toward the wood bin to get kindling for a fire. But halfway across the kitchen, he suddenly realized there was something different about the room. He looked around but couldn't quite pinpoint the difference. He frowned, hands on hips, looking about him.

Sunshine spilled through the high windows, reflecting off the whitewashed table and wooden floor. And he suddenly knew. The room was spotlessly clean. All the dirty dishes had been washed and put away. Paintbrushes, rags, and bottles of linseed were nowhere to be seen. His mud-encrusted painting had been placed neatly in one corner. The tabletops and floors gleamed. There wasn't a speck of dust anywhere.

His guest had obviously not paid any attention to his refusal of her offer. He wondered where she'd put his paintbrushes. He gave the table a frustrated kick with his boot and muttered three of the most obscene curses he knew.

He had spent the past week making sure the girl didn't die, and here she was, barely out of the sickroom, cleaning house. *His* house. Hadn't he specifically told her that he didn't need or want a housekeeper? He didn't want her messing about with his things, putting them in all the wrong places.

He knew exactly what she trying to do. *Mais oui.* She was trying to show him how much more comfortable his life would be if she remained and kept house for him. Well, he had no intention of allowing it. If she was well enough to clean his house, she was well enough to leave.

Alexandre had worked himself into a righteous fury by the time he finally noticed the sound of humming. It was low, but he could hear it distinctly. He marched across the kitchen to follow the sound, determined to tell the girl exactly what he thought of her little plot.

He found her in the dining room. Her back was to him. She had tied her skirt up several inches off the ground to keep from tripping over it and beneath the skirt the hem of her petticoat brushed the floor. On the table nearby was a pail of water and a pile of rags. She was still humming, her hips swaying as she moved backward across the room. The broom in her hands was being put to vigorous use, raising clouds of dust as she swept the floor.

Alexandre frowned at her back, his frustration growing. Seeing her cleaning like a servant, remembering how ill she had been only a few days before, fueled his anger. When he spoke, his voice was hard and furious. "What do you think you're doing?"

Tess jumped and whirled around, her eyes wide as they met his. She swallowed hard and clutched the broom close to her breast, looking at him in a startled fashion.

"Sacre tonnerre!" he shouted, exasperated. "Have I not spent the past week trying to keep you alive?" He gestured furiously as he spoke. "Your second day out of bed, you start working like a scullery maid! *Mon Dieu!*"

She didn't answer but continued to stare at him with wide eyes.

"Did I not make myself clear yesterday, mademoiselle? Did I not say that, no, you could not be my housekeeper?" He came toward her with long strides, and she backed away as he advanced, her eyes growing wider with every step.

When her back hit the wall and she could retreat no further, she lowered her gaze and stared at the floor. "I'm sorry," she mumbled, refusing to look at him.

Her humble response surprised him. He hadn't expected this sort of reaction. He would have thought she'd try to persuade, coax, or plead her cause. He looked down at the slender hands holding the broom and saw that they were clutching the wooden handle tightly. Their trembling reaffirmed his thoughts of the night before. She was afraid of him. He folded his arms across his chest and frowned down at her, feeling both irritated and dismayed.

After a long moment, she raised her head slightly to look at him. He saw the fear in her eyes. And something more. Resignation. Sadness. A deep well of sadness. Alexandre was startled. He remained motionless, staring at her, not quite sure what to do.

Finally, he reached out to grab the broom from her. She flinched, releasing her hold on the handle and shrinking back against the wall.

Before he could stop the words, he found himself saying, "If you are going to be my cook as well as be my housekeeper, you'd best start dinner, mademoiselle." He paused, then added, "If you feel well enough?"

She almost sagged with relief and nodded. He watched the fear and the sadness melt from her eyes, and he let out his breath in an exasperated sigh. Like it or not, he had acquired a housekeeper.

He set aside the broom and turned away. "Come with me," he ordered over his shoulder and walked out of the room.

Tess obediently followed. She wanted to thank him for his kindness, she wanted to tell him how grateful she was, but she stared at his broad, rigid back and decided to say nothing. He was a difficult man to understand. One moment he was raging at her and the next he was agreeing to her proposition.

When she had seen his anger, she had been sure he would hit her. She had been sure he would toss her out then and there. She thought of what Nigel would have done, and she shuddered. But that was all behind her, she reminded herself. Nigel could not hurt her ever again. He could not hurt her baby.

When they reached the kitchen, Alexandre halted and pointed to a pail that stood on the table. "Dinner, mademoiselle."

Tess walked over to the table and peered into the pail. Four crabs lay inside, covered with water. She stared down at them, realizing for the first time that while the cleaning part of her new position was simply a matter of common sense, the cooking was going to be difficult. She glanced up at him, but he only leaned one hip against the table and folded his arms across his chest, watching her.

She looked down again at the crabs and saw one of them twitch sluggishly in the water. She jumped back, startled. "They're alive!"

"Of course. I just caught them." His eyes rested on her thoughtfully.

Tess swallowed hard, trying to recall the many ways she had seen crab served. In salad, of course. Stuffed. Covered with sauce. None of that was much help, however, in trying to determine how to cook it.

She worried her lower lip between her teeth, knowing she had to pretend she knew exactly what to do. If he discovered that she couldn't cook, couldn't even boil water for tea, he'd change his mind. He'd toss her out. Then what would she do?

She straightened her shoulders and turned to him. "Have you a cookbook?"

He lifted one dark eyebrow. "I'm afraid not. It is fortunate you already know how to cook, *n'est-ce pas?*"

"Yes . . . mm . . . it is." Tess uttered the lie without a blush. "But I'm not familiar with your Provençal cooking. Have you any recipes?"

He shrugged. "It doesn't matter how you cook them. Your English way will be fine. You'll find potatoes and carrots in the garden." Gesturing toward the wood bin beside the cast iron stove, he asked, "Shall I light a fire for you?"

"Please." Tess watched carefully as he built a fire in the stove, hoping she could figure out how to cook something on it. When he had finished and closed the hinged door, he stepped aside. Leaning his back against the wall, he again folded his arms across his chest and waited.

Was he going to stand and watch her the whole time? Tess stepped forward. "Well," she said, hoping her voice sounded brisk and efficient, "I'm sure you have many things to do. Painting or sketching or something. I'll fetch you when the meal is ready." She waved him toward the door.

"Very well." His lips curved in a smile as he took the hint and moved to the door leading into the hall. "I will be upstairs in my studio," he told her. Stepping through the doorway, he paused, glancing over his shoulder at her. "Mademoiselle? You might try boiling them." And with that small piece of advice, he was gone.

Tess lost no time. Hastily, she began searching the kitchen, looking for a recipe box or book. She knew there were such things. As a child, she had watched Molly, the family cook, pouring over recipes many times, recipes carefully preserved in a cookbook. Surely the French had such books, too. Alexandre had said there were none, but he was a man. What did he know?

Opening one cupboard after another, she familiarized herself with what they contained as she searched. Pots, pans, utensils, but no recipes. With a sigh, she placed her hands on her hips and glanced around. How on earth was she going to manage this without any sort of instruction?

She glanced toward the stairs, remembering she had noticed two doors at the bottom. One door went outside, but did the other perhaps lead to a cellar? She lit a lamp and went down the stairs.

Not a cellar, she discovered, but the storerooms of the original castle keep. She found no cookbook or recipes, but she did find a bin of apples beside the stairs. Dessert, she decided.

Behind the bin was a wine rack, filled with dusty bottles. Tess held the oil lamp high and pulled one of the bottles from the shelf. Blowing off the dust, she studied the label. "Dumond Red," she read aloud. "1814."

This wine must be from the now-deserted vineyards. She tucked the bottle under one arm, then gathered some of the apples in her apron and went back upstairs.

Locating potatoes and carrots in the garden was not easy. As a child, she'd spent many hours helping old Herbert in the cottage garden of the vicarage. She knew what potato and carrot tops looked like, but finding them amid all the weeds was difficult. Soon, she vowed, she'd come out here and weed the garden.

Back in the kitchen, she set the carrots and potatoes she'd gathered beside the apples, then walked over to the table and stared down at the crabs. They were moving slowly in the water. They looked quite menacing, with their huge claws and spiny shells. "Boil them," Alexandre had said.

After finding a kettle large enough for the crabs, Tess filled it from the water pump in the courtyard below. She set the pot on the stove to let it boil, then peeled the potatoes and carrots, cutting her finger in the process.

By the time she had finished with the vegetables, the water in the huge kettle was still not boiling, but it would be soon enough, she supposed.

"Cooking isn't so hard," she told herself, hauling the bucket of crabs over to the stove. The words were barely out of her mouth when she realized she had a new problem. How was she going to get the crabs into the pot? She wasn't about to put her hand in that pail and get pinched.

Hanging on hooks beside the stove were several long-handled utensils. Grasping one in each hand, she carefully lifted one crab out of the pail and dropped it into the kettle of now-steaming water.

When the crab screamed, so did Tess. Horrified, she listened to the squealing sound and heard the helpless scratching against the sides of the pot as the crab tried to escape.

It wasn't until the water in the kettle began to boil that the squealing stopped. Tess had a difficult time bringing herself to throw the other three spiny creatures to such a horrible fate. But she did it, apologizing to each one as she dropped them into the bubbling water. She was relieved that the other three did not scream.

An hour later, exhausted and nursing her cuts and burns, Tess arranged the cooked crabs on a large platter, still feeling somewhat sick at how they had met their fate. Trying not to think about it, she carried the platter into the dining room where she had set two places at opposite ends of the long dining table. She placed the dish in the center of the table then returned to the kitchen.

An unpleasant smell greeted her as she entered the room, and with a groan of dismay, she raced to the stove. The potatoes had boiled dry and their scorched smell permeated the kitchen. With a sigh, she pried them from the pan with a fork and cut off the browned edges. They look all right, she decided, spooning them into a bowl.

Turning her attention to the boiled carrots, she removed them from the fire and arranged them on a plate. She sprinkled some thyme from the garden over them for artistic affect.

She opened the oven door to check on the apples baking in a juice of sugar, brandy, and cinnamon, a recipe she'd invented out of necessity because she'd had no idea what else to do with them. But they smelled heavenly and were turning a nice, delicate shade of brown. Pleased, she closed the oven door, then carried the bowls of vegetables into the dining room, placing them beside the crabs.

Surveying the table and the steaming plates of food, she felt foolishly proud of herself. She had done it. She had cooked an entire meal by herself. For the first time in over two years, she felt as if she had truly done something worthwhile. As Nigel's wife, she had been an ornament, whose major accomplishments were looking beautiful and being obedient. Cooking, she decided, was much more satisfying. After flicking a speck of dust off the table with the edge of her skirt and taking another moment to admire her achievement, she went to fetch Alexandre.

The first thing he noticed when he entered the room behind her was the wine. He picked up the bottle on the table and looked at it, then glanced at her. "You found this in the cellar?"

She nodded.

"Four years," he muttered. "Let's hope it hasn't turned to vinegar."

He uncorked the wine with the corkscrew she had laid beside the bottle, then poured a bit of the wine into a glass. He lifted the glass, staring at the apricot-yellow liquid. He swirled it in his glass, then waved it beneath his nose. "Perfect," he murmured. "Just a hint of blush."

She frowned, puzzled, and walked over to stand beside him. "The label said it was red wine."

He smiled slightly, staring at the wine. "It is. Dumond Red. Made with Muscat white grapes. The pink blush is from adding a slight amount of Muscat Hamburg. Not a high-quality grape, but being red, it gives the wine its unique color."

He swirled the wine in his glass once more, then sampled it, giving a satisfied nod. He picked up the bottle and poured wine into her glass.

Taking the glass he offered her, she took a sip of the wine as he watched. It was marvelous, with a mellow full-bodied flavor. "I like this wine," she told him, licking a droplet from her upper lip. "It's sweet."

"It's a good vintage," he replied. "The sweetness comes from the way we harvested our grapes. At harvest time, we would twist the stems and leave the bunches of grapes to hang on the broken vines for several days. Then we would pick them."

She wrinkled her nose, staring down at the wine. "But the grapes would rot."

"Precisely."

She gave him a skeptical stare. "You made your wine from rotten grapes?"

He laughed at her distasteful tone. "Not all of them were rotten," he assured her. "But it is a very old technique here in the Midi, dating back many centuries. It is hot here in the south and heat destroys the wine, causing it to spoil too fast," he explained. "If a good percentage of the grapes are overripe, the sugar content of the wine is much higher, making it a stronger wine and preventing it from spoiling."

"I see." She glanced down at the wine and took another sip. Looking back up at him, she said, "Whatever you do, it works. I don't particularly care for wine, but I like this."

"I'm glad you like it, mademoiselle."

"Since you are so good at it, why don't you make wine anymore?" she asked softly.

He froze, the glass poised in midair. Then he took another swallow and said, "I will never make wine again." Frowning down at the food on the table, he said, "We should eat this before it gets cold."

She began to serve the food, not missing the fact that he had changed the subject without answering her question. Accepting the plate she handed him, he went to his seat at the head of the table.

Tess took her own plate and walked to her place at the other end. Down the long length of table that separated them, she watched anxiously as he broke apart the legs of the crab on his plate. As he took the first bite, she held her breath, watching him chew. And chew. And chew.

Something was wrong. Hastily, Tess broke apart her own crab, her anxious curiosity overcoming her squeamishness. The meat, which was supposed to be tender and sweet, had the texture of rubber and no taste whatsoever. Across the table, their eyes met as they both valiantly chewed the crab and said nothing.

Tess finally gave up the struggle and swallowed the bite whole with a gulp of wine. Hoping the vegetables were better, she pushed her fork into a bite of slightly brown, boiled potato. The potatoes at least had a taste. Scorched.

With growing dismay, she sampled the carrots. They were not scorched. They were still raw and had the pungent flavor of too much thyme. She crunched bravely, but tears of humiliation stung her eyes. She had made a true mess of things. Alexandre would surely turn her out. Or he would find some other way to punish her.

But Alexandre said nothing. He politely ate what was on his plate and the longer she watched him, the more miserable she felt. All her earlier optimism had long since vanished. She was a failure. He would surely treat her like one.

Finally, she could stand the oppressive silence no longer and rose. "Would you care for dessert?" she asked in a tiny voice.

Alexandre swallowed another gulp of wine and rubbery crab. "Certainly."

A man about to be executed probably spoke in that same brave tone of voice, she thought, heading for the kitchen. Almost timidly, she opened the oven door. The apples were golden brown and simmering in their juice, and the smell of cinnamon filled the air. They seemed to be done. Unwilling to trust her own eyes, she pushed a fork into the fruit. It was tender, but not mushy. Relieved, she put the apples into a serving dish, poured some of the sauce over them, and took the dish into the dining room.

"What is this?" Alexandre asked as she set the bowl beside his plate.

"Baked apples," she answered, spooning some of the fruit onto a dessert plate for him and one for herself.

"It looks quite good."

"Really?" She looked at him and saw him nod. His smile was so reassuring, so *understanding*, she felt the tears well in her eyes again. He didn't seem angry, and somehow that made her feel worse than before. Taking her plate back to her end of the table, Tess sat down, but didn't make any move to eat. She stared down at her plate through a blurry haze. Even if the dessert was good, it wouldn't matter. She couldn't cook, and he knew it.

But when Alexandre picked up a fork to sample her dessert, Tess couldn't help observing him from beneath her lashes. Perhaps, she thought, the dessert was good. Perhaps he would like it. She watched him bring the fork to his lips.

When he choked on the apples, she couldn't bear it and jumped to her feet. "It's a lovely evening. I think I'll take the air." She practically ran out of the room.

Alexandre found her in the courtyard, sitting on a stone bench, looking the picture of dejected misery. The setting sun reflected the tears on her cheeks and caught the fiery halo of her hair. Her profile was pensive.

He watched her for a long time, wishing he had his sketchbook. The vulnerability he sensed in her was never more clear than at this moment. He felt a sudden, unwanted desire to comfort her. He stepped into the courtyard, his boot heels crunching against the broken flagstones.

Tess started at the sound. She sniffed, turning her face away as his shadow fell over her. She brushed a tear from her cheek. "What was wrong with the apples?"

He smiled down at her. "I don't know about you, but I prefer a bit of cinnamon with my apples, not a bit of apples with my cinnamon."

"I used too much spice?"

"A bit." He studied her discouraged expression. "It isn't so bad," he tried to tease her. "We could put it in jars and use it for potpourri."

Her answer was a choked sound, half laugh, half sob.

"It was only a meal, mademoiselle," he said quietly.

She shook her head. "No, it wasn't. Not for me."

He frowned, not understanding her enigmatic remark, but he did not pursue it. Instead, he put a hand on her shoulder and pushed gently, urging her to move over. When she did, he sat down beside her. "I should not have let you do so much on only your second day out of bed. You should have been resting."

"I doubt that rest will make me a better cook." Her tone was wry.

He chuckled. "Perhaps not."

They sat in silence for awhile. The sun slowly disappeared, leaving the courtyard in dusky twilight.

Finally, it was she who broke the silence. "Are you going to send me away?"

His jaw tightened. He should. For his own peace of mind, he really should. "No."

Her sigh of relief was audible. "Thank you."

"I have two conditions," he added, casting a sideways glance at her. He saw her stiffen.

"What conditions?" Her voice was low and wary.

"No hard work until you are feeling better, for one."

She considered that for a moment, then nodded. "I agree. But tomorrow you must show me what tasks I can do." She took a deep breath. "And the other condition?"

He turned to face her. "I do the cooking."

Her teeth flashed white in the dusk of evening as she smiled. "That would hardly be fair. If you are employing me as a cook and housekeeper, I should do the cooking, too. I want to earn my keep."

He considered her words. He didn't care what tasks she did or didn't do, but he knew that for the sake of her pride, it was important to her. "Very well." He paused, then added, "Tomorrow I will begin teaching you how to cook."

"You will?"

He rose to his feet. "If I don't, we'll both starve."

5

When Tess awoke the next morning, she found a bucket of fresh water and a silver-backed mirror and brush outside her door. Beside them was an untidy pile of dresses, underclothes, and shoes. She smiled down at the collection of things Alexandre had left at her door, knowing he meant what he had said the night before. He was going to let her stay.

She shed the blue muslin dress she'd been wearing the past two days, washed quickly, then donned a fresh chemise, petticoat, and a high-waisted gown of peach muslin. After giving her tangled curls a vigorous brush, Tess headed downstairs, hoping Alexandre had not forgotten his other promise.

She found him in the kitchen making tea. "Good morning. Thank you for the water."

He glanced over his shoulder at her, then turned back to the stove and continued pouring hot water into the teapot. "I have to bathe as well. It was no trouble. I see you found the clothes."

"Yes, thank you." She wanted to ask about the clothes, about the girl in the portrait. But she was reluctant to pry.

Alexandre's manner did not invite questions. Besides, he might start asking her questions, and that thought forced Tess to put aside her curiosity. They both had secrets, it seemed.

"Are you ready for your first lesson?" Alexandre's voice intruded on her musings, and Tess came out of her reverie to find him standing in front of her, holding out a cup of tea. She nodded, taking the cup.

While Tess drank her morning tea, Alexandre took a basket and went out. When he returned a few minutes later, the basket was filled with vegetables and herbs. Tess set down her empty cup and gave him an inquiring glance. "What do we do first?"

"We will start, I think, with an omelette. But first, we must milk the goat and fetch the eggs. Come." Taking one small pail and one large one from their hooks on the wall, he moved to the back door.

Tess followed him out into the bright morning sunlight toward the group of crumbling buildings she had passed on her walk the day before.

Alexandre led her into the fenced pen, where he set down the large pail. The hens, out of their night roost, scattered as he walked past them toward the coop, the small pail still in his hand. Tess moved to follow him inside, but the smell that greeted her through the doorway made her want to retch. It had obviously been a long time since the coop had been cleaned. Hand over her mouth, she choked, "I'll wait out here."

"If you are going to be the cook, tending to the chickens will be your responsibility," he answered. "Come."

She felt her stomach turn and she was certain her face had gone green. "I can't." She pressed her other hand to her abdomen, fearing her tea was going to come back up. "The smell . . ."

Alexandre waited a moment, but when she did not move to follow him, he shrugged and turned away, entering the coop. When he reappeared, the small pail was filled with eggs, and he handed it to her. He then walked back inside, returning with a bucket of feed, which he began to scatter about for the hens. When the bucket was empty, he tossed it back through the doorway and left the yard, picking up the large pail on his way out of the pen.

She followed, glad to be away from the overpowering smell, as Alexandre passed the barn and entered the pen on the other side, where a gray and white goat bleated at him. He paused and looked at Tess. "You can't cook, you don't like hen houses. I don't suppose you've ever milked a goat?"

She shook her head with an apologetic smile. "I'm afraid not."

He beckoned her to come inside the pen. "You're going to learn."

Tess set down the pail of eggs and pushed open the gate, walking over to stand beside the goat. Alexandre went into the connecting barn, returning with a length of stout rope and a stool. He tethered the animal to the fence with the rope and pulled the stool forward. He patted it with his hand. "Sit down," he told her.

She complied. The goat bleated again, trapped between Tess and the fence, and butted her head to Tess's shoulder. "Stop that, goat," Alexandre ordered, pushing the animal's head away.

Tess grinned at his words. "Goat?" she asked. "Doesn't she have a name?"

Alexandre shrugged and placed the pail under the goat's legs. "None that I know of," he answered and squatted beside her. "Now, grasp—"

"We'll call her Sophie," Tess interrupted, reaching up to pat the goat's flank.

"Pay attention, mademoiselle," he ordered and proceeded to explain how to milk a goat. Tess listened carefully, watching as he squeezed and pulled the teats of

Sophie's udder with gentle hands. Milk splattered into the pail. "You try it."

She did try, doing exactly what she had seen him do, but nothing happened. Patiently he explained again and Tess tried again, but still nothing happened. She frowned, sitting back on the stool. "What am I doing wrong?"

"Nothing. It just takes practice."

After several more tries, Tess had still gotten no milk, and Sophie stirred and bleated, impatient with her clumsy efforts. But Alexandre exhibited no impatience. He leaned forward and said, "Let me show you." Then he reached out, closing one hand over hers.

Tess jerked involuntarily at his touch, and she felt his hand tighten. She drew in a sharp, panicky breath.

"Squeeze, mademoiselle," he told her. "Squeeze and pull."

She tried to concentrate on what he was saying, but his arm entwined over hers, his palm against the back of her hand, his fingers pushing hers into the proper motions, all unnerved her. He was so close.

She focused on the movement, feeling her hand work with his, hearing the milk hit the side of the pail. When he let go, she continued to pull, and the milk continued to flow. "I did it!" she gasped and pulled again, watching more milk squirt from Sophie's udder.

With an exclamation of delight, she released her grip on Sophie to clap her hands together, all her earlier tension momentarily forgotten. She turned to the man beside her with a triumphant grin. "Alexandre, I really did it."

He returned the smile with one of his own, and Tess stared into the face only inches from hers. He had a beautiful smile, a genuine smile that flashed even white teeth against his sunbrowned face and crinkled the crow's feet at the corners of his black eyes. Her breath caught in her throat.

Both of them looked away at the same moment. "Very good, mademoiselle," he told her, breaking the self-conscious silence. "But you had better finish soon, or Sophie will probably kick you."

When the milking was done, Alexandre led Sophie out to the pasture. He tethered her to the tree stump, just as Tess had seen her tied the day before. When he left the goat and turned to go back to the château, Tess followed.

As they passed the patch of wild berries, he paused to look at the canes. "Not ripe for a month, at least." He shook his head with obvious regret and cast a sideways glance at her. "I love blackberries," he confessed.

She found herself smiling. "So do I."

"When they're ripe," he added, turning to continue on toward the house, "we'll make blackberry tarts."

Back in the kitchen, he set the pails of milk and eggs on the table, then stoked the fire in the stove. "When you cook eggs, you must have a low fire," he told her, as he poured a bit of olive oil into a cast-iron skillet and began to swirl it in the pan.

Tess listened as he explained how to control the heat of the fire in the stove. She watched as he made a stuffing for the omelette of spinach, wild mushrooms, and shallots. He showed her how to sauté the vegetables in olive oil with a clove of garlic. As they worked, she listened to him explain everything, simply enjoying the sound of his voice. Rich, languorous, warm, and very French, like the Provence sun. He had, she decided, a very nice voice.

She watched as he cracked eggs into a bowl rapidly, expertly, with his left hand. A man's hands were something Tess had learned to notice and to fear. Alexandre had large hands with the long, tapering fingers of an artist. She had felt the strength in those hands and it had frightened her, but she had also felt the gentleness. A man's hands didn't seem so frightening now.

He beat the eggs vigorously with a fork, ladled in a bit of milk, then poured them into the pan heating on the stove. She noticed how, when the eggs were cooked, he added the spinach stuffing and folded the omelette over with an expert flick of his wrist. Curious, she asked him, "How did you learn how to cook?"

Alexandre turned a pepper grinder over the pan, lightly dusting the omelette with the black spice. He was silent so long, she thought he wasn't going to answer her question. But he finally said, "When I was twenty-one, I went to Italy. I wanted to paint, I wanted to study the masters. But I had no money and no one to sponsor me. I needed employment."

A tiny, wry smile tilted the corners of his mouth. "I happened to meet an Italian nobleman who was in desperate need of a French chef. As you know, French chefs are always in great demand. I convinced him that I was perfectly suited to the task." His smile widened into a wicked grin as he added, "I couldn't cook at all."

Tess stared at him in astonishment, then she began to laugh. "You're joking!"

"*Non,*" he denied. "I'm not."

"But . . . but," she choked, still laughing, "what did the nobleman do when he found out? Didn't he throw you out in the street?"

"No. In fact, later he became my first sponsor. I painted portraits of his entire family."

"Wasn't he angry at being deceived?"

"Of course."

"But then why—"

"Perhaps," Alexandre said softly, his eyes meeting hers, "he felt that everyone deserves a chance."

Tess pondered his reply as he slid the omelette from the pan to a plate. When he carried the food to the table, he walked past her and said something more. His voice was so low, she barely heard his words. He said, "You should laugh more often, mademoiselle."

*   *   *

That afternoon, while Alexandre went off to sketch, Tess continued her battle against dust and cobwebs. She dusted furniture, swept floors, washed down walls, and opened windows to rid the château of its musty smell. Although her progress was slow and she had to take frequent rest breaks, she managed to thoroughly clean three rooms by late afternoon.

Wringing out a rag in the bucket of water beside her, Tess gave the tiny window panes of the library one last swipe. She then rubbed the glass with a dry rag until it gleamed. With a satisfied nod, she turned away from the window and bent to reach for the handle of the bucket.

A sudden pain shot through her lower spine and she winced, pressing a hand to the small of her back. Lifting the bucket with her free hand, she went back through the kitchen and down the stairs.

Pouring out the bucket of dirty water, Tess looked up and saw Sophie standing in the garden, munching happily on herbs and weeds. Tess groaned in dismay and dropped the bucket as she watched the goat devouring the garden with obvious relish. She knew she'd have to catch Sophie, but when she moved forward with that intention in mind, the goat skipped nimbly out of reach.

Twenty minutes later, panting and disgusted, she led the disgruntled Sophie back to her pen, her hand firmly clutching the collar of rope around the goat's neck. The other end of the rope, now chewed through, dragged on the ground behind them. "You should be ashamed of yourself," she told Sophie, who only glared back at her, unrepentant.

Tess untied the rope from Sophie's neck, coiled what remained of it, and took it back into the barn.

Unlike the hen house, the barn smelled only of dust and disuse. It was empty, with nothing but a few rusty tools and burlap bags lying about. Tess walked between the stalls and was reminded of the empty rooms of the castle. They, too, were dark and dusty. And lonely.

She tossed the rope into one of the empty stalls and turned to leave, when a faint cry stopped her. Frowning, she didn't move, and the cry was repeated. She stepped forward, looked into the next stall, and gave a gasp of delight. Standing in one corner on shaky legs was a tiny kitten, meowing piteously.

She walked into the stall and dropped to her knees beside the small orange ball of fur. Its eyes were open, but Tess knew it was still very young. "Oh, poor baby," she breathed, lifting the kitten gently in her hands. "Where's your mama?"

The kitten answered with another meow.

"All alone?" she asked, rubbing her thumb over the animal's head. Setting the kitten down, she rose and left the stall. She searched the barn and stables thoroughly, but she found no other kittens and no sign of the mother cat.

She walked back to the château, cradling her tiny new friend in her hands. Before going inside, she paused beside the well and drew up the bucket. She knew Alexandre had put the milk left over from breakfast in a sealed jar and had lowered it into the well before leaving that morning. And she knew the kitten was probably hungry. Taking both milk and kitten, Tess went up the stairs.

Holding the kitten against her breast with one hand, she set down the jar of milk and took a small bowl from one of the cupboards. She knew the kitten was too young yet to drink straight from the bowl, so she fetched a clean rag from the buttery. Sitting down at the table, she dipped a corner of the rag in the bowl and began to feed the kitten. "I'm going to call you Augustus," she told him, waiting patiently as he sucked the milk-soaked cloth she held to his mouth.

As she fed the baby cat, Tess felt a sudden flutter in her abdomen and smiled. A fierce wave of maternal love stole through her, as she cradled the kitten to her breast and felt the movements of the child in her womb. Softly, she began to hum to both her babies.

When his hunger appeared to be sated, she set Augustus down on the floor and watched as he ambled across the room, found a spot in the center that suited him, and curled up into a little ball. He promptly fell asleep.

Tess was still watching him and still smiling when Alexandre came home. She heard his footsteps on the stairs and rose as he entered the kitchen. She saw the direction of his steps and cried, "Stop! You'll step on Augustus!"

"What?" Alexandre came to an abrupt halt and looked down at the small fur ball at his feet. Augustus was asleep and oblivious to the boot that had almost flattened him. "A cat," Alexandre muttered, his lip curling. "I hate cats." The look he gave Tess was belligerent.

Her eyes widened with deliberate innocence. "He's only a baby."

They stared at each other across the kitchen.

"I hate cats," he repeated.

"I found him in the stable," Tess explained as she picked up the bowl and rag from the table. "Crying. The foxes probably got his brothers and sisters. I don't know what could have happened to his mother." She looked at Alexandre, who was staring down at the cat with distaste. "He's all alone," she murmured in a mournful voice, "with nobody to take care of him."

Alexandre looked at Tess again. He sighed, raking a hand through his hair, watching her watch him. He opened his mouth to reply, then closed it abruptly. Without a word, he stepped over the kitten and strode across the kitchen, through the door and out of the room, his boot heels stomping on the wooden floor. His muttered words floated back to her. "I hate cats."

Tess smiled as she watched him depart, then she walked over to Augustus, who was now awake and mewing softly. She scooped up the tiny animal in her hand and rubbed his nose with her own. "Don't worry," she told the kitten. "I think he's going to let you stay, too."

The following day, Alexandre sent Tess out to milk the goat and feed the chickens on her own. She wrinkled her nose distastefully at the thought of the smelly hen house, but she took the pails and went without complaint. The chickens, as Alexandre had told her yesterday, were her responsibility now.

"Good morning, Sophie," she greeted as she entered the pen and gave the goat an affectionate pat. Sophie butted her head against Tess's hand and bleated in reply.

Tess milked the goat, finding her task much easier than she had the first time. Sophie seemed to appreciate the difference too, and she didn't shy impatiently away or complain with indignant bleats.

Tess set the full pail of milk aside and led Sophie out to graze, wondering if she was going to be chasing the stubborn goat again this afternoon. She made a mental note to suggest repairing the fence around the pasture, then she headed for the hen house.

The hens squawked and fluttered about her as she moved past them. She hesitated at the doorway of the coop, but this morning there was no foul stench to greet her. She inhaled deeply, but the only smells were fresh morning air and a faint tinge of vinegar. She stepped inside.

The coop was clean. Astonished, she stared at the loose, freshly raked dirt beneath her feet and the shelves of neatly piled straw where the hens roosted.

Alexandre must have cleaned it yesterday while she had thought him off sketching somewhere. Tess swallowed hard, feeling a sudden desire to cry. It was a simple act of consideration, of thoughtfulness, but Tess found it hard to believe a man capable of such a thing.

She thought about the way he had taken her in, cared for her during her illness. He hadn't wanted to. He'd made that clear enough. But he had done it anyway. He had eaten that dreadful meal she'd cooked without complaint. He hadn't wanted to let her stay, hadn't wanted to teach her to cook, hadn't wanted a cat. Yet, here she was, in his house, learning to cook, taking care of the cat. She and Augustus had both been allowed to stay.

A tiny little glow of warmth flickered inside her until a cold breath of doubt blew it out. Why was he being so kind to her? Was it so that he could torment her with it later? A memory flitted through her mind, a memory of dresses and the horrible, ripping sound of silk torn from her body. She closed her eyes.

"Pink! With your coloring?" Nigel's voice, filled with contempt, echoed in the hen house. "Just once, I give you leave to select your own gown for a ball, and this is what you choose?" She could see the heel of Nigel's Hessian boot grind remnants of a silk gown into the plush Persian rug. The gown had been peach, not truly pink. But Nigel hated pink, and he had wanted an excuse, any excuse, to punish her. "Your taste is appalling, madam."

Tess could see herself staring down at the ruined gown she had chosen, her arms wrapped around her half-naked body. She could feel the jarring pain of that first blow. She should not have been happy at the unexpected freedom he'd given her. Hadn't she learned he gave her things only for the pleasure of snatching them away? She had not been able to attend that ball.

Nigel had taught her well. Any act of kindness was suspect. Torment was sure to follow, or payment extracted. A man didn't show kindness for nothing. She shivered. What payment did Alexandre expect?

6

While Tess was out with the goat and the chickens, Alexandre picked vegetables in the garden. He then returned to the kitchen, washed them and began slicing them, trying to keep the cat out from under his feet. Augustus had other ideas, however, and continued to be a nuisance, rubbing his ankle and meowing for attention. For the fifth time, he picked up the kitten and moved him to an out-of-the-way corner. The silly thing was probably hungry. "You'll have to wait," he told the mewing animal and turned back to his task. "I'm letting the mademoiselle keep you," he threw over his shoulder, "but I'll be damned if I'm going to feed you."

But Augustus wouldn't stay out of the way, and Alexandre was finally forced to capitulate. He allowed Augustus the dubious pleasure of lying on top of his foot, kneading the boot leather and purring.

He couldn't help wondering what the petite mademoiselle would say about the hen house. Of course, he hadn't done it for her. It had needed mucking out and he had been meaning to get to it for quite some time. Her slightly green expression had merely reminded him. Still, a tiny little part of him, a part he didn't want to think much about, hoped she would notice and appreciate what he had done.

When she returned to the kitchen, he watched her out of the corner of his eye as she took the pails of milk and eggs to the table. She didn't say a word.

When she was out of his line of vision, he turned his head to look over his shoulder. Her back was to him so he could not see her expression. The line of her back was rigidly straight, but her head was bowed, and her hands gripped the table, a tense gesture he was coming to expect. She was so quiet. "Mademoiselle?"

Her head came up. He heard a choked sound. "Yes?"

He set down the knife and turned, disentangling Augustus from beneath his feet. He walked over to stand beside her. She didn't move. He leaned forward and bent his head to see her expression, but she felt the movement and turned her face away. "Are you not well?" he asked.

"I'm fine."

Alexandre reached out a hand and touched her shoulder. He felt her tremble. But she didn't pull away. She simply stood there. "Mademoiselle," he said, worry making his voice impatient, "what is it?"

"You . . ." She paused, then choked out, "You cleaned the hen house."

"It needed cleaning." He didn't like this, the way she stood so still, so rigid, as if to keep control over powerful emotions he couldn't fathom.

"Was that the only reason?"

Her words were so low, he bent his head to catch them. Then he frowned. He didn't want to answer her questions. He didn't want to admit, even to himself, that he had done it to see her smile.

He didn't even want her here, he told himself. All he wanted, all he'd wanted for three years, was to be left alone. But a voice in his head mocked him. *So, why are you making it so pleasant for the girl to stay?*

He dropped his hand from her shoulder and turned away. "Of course," he answered her question diffidently, picking up the knife on the counter. "What other reason could there be?"

He got no reply to that, and when he glanced at her again, she was still standing there, head bowed, tense and silent. He resumed his task, chopping scallions into smaller and smaller pieces, feeling irritated and more than a little confused by her reaction. He didn't know what he'd expected her to say. He didn't know how he'd expected her to react. But one of her infrequent smiles and a "thank you" would have been nice.

A routine had been established those first two mornings, and Tess and Alexandre continued the pattern during the two weeks that followed. Every morning there was fresh water outside her door. After she had bathed and dressed, she came down to the kitchen, where Alexandre waited with freshly brewed tea. Then, while she milked the goat and fed the chickens, Alexandre gathered vegetables and herbs from the garden for their morning cooking lesson. They had two lessons each day, morning and evening. He taught her how to make sauces and soufflés, how to use herbs and spices, how to plan meals. But everything was done in a stiff and uncomfortable fashion, without the camaraderie of that first morning in the kitchen.

In the afternoons, while Alexandre went off to paint or sketch, Tess spent her time cleaning, or mending, or doing laundry. Occasionally, when she was sweeping the upstairs floors or putting away laundry, her gaze would stray to the locked doors at the end of the corridor, and she would wonder what lay within those rooms. But she did not have much time to dwell on the matter. There was plenty of work to be done.

She found herself free to do whatever work she felt like doing. There was no one telling her what to do or how to do it. There was no one to gainsay her if she wanted to go for a walk or take a nap. There was no Nigel to humiliate her with belittling words, no Nigel to humble her with a kick or a blow, no Nigel to torment her with her own unworthiness.

It was freedom and it should have been glorious. But Tess found herself waiting. She waited for Alexandre to begin making demands. She waited for him to disapprove of the way she had done something. She waited for him to treat her as Nigel would have done. She expected it, certain that it was only a matter of time. She worked harder and harder with each day that passed, hoping to avoid the inevitable, hoping to make everything so perfect Alexandre would have no excuse to criticize, no reason to hit.

But her pessimistic expectations came to naught. Alexandre never said an insulting word to her. In fact, he hardly spoke to her at all. He never lost his temper because he hardly seemed to notice what she did.

It's like walking on eggs, she thought, leaning forward and yanking another ragweed plant out of the ground. She tossed it onto the pile of weeds by her side and straightened up. She pressed a hand to her lower back as she surveyed the huge patch of garden in front of her, filled with waist-high weeds.

The feeling was familiar. During her two years of marriage, she'd walked on eggs most of the time, waiting for the inevitable with that tense feeling of dread. Now, she was in a different house, and it was a different man, but she was still waiting.

Tess leaned forward again, placing one hand to her rounded belly and grasping the base of another weed with the other. She pulled it from the ground, root and all. This time she winced as she straightened, and she began to massage the base of her spine. She'd only pulled a few weeds and already her back was beginning to ache. She knew it would be less painful if she wore stays. But she thought of how uncomfortable the baby would feel, compressed within a confining corset, and she couldn't do it. She couldn't sacrifice the baby's comfort for the sake of her own. Working in the garden was definitely not doing her back any good, but she wanted to get the weeding done today.

The afternoon sun felt warm on her neck and the pleasant hum of bees surrounded her as she worked. The bright red of a ladybug on the leaf of a weed caught her attention. She pushed the insect gently off the leaf before pulling the weed from the ground. A long-ago voice reminded her, "Ladybugs are good to have around, Tessie."

She smiled, remembering. Old Herbert, laying out bedding plants with gnarled hands, showing his five-year-old assistant how to train pole beans, letting her plant the nasturtiums and sweet peas because she could easily hold the large seeds in her tiny fingers.

The vicarage garden had been one of her childhood joys, one of many. She could still remember sneaking scones from Molly's kitchen, and her partner in crime had usually been her father. "I should feel guilty," he would say as they ate the stolen scones under the hickory tree by the stream, far from the cook's exasperated scolding. "A vicar should set a good example." But Molly had often found an empty plate where scones should have been.

She could remember her mother stitching samplers with her, teaching her how to sew and embroider. She could hear her mother's voice telling Herbert firmly every spring, "No asters in the flower beds. I want geraniums." But there had always been asters around the vicarage.

And there had always been love and laughter in her house and in her life. Even after her mother's death when she was fifteen, even after her father became so very ill, love had carried her through. Until she married Nigel. Then love wasn't enough.

Her father had approved of the match. "He'll take care of you after I'm gone, Tess. You'll be a countess. You'll never want for anything."

She hadn't married Nigel because he was an earl. She had married him because she had loved him. The moment she had first seen him, sitting across the aisle of the parish church in Ainswick, she'd been in love. He'd come to Northumberland to visit his mother, but during the days that had followed, it was Tess who had become the object of his attention.

Those days of courtship had been exciting and heady. Sweet words and tender endearments had come so easily from his lips. Swept off her feet by an earl's attention, she had never realized how meaningless the words were.

Tess stared down at the weed in her hand. Somehow, fate had played a cruel joke on her. Fate had given her two loving parents who had shown her what life and marriage and family could be like. In marrying Nigel, the man she loved, she had assumed her new life would have all the love and happiness of her old one. But her joy and her innocent assumptions had been snatched away during her honeymoon. And in that first month of marriage, coldness and brutality and pain had taken their place. Her life had left her unprepared for such sordid emotions. Her love and her innocence had both died a quick death.

Not even her father had been able to help her. He had died during her wedding journey. And there was no one else, a fact Nigel had never let her forget. "You're the

PRELUDE TO HEAVEN   73

daughter of a dead vicar," he'd sneer. "A nobody. You have no money, no family. You have nothing. Without me, you are worthless."

Tess dropped to her knees and yanked another weed from the ground. She threw it onto the pile, anger bubbling inside her. She had done nothing to deserve the horrible things Nigel had done to her. She had done nothing to deserve the humiliation, the abuse, the degradation. She had done nothing wrong. Nothing. She wasn't worthless. She would work hard and she would prove it.

She began to work frantically, pulling one weed after another, remembering how Nigel had forbidden her to do one of the things she loved, gardening. "I have made you a countess!" he'd shouted down at her the first and only time he'd found her on her knees in a flower bed. "Do you want to have callouses and dirty hands?" He had dumped the basket of weeds over her head. "Do you want to be a bloody gardener, countess?" He had pushed her down, grinding her face in the dirt. "Do you? Then you should look the part." She could still taste the dirt in her mouth.

Tess pushed herself harder, pulling weeds as if each one were a piece of Nigel's flesh. She grasped each weed and tore it from the ground, crushed it in her hand, then threw it onto the growing pile. On she worked, not stopping until she reached the end of the row.

Breathless and sweating, she paused for a moment and sat back, staring down at her dirty, green-stained hands with both pride and fury. What would Nigel say if he could see her now? She wondered if men could see earth through the flames of hell. She hoped so. She truly hoped so.

Alexandre marched through the courtyard, slapping the straw hat he'd brought out for her against his thigh as he walked. He'd seen her through the window, weed-ing the garden with a frantic energy that alarmed and angered him.

She'd promised him she wouldn't do any hard work. But every day, she seemed to work longer and harder, pushing herself to do more and more and more. He didn't know what was driving her, but it was going to stop. "Mademoiselle!"

His shadow crossed her. She did not pause in her task, but continued pulling weeds savagely out of the ground.

"I didn't make you my housekeeper to acquire a slave," he told her. "Stop this."

She didn't stop. Her frantic pace seemed to increase. "I have to get this done today. I have laundry to do tomorrow."

He knelt beside her, slamming the hat to the ground, and grabbed her wrist. "I said stop."

She wrenched her wrist free. "But there's so much to do, Alexandre." She pulled another weed. "I have to get the garden finished today. I still haven't mended all your shirts. And there's dusting and laundry and—"

"Mademoiselle!" He grasped her shoulders and turned her towards him. "Stop it!"

She twisted free, scrambling backward on her knees. If he was going to strike her, punish her, she wished he would just get it over and done. "Don't tell me what to do!" she flared, suddenly defiant, wanting to provoke him, unable to stand the suspense. "No one tells me what to do!"

"Damn!" He reached out and seized her wrists in an iron grip. "I am your employer, no? I will tell you what work you can and cannot do. And you will do as I say. No more gardening."

She froze, her wrists locked in his hands. She looked up at him, and all the fight went out of her as quickly as it had come. Her face, flushed a moment ago, was suddenly pale. "Are you telling me I can't work in the garden anymore?"

"That's exactly what I'm telling you," he said sharply. Letting go of her wrists, he raised angry hands to the sky. "*Mon Dieu!* What are you thinking of? Out here during the warmest part of the day, on your knees and pulling weeds in your condition?" His voice rose with his anger and agitation. "Have a care for the babe you carry, mademoiselle! No more!"

He was so frustrated and preoccupied with his lecture that he did not see the fear in her eyes. But when he seized the hat and moved to slap it down on her head, she ducked and flinched, uttering a frightened cry as she held up her arm in a defensive gesture.

He paused, the hat in midair, and stared at her, dismayed. Did she think he was going to strike her? His dismay increased when she said frantically, "I won't work in the garden if you don't want me to! I won't, I promise!"

Her fear again. Drawing a deep breath, he gently pulled her arm down and placed the hat on her head. "This must stop, mademoiselle. You are working much too hard. I won't have you injuring yourself or the babe."

He watched her slowly relax. Her gaze lifted to his face and he added in a gentler tone, "I don't want to spend another week nursing you when you drop from exhaustion. Is that understood?"

She nodded.

He rose and pulled her to her feet. "I will take care of the garden, mademoiselle." Tucking her arm within his, he led her several feet away to the base of a huge chestnut tree. "You will sit here in the shade and rest," he said, as she lowered herself into a sitting position at the base of the tree. "And from now on, mademoiselle," he added over his shoulder as he turned and walked back toward the garden, "when you go out into the sun, always wear a hat. Your skin is fair, and the Provence sun is fierce. You will burn if you are not careful."

He began weeding the garden, trying to figure out what it was about him that she feared so much. True, some of the villagers feared him, but Tess couldn't know about that.

Still, there was something about him that terrified her. He knew he was a large man, much larger than the petite girl now sitting under the chestnut tree, but he didn't think he was a man who frightened women. Certainly, he'd never frightened Anne-Marie. They had quarreled nose to nose, shouting at the top of their lungs many times. Never had she flinched or trembled. But then, he and Anne-Marie had known each other since childhood. To this girl, he was a stranger. She couldn't know about him, or she would never have come here. But perhaps she could simply look at him and know what he was responsible for.

Every time he glanced in her direction, she was staring at him, a confused look on her face, as if she were trying to understand his behavior the same way he was trying to understand hers.

He wished that what he had done three years ago could be undone. But it couldn't. He couldn't forget the past, he couldn't erase it. It would always come back to haunt him. And he would never be able to forgive himself.

He had raised his voice. That was all. Tess couldn't fathom it. She had provoked him deliberately, unable to stand the suspense. But he hadn't hit her. Even his grip on her wrists, though firm, had not been rough.

She settled the hat far back on her head and leaned against the tree, watching him. He worked at an unhurried but steady pace, his tall body bending to pull a handful of weeds then straightening to toss them aside with a rhythm and economy of movement that was somehow fascinating to watch. She thought of her own clumsiness, her awkward bending. Yet, for him, it seemed to take no effort at all. In only a few minutes, he had pulled more weeds than she had done in the previous hour.

He straightened again, glanced at the sun still high overhead, then undid the three buttons of his shirt. Pulling the white linen shirt over his head, he tossed it aside, brushed his forearm across his forehead, and bent again to his task.

Tess noticed the flex and play of his muscles beneath his skin as he moved. Strength rippled along every chiseled contour of his body, from the long legs encased in tight black trousers, to the knotted muscles of his bare chest and back, over wide shoulders and powerful arms.

So different from Nigel. Taller, wider, brawny where Nigel had been wiry.

But he was the same. He was a man.

She thought of how Nigel had thrown her across the room with one push, had sent her spinning with one blow, had cracked her ribs with one kick. Nigel had possessed lightning-quick strength, the ability to lash out, inflict pain, and withdraw. Like a whip.

She watched Alexandre work, thinking of how he'd lifted her so easily, carried her up those stairs as if she weighed no more than the weeds he was now tossing aside. Alexandre had a hard, unyielding strength. Like a wall.

How could a woman defend herself against that kind of power? She knew what a man's strength meant, how it could hurt.

But Alexandre hadn't hurt her.

He could. He could decimate her with one stroke, more easily even than Nigel could have done. But he hadn't.

Skeptical and wary, she wondered why. She had been in his house for three weeks. He'd shown displeasure, more than once. He'd shouted at her, more than once. But never had his angry words been insulting. Never had his hand reached out to hit her. Not even once.

He was still weeding, standing in the middle of the garden now, moving between the rows at that same steady pace. A fine patina of sweat made his brown skin gleam like polished oak. His long ebony hair had come loose from its ribbon and tumbled over his back and shoulder. He reached up, once again wiping the sweat from his brow.

He looked hot and thirsty. Here she was, sitting in the shade, watching him do her work for her. He wouldn't let her help, but the least she could do was fetch him some water.

Tess rose and walked down the path to the well. Pulling up the bucket, she removed the jar of that morning's milk, setting it in the shade, and unhooked the bucket from the rope. She took the ladle from its hook beside the well and carried both bucket of water and ladle to the garden.

Alexandre had paused, watching her approach. As she walked through the garden to where he stood and set down the bucket, she saw that wide, genuine smile curve his lips and crease the corners of his eyes. "I thought you might be thirsty," she said, feeling almost shy as she handed him the dripping ladle.

His smile widened in appreciation. "*Merci.*" He took the ladle, swallowed its contents in one draught, and refilled it again.

When he dipped the ladle in for a third time, she chuckled. "I think I was right."

But he didn't drink it. Instead, he held the ladle out to her. She took it and swallowed several mouthfuls, then handed it back to him. "Thank you."

"Do you want any more?" he asked. When she shook her head, he added, "Then stand away."

When she stepped back, he set the ladle aside and lifted the bucket. He poured the remaining water slowly over his head. "Ahhh," he said with obvious pleasure.

Tess stared, watching the water flow over him, forming tiny rivers between the muscles of his body, clinging in droplets to the hair of his chest, glossing his smooth brown skin.

A queer little ache hit her in the belly, forming a knot of heat and radiating outward, to the back of her throat, to the tips of her fingers, to the balls of her feet. She felt suddenly odd, restless and fluttery. It was an unfamiliar, uncomfortable feeling. But it was not unpleasant.

She watched him shake his head vigorously from side to side, then fling it back. Drops of water spattered her like a light drizzle of rain, wetting her dress and cooling her skin. She took a hasty step backward and the feeling was gone.

The long strands of his hair curled and clung to his shoulders like the variegated marks of marble until he raked a hand over the crown of his head and pulled them back. Then he handed the bucket to her. "Thank you again, mademoiselle. Now go back and sit. Rest yourself."

"Can't I help you?"

"I think you've done enough work for one day. Besides, I'm almost finished." He nodded toward the chestnut tree. "Lie down in the shade. Have a nap."

Without a word, she turned and walked over to the tree. Pulling off her hat, she tossed it aside. She sat down, stretched out her legs, arranged her skirts and leaned back against the trunk. Resting her folded hands on her roundness, she continued to watch him. She couldn't take a nap now. Not while Alexandre did the work she should have been doing. Not while he could see how lazy she was being. But the day was warm, and she did feel very sleepy, and some things were difficult to resist. Within five minutes her eyes fluttered shut, and she drifted off to sleep.

Alexandre watched her as he worked, noting with a smile the moment her head dropped slightly to the right and her hands fell to her sides. He glanced down the last row. He'd finish this, he decided, then join her. He continued down the row, finally pulling the last weed with a heartfelt sigh of relief. He hated gardening.

He tossed the weed aside and walked over to the chestnut tree. She was sound asleep, but leaning back against the rough bark could not be comfortable. He sank down to the ground beside her.

Leaning forward, he grasped her shoulders and turned her body so that she could lie down. She stirred but did not awaken. He laid her head gently in his lap and then stretched out fully, his body perpendicular to hers. His belly wasn't the best pillow he could offer her, he supposed, but it would do.

7

Tess explored the winery on the following day. This was the first moment of free time she'd allowed herself in over a week, and her walk had led her through the vineyards. The vines were vigorous. But, unattended, they were badly in need of pruning.

She walked down the slope between rows of lush vines, which grew wild and unchecked along their poles, thinking what a shame it was. The vineyard could have been productive. But Alexandre didn't seem to care.

Alexandre. When she had wakened from her nap the day before, she'd found herself with her head resting on his stomach. Shock, fear and embarrassment had all shot through her as she had moved to sit up. But his hand had reached out in sleep to gently stroke her hair, and she had remained where she was, slowly coming to the realization that she was enjoying it. She'd enjoyed the feel of his strong fingers pulling through her curls. She'd enjoyed the feel of his flat, hard stomach beneath her head and the deep, rhythmic sound of his breathing.

She stopped walking, staring with unseeing eyes at the grapevines before her. In her mind she saw his face, relaxed in sleep. By that time, she'd been sitting up, arms hugging her knees, watching him. She saw how his thick lashes rested like tiny black fans beneath his closed eyes. She saw the shadow of stubble that was beginning to form along his square jaw. She had reached out her hand, wondering if his cheek would feel rough with the texture of fine sand or soft like a ripe peach, but she'd snatched her hand back without finding out.

She saw the rise and fall of his wide chest. She saw the triangle of black hair that tapered with his torso to his narrow waist, disappearing into the black of his trousers. She saw his long hair weaving through the blades of grass around his face in a tangled tapestry.

When he had woken, she'd watched the lazy way his arms had moved above his head, his body giving a tiny shudder of stretching muscles. She hadn't seen any more because she'd turned her face away, leaning back against the tree with eyes closed, feigning sleep. But she'd heard his deep, regretful yawn, sensed his languorous, sleep-drugged movements as he'd sat up.

Standing in the vineyard, thinking about yesterday, brought back that odd little ache in the pit of her stomach. She pressed one hand to her round abdomen, and she wondered why she'd never felt that way when she'd looked at Nigel's lean, hairless chest.

But she knew why. The sight of Nigel's naked chest had meant only one thing, and that thing had meant more humiliation, more pain.

She closed her eyes for a moment, willing herself not to think of Nigel. His arrogant, handsome face formed in her mind, but it quickly faded, replaced by another. A face not so handsome, but somehow more compelling. A face that frowned with the anger of genuine concern, not the rage of thwarted whims. A face that didn't use handsomeness to charm and to beguile, but that smiled with the genuine pleasure of a simple task well done.

Tess opened her eyes, seeing more than a vineyard. She suddenly saw something else. She saw that one man wasn't always just like another. She realized that a man's hand could do things other than inflict pain. It could spoon soup into the mouth of a sick woman, could paint life into a blank canvas, could provide a gentle caress. She had been seeing Alexandre as if he were just like Nigel. But he wasn't like Nigel at all.

She remembered other men. Her father, whose hand had composed sermons and snatched scones from Molly's kitchen. Old Herbert, whose hand had planted flowers with loving care. She had forgotten that a man's hands could be gentle. Nigel had erased such things from her mind. But Alexandre was helping her to remember.

The nearby sound of a bird rustling its wings broke into Tess's reverie. She started, looking over at the big black crow perched atop the pole beside her. "I'm afraid it's too early for you to feast on grapes, my friend," she told the bird with a smile. "You'll have to wait a few months."

Its only answer was a loud, irritated squawk before it lifted its wings and flew away in search of food elsewhere. Tess resumed her walk through the vineyard, feeling lighter of heart and more optimistic about life than she had felt in a very long time.

She found the gray stone buildings that formed the winery itself. They stood empty in a valley at the center of the vineyards, looking as desolate as the château, the barn, and the man who owned them. She entered the first of three buildings.

What a waste, she thought, walking between rows of huge vats, the sunshine pouring through the doorway lighting her way in the cool, windowless room. She knew little of wine making, but there seemed to be a vast array of equipment and supplies. Once, this winery had been productive and busy. Thrifty by nature, Tess simply could not understand why such a viable source of income remained unused.

Shaking her head, she emerged from the building into the bright sunlight. It truly was a shame. She turned toward the other buildings, intending to explore them as well, when she halted abruptly.

Several yards away, in the shadow between two buildings, stood a donkey. The animal carried nothing, but its back was swayed from too many past burdens. The bones of its ribs and flanks plainly showed its years of hunger. Tess's heart constricted with pity. She took a step forward, and the donkey shied back with a frightened bray.

She reached out her hand and moved forward more slowly, speaking to the animal in a soft voice. "It's all right, love. Don't be afraid."

The donkey didn't shy this time. It simply raised its head, staring at her with wide, sad eyes, as if too tired to care. She stepped closer and saw the reason why.

Its back and sides were crisscrossed with the scars of a whip. Dried blood caked the most recent ones. A deep wave of anger, hot and strong, shimmered through her. More than anger. Empathy.

Tears stung her eyes and she reached out a tentative hand to stroke the donkey's neck. "Oh," she choked, "you poor, poor thing."

The donkey hung its head, as if ashamed. Tess knew. Oh yes, she knew.

She wrapped her arms around the donkey's neck, buried her face in its short, ratted mane. And she cried.

It was a long time before she lifted her head. She brushed aside her tears with a hasty swipe of her hand. "You ran away, didn't you? Don't worry, sweetheart. I'm going to take you home with me." She stroked the animal with a gentle hand and vowed, "No one will ever hurt you again. I swear it."

Grasping the mane, she led the animal toward the château. It followed obediently, resigned to whatever fate lay ahead.

It was late afternoon. The sun was falling behind the rocky hills in a blaze of crimson and salmon against the azure blue of the sky.

She led the donkey to the stable and into one of the stalls. Giving it a final affectionate pat, she said, "I'm going to get you something to eat. I'll ask Alexandre if there's hay anywhere about."

She made her way back to the château in search of Alexandre. She passed through the kitchen, only vaguely noticing the appetizing smell of something on the stove.

She found Alexandre in his studio, cleaning paint-brushes. He paused, brush in hand, as he watched her head and shoulders emerge from the spiral staircase in the corner. "*Bon soir,* mademoiselle. Is it time for us to prepare *le diner?*"

Dinner was the last thing on her mind at the moment. She shook her head impatiently. "Do you have any hay?"

"Hay?" A puzzled frown creased his brow at her curious request. "It's summer, mademoiselle. Sophie won't need hay until autumn."

She sighed. "You have none, then?" When he shook his head, she asked, "What about grain?"

He set down the brush, turning to face her. "There is a bag of oats in the barn. What is all this about?"

Tess hesitated, suddenly realizing that he might not be pleased about the donkey. Wildly, she wondered if she could hide the animal. Silly. He'd find it within a day.

She thought again of the abuse the donkey had suffered. Surely, if Alexandre saw it, he would let her keep it. "Come with me. I'll show you."

She took him out to the stable. As they approached its stall, the donkey lifted its head, but its ears hung down like long, limp blades of grass. Dispirited, it stared at them without moving.

"I'm back," she told the animal softly, reaching out to scratch between its ears. "I think I'll name you Flower."

"A donkey?" Alexandre's voice slashed through the air. "You brought home a donkey?"

She turned back to him. He stood with hands on hips, a frown on his face. She'd been right. He was not pleased at all. "I found her in the vineyards. You can see she's been shamefully abused—"

"Who's going to take care of it?" he demanded.

"I will."

"You work too hard as it is."

"Alexandre, feeding one donkey is hardly work."

"And after you're gone? Then what?"

Tess swallowed hard at the stinging words that reminded her that her situation was only temporary, that this wasn't her home. "I'll take Flower with me."

She watched the muscle work at the corner of his jaw. "I don't want a donkey named Flower."

"Then you give her a name."

"I don't want to name her. I don't want her at all!" His scowl was fierce.

Tess stared him down bravely, even though her knees felt like giving way. "Then her name is Flower. And we are going to keep her."

"We are not. It probably belongs to one of the peasant farmers hereabouts. He'll want it back. These people are poor. They need their animals."

Tess folded her arms beneath her breasts and widened her stance stubbornly. "Whoever owns this donkey forfeited all rights to it by treating it so cruelly."

"That doesn't signify. A man has the right to do what

he wants with his animals. It isn't our place to interfere."

Tess wanted to scream. *That's what men say about their wives, too!* Firmly putting aside any fear of Alexandre's anger in her concern for Flower's welfare, she said, "If the animal really meant anything to the owner, he wouldn't have abused her like this. Men should . . ." She swallowed hard. "Men should protect and take care of what belongs to them." She waved an angry hand in the donkey's direction. "Look at her, Alexandre! Abused and starved. Have you no pity?"

Alexandre looked from her to the pathetic donkey and back again. "You feed it, then. You take care of it. If its owner comes looking for it, we will give it back. If not, you'll take it with you when you leave." Turning, he walked out of the stable.

He went back to the château, her words echoing in his head. *A man should take care of what belongs to him.* He passed the now well-ordered garden, knowing he'd have to keep on weeding the damn thing.

He marched up the back stairs and across the now-clean kitchen. He still didn't know where she'd put those paintbrushes. During the past few weeks, he really hadn't given the matter much thought. He had other paintbrushes, of course, and he hadn't bothered to ask where she'd put them. But at this moment, the fact that they were missing irritated him greatly.

His boots stomped across the now dust-free floors as he headed for the only place in this house that still seemed to be his. He began ascending the stairs to his studio. She wanted a donkey? Fine. She could be the one to take care of it.

He stopped abruptly on the first landing. He stared down at the jar of wildflowers on the hall table below. His gaze moved to the door into the dining room, to the basket of plums that now stood on the table. Seeing those womanly touches, he felt frustrated. He shouted,

"I just want to be left alone!" The words echoed in the empty château.

Then a faint meow of protest answered him. He looked down to the foot of the stairs. There, on the bottom step, was Augustus. Too tiny to skip nimbly up the steep stairs, the kitten was struggling on the first step, trying to follow him.

Alexandre watched as Augustus rested his forepaws on the second step and lifted one back leg again and again, trying to hoist himself up. But he kept slipping off, unable to sink his tiny claws into the stone surface. Persistence paid off, however, and he finally made it, rolling on to the second step. Then he began to tackle the third.

Alexandre raked a hand through his hair, and the ribbon tying it back came loose, falling to the floor. *A man should take care of what belongs to him.* "No!" he told the kitten, pointing toward the kitchen. "Go back."

Augustus meowed and climbed up on to the third step. Then the fourth.

Alexandre slammed his palm against the wall in exasperation, wondering exactly when he'd lost control of his own life. He didn't want a pregnant woman living in his house. He didn't want a donkey. He didn't want a cat. A goat and some chickens were all he could handle.

They were all things a man had to be responsible for. Tess was right. A man should take care of what belonged to him. But the woman didn't belong to him. The donkey didn't belong to him. The cat didn't belong to him. He didn't want to take care of them. He wasn't any good at it.

"Go back!" he repeated his command, glaring down at the tiny animal.

Augustus gave a plaintive wail for help and kept climbing.

Alexandre watched the kitten struggle for a moment

longer, then uttered a curse and came down. He scooped up the kitten with one hand. Turning, he marched back up the stairs. "Your trust in me is sorely misplaced, *mon ami.*"

Augustus meowed and burrowed into the crook of his arm, not at all intimidated by that comment.

When Tess came into the house after feeding Flower a bucket of oats and getting her fresh water, Alexandre was not in the kitchen as she expected, waiting to start their evening cooking lesson.

She noticed again the appetizing smell and walked over to the stove. Lifting the lid of the pot, she saw pieces of chicken simmering in water, making a rich stock. She placed the lid back over the pot with a thoughtful frown.

He was probably in his studio. She knew he wasn't happy about the donkey. He didn't seem to want the company of anyone, not servants, not her, not the animals. He was such a solitary man. She wished she knew why.

Tess bit her lip, uncertain, not knowing if he'd simply forgotten about their cooking lesson or if he was avoiding her. She didn't want to disturb him if he wanted to be alone. But it hurt to think he'd forgotten about her.

Turning away from the stove, she walked into the buttery. She knew enough now about cooking to make a meal by herself. She could make dinner and take it up to him. She set to work.

Some time later, Tess carried a tray laden with food up to the tower. She had the hem of her skirt draped over one arm so she wouldn't trip and gripped the heavy tray in both hands as she carefully climbed the stairs.

She smiled, looking down at the tray. Three weeks ago, she had failed at making a meal. This time, she had done it with ease. On the tray were two steaming bowls of chicken stew, a baguette of bread, an apple walnut torte, a bottle of Alexandre's wine, two glasses, two napkins, and flatware. Granted, it was a simple meal, but she was still rather proud of herself. More than that, she was pleased she could do something nice for the complex man who'd done so much for her.

Alexandre must not have heard her coming. When she reached the last few steps of the spiraling staircase and emerged into the room, he wasn't looking at her. He was staring at the canvas resting on the easel before him as his left hand moved a brush across it. His face was in profile to her, but she could see his intent expression, the frown of concentration that drew his brows together.

Night had fallen, and the room was ablaze with the light of many lamps, making it as bright as day.

Alexandre's movements were rapid, almost frenzied, as he dipped the brush into the paint on his palette and moved it across the canvas without hesitation. There was an intensity about his movements, a passion that radiated from him, and she hesitated by the stairs, unwilling to interrupt.

She heard a soft meow and turned her head to see Augustus amble across the room. The kitten did not share her own hesitation, however. He moved between Alexandre's feet, rubbing his body against the man's boots and meowing plaintively.

"Not now, *mon ami*," Alexandre told the kitten, his attention fixed on the canvas before him.

Augustus responded with another meow.

"I know you're hungry," he said, not pausing in his movements. "You'll have to wait."

The kitten curled his body over Alexandre's right foot, his chin resting on the tip of the boot, his tail curled around the ankle. He gave one last disgruntled meow and fell asleep.

Tess couldn't stifle the giggle that bubbled from her throat.

Alexandre turned his head to give her a quick, impatient glance. She was still smiling at the sight of this huge man with a tiny kitten napping on his boot. Slowly, the impatient look left his face as he looked at her and realized what an incongruous picture he must make. An answering smile tugged at the corners of his mouth as he turned back to his painting and resumed his work.

She stepped farther into the room. Clearing a space on one of the tables, she set down the tray. "This is the man who hates cats," she teased.

Alexandre kept painting. "The cat, unfortunately, does not hate me." His tone was rueful.

"He has excellent judgment, I think," she whispered, so softly he did not hear. She poured the wine into the glasses and asked over her shoulder, "Are you hungry? I've brought you something to eat."

He glanced at her again, one black eyebrow rising skeptically. "Did you taste it first?"

"I did." She smiled at him. "It's delicious. I think I'm becoming an excellent cook."

He looked down at Augustus. "My cook," he told the kitten, "is very talented. Modest, too."

Augustus meowed.

Alexandre glanced toward the table. "I'm afraid not, *mon ami.* I see no milk on the tray."

Augustus' responding meow was so disgusted, Tess laughed aloud. "I'm terribly sorry," she told the kitten. "I didn't know you were up here."

She looked up at Alexandre, who was watching her. The reluctant smile she'd pulled from him had widened into that full, heart-stopping grin, the one that always seemed to catch her by surprise. Once again, she felt that strange little ache. More than that, she felt an indescribable longing for something, something she fancied she should recognize, but didn't.

Picking up one of the wine-filled glasses, she took it to him. He set the brush and palette on the table to his left, then reached out his right hand. His fingers brushed hers as he took the offered glass, but Tess didn't tense at the brief contact. She found herself savoring it.

He took a sip of the wine, then strolled past her to the table. "What have we here?" He studied the tray for a moment, then he looked at her. "I see you turned my chicken into stew."

She walked over to stand beside him. "Yes, I did." With a smile, she added, "It's the only chicken dish you taught me how to make."

He gave her an answering smile and set his glass on the tray beside hers. "We should eat this excellent meal before it gets cold." Glancing around, he added, "We'll have to sit on the floor."

"Why aren't there any chairs up here?"

He shrugged. "I'd never use them. If I'm working, I'm either painting or pacing the floor in frustration." Lifting the tray, he walked to an open space across the room. He set the tray on the floor then reached out an arm to her. Tess walked over to him, and he assisted her in lowering to a sitting position. He sat opposite her, the tray between them.

Picking up a spoon and a bowl of the stew, he sampled her solitary cooking effort. "*Très bon,*" he complimented, dipping his spoon for another taste.

A thrill of pride and gratification shot through her. "You're only saying that because it's your recipe," she teased, picking up her own bowl.

As they ate, Augustus walked over to the tray and let out a loud wail. He began to circle them, voicing his displeasure with plaintive meows.

Alexandre paused in the act of lifting the spoon to his mouth, and his face took on a stern expression. "Augustus, lie down and be quiet. The mademoiselle will feed you when we are finished."

The kitten immediately fell silent. He walked over to Alexandre and rubbed his head against the man's knee with an affectionate purr.

Tess watched them happily. "You have made a friend, I think."

He sighed. "It would seem so."

She glanced around the studio. Her gaze moved to the stack of linen-wrapped portraits that leaned against the wall, and she wondered again about the woman. But she did not ask about her. Instead, she broached another subject. "Is this your ancestral home?" she asked, tearing a piece from the loaf of bread between them.

He nodded. "The Dumond family has held this land for five centuries."

"How did you manage to keep it during the Revolution?"

"I didn't." He paused a long moment, and Tess thought he was not going to say any more. Then, very softly, he added, "Robespierre accused my father of treason. The Jacobins executed both my parents in Paris in 1792. I was five years old."

Tess drew in a sharp breath. "I'm so sorry," she whispered. She, too, knew how painful it was to lose one's parents, but to lose them must have been especially difficult for a five-year-old boy.

He didn't hear her. His words flowed faster now as if he suddenly needed to talk. "I was here at the time and Lucien, my father's wine master, adopted me. I lived with his family while I watched my lands taken over by a wealthy bourgeois who only came here once a year. The rest of the time, Lucien managed the estates for him."

"How did you get the land back?"

He picked up a knife from the tray and began slicing the apple torte into sections. "When Napoleon began his Egyptian campaign, he took possession of my home for military purposes. Because my land sits right on the Mediterranean Sea, it made an excellent military outpost."

He gestured to their surroundings. "This tower was originally one of four, but in the sixteenth century Provence law declared that towers were too ostentatious, and all four towers had to be torn down. Napoleon rebuilt this one as a watchtower to the sea. While I was in Italy, Lucien continued to manage the lands for Napoleon until 1814, making brandy and other wines for the army. When the Corsican fell and Louis came to power, I returned from Florence and petitioned the king to restore to me my lands and title. He agreed. I have lived here ever since."

"Title?"

He bowed his head to her. "Mademoiselle, allow me to formally introduce myself. I am the Comte de Junot."

But who is the girl in the portrait? Tess looked down at the dark blue pool of muslin surrounding her. *Who wore this dress?*

But he said nothing more, and their meal was finished in silence.

While Alexandre helped himself to a second slice of apple torte, Tess started to rise to her feet. He immediately moved to help her, but she waved him to sit. "I can still stand by myself," she told him, getting to her feet. "Although," she added, "in a few weeks that will all change." She ran a hand over her abdomen, gently stroking where the baby nestled.

Alexandre's mouth went dry at her words, at her soft, loving voice. He tried to swallow the mouthful of apple torte, failed, and grabbed for his wine glass to wash it down. Mesmerized, he watched her small hand move so tenderly over her swollen belly. He saw the soft, maternal expression on her face as she gazed down. She looked like a Bellini madonna. He couldn't breathe.

A squeezing pain constricted his heart as memories

invaded his mind. Memories of another woman's face, a look not so loving. Her terrified words. *"I hate this baby. I hate it . . . hate it . . ."*

"Alexandre?"

He came out of the past with a start. Tess was looking down at him with concern, her stroking hand stilled now, resting on her roundness. He rose abruptly and brushed past her to the painting he had yet to finish. "Thank you for the meal, mademoiselle," he said, his voice sounding harsh to his own ears. "But I have work to do."

It was a clear dismissal. Tess swallowed past the painful lump of hurt in her throat, unable to understand what she had said wrong.

She left the tray on the floor. Instead, she picked up Augustus and left the studio without a word. As she descended the stairs, she glanced up for one last look.

He didn't even notice her departure. He was stabbing at the painting with savage brush strokes, oblivious to everything but the images he was creating on canvas.

8

By the time Alexandre laid the last brush stroke to the painting, the sea and sky to the southeast were beginning to blush with the delicate pink of dawn. He dropped the brush into a jar of linseed oil and rubbed his tired eyes with the tips of his fingers. The painting was finished. His obsession was gone, his passion was sated.

In a few days, when he could be objective, he would examine his night's work, adding the final touches. But the essence was there, on canvas. He walked over to the eastern window. Leaning one shoulder against the window frame, he folded his arms over his chest and watched the sunrise, feeling suddenly bereft and empty.

It was always that way when he finished a painting. How he hated these times. His arm ached, and his body was weary. He should sleep, but he knew from experience that peaceful sleep would elude him just now.

The mademoiselle would awaken soon. He should fetch the water for her. It was something he did every morning. It was the least he could do. After all, she cleaned the chamber pots. He'd rather haul twenty buckets of water up the stairs than clean chamber pots. There were, he decided, some positive aspects to having a housekeeper.

And she always thanked him for the water. Every morning when she came downstairs for their cooking lesson, she thanked him. She was a woman who seemed to take very little for granted.

He could understand that. Life had taught her a fine lesson. She had given her trust to some man who had used her and left her to face the shame and responsibility alone. What kind of man would do such a thing? If the babe were his . . .

Alexandre sighed and straightened away from the window. It was a crass and ugly world when a man could desert the woman who carried his child.

Tess was awakened by a cramp that caught her low across the belly. She sucked in her breath sharply, holding a hand to the round swell of her abdomen. Rolling from her side to her back, Tess realized that did absolutely no good and turned back to her side, knowing the cramp would soon pass. After a moment, the pain eased, and she rose from the bed.

Cupping her hands beneath her roundness, she sighed. "I'm getting so fat," she murmured ruefully to Augustus, who was curled on one of the pillows of her bed. "I'm probably starting to waddle when I walk." She moved her hands up and down, rubbing the itchy skin of her abdomen. Sometimes, she thought, pregnancy was very inconvenient.

The water Alexandre usually left for her was not outside her door, but it was still quite early. He might still be asleep. Tess dressed and took Augustus downstairs to the kitchen.

She hoped he would not still be angry. She knew he'd been irritated about the donkey, but during their meal together in the studio, they had seemed to deal together rather well. Then, all of a sudden, he had turned brusque and cold. It was as if a wall had slammed down between them.

She set Augustus on the floor, and the kitten immediately let out a loud meow. "Not yet," she told him. "I have to milk Sophie before you can eat."

She took the two pails from their hooks on the wall and headed for the hen house. But she set the pails down beside the gate into the chickens' pen and went to the stable first. She wanted to look in on Flower.

The donkey was standing in the stall, her head hung low. Tess walked over to her and gently scratched between her ears, murmuring a soft greeting. She noticed the flies gathering around the still-fresh wounds on Flower's back and knew she had to do something about it. Perhaps bathing the animal would help.

Taking the coil of rope that lay in the corner, Tess led Flower outside and around the corner of the stable, where she tethered the donkey to a post. Then she went to the well for water.

Alexandre stood by the window, watching the sun until it rose above the sea. He then extinguished the lamps that still burned and left the studio. Making his way downstairs, he entered the kitchen. Augustus was standing by the back door, meowing loudly. "Hungry, *mon ami*? The mademoiselle may not wake for a while."

Augustus let out a wail as Alexandre took the two water buckets from their place beside the kitchen door and went downstairs, where he filled them from the pump.

After leaving one bucket of water at Tess's closed door, he took the other to his own room, thinking he really ought to get the bathtub out of Anne-Marie's room for Tess's use. He hadn't thought about it before. If he wanted a full bath, he simply walked down to the sea. But being *enceinte* she'd find the steep path to the sea too difficult. Besides, a woman ought to have a bathtub.

After a bath and a shave, he returned to the kitchen. Augustus was still standing by the back door, mewling indignantly. Taking a basket from the cupboard, Alexandre stepped carefully over the kitten and went down to the garden for fresh herbs and vegetables.

Because of the heat, the summer vegetables were already ripe, and he decided he'd teach the mademoiselle how to make ratatouille today. He began to rummage for onions, eggplant, sweet peppers, tomatoes, and zucchini.

As much as Alexandre hated gardening, he also loved good food. His philosophy was simple: plant a lot of everything and harvest whatever the insects and weeds didn't kill. There was always enough. But as he gathered the vegetables, he was forced to admit that finding them was much easier when there were no weeds to get in the way.

He pulled one last pepper. As he straightened, he heard the sound of a cock crow and glanced toward the hen house. His gaze moved to the stable and he dropped the pepper into the basket with a sigh of irritation. The door was open. It was likely that Tess had forgotten to close it the night before and her precious donkey had probably wandered off.

He walked past the barn to the stable and was just about to step inside, when the sound of Tess's voice stopped him. He turned and walked past the open door, following the sound of her voice around the corner. He halted abruptly at the sight that greeted him.

The donkey was tethered to a fence post, facing him. Standing beside the animal was Tess, a bucket of water beside her and a rag in her hand.

His gaze moved over her and a wry smile touched his mouth. She had tied her long skirts up around her knees, revealing the white petticoat beneath, its lace hem dragging in the dirt. As she squeezed water from the rag over the donkey's scar-crossed back, she talked softly to the animal as if they were sharing confidences.

". . . and everything will be all right now," she said. "You'll see. Alexandre and I will take good care of you. Nobody is going to hurt you any more."

He felt a sudden twinge of guilt, and he tried to brush it aside. He didn't want a damned donkey, he told himself. The animal obviously belonged to someone. At the first opportunity, he'd seek out the fellow and give him back his property.

He stepped forward. "*Bonjour,* mademoiselle. You're up early this morning."

She froze, her hand poised over the donkey's back. "Good morning," she answered without looking at him. "I was just giving the donkey a bath," she added unnecessarily.

"So I see." He heard a soft snort and turned his gaze back to Flower. He stared at the animal, really seeing her for the first time. Last night, he'd been too frustrated to notice much about her.

Soaking wet, she seemed even more pathetic than she had the night before. She was so thin, her ribs looked ready to break through her hide. The scars of abuse were painfully obvious. Tess had told him the animal had been abused and starved, but he hadn't been listening. He hadn't been looking. He was looking now.

The donkey was looking back at him. Her big brown eyes were dull and glassy and sad. No animal he'd ever seen looked more in need of help than this one.

He walked over to Tess as she continued to rinse the donkey's wounds with the rag. He glanced down at the bucket. "Plain water? *Non,* mademoiselle, that will not be enough."

She paused again and turned her head to look up at him. "I don't know what else to use," she confessed.

"I'm not very skilled in the medicinal arts. I love growing herbs, but I don't know much about how to use them."

He looked down into her face. Her eyes held him with that look again. That look that pleaded for understanding and help. He was beginning to fear that look. It did things to him. It tried to convince him of things he didn't believe in anymore. He sighed and reached out to take the rag from her hand. "Get something to dry off the animal. I will make an ointment for the wounds."

He saw the smile light her face, he saw the warmth of trust in her eyes. "We're not keeping it," he reminded her sternly. "When its owner comes looking for it, we are going to give it back."

She nodded, still smiling. "Whatever you say, Alexandre."

Nigel Ridgeway was not a happy man. He stared down at the letter that had come in the morning post, scanning the lines of Martin Trevalyn's handwriting with growing irritation. Pushing aside his breakfast of kippers, bacon, and toast, Nigel read the letter once again, unable to believe that they had still found no trace of his wife.

Trevalyn had been in Paris for nearly two weeks now and had uncovered only one tiny scrap of information. It was now confirmed that she had been in Paris, staying at an inn on the outskirts of the city for several days. But her stay had been in April, three months ago, and Trevalyn had no clue as yet where she had gone from there. He scowled down at the spidery handwriting.

"Is something wrong, Nigel?"

The earl gave a distracted glance at the woman seated at the opposite end of the table. He'd forgotten his mother was even there. But then, that wasn't surprising.

The dowager countess was a small woman who looked

much older than her fifty-three years. Though she sat rigidly straight in her chair, there was something about her that reminded him of a drooping flower. Perhaps it was the way she could never look him in the eye, or the apologetic way she spoke, or the perpetual expression of martyrdom she wore. She irritated him immensely. She always had. "No, Mother," he answered, "nothing at all."

He returned his gaze to the letter in his hand. He was not worried about finding Teresa. She had run away twice before, and he'd had no trouble locating her. She couldn't get far on the meager sum she'd gotten for the emeralds, in any case. But he had hoped to find her long before now. Before someone found out the truth.

He crushed the letter in his fist and tossed it onto his plate, where it landed atop a slice of marmalade-covered toast. "Sullivan!" he shouted, rising from his chair.

The valet appeared within moments. "Sir?"

"We are going to Paris immediately. Begin making the necessary preparations."

"Paris, sir?"

"Yes. Since I have no idea how long we will be forced to remain there, pack enough for an extended stay." He paused, then added, "Have Lady Aubry's maid pack some of her things as well."

It wasn't Sullivan's place to ask questions. "At once, my lord." He bowed and left the room to carry out his orders.

"Nigel?"

He gave his mother another distracted glance. "What?"

"Since you are going to France, I will return home to Northumberland immediately."

"Fine." He didn't care what she did. That wasn't important right now.

He stared down at the crushed letter on his plate. If that bumbling nodcock Trevalyn couldn't find Teresa, he would. Oh, yes. He'd hunt her down from post to pillar, but he'd find her. He always did. It was only a matter of time.

Tess rested the basket of wet laundry on her hip, watching Alexandre chop wood. She loved watching him work. There was something about the way he moved that always made her pause in her own tasks to stare at him. His shirt was off and as he swung the ax, she saw the muscles of his chest flex.

He tossed the split wood to the pile nearby and set another log on the stump. He stepped back, focused his aim, and swung the ax, cracking the log straight down the center. After two more quick blows of the ax, the log split and the two pieces tumbled to the ground. He chopped wood the same way he weeded the garden, at an unhurried but steady pace, without wasted energy.

She moved her basket to the opposite hip and leaned back against the stone wall of the courtyard behind her. Her gaze shifted to the pasture where Flower and Sophie grazed, free to move about since Alexandre had repaired the fence a few days before. The two had gotten off to a rather bad start when introduced, but Sophie had quickly asserted her authority, and poor Flower had capitulated without so much as a whimper. Now, only two days later, the pair dealt quite well together.

A movement by the tumble-down gatehouse beyond the pasture caught her attention and Tess straightened. A man was walking down the path toward the château. She knew instinctively that he was coming for Flower.

She dropped the basket and started forward, her heart pounding in her breast. But then a thought struck her and she stopped. She couldn't let anyone know she was staying here. She didn't know if authorities of the British crown still hunted for her, but she couldn't take the chance of letting them discover her whereabouts. If this man saw her and was later asked about her, he would tell the authorities she was living here.

Tess darted back into the courtyard. She peeked her head around the corner and jammed a fist into her mouth, watching helplessly as the man moved closer. The harness in his hand confirmed her suspicion.

The arrival was also noticed by Alexandre. He'd seen the man come through the gatehouse that led to the vineyards. But he continued to chop wood as the man came closer.

Alexandre took a deep breath and swung the ax, watching the blade sink into the stump, then turned toward the visitor, who had stopped a good ten feet away. "*Bonjour,*" he said, wiping his palms together. "What can I do for you, monsieur?"

The man was short and stout, with a thick mustache. His clothes were tattered and stained with dirt and wine. Alexandre did not miss the nervous way he twisted the strap of leather harness in his hands.

Alexandre's eyes narrowed at the sight of the other man's apprehension, and he placed his hands on his hips. "Monsieur? You are trespassing on my land. I suggest you state your business."

The man pointed toward the pasture. "I have come for my donkey."

"Indeed? And what proof have you that the animal is yours?"

The little man drew himself up, indignation replacing his trepidation and making his long mustaches quiver. "The animal is mine. She has my mark on her flank."

"She has your mark, right enough," Alexandre agreed, thinking of the scars on the donkey's back, thinking of the pain his own hand had caused the animal when he'd rubbed the ointment into her wounds. "The mark of a whip."

The man bristled. "The donkey is mine. I want her back. If you do not hand her over to me, I will go into the village and see the *maire*."

Alexandre opened his mouth to tell the man that would not be necessary and that he could take the donkey. But suddenly he imagined the look he'd see on Tess's face when she discovered her Flower was gone. He imagined how her eyes would stare accusingly up at him.

No. He couldn't do it. The donkey would have to stay. A donkey that would probably drop dead before it could be of any practical use. And he knew the reason for his change of heart was to avoid seeing hurt in a pair of dark green eyes.

"How much?" He barked out the question, not missing the man's shudder of fear. "How much for the donkey?"

The man stared at him in some surprise. "You want to buy her?" When Alexandre gave a sharp nod, he said, "One hundred francs."

Alexandre snorted. "One hundred? The animal's not worth ten."

"Livestock is scarce, monsieur." The little man shrugged. "One hundred francs."

"Twenty."

The man gestured heavenward. "I couldn't replace her for that! Eighty."

"If you take her back, you'll continue to mistreat her, she'll die and you'll have no donkey and no money. Thirty."

"Fifty. I'll go no lower." Despite his fear of Alexandre, the man's stance and tone of voice were firm.

Alexandre glanced up and found himself the victim of another pair of eyes. Brown, sad eyes staring at him from the pasture. He muttered a curse. "Fifty, then. Wait here."

He turned on his heel and walked toward the house. He passed Tess in the courtyard, knowing she'd probably heard the entire conversation. But he didn't stop. He went into the château.

When he returned a few moments later, he carried a small pouch. He thrust it toward the man. "Fifty francs. Now go."

The man grabbed the money, and Alexandre grabbed the harness. The man departed, scurrying back the way he had come. As Alexandre watched him disappear from view, he heard a sound behind him. Turning, he saw Tess standing a few feet away, her tear-filled eyes the color of wet leaves, her smile of gratitude like a shaft of sunlight. *Mon Dieu!* She was looking at him as if he were her *preux chevallier.* He felt suddenly suffocated.

He was no knight in shining armor! *Disillusion her,* he told himself desperately. *Tell her the truth about yourself. Tell her about Anne-Marie. Tell her every shameful detail, and see how she looks at you then.*

He couldn't do it. He said, "I have to finish chopping the wood." Turning back to the stump, he seized the ax and began to split the logs at a fast and furious pace. It seemed an eternity before she finally walked away.

9

He was avoiding her. There was no doubt in her mind. Tess set down the note he'd left on the kitchen table and slumped dejectedly into a chair. He would be gone all day, the note said. There would be no cooking lessons, no camaraderie, no Alexandre again today.

For over a week now, ever since he'd bought the donkey, he'd been doing his best to avoid her. He rose before she did and returned long after her sleepy eyes forced her into bed. Sometimes, she would find a bucket of freshly caught fish on the table when she came down to the kitchen in the mornings. Sometimes, she would find a chicken or pheasant, freshly plucked and butchered, when she returned from her afternoon walk. One day, she came down to find a bathtub in the kitchen with a note that told her she could use it if she wished. But she hardly ever saw him. When she did, they exchanged only brief words before he mumbled some excuse and went off.

In the evenings, she would sit at the kitchen table with a basket of mending, waiting for him to come

home. But he never returned until she had extinguished
the light and gone to bed. She knew because she would
not fall asleep until she heard his soft footsteps pass by,
until she heard his door open and close.

She had no idea what he did all day, but it was clear
she was not allowed to be part of it. Why? What had she
done?

Tess went over all the events leading up to his sudden
withdrawal and could find no explanation. All she knew
was that she didn't want to eat her meals alone any
more. She didn't want to have only the animals to talk
to.

She sighed and leaned forward, resting her elbow on
the table and her chin on her hand, feeling quite dismal.
The truth was that she needed Alexandre, but he didn't
need her. She needed his company, his strength, his
help. But he required nothing from her. Not even her
friendship. This week had made that plain.

He was a good man. But he was also a complicated
man. Unreachable. There were moments when he let her
into his solitary world, but they were brief. The walls
around him always came up again before she'd even realized they'd fallen down. Why?

He was a lonely man. But he made no effort to seek
out the company of anyone. In truth, he went to great
pains to avoid contact with the outside world. He went
to great pains to avoid *her.* Why?

But Tess knew she had no answers. Only questions.

Augustus strolled over to where she sat and rubbed
his head against her leg, meowing. She peeked beneath
the table and said, "I know. I miss him, too."

As she did her morning chores, Tess wondered for
perhaps the hundredth time what she could do to bridge
this chasm between them, to make them friends again.
She milked the goat, fed the chickens, retrieved the day's
eggs, and fed the donkey. But no ideas came to her.

Alexandre had done so much for her. She wished she could repay at least a tiny portion of that by doing something special for him. Perhaps, if she could think of just the right thing, he would stop avoiding her, and they could become friends again.

After taking Sophie and Flower out to graze, she left the pasture and headed back toward the château. She passed the berry patch and turned toward the barn, where she had left the milk and eggs sitting in the shade. The trouble was, she didn't know what Alexandre liked, she didn't know what he would enjoy . . .

She stopped abruptly on the path and turned back, staring at the wild tangle of the berry patch. She could see the purple-black of the first huge berries on the tall canes, ripe in the July heat. Birds were flying overhead and swooping down to gobble their share of the sweet-tart fruit.

"Perfect," she whispered. "Absolutely perfect."

Two hours later, Tess carefully wrapped blackberry tarts in linen napkins and placed them in the basket before her on the kitchen table. Under the tarts, the basket contained roast chicken, bread, cheese, and wine, everything needed for a picnic. All she needed now was Alexandre, and she had no idea where he was.

She placed a cloth over the top of the basket. Hooking it over one arm, she moved toward the door, pausing to grab her straw hat, which hung on a hook in the wall. Augustus, who was lying beneath the table, lifted his head and stared at her. "Well, come on," she told him, beckoning with the hat. "Don't dawdle. We may have to do quite a bit of searching before we find him."

The kitten had doubled in size since she'd found him in the barn a month ago. He skipped behind her down the stairs with ease. When she paused at the gate, he halted beside her. She looked down. "Which way, do you think?"

Augustus sat back on his haunches, yawned and lifted his paws to clean his face.

"Hmm . . . You don't know?" She looked around, deciding to take the path that led toward the sea, hoping perhaps she could see him without having to walk down the steep hillside.

But he wasn't there. Tess then tried the vineyards. Then the foothills of tall umbrella pines, cork oaks, and wild lavender that lay to the north. But after two hours of searching and calling his name, she still had not found him.

Feeling somewhat silly for thinking she could find him when she had no idea where to look, and also feeling very disappointed that she hadn't managed it anyway, Tess paused in a dry stream bed.

She was feeling hot and tired. Two hours of walking through the hills in the summer heat when she was six months pregnant had probably not been wise. Setting down the basket, which was becoming heavier with every step, she picked up Augustus, cradling the kitten in the crook of her arm. She pushed her hat back on her head and glanced around, her gaze roaming over the meadow behind her, the rocky, tree-dotted cliffs above her, and up and down the dry stream bed in which she stood.

"Alexandre?" she called. But only silence was her answer. She sighed, stroking the kitten's soft orange fur. "Where could he be?"

Feeling quite discouraged, she picked up the basket and turned back. He'd probably gone to the village. "It was silly idea anyway," she told the kitten, picking her way carefully across the dry, rocky stream bed.

Alexandre stared down at the book in his lap, unable to focus on the words of Voltaire. He settled back more comfortably against the ancient olive tree and crossed his legs, his eyes roaming the rocky hillside and meadow below.

He knew he couldn't keep avoiding her. But he didn't want to see her look up at him that way. With trust he didn't deserve, with expectations he couldn't fulfill. It hurt. It reminded him too much of what he'd once thought himself to be. He couldn't be any woman's hero. Not anymore.

He glanced down at the shirt he wore. It was one of the freshly laundered white linen shirts he'd found neatly folded on the chair of his bedchamber when he had finally come in late last night. He had returned much earlier, but he had not gone up. From the courtyard, he'd seen the light burning in the kitchen window. He'd sat on the stone bench, looking up at her silhouette bathed in the lamplight. She'd been sewing, mending one of the shirts he now wore, he fancied. Through the open window, he'd heard her humming as she worked. Occasionally, she had risen and walked across the room to fetch something and he'd seen her pause to run a hand in that loving gesture over her roundness before sitting down to resume her task.

He slammed the book shut and set it aside. She waited up for him. Every night. No one had waited up for Alexandre Dumond to come home for a very long time.

His gaze moved down the pair of black trousers he wore, trousers she'd left beside the shirts, to rest thoughtfully on his boots. The black leather now gleamed from the polish she'd given them. He should tell her she didn't have to do these things. He should tell her she didn't have to earn her keep. He should tell her she didn't have to wait up for him.

"Alexandre?"

The sound of her voice calling his name caused him to lift his head. He could see her far below, standing in the dry stream bed, looking around. In the crook of her arm was a bright orange spot he knew to be Augustus. Beside her was a picnic basket.

What she doing out here searching for him? Didn't she know better than to go tramping around in the heat? She was probably lost.

He watched as she picked up the basket and turned to retrace her steps. Her shoulders drooped as she trudged across the stream bed. He watched her take another step, stumble and pitch forward, falling to the loose, stony ground. The picnic basket flew from her hands, and its contents spilled out as it rolled away.

Sacré tonnerre! He was on his feet, moving faster than he'd ever moved in his life. A glimpse of stone stairs and a flash of tumbling blond hair and blue skirts danced through his memory as he ran, stumbled, and slid down the hillside. His heart was in his throat as he watched Tess roll over slowly onto her back with a soft moan. *Just like Anne-Marie.*

Was she going to miscarry? *Mon Dieu! Don't let her be hurt,* he prayed to a God he knew wouldn't listen. As she sat up, he fell to his knees beside her, breathing hard, hearing her dazed moans with a sick feeling of dread. Reality that had turned to a dream was becoming reality again. He reached for her.

"Tess! Tess! Are you all right?"

She opened her eyes and drew a deep breath through her nose, expelling it slowly through her mouth. "I think so." Her voice was shaky.

He pushed her gently down onto her back, running his hand over her abdomen. "Do you feel any pain?"

She drew several more deep breaths before she nodded. "My ankle. I think I twisted it."

"Your . . ." He swore. "But the babe, Tess. What about the babe?"

She started to sit up again, but he pushed her back

down. "Don't move," he ordered. "Lie here for a moment."

"Alexandre, I'm all right." She sat up, cupping her hands beneath her roundness. "The baby is fine."

He didn't believe her. "How do you know? What if it isn't? *Mon Dieu.*" He pushed the hair out of his eyes and swore again.

"Alexandre." She placed a hand on his arm and smiled with reassurance. "The baby is fine. Babies are very resilient, you know."

"I don't know anything of the sort!" he snapped. "Tess, you took ten years of my life when you fell. Do you realize that?"

"You saw me fall?" Her smile faded. "You were watching me. You knew I was here." He heard the hurt in her voice, saw the accusation in her eyes.

He rolled his eyes heavenward. Who cared about that now? He moved away from her side, toward her feet. "Which foot hurts?"

She didn't have to tell him. Her cry when he lifted her right foot was his answer. He pushed her skirts higher up her legs and pulled off the leather slipper she wore. He cradled her foot in his lap, running his hand over her stocking-clad ankle. "I don't believe it's broken, just sprained."

"Why?" she asked softly.

He knew what she was asking. He ignored the question. "Are you certain you're all right? The babe is all right?"

When she nodded, he moved to her side and put his arm beneath her knees with the intention of lifting her, but she put a hand on his arm to stop him. "Wait! Augustus?" She glanced around. "Where is he?"

Alexandre looked over the top of her head and saw the kitten sitting several feet away, watching them. "He's right over there." Rising to his feet, Alexandre retrieved the basket and lifted the kitten, gently putting him inside. He placed Tess's slipper and hat in the basket as well. The food and broken bottle of wine, he left where they were. Placing the basket in her lap, he said, "I'm going to carry you back to the house. Are you certain you don't feel any pain with the babe?"

"I'm certain."

He lifted her into his arms, basket, kitten and all, and rose to his feet. But he had a difficult time standing. Now that it was over, his knees threatened to give way. A tremble ran through his body as he stood motionless, holding her against his chest, thinking about what could have happened. "*Sacrebleu,*" he muttered, resting his chin atop her head. "You scared me."

"I know. I rather scared myself."

Holding the basket with one hand, she curled her free arm around his neck. She rested her head against his shoulder.

His arms tightened protectively as he turned and began walking in the direction of the château. "Don't ever do it again," he ordered.

Neither of them spoke until they reached the house. Alexandre carried her up the stairs into the kitchen and set her gently in a chair as she placed the basket on the table. "I'll be right back."

She watched him grab a bucket and head down the stairs. When he returned, the bucket was full of water. He set the bucket beside her feet and dropped to his knees. She watched as he removed her other shoe and both her stockings, sucking in her breath sharply at the pain in her ankle.

He glanced up with a frown of concern, then looked back down at her bare feet resting on his thighs. He took her right foot in his hands. "Can you move your toes?"

She complied, biting her lower lip. She watched as his brown fingers ran lightly over the white skin of her instep, and she shivered, but not from pain. The touch of his fingers did strange things to her insides.

He pulled the bucket forward, guiding her foot into the cold water. As she felt the water cover her swollen ankle, she uttered a relieved sigh and lifted her other foot into the bucket as well.

"Oh," she breathed, leaning her back against the wooden one of the chair. "That feels good."

"If you didn't go traipsing all over the countryside, you wouldn't have sore feet," he pointed out. "Or a sprained ankle."

She lifted her head. "I wouldn't have gone traipsing all over the countryside," she returned with some spirit, "if I hadn't had the silly idea of being nice and taking you a picnic lunch."

He grinned at her feisty tone. "I'm sure it was a very tasty meal."

"It was," she grumbled. "I made roast chicken with tarragon. And there was bread and cheese. I even made blackberry tarts, *your* favorite."

His grin faded. "You made me blackberry tarts?"

She sniffed. "I did."

Rising to his feet, he said, "I'm going to get some herbs to make a poultice for that ankle." He paused at the door. "Tess?" When she looked up, he said, "When your ankle is better, I'd like some more blackberry tarts."

The warm glow in her heart lasted all day.

"But I want to move the rook. Shouldn't I take your knight now, while I have the chance?"

Alexandre shook his head. He pointed to one of the pieces on the chessboard between them. "If you do, you leave your queen unprotected."

"I didn't see that." Tess frowned down at the board, her thick, chestnut brows drawn together in concentration.

It was her first chess lesson and she wasn't doing too badly. He'd checkmate her in about three moves, but she'd managed to last quite a while. He watched her reach out toward the board and hesitate, her hand poised over her remaining bishop. She bit her lip uncertainly and glanced at him. He smiled. "Don't keep looking to me for help. If I continue telling you what to do, you won't learn."

"Beast." She stuck out her tongue at him and moved the bishop.

Without hesitation, he reached out and moved a pawn two spaces forward.

He studied her in the lamplight as she contemplated her next move. The evening breeze from the open window of the library ruffled her unruly curls and the lamplight gave them the glow of burnished copper. Her chair sat at an angle with her feet resting on a padded footstool. He'd bound her swollen ankle with a poultice of crushed comfrey leaves that had reduced the swelling, but she wouldn't be able to walk on it for several days.

He frowned. She'd scared the life out him when she'd taken that tumble this afternoon, and he realized with a pang of guilt that he shouldn't have left her alone all this time. He closed his eyes and swallowed hard. Anything might have happened. What if she'd taken that fall somewhere else and he hadn't been there? What if she'd had a miscarriage? His mouth went dry with fear, and he reached for the glass of wine at his side.

He had to stay close by. He couldn't leave her alone again. He couldn't let anything happen to her.

He set down his glass and looked at her face. She was still studying the board, trying to decide on her next move.

The month she'd been in his home had brought about subtle changes to her face and form. She was gaining weight, losing that thin sharpness. Her abdomen was larger, rounder. Her eyes were still haunting and huge, but there was no tinge of fear in their forest green depths. Her skin was still pale, but it was the healthy tint of fresh cream, not the sick gray pallor he'd first seen. Her bow-shaped lips now curved often into a smile. The planes of her face were still sharp and thin, but they were softening. Alexandre the artist had known all along that she was a beautiful woman. But Alexandre the man suddenly realized it.

It was inevitable—he had to paint her.

"Alexandre?"

He started. "Hmm? What?"

"It's your move."

"Oh." He glanced down at the board and moved his knight. "Checkmate."

Resting her elbow on the table, she cupped her chin in her hand and sighed. "I knew I should've taken that knight."

He laughed. "If you had, I'd have had you three moves ago."

She smiled at the sound of his laughter. "Let's play again."

"Are you sure you want to? You've had a difficult day and should probably rest."

"The way I'm playing," she told him ruefully, "this game won't last long."

"You're doing quite well for a beginner," he assured her as they began moving the pieces back to their original positions. "How is your ankle?"

Glancing to the side, she wiggled her toes experimentally above the white linen binding. "The pain is nearly gone. What did you put on it?"

"Comfrey leaves. It works well for sprains. A poultice of it reduces the swelling."

"Really? Could you show me how to make one?"

"Are you planning to sprain your other ankle?" he teased.

She shook her head. "No. Once was enough. But . . ." She paused, then added, "It's only that I'm . . . well, my ankles are swelling anyway. The heat and the baby and everything . . ." Her voice trailed off in painful embarrassment.

"I noticed that," he said, realizing for the first time that when she was embarrassed, her flushed cheeks revealed a light dusting of freckles. "I'll show you how to make the poultice tomorrow."

"I'd be ever so grateful. Thank you." She cocked her head, looking at him. "You made an ointment for Flower, too. How do you know so much about medicinal herbs?"

"Babette." He smiled, remembering. "Two years ago, I became very ill. Some sort of fever. I thought I was going to die. I had no idea how to take care of it. When I recovered, I went to see Babette and asked her to teach me about herbs, so that if I ever became ill again, I would know what to do."

"But who is this Babette?"

"She was the local witch, of course. She's dead now."

"A witch?"

"That's what they say. Really, she was just an old woman who knew a great deal about a lot of things. She had gypsy blood, I believe. But everybody said she was a witch. As a boy, I was terrified of her."

Tess nodded. "We had a woman like that in Ainswick, the village where I grew up. Her name was Mildred Spence. People thought if she muttered something about your cat and looked at you in a strange way, the cat would die. Things like that. Every village probably has an old woman like Mildred." She laughed. "My father used to get so frustrated by the superstitions. He was the vicar in Ainswick. But people seemed to believe as much in the word of Mildred Spence as they did in the word of God."

He was contemplating how he could capture on canvas the glow that lit her eyes when she laughed. He'd thought several times of doing of a sketch of her, but until now, painting her portrait was something he had not even considered. He hadn't thought she'd be staying that long. He was lost in thought, and it took a few moments for her words to sink in. She had mentioned her father, and this was the first time she'd ever confided anything about herself or her past. "Your father was a vicar?"

"Yes, he was."

"Did he teach you Greek?"

She stared at him across the table. "Yes. How did you know?"

"That night when you fell asleep in the library, you had been reading Aristotle."

"I'd forgotten about that." She fingered a chess piece thoughtfully. "My father had a passionate interest in the Greek philosophers. He didn't see any reason why I shouldn't be able to understand and appreciate their writings, so he taught me to read and write Greek."

She shifted in her chair and set down the chess piece, looking suddenly uncomfortable. Gesturing toward the board, she asked, "Shall we start our game?"

Her discomfort and her change of subject were not lost on him. He asked no more questions. But he wondered what a vicar's reaction would be to a pregnant, unwed daughter. He wondered very much.

Nigel turned his gaze away from the window of his hotel suite, a window that gave a marvelous view of the Seine River. He glared at Martin Trevalyn. "She couldn't have just disappeared. There has to be some trace of her."

Martin shifted his weight from one foot to the other and coughed. "Yes, sir," he agreed. "I believe there are only two directions she could have taken from here. She could have gone east, toward Germany or Switzerland. Or she could have gone south, toward the French coast or Spain."

Nigel immediately eliminated the first hypothesis. He shook his head. "She must be traveling on foot. She couldn't possibly have had enough money for coach fare, and she couldn't have crossed the mountains on foot, especially since the snow there wouldn't have melted until June. She left Paris earlier than that."

"South, then." Martin consulted the map on the table. "Italy, perhaps, or Spain."

"Lady Aubry doesn't speak Spanish." Nigel shook his head impatiently. "It doesn't signify in any case. Until we find confirmation that she has gone south, we cannot concern ourselves with guessing further. Trevalyn, I want your sources to begin inquiring on the road from Paris to Lyon. If we can confirm she has been seen heading in that direction, we can proceed."

"Yes, sir." Martin folded the map and put it in his leather case. He pushed up the gold-framed spectacles that were sliding down the bridge of his nose and glanced at the earl, who was once again staring out the window. He was emboldened to add, "Lady Aubry seems to be making a great effort to hide. She does not want to be found."

Nigel turned, his handsome face hard and uncompromising. "What Lady Aubry wants is hardly your concern, Trevalyn. She is my wife and her place is at my side. I want her found and that is all you need to worry about."

"As you say, sir." Martin bowed stiffly and left the earl to contemplate the beauty of Paris' Left Bank.

10

"*This is silly,*" Tess told Alexandre, as he carried her across the meadow, through the knee-high grass. She had one arm curled about his neck while she clutched the picnic basket and straw hat in her lap with her free hand. "I think my ankle is healed. It doesn't hurt when I put weight on it."

"It's only been two days," Alexandre reminded her. "I don't want you walking on it for another day."

Tess didn't argue. She rather liked being carried about by Alexandre. It felt quite nice to be lifted into his strong arms, carried so easily when she felt so fat and awkward. Besides, she could rest her cheek so comfortably in the dent of his shoulder. She could enjoy the scent of him—lavender and linseed and something more—to her heart's content. Yes, she liked this very much.

He set her down in the midst of wildflowers and gold-green grass. He took the basket from her lap and set it aside as she placed the straw hat on her head.

"Why did you bring me out here?" she asked, reaching over to peek under the cloth that covered the basket.

"I think your idea of a picnic was a very nice one. Don't move. I'll be right back." She watched him turn and walk back to the château, knowing there was more to this than a picnic.

When she caught sight of him returning, she saw that he carried a chair from the kitchen, his sketchbook and his leather pouch of charcoal pencils. "A picnic, hmm?" she teased as he approached. "You want to work. You only brought me along to make sure I wouldn't get into trouble."

He set down the chair and dropped his sketchbook and pencils to the ground. He lifted her and placed her in the chair. "If I did, could you blame me? Who knows what you might think of next? I might come home to find you had stolen some poor farmer's lamb so he couldn't butcher it for his dinner."

She wrinkled her nose at him. "It's past lambing season."

He shot her an amused glance. He looked up at the sun overhead, then back at her. Tucking the pencil behind his ear, he picked up his sketchbook.

Tess glanced around, noting the crumbling ruins of a Roman temple at the edge of the meadow. "What are you going to sketch? The ruins?"

He shifted a bit to the left and glanced at the sun again. "*Non,*" he answered, cocking his head to one side, looking at her. "I am doing a preliminary sketch today for a painting. I am going to paint you."

"Me?" Dismayed, she frowned at him. "Oh, no! You can't!"

He raised an eyebrow in surprise. "Why not?"

"I don't want you to paint me." She brushed a self-conscious hand over her belly and ducked her head. "I'm fat," she mumbled.

He abruptly dropped the sketchbook and came toward her. Bending down, he grasped her chin and lifted it. "You're not fat," he told her sharply. "You're pregnant."

Bewildered by his vehement tone, she stared at him. He was frowning at her, looking quite displeased. Then he dropped his hand and turned away. "You're not fat," he repeated in a low voice.

"Well, I feel fat." Hoping to lighten his suddenly dark mood, she added, "You'd feel fat, too, if you waddled like a duck."

Glancing over at her, he saw the smile on her face. His frown disappeared and one corner of his mouth lifted. "I probably would," he agreed.

Pulling the pencil from behind his ear, he picked up the sketchbook. He studied her for a long time.

Disconcerted by his silence and his stare, Tess shifted her weight in the chair.

"Are you uncomfortable?"

She shook her head. "I'm fine."

Resting the sketchbook in the crook of his arm, he nodded and began to move the pencil across the paper.

She settled back in her chair and took a look around. The meadow was a riot of color—blue cornflowers, red poppies, white meadowsweet, and rippling golden grass. Behind her, the three remaining columns of the temple rose like spires toward the blue sky above. The forest of chestnut, cork, and pine that surrounded the meadow hid it from the world as if it were a very special secret.

"It's very pretty here," she commented.

Alexandre did not look up. "This is the Meadow of the Fairies." He paused in his sketching to explain. "This has always been considered a magical place." He gestured to the ruins behind her with his pencil. "Even the Romans thought so. People say that sometimes the fairies come here and sit on the petals of the flowers."

She laughed. "The fairies?"

"Don't laugh. They say if you see the fairies in the flowers, you have found happiness and good fortune.

But if you laugh at them and don't believe in them, they will bring you sorrow."

"Have you ever seen the fairies?"

"Yes," he said softly, and resumed sketching. "I saw them once." With those words, silence fell between them.

Often, he would look up to study her face for a moment, then he would resume sketching in the book. After a long period of silence, she asked the question uppermost in her mind. "Why do you want to paint me?"

He didn't look up. "Why shouldn't I paint you?"

That was no answer. "I suppose there is no reason why you shouldn't. I simply wondered why you would want to."

"I don't do many portraits now. I don't often have a subject." He paused, then added softly, "But a woman *très jolie* is too tempting an opportunity to pass by."

His words took her breath away. "Pretty? You think I'm pretty?"

He continued to sketch. "Very pretty. Now stop fishing for compliments, mademoiselle, and pour me a glass of wine, *s'il vous plaît.*"

She threw a cornflower blossom at him. The blue dot bounced off his hair and landed on the sketchbook. He pushed it aside and kept working.

Très jolie. Tess smiled, hugging the words to herself as she reached into the basket beside her for the bottle of wine.

He stepped forward, tucking his pencil behind his ear, studying the sketch. He reached out his left hand and took the glass she offered him, while continuing to gaze at the sketch. He glanced at her and took a sip of wine. Then he set the glass on the ground beside him, pulled the pencil from behind his ear, and resumed sketching.

"May we eat while you work?" she asked, reaching again toward the basket beside her.

He shook his head. "*Non.* Wait. I am nearly finished with this."

"Already?"

"This is only a preliminary sketch. I will probably need to do several of these before I begin the portrait." He sketched for several more minutes, then laid one last stroke to the paper and tucked the pencil behind his ear. He studied the sketch for a few moments, gave a satisfied nod, and closed the book.

"May I see it?" she asked.

Alexandre opened the book again to the proper place and handed it to her. She studied the page thoughtfully. It was only a sketch of her face. He hadn't drawn the entire scene. It was rough, but her likeness was very clear.

"May I look through the rest of this?" When he nodded, she flipped to the first page and began looking at his other sketches. Most of them were landscapes of the surrounding countryside, each with something unusual as the focal point. There was one of a rocky hillside where a lone olive tree grew, its twisted branches rising toward the sky in the shape of a praying woman. Another of a peninsula jutting out into the sea, its abandoned, crumbling lighthouse standing like the profile of an old sailor. A rocky wall between two fields where the shadows on the stones formed the delicate shape of a girl's face. She would never have seen in these ordinary things the shapes and forms of the extraordinary, but Alexandre did. "You truly have a gift," she said, handing the sketch book back to him.

"*Merci.*" He took the book and dropped it to the ground, then reached down into the basket for a hunk of cheese and the mustard pot. He spread a dab of mustard on the cheese with his knife.

"Why aren't there any sketches of the winery?" she asked.

His hand stilled. Slowly, with great care, he wiped the side of the knife onto the cheese and set the knife back in the basket. "The winery is closed, mademoiselle," he told her, sinking to the ground to sit cross-legged in the grass. "There is nothing to sketch there." He paused. "Not anymore."

Tell me, she pleaded silently. But he said nothing more, and their picnic was finished in silence.

Tess's ankle was completely healed by the following day, but during the days that followed, she found herself prevented from resuming the frantic pace she had set for herself. Alexandre simply would not let her. If she washed clothes, he was there within minutes, rolling up his sleeves, insisting on taking over the vigorous scrubbing and relegating her to the easier task of hanging the clothes on the line. If she dusted the bookshelves, he was there to dust the top ones so she would not have to climb the ladder. If she wanted to muck out Flower's stall, she would reach the stable only to find that Alexandre had already done it for her. When she wanted supplies from the village, he got them for her, but he never went anywhere without telling her exactly where he was going and how long he would be gone. He was never gone for long.

He did several more sketches of her. He did not use his sketchbook, but drew her likeness on larger pieces of drawing paper. Each one was more complete than the last. "I don't think you are ever going to do the actual painting," she would declare, as they would walk back to the house after another session.

He would only shake his head. "I want it to be exactly right," was all he ever said.

It was fortunate that Alexandre was so attentive. Tess continued to keep the house as tidy as possible, but as the days passed, she found herself able to do less and less. She tired more easily, and her back ached all the time. Her walk became more ungainly, she had continual heartburn, and she seemed to always be dropping things. She became more absentminded, frequently walking into a room and forgetting why she was there. One evening in mid-August she found herself in the library, contemplating just such a predicament.

"Now why did I come in here?" she muttered, placing her hands on her hips and looking around the room with vexation. She thought and thought, but couldn't remember. She was just about to give up and leave the room, when the low murmur of voices speaking in French floated up to her through the open window.

"What if he sees us?"

"We run, Pierre, as fast as we can."

Tess frowned. Walking over to the window, she leaned out. Directly below, two boys about ten years of age were crouched beneath her window. They were hidden from any view but hers by the shrubbery surrounding them and the shadows of twilight. She watched as one of the boys lifted his head above the bush and took a furtive look around the courtyard.

"I don't see him."

"Maybe we should go back, Jean-Paul. We've made it into the courtyard. Won't that be enough?"

"The dare was to get into the house," the boy called Jean-Paul pointed out. "We've got to get in somehow."

Tess listened to them in puzzlement. Why were they afraid to come into the house? If they wanted to see Alexandre, they could just come in. She strained to listen as the boy called Pierre mumbled, "I don't like this. What if it's true what they say about him?"

"It's true. You know it is." Jean-Paul took another look around. "I don't think he's here. C'mon."

He started to move, but Pierre grabbed his shirt. "But what if he catches us?"

"He won't."

"Jean-Paul, I'm scared."

"Don't be such a ninny."

"If *Maman* finds out, we won't get any supper. Papa will give us the willow switch, I know it," he wailed.

"Shh! Stop being a baby. C'mon." Jean-Paul moved out from behind the shrubbery and started for the door leading to the kitchen stairs.

Pierre followed, mumbling, "I don't like this."

Tess walked to the opposite window and watched the two boys move furtively toward the back door. A dare? Why were they scared of Alexandre? And why should their papa beat them for coming to visit him?

Jean-Paul opened the door and moved to come inside the house, when a sudden cry from Pierre stopped him. Tess watched as both boys whirled around to find Alexandre striding into the courtyard.

"There he is!"

"Run, Pierre! Run!"

With several whoops of terror, the boys ran toward the far end of the courtyard, scrambling over the stones of the crumbling wall to race away across the meadow as fast as their legs could carry them.

Still confused, Tess turned her head to look down at Alexandre. He was staring after the two boys with an expression on his face that tore at her heart. He suddenly looked very, very sad. His wide shoulders sagged as he sank onto the stone bench beside him. As she watched, he slowly lowered his head into his hands.

Just then, the baby kicked, and Tess placed a hand to her roundness. But she didn't stop to savor the movement as she usually did. Alarmed by Alexandre's reaction to the two boys, she walked out of the library, through the hall to the kitchen and down the stairs as fast as she dared.

She paused at the door left open by Jean-Paul and

studied Alexandre, who still sat on the bench, cradling his head in his hands. She didn't know why the two boys had been afraid. At this moment, she didn't care. All she cared about was that their fear had made the shoulders of this proud, strong man slump and had brought a terrible sadness to his face. She had no idea what she could say, what she could do. But she had to do something.

She felt the baby kick again, thumping against her ribs. She walked toward Alexandre without even thinking about what she was going to say or do. He looked up as she approached, and she saw him sit up with a stiff, abrupt movement, not looking at her.

She halted beside him. Bending slightly, she grabbed his hand, and without speaking, placed it at the top of her abdomen, right where the baby was kicking.

"Isn't it wonderful," she said in an aching voice, spreading her hand over his and looking down at his lowered head.

The baby landed a powerful jab at her ribs and Tess drew in a sharp breath. But when Alexandre lifted his head to look up at her, she smiled. The sadness was gone from his features and an expression of surprised awe had taken its place. They remained there for a long time, motionless as the shadows of night darkened the courtyard and the stars came out.

11

That night Tess found it difficult to sleep. The incident earlier that evening with the two boys replayed itself in her mind again and again. She couldn't stop wondering why two young boys would be terrified of Alexandre. She couldn't stop wondering if that was why he isolated himself from the outside world.

Tess rolled onto her opposite side, punched her pillow, and closed her eyes. *Who was the woman in the portrait?*

With a groan of frustration, Tess opened her eyes and sat up. It was no use. She couldn't sleep. She rose from the bed and slipped a matching wrapper over her night dress. *Who wore this?*

A pregnant woman, to be sure. Tess fingered the generous folds of delicate material thoughtfully. His wife, probably. But if that were true, what had happened to her? What had happened to their child?

She walked to the open window and stared out at the fat yellow moon floating in a black velvet sky. She ran a hand over her abdomen. There were, she acknowledged with a sigh, more important things to think about right now than Alexandre's past. Her own future and that of her baby.

She wanted to stay here. She wanted to live with Alexandre in this house. She wanted to raise her baby here. Not because she had nowhere else to go. Not because she was trying to hide. She wanted to stay here because Alexandre was here. Alexandre would be wonderful with the baby. He would be overprotective perhaps, especially if the child were a girl, but he would—

She stopped building her fairy-tale castles. Alexandre had said nothing about her staying here permanently. He probably didn't want to take on the responsibility of another man's child. He probably didn't want her and her baby to stay.

Suddenly the summer breeze floating in from the sea seemed cold. Tess stepped away from the window. She had to talk to Alexandre about the baby. She had to find out exactly what her position would be once the baby was born. And she had to begin preparing for the actual birth. Arrangements had to be made. Arrangements for a nursery, for clothes, for help.

She would need a midwife. Tess bit her lip worriedly at that thought. She hadn't really thought about it before. If she arranged for a midwife, the woman would know about her. She could be found.

She took several deep breaths, stilling her sudden panic. It had been five months since she'd fled England. If the Crown was searching for her, wouldn't they have found her by now? Perhaps she was safe.

There was no choice. She had to have a midwife. There was no other way. And there were other things she needed as well. She had waited far too long already.

She went downstairs, moving carefully in the dark. In the kitchen, she lit a candle. Finding notepaper, quill, and ink, she sat down at the table and made a list of everything she could think of.

She lifted the paper, blowing on it to dry the ink, then scanned the list in the candlelight, hoping she hadn't forgotten anything. It was a lengthy list, but what she needed most was not on it. She needed Alexandre. She needed his support. She needed his strength. Tomorrow, she would talk to him. He would help her make arrangements. Tess tried to reassure herself that everything was going to be all right. But it was still a long time before she finally tucked away her list, blew out the candle and went to bed. She drifted off into a troubled sleep.

"I'm going into the village today," Alexandre told her the next morning after the chores were done. "Is there anything you need?"

Tess paused in the act of ladling milk from the pail into a bowl. "Yes, I need several things," she answered, setting the bowl on the kitchen floor for Augustus. The kitten pounced on it with relish.

Alexandre waited, watching as she wiped up a bit of spilled milk with a rag and turned to him. She pulled out two of the chairs from the table. "Could we sit down? I would like to talk with you for a moment before you go."

Every muscle in his body tensed at her serious tone and her formal manner. He knew she'd seen what had happened the night before. He'd seen her looking out of the library window. Was she going to ask him about the two boys? Was she going to ask him why they had run screaming when he'd approached? Was she going to ask why they were so afraid of him? And what on earth was he going to tell her if she did?

He sat down. She took the other chair and folded her hands over her roundness. She didn't speak for a long moment, then she said, "I have made a list of things I need, but I wanted to talk with you first." She looked up at him. "Alexandre, I need you to make arrangements for a midwife."

He stared at her in complete astonishment. He hadn't even thought of such a thing. "Now?" Panic closed over him. "Tess, are you . . . ?"

She smiled at him. "Alexandre, the baby isn't due for two more months. We have plenty of time. But I have to start getting things ready. I should have started long before now."

A midwife. *Mon Dieu.* He thought about going into the village and asking old Françoise to come to his home to deliver a baby. She wouldn't come here. Not after Anne-Marie. She wouldn't come.

He looked at Tess, who was watching him with that look again. She needed his help, her eyes said. He couldn't seem to force out any words to tell her Françoise wouldn't cross the street to speak to him, much less deliver a baby for him. He swallowed hard and nodded, wondering what the hell he was going to do.

"I need some other things," Tess went on, pulling a sheet of notepaper from the pocket of her apron. "Talk to the midwife and make certain I haven't forgotten anything. She will probably want to see me beforehand in any case."

He took the paper and scanned the list of items in her small, neat handwriting. Cotton wool, bolt of plain muslin, bolt of cambric, bolt of flannel, yarn, strong twine, pledgets, buttons . . .

"Buttons?" he choked out.

"I have to make some clothes and things for the baby," she explained in that soft, loving tone she always used when she mentioned the child. Then her voice became hesitant as she added, "I had a bit of money left when I arrived here. If it isn't enough—"

"It doesn't matter," he cut her off with an impatient wave of his hand. "God, Tess, the money doesn't matter. It's just . . ." He sighed, knowing he could never tell her how the thought of babies being born made him go stone cold with fear.

He listened as Tess went on, "There is a room upstairs by the servants quarters that appears to be a nursery. But it's so far away from my room that it will not be suitable for the baby. I thought I would use the little room off of my own for the baby. May I make that into a nursery?"

Alexandre closed his eyes, listening to her soft voice as she spoke of nurseries and babies, as she asked his permission to make a home for her baby. Did she even have to ask? Of course, she could stay. She and the baby, too, as long as she wanted. But the look he saw on her face when he opened his eyes reminded him again that she took nothing for granted. "I think," he said, folding the list and shoving it in his pocket, "the little room off of your chamber will make a fine nursery."

He was gone before she could even thank him.

The road to the village was long and winding and led past the vineyards. Alexandre never used it. Instead, he took the more direct path along the beach. As he walked toward Saint-Raphael, he thought of having to approach Françoise, and just the thought of it brought a sick feeling to his gut.

He hadn't seen the old woman since Anne-Marie's death. But he knew what she thought of him. What they all thought. How could he stop at her cottage and explain Tess to her, ask for her help after what he had done? How could he look at her and see the accusation in her eyes? And even if he could face her, even if he could tell her about Tess, he knew she wouldn't come.

He passed the path from the sea up to her cottage and went on. There had to be some other way.

By the time he reached the village, Alexandre knew there was only one thing to do. He purchased quill, ink, wax, and paper. He wrote a letter, sealed it, and posted it. When he asked, he was told the letter would go out when the carrier passed through the village three days hence on the weekly mail run from Nice to Marseilles. Then he went on to the draper's, where he bought everything on Tess's list and earned several curious, apprehensive stares in the process. But no one asked any questions. No one ever asked him any questions.

"I'm not certain this is a good idea at all," Tess informed Alexandre as he set up his easel in the meadow. She wriggled in the chair he'd brought out for her. "Wouldn't you rather paint a portrait of Augustus?"

He glanced at her hopeful face, then down at the kitten curled in a ball at his feet. "An excellent suggestion," he agreed, bending to pick up the animal. He walked over to her and placed the kitten across her knees. "Augustus should be in the portrait as well."

"I was hoping you would paint him *instead* of me," she grumbled as he walked back to his easel.

He turned to her, raising his hands to the sky in mock despair. "When I painted in Florence, women would wait months to sit for me. Never before has a woman told me she did not want to be painted by Dumond." He sighed heavily and shook his head. "Tess, you have wounded me."

She smiled, loving the way he said her name. For so long he had referred to her only as mademoiselle. But the day she'd taken that tumble, he had called her Tess for the first time. He had called her Tess ever since.

He had done the final sketch the day before, this one

on the canvas now perched on his easel. He had blocked
out the basic shape of her and the surrounding scenery.
Now, he took his pencil and added a few more touches
to the sketch. She assumed he was sketching Augustus
into the portrait.

When he had finished that, he proceeded to mix paint
colors on his palette. When he was satisfied with the colors, he turned to her, brush in his left hand, palette in
the crook of his right arm, ready to begin. He stared at
her long and hard for a moment, then turned to the easel
and dipped the brush into a blob of oil paint. He laid the
first stroke across the canvas.

Fascinated, she watched him work. Often, he would
look at her, then at the canvas, then back at her. His
brush would be motionless for long moments, but she
could still feel the passionate energy that emanated from
him.

His brows were furrowed in concentration. The ribbon slipped from his hair and was carried away by the
summer breeze, but he didn't bother to retrieve it. When
his long hair blew across his face, he merely shook his
head back to keep it out of his eyes. He only spoke when
she stirred restlessly in her chair and all he said was,
"Don't move."

After keeping still and watching him for quite some
time, Tess found her attention wandering on to other
things. She began making lists in her mind. She would
need shirts, caps, frocks, bedgowns, and blankets for the
baby. She would have to make plenty of napkins, too.
She thought of the fabric Alexandre had bought for her
the day before, and she smiled. He had brought home
fabric, ribbons, and thread in coordinating colors. Even
the buttons matched. Wasn't that just like an artist?

She glanced at Alexandre, but he seemed oblivious to
everything except the painting. It was some time later
before he finally stopped working and tilted his head

back to glance at the sun. Then he set down the brush. "The light is changing. We will stop now."

Tess stopped making lists. "Are you finished?" she asked, tilting her head first to one side then the other, trying to remove the kink that had formed in her neck from sitting so long.

"*Non.* It will take several days, I think. Perhaps as much as a week." He wrapped the brush in a rag and dropped it into the open leather case that lay at his feet.

"Could I see it?"

"No, you can't. I never allow the subject to see a portrait until it is done. A lesson I learned long ago." He closed the case and brought it to her as she removed the kitten from her lap and rose to her feet. "If the subjects see the unfinished work, they are always disappointed or even critical. So I always make them wait until the portrait is finished."

Curious, she leaned around him, trying to see, but he blocked her view. "Tess . . ." His voice trailed off with the warning. Then he said, "Take my paints and the kitten and go back to the house. I will follow."

She made a face and turned toward the château. She knew he was behind her, carrying the canvas. When they reached the house, he left her in the kitchen and took the portrait up to his studio. When he returned downstairs, he went to fetch the easel and chair, pausing in the doorway to say, "It won't do you any good to peek. I've locked the door to the tower."

She made no reply, but her exasperated glare made him chuckle as he walked away.

Over the next several days, Alexandre continued to paint her portrait in the meadow. Then he confined himself to his studio for another two days, putting the final touches to the painting.

Nearly a week after he had begun the portrait, it was finished. He dropped the brush into a jar of linseed oil and turned away from the easel. He didn't pause to look closely at the canvas, but then, he never did. He always waited a few days to give himself perspective before he studied the finished work.

As usual, he felt tired and drained. What he needed was a swim. On his way downstairs, he paused at the door of Tess's bedchamber. Since it was midafternoon, he expected to find her taking a nap, as she was wont to do at this time of day. But she wasn't in her room.

He found her instead in the kitchen. The worktable before her was littered with scraps of fabric, snippets of thread, and other sewing materials. She was sitting in one of the chairs, a piece of soft white flannel printed with thin green stripes in her lap, to which she was sewing a length of willow green ribbon. She glanced up as he entered, then returned her attention to her sewing.

"What are you making?" he asked, coming up to stand beside her.

Spreading out the flannel for him to see, she answered, "A skirt for the baby."

For the baby. Her voice was so soft. Tender. He leaned closer. He watched her hands pulling needle and thread through the ribbon and fabric of what seemed to be the hem, making tiny, meticulous stitches. A deep wave of longing hit him, a sudden yearning for what he had missed, a painful desire for what he'd almost had a long time ago.

She went on, "Thank you for the fabric. This printed flannel and green ribbon will be nice for either a boy or girl, don't you think?"

Boy or girl, that wasn't why he'd picked out that particular color. He'd chosen green because he thought Tess's child would have Tess's auburn hair, and green would suit the baby well.

Her needle glinted in the afternoon sunlight pouring through the high kitchen windows. "There will be enough for blankets, too," she said.

Blankets. Alexandre turned away, mumbling vaguely that there was work to be done. He went back upstairs, knowing there was something else he needed to do, something more important than work. Going into the bedchamber he was now using, he took a key from the top drawer of the dressing table, the key to a room no longer used, no longer needed. He left the room, walking to one of the two locked doors at the end of the corridor. He unlocked one and went inside.

He knew exactly where it was. In the wardrobe, packed away with so many other things. He entered the small adjoining chamber. Pushing aside packed crates and trunks, he knelt down before a tiny wooden cradle.

He reached out and ran his finger along the dust-filled carving and painted flowers. The cradle was the only thing in the house that had been the baby's. He'd given away all the clothes and toys, unable to bear the idea of having them in the house. But he had not been able to part with this.

Giving the cradle a push, he watched it rock back and forth for a baby that had never been lulled to sleep by its gentle movements. He stared at the rocking cradle and remembered.

I don't want a baby. Her voice came back to him so clearly. He could recall her every word, as if it were only yesterday. *What if something goes wrong? I'll die, just like Louise. I'll die.*

The cradle rocked with every word. *Die . . . rock . . . die . . . rock . . . die.*

The rocking stopped. Alexandre curled his fingers into the cut-out hearts at the head and foot of the cradle and lifted it. Leaving the room, he set the cradle down long enough to lock the door, then took it into Tess's chamber, placing it in her newly made nursery.

He found a rag and wiped away the dust until the polished oak gleamed, until the painted flowers of red, blue, and yellow were bright again. Then he left the room and went for his swim, wishing the water could wash away the pain in his heart and the guilt in his soul.

Tess knotted the last stitch and cut the thread. She smiled down at the finished skirt for a moment, then folded it neatly and added it to the growing pile of baby clothes in the basket beside her. She took all the tiny scraps of leftover material and put them in the linen bag she had made for that purpose, knowing she would use them to make stuffing for toys. Gathering her scissors, thread, and box of pins, she added them to the basket and took it upstairs.

Humming softly under her breath, she entered the nursery and halted at the unexpected sight before her. On the floor beside the table she'd brought in from her bedchamber stood a cradle.

Setting the basket on the table, she stared at it in astonishment. It was a lovely thing of polished oak and painted flowers. Alexandre must have put it there that morning.

Alexandre.

Tess leaned down and ran a hand over the wood, knowing that her thoughts had been correct. He'd had a wife and a baby once. But what had happened to them? Did the wife have a baby and run away, taking the baby with her?

Tess shook her head. No, she couldn't imagine such a situation. With a man like Alexandre, there was no need to run away. He was a good man, a kind man, a man who would love children. The look on his face as he had felt her baby kicking told her that. The woman must have been expecting a child, but both she and the baby had died during the birth.

That would explain many things, including the cradle before her. She thought of him, all alone in this empty house, grieving for a dead wife and child.

Her heart constricted with pain. He had given her this cradle because he had no use for it now. He had no baby now.

She wanted to go find him, thank him for his gift. She wanted to tell him she knew, that she understood. But he was so private. He would be embarrassed by her sympathy. He wouldn't want her pity. Tess left the room with no idea what he did want. She wished she did.

But she managed to thank him for his gift without causing him any embarrassment. She did it in an off-hand, casual fashion as they prepared dinner together in the kitchen. He didn't offer any explanations for the cradle's existence, and she didn't ask for any. But her heart ached for him just the same.

It was several days before Alexandre finally let her see the portrait he had done of her. When he lifted the linen sheet from the easel, she stared at the painting, unable to believe she was looking at herself.

He had captured perfectly the reddish-brown shade of her hair peeking beneath her hat, the brilliant colors of the flowers surrounding her chair, the pale orange of Augustus' fur as he sat on her lap.

He had made no effort to conceal her faults. She still had a chin that she thought too pointed. Her nose still had that funny little dent at the tip that had irritated her since childhood. He had made no effort to minimize her pregnancy either. And yet, her features and form had a softness she'd never seen before when she looked in a mirror. There was a glow about her she knew was an artist's fancy. She didn't feel like she glowed. Most of the time, she felt tired and achy and fat. "I can see why women waited months to be painted by you," she told him truthfully. "You make us look quite nice."

He laughed. "Nice? Nice is all you can say?" His eyes teased her. "I suppose that's better than awful."

"It's hard to be objective about a painting of yourself," she told him, staring at the portrait. "But I like it."

"That is what matters most." Leaning closer, he confessed, "I'm quite fond of it myself. I think I'll hang it in the hall."

Tess groaned. She wasn't sure she liked it quite that much. But after Alexandre had gone to do some chores outside, she continued to study the painting. There was something about it that she felt, but couldn't see. Something she ought to see. She leaned closer, studying the wildflowers surrounding her chair, and caught her breath.

There, barely discernible on the petals of a red poppy, was a tiny, delicate figure with wings. It was a fairy.

12

When Tess went for a walk the following day, Alexandre accompanied her. It was a golden-brown day in late summer, hot and dry. He walked a slight distance behind her, watching the sway of her hips as she moved through the meadow. She really did waddle, he realized. The warm Provence breeze flared the skirt of her blue muslin dress to one side and threatened to send her straw hat flying until she finally tied its wide blue ribbons beneath her chin.

She bent to pull a handful of the last wildflowers, and he noticed how she always placed a hand to her round abdomen as she leaned down. There were other things he noticed, too. The way she would stand sometimes, hands on the bulk of her belly, breathing deeply. When she did that, he knew the baby was kicking. Sometimes, he wished she would let him put his hand there again, feel the movement, but he never asked.

He noticed how she spent more time resting than she ever had before. He knew she tired easily, and that worried him. Everything about Tess having this baby worried him. But Tess never seemed afraid or apprehensive about having the baby. If she was, he never saw it.

He quickened his pace to catch up with her as they passed through the meadow and into the forested foothills of chestnut trees, cork oaks, and pines. "Is all of this your land?" she asked as they paused beside a pond set amid the trees.

He nodded. "From the sea to the foot of the *Massif des Maures*."

"The mountains?"

"*Oui.*" He turned, pointing to the west. "And from here past the vineyards to the road leading into Saint-Raphael."

They turned, heading in the opposite direction from the vineyards, passing out of the trees and into another meadow. A stream, low in the late summer heat, meandered through the green and gold grass. He said, "This stream is the border between my land and the farmer beyond."

She looked across the stream at the sheep, which grazed on the peasant's land. Some distance away, she could see a boy guarding the sheep with the help of two dogs.

"We have walked a long way," he commented. "You must be getting tired. We should go back."

She nodded, following as he began to walk back the way they had come. "I am rather tired," she admitted. "It's quite hot today." She pulled at the ribbons beneath her chin, untying the bow, then pulled off her hat and began to fan her face with it.

As they came out of the trees and into the Meadow of the Fairies, Tess suddenly stopped, staring to the right. His gaze moved past her, but he saw nothing unusual. "What are you looking at?"

She didn't answer but began walking in that direction. He followed her for several feet before he saw what had caught her attention. It was a large white goose, sitting in the shade of a plane tree. It must have wandered over from the peasant's land nearby. As she approached, the bird began to flap its wings in alarm, but only one wing moved. The other hung helplessly by its side.

Tess paid no heed to the goose's attempt at bravado. She dropped her hat and began to speak softly to the bird, holding out her hand in a coaxing fashion, moving forward until she was able to kneel beside it. Alexandre followed.

He watched as she continued to talk to the goose, and he was amazed when it allowed her to gently examine its wing. After a long moment, she reached out an arm, and Alexandre helped her to her feet. She turned to him, looking up into his face.

He saw that look in her eyes. Knowing exactly what she was thinking, he tried to forestall her. "No. Absolutely not."

She said nothing but continued to look up at him.

"No," he repeated firmly.

She glanced at the wounded goose then back at him and said, "If we leave her here, the foxes will eat her."

"Tess, I don't want any more animals!"

She said nothing, but she didn't have to. Her eyes said it all.

He had lost, and he knew it. Looking down at the goose, seeing its limp wing hanging in a pitiful fashion, he sighed, knowing he couldn't fight Tess's kind heart. "I suppose I could fashion a splint of some sort for its wing," he said doubtfully.

Her smile was a heady reward. "Thank you," she whispered, standing up on her toes to curl her arms around his neck. She buried her face against his chest. "Thank you." Her voice was muffled against the front of his shirt.

He tensed at the intimate contact. Every contour of

her shape became burned in his memory as he slowly lifted his arms to wrap them around her. He could feel the roundness of her belly against his hip, the softness of her breath warming his skin through the white linen shirt.

He moved his hands up and down her back. It felt so good to hold, to be held. It was warmth and sunlight after living for years in the shadows. He bent his head, hesitated, smelled the fragrance of her hair and closed his eyes. His lips touched the silk of her curls. Afraid to let her go, afraid to wait until she pushed him away, he remained motionless, drinking in the scent of her, the feel of her, stealing as much as he could.

Her arms moved, sliding away from where they curled around his neck. *Non.* His arms tightened around her shoulders in a silent protest. But she didn't pull away. Instead, her hands moved slowly down his chest. His muscles tightened, quivered with her touch, as her hands slid over his hammering heart, over his ribs, around his waist.

He moved his head lower, touching his lips to the pulse in her temple. His fingertips brushed lightly up her spine, to her neck, to the line of her jaw. He cupped her cheek in his palm, lifted her face with both dread and anticipation, waiting for rejection in her eyes.

It wasn't there. All he saw was acceptance. Hope, something he had lost long ago, was regained. When she turned her face into his hand and pressed her lips to his palm, he felt his hardened, brittle heart shatter into pieces at her feet.

His fingers raked through her hair. Pulling her head back, he lowered his head slowly, giving her plenty of time to turn aside if she chose. But her lips parted in silent invitation, and he hesitated no longer. He brushed his lips over hers, his eyes open to see hers flutter shut.

There was no fear in her now. Somehow, over the

long days of summer, it had disappeared. He felt her hands against his back pulling him closer. He deepened the kiss, savored the forgotten softness of a woman's lips, tasted the special sweetness that was only Tess.

The pain of his lonely, empty life was forgotten as he held her in his arms. The deep ache, assuaged before only by a brush and canvas, was destroyed by her kiss. Alexandre Dumond was reborn.

Tess couldn't believe what was happening. Wonder was what she felt, wonder and awe. The queer little ache deep within her was longing. She recognized it now, a longing for something she had never experienced at a man's intimate touch. Tenderness.

The kiss became fuller, deeper as Alexandre's tongue touched hers. She rose up once again on her toes and tilted her head to deepen the kiss even more, moving one hand up to his neck, to tangle in his hair.

Alexandre . . . Alexandre . . . His name was a prayer on her lips, a prayer that her new life would last forever, that her feelings were shared ones. She had never known a kiss like this, but she wanted kisses like this for the rest of her life.

It was he who finally broke the contact, moving his lips from hers to touch them to her cheek, her forehead, her hair. His arms relaxed for a brief instant, then tightened again as he cradled her head against his chest. She stood in the circle of his embrace, savoring for one last moment the feel of his arms holding her, cherishing her.

But she had to know. Lifting her head, she gazed up into his face, unable to hide her feelings, hoping he felt it, too. She thought it was there, in the black depths of his eyes.

They stared at each other, shaken, reluctantly pulling back by degrees until only fingertips touched, until rapid breathing slowed, until pounding hearts resumed a normal rhythm. Then, at the same moment, both of them pulled back one more fraction of an inch, and the contact was broken. Once again, they were separate, isolated entities.

Tess longed to hurl herself back against him, to find again the warmth of his arms. But instead she turned away, looking down at the injured goose that had been forgotten in the wonder of other discoveries.

"We'll have to carry her home," she told Alexandre. "She won't simply follow us."

He nodded and moved toward the bird with the intention of lifting it, but the goose honked belligerently at him and nipped at his hand. He gave her a wry glance. "Any other suggestions?"

They finally managed to carry the bird home by fashioning a sort of hammock, using Tess's petticoat and two tree branches. But after carrying the bird back to the château, they found they had a new problem.

Alexandre tried to examine the bird's broken wing, but the goose struggled and honked and batted her good wing at him every time he came near. "Ouch!" he cried, jumping back after the goose again nipped his hand. "This bird hates me," he told Tess, sucking his injured finger.

The goose, however, did not seem to hate Tess. In fact, when she came close and reached down to touch her, the bird didn't protest or struggle in the least. Tess glanced at Alexandre, who was now standing a good five feet away, looking quite irritated. "I think I'll have to do this," she told him.

"I have a better idea," he said. "Why don't we just cook it for dinner?"

Horrified, she stared at him. But then she saw the teasing glimmer in his black eyes. "Very amusing," she answered. "You're only saying that because the goose doesn't like you."

"Very true. But I like goose. Roasted, with stuffing and—"

"Alexandre," she interrupted, "this is serious. What do I do?"

"I don't really know," he confessed. "I've never set a bird's broken wing before." He looked down at the goose, his expression turning thoughtful for a moment, then he said, "We'll need some linen to bind it and a leather strap."

After finding the necessary materials, they set to work. Alexandre asked Tess to measure the length of the broken bone, and when she did, he cut a piece from the leather harness they'd found in the barn slightly longer than the measurement she gave him. Using his razor, he cut two lengthwise slits, one at each end of the strap.

Tess sat down on the floor beside the goose, located the broken bone, and following Alexandre's improvised instructions, she set it in a flexed position. Alexandre tried several times to assist her, but the goose struggled and protested every time he came close.

Tess hooked the ends of the strap over the joints on each side of the broken bone as Alexandre instructed her, carefully fitting the joints into the slits he had cut in the leather and securing the bone firmly in place. She then bound the wing tightly to the goose's body using the strips of linen.

"The important thing is to make certain the wing stays set so that it will heal," he told her when she had finished, leaning as close as he dared to examine her handiwork. "Is it tight?"

"Yes."

"Good. Look at it every day to make certain it isn't coming loose."

Tess nodded as he helped her to her feet. Both of them watched as the goose walked around in a circle, honking and flapping her good wing. But the broken one seemed securely in place for the moment.

"She seems to be all right," Tess said.

"Yes."

The silence was deafening. Embarrassing. Now that the goose was taken care of, there was only one other event of the afternoon to think about.

Tess looked at Alexandre, felt herself blushing, and thought she was fat and awkward.

He thought she was beautiful.

She thought he was the strongest, gentlest man God ever made.

He thought he was a lost cause.

They stared at each other, their own insecurities convincing them that the feelings they had shared were imagined. Both spoke at once.

"I'll take the goose out to the barn," she said.

"I'll pick vegetables for dinner," he said.

And as both of them went to do their respective chores, they wished they had the courage to prove themselves wrong.

"I'm going into the village this morning," Alexandre told Tess the following day. "Is there anything you need?"

She glanced up from her task of feeding the chickens and paused, a handful of feed in her hand. Their eyes met for a moment across the fence. Then she shook her head. "No."

"I'll be gone for several hours." He didn't wait for a reply but turned away, unable to gaze into her eyes and see the tenderness there.

As he walked down the steep path toward the sea, he tried to keep thoughts of the day before out of his mind, but he couldn't. Last night, he had sought refuge in his studio, but not even his work could keep him from thinking of her.

Even now, he could still feel the warmth of her

against him, he could still smell the fragrance of her hair, he could still taste the sweetness of her lips. She was pregnant with another man's child, and his own feelings of desire shocked him.

Yet, he ached to hold her in his arms once again, to kiss her again, to believe in love again.

He had to put some distance between them. Because eventually she would learn what had happened to Anne-Marie.

When she discovered the truth about him, he would see the same condemnation in her eyes that he saw in the eyes of the villagers. He would see her fear return, the same fear that had caused those two boys to run away from him. He would lose her trust, she would stop believing in him.

He wasn't what she thought he was. She believed he was some sort of hero. Foolish, foolish man, he told himself, knowing that when he'd held her in his arms, he had believed it, too.

Tess dropped the baby's cap she'd just finished into her sewing basket and carried the basket upstairs. It had taken her all morning to complete it. Her attention had continually wandered from her sewing to Alexandre. She had paused with every other stitch to savor the wonderful feeling of being cherished in his arms, something she had never thought she could experience, something she could never have imagined.

She passed through her bedchamber into the tiny adjoining nursery and set the basket on the table. She looked down at the cradle he had given her. What a lovely gift it was. But if his wife and baby had died, it must have been very painful for him to give that baby's cradle to her. She wondered what his wife had been like.

She thought of the laughing eyes and beautiful face of

the girl in the portrait. Jealousy, an intense, violent assault of it, shot through her. Shaken, she walked out of the nursery, out of her bedchamber.

She went to the rooms at the very end of the corridor, the ones that were always locked. She stopped before one door, staring at the heavy oak panels. She had never been more than mildly curious about these rooms before, but suddenly she wanted to know what was inside them more than she'd ever wanted anything in her life.

Turning back, she went into Alexandre's room and began to search. There had to be a key somewhere. She knew she shouldn't do this. The rooms were locked, and what lay within was none of her affair. She was where she had no business to be, and it was wrong. But the wicked imp of curiosity and jealousy pushed aside the virtuous upbringing of a vicar's daughter. She had to know.

The key was tucked away in a drawer, far in the back, beneath layers of Alexandre's clothing. She grabbed it before she could change her mind and marched back down the corridor. She unlocked one door.

It was clearly a woman's room. The quilt on the huge bed showed a floral design in pastel colors, muted by a layer of dust. The armoire contained a few dresses, but most of them were probably now in Tess's own room. The drawers were filled with an untidy jumble of delicate lacy undergarments, ribbons, handkerchiefs, fans, and other falderals. The fading scent of lemon-verbena sachet spilled from the drawers. A jewel case of carved ivory sat on the dressing table.

At one end of the room, a door led into a wardrobe chamber. At the other end was another door. Opening it, she stared into the adjoining bedchamber, furnished in a much more masculine style.

It was true. These were the connecting chambers of a married couple. At one time, Alexandre had shared these rooms with someone. His wife.

He was grieving for a dead wife. Now that the idea was firmly in her head and the proof lay clearly before her, she knew it was true. How could she compete with another woman's ghost? Tess buried her face in her hands, knowing she couldn't. But she wanted to.

She wanted to drive that other woman out of his mind, out of his heart, because she wanted to take her place. She was in love with Alexandre.

How had this happened? A few months ago, the thought of a man, any man, had terrified her. Love between a man and a woman was something she had ceased to believe in. But Alexandre had changed all that. Changed it with hands that were strong, but gentle. A voice that was as rich and warm as the sun. A smile that warmed her heart. One by one, he had taken away her fears. Day by day, he had shown her that a man could be protective, thoughtful, and caring.

She wanted to banish the ghost of that woman from Alexandre's life, relegate her to the past where she belonged. She wanted—

"What are you doing in here?"

Tess jumped at the sound of Alexandre's voice. She dropped her hands and whirled around to find him standing in the doorway. His expression told her more clearly than his harsh tone how angry he was.

Though she was trembling, Tess drew herself up with as much dignity as someone caught sneaking about could muster. She swallowed hard and said nothing. She simply looked at him, wishing he could trust her, that he would tell her about these rooms, about this woman.

She trusted him. She knew that no matter how angry he was, he would not hurt her. She loved him. She knew that no matter what he said to her now, her feelings would not change.

He saw that look. That look that told him she expected him to live up to the pedestal she'd placed him on. This was the moment he'd dreaded for so long. This was the moment when she'd see him for what he was. The thought made him more angry than before. Damn her for delving into the past, for having a woman's curiosity, for ever coming into his life.

"You have no right to be in here," he told her, slamming his palm against the open door in his fury. The door swung back against the wall with a loud bang that made her jump. But she didn't shrink back. She just continued to look at him.

"Who was this woman?" she asked in that soft voice that shattered him.

He forced the words out. "She was my wife."

Tess didn't look surprised. She even nodded. "I guessed that. What happened to her?"

Don't. I don't want to tell you about Anne-Marie.
"She died."

"How did she die?" Tess whispered.

She wasn't going to let it be. She was going to keep after him until she got the sordid truth. She wanted the truth? She really wanted to know? Then he would tell her. He folded his arms across his chest, look straight into her eyes, and said bluntly, "I killed her."

13

Tess staggered back as if he'd slapped her. Of all the things she might have expected him to say, that wasn't one of them. She grabbed for the closest thing to hang on to, the door jamb to the adjoining chamber, as she felt herself sliding off the face of her fragile new world. Killed his wife? What was he saying?

She closed her eyes, waves of the old fear running through her. Could Alexandre really have done such a thing? How? Why? She saw Nigel come before her eyes with the look of murder on his handsome face. She struggled for control, thinking of Alexandre, and Nigel faded from view. She saw Alexandre rubbing ointment into the wounds of a donkey he didn't even want. She heard the terrible fear in his voice when she'd taken that tumble in the stream bed. She felt his fingers move with such gentle care over her sprained ankle. She saw the awe on his face when he'd felt the baby kicking. So many things, so many moments that told her what he was saying now couldn't be true.

Things weren't always what they seemed. She, of all

people, knew that much. She had shot her own husband, hadn't she? And she'd had sound reasons for doing so, reasons that might not stand up in a court of law, but that were valid just the same. Alexandre must have had reasons, too. Determined to tell him exactly that, Tess opened her eyes. But he was gone.

"Alexandre?" she called, racing for the door. She stepped out into the corridor, but he had disappeared. Sagging against the stone wall behind her, she knew she had made a fine mess of things. He must have sensed her momentary doubt, fleeting though it had been. He must have seen that brief shock of fear in her face. She must have looked at him the way those two boys had looked at him. *O, God.*

She turned and leaned forward, pressing her forehead to the cool stone wall. She had to go after him, talk to him, but she knew from experience that if Alexandre did not want to be found, she would never find him. She would simply have to wait until he came back.

A soft meow sounded behind her, and Tess turned to see Augustus sitting at her feet. With a sob, she picked up the kitten, burying her face against the soft orange fur. "He'll be back soon," she murmured. "Very soon."

But the words sounded hollow to her own ears. And they gave her no comfort whatsoever.

Alexandre walked and walked, without any conscious idea where he was going or what he would do when he got there. But no matter how far or how fast he walked, Tess's horrified gaze followed him.

He'd known this moment would come. He had dreaded it, he had tried to prepare for it. But no amount of preparation could dilute the pain that had sliced through him when he'd seen the look on Tess's face.

I killed her. I killed her. His harsh self-accusation

kept time with his long strides as he walked through the meadow where he and Tess had so often sat with a picnic while he sketched and painted her portrait.

His steps slowed at the edge of the meadow, and he sank beneath the plane tree where he had kissed her only yesterday. Despair swamped him. Why couldn't she have been different? Why couldn't she have contradicted all his expectations? But he had been right all along. Her trust was gone, replaced by fear.

How could I have expected anything else? he thought with self-loathing. The truth was the truth. And no matter how he had said it, no matter how she had learned it, he would never be able to change the fact that he was responsible for the deaths of his wife and child.

Tess didn't see Alexandre for three days. She waited up every night until it was nearly dawn for him to come home. She went to his room every morning and gazed dejectedly at the bed he hadn't slept in. She ran to the library window every ten minutes, hoping to see him walking up the path. But he never did. Remorse gave way to worry. What was he doing? Was he all right?

She didn't see Alexandre, but he saw her. Every morning, he watched her drag water from the pump up the back stairs. Every day, he watched her pick vegetables in the garden, bending and stooping with difficulty. Every evening, he watched her lead Sophie and Flower back from the pasture to the barn. Every night, he watched her sit by the kitchen window, sewing clothes for the baby with the fabric he had brought home for her.

For three days, he watched, guilt-ridden to see her doing her own work and his, too. Guilt-ridden to see her fetching water and picking vegetables when she was seven months pregnant. But too ashamed to face her again.

For three days, guilt wrestled with shame. Guilt finally won. He came home.

Tess saw him before he'd even made it to the garden. Staring out the library window for perhaps the hundredth time that afternoon, she saw him come up the path from the sea. Relief washed over her, and she mumbled a prayer of thanks as she left the library. *He's come back. He's finally come back.*

Wasting only a moment, she paused beside the looking glass in the hall to comb her hair with hasty fingers and calm her pounding heart.

She walked down the back stairs and through the courtyard to the rickety gate and waited, her eyes studying him with worry as he came up the path toward her. His long hair was tangled, and his jaw was shadowed with a three-day growth of beard. His clothes were rumpled and stained. She wondered if he had eaten, where he had slept. But it was his expression that caused her the most concern. He looked tired, not only in body but also in spirit.

She wanted to reach out her arms and hold him. She wanted to tell him that the past didn't matter, only the present. She wanted to tell him that she loved him. But when she smiled, he did not return the smile. Instead, he walked right past her through the gate and turned toward the château without saying a word. It was almost as if he hadn't even seen her.

Her smile faded. She pressed her clenched fist to her lips, watching his back as he walked away.

The next morning, the water was outside her door. She found a basket of vegetables on the worktable when she came down to the kitchen. But Alexandre was not waiting there for her with freshly brewed tea. He was probably in his studio, using his work as a reason to avoid her, just as he had done the night before.

Tess frowned down at the basket. She was not going to let him do this. Somehow, there had to be a way to reach him.

Turning away from the table, she took the pails from their hooks on the wall and went out to do her morning chores, trying to decide what she could do to break down his walls.

Talking to him would not help. Telling him she loved him, telling him she didn't care what had happened to his wife, wouldn't change anything. He wouldn't believe her. She would have to show him that she loved him.

As she went about her daily tasks, Tess came to the conclusion that showing him how she felt, how much she loved and trusted him, might not be enough. He might not be able to forget the past. He might never be able to return her love. But she had to try.

And time was her ally. He wouldn't send her away. She knew he would let her and the baby stay with him as long as they wanted. Perhaps, over time, he would forget. Perhaps, over time, he would accept a new family. Perhaps, someday, he would love her as she loved him. Perhaps.

At sunset, Tess went out to the pasture to bring in Sophie and Flower. Standing beside the animals, she suddenly heard the clatter of horses' hooves and carriage wheels. Turning, she watched in astonishment as a traveling carriage, its top lowered, came down the drive and past the pasture, headed for the barn and stable. Sudden panic seized her. What if the British authorities had found her?

Shading her eyes, she could see two people in the carriage, a man and a woman, and her panic eased somewhat. If a man had come to arrest her, he would hardly bring a woman with him. But who were they?

She left the pasture and walked toward the stable, her heart still pounding with apprehension. She watched the man alight from the carriage and reach out his arms to assist the woman. She noticed the two trunks strapped to the back of the carriage. Had these people come to visit Alexandre? How odd.

As she approached, the couple noticed her. Both of them turned towards her at the same moment, and Tess could see her own astonishment reflected in their expressions. The couple exchanged a quick, puzzled glance, then the woman stepped forward.

"*Bonjour,* madame," she greeted Tess in French. "Is Alexandre at home?" Beneath the turned-up brim of a straw bonnet, the woman's brown eyes gave Tess a quick appraising glance, then she smiled. "I am Jeanette Caillaux, and this is my husband, Henri."

Jeanette placed a gloved hand on the arm of the handsome man who stepped up beside her. He bowed. "Madame."

Tess knew she was staring, trying to assimilate the fact that Alexandre had visitors. "My . . . my name is Tess," she stammered out. "I am . . . the housekeeper."

The pair exchanged another quick glance, then Jeanette repeated her question. "Is Alexandre here?"

Tess flushed, knowing she must seem like a complete idiot. "Of course. He is in his studio. Come with me."

Henri said, "I will take care of the horses and join you inside."

His wife nodded and followed Tess as she turned, walking toward the château. She fell in step beside her, but neither woman spoke.

Who were these people? Tess couldn't fathom it. She led the woman into the château, where they paused in the hall at the foot of the wide staircase. "I will tell him you are here."

Jeanette did not reply and Tess glanced at her. The

other woman was staring at the portrait of Tess that hung on the wall. "When did Alexandre do this?" she asked, her voice barely above a whisper.

"He finished it a few days ago." Tess turned to go up the stairs, but Alexandre's voice on the landing above stopped her.

"*Bonjour,* Jeanette."

Both women looked up as Alexandre came down the stairs. Jeanette turned away from the painting and reached out to clasp his hands warmly. "Alexandre! How wonderful to see you! But what is this all about?"

He kissed her on both cheeks. "I hadn't expected you to arrive so soon."

"Well, what did you expect, then?" She laughed. "Such a mysterious letter! Henri and I did not wait a moment. We packed our trunks and"—she raised one hand in a delicate flourish—"*voilà!* Here we are, dying to know what affair of yours demands our immediate attention."

"Where is Henri?"

"He is putting the horses in the stable. He will join us shortly." She gave him a stern look. "If you had servants—"

"I do. I have a housekeeper."

"That hardly constitutes a household staff. I can't understand—"

"Jeanette," Alexandre interrupted, "now is not the time for one of your lectures about my way of life."

"Well, you could at least have allowed me to bring servants of my own."

Tess watched the two of them talk with easy familiarity, more puzzled than before. With any other man, it would have been perfectly understandable. These people were friends invited to come for a visit. But with Alexandre, it was a puzzle indeed. He had written to them, he had invited them to come here. Why?

"Tess and I have met, as you can see." Jeanette's reference to her startled Tess out of her reverie. She cast a questioning glance at Alexandre, but he was not looking at her. He was looking at Jeanette. "Come," he said, linking his arm through the woman's. "There is much we need to discuss." Over his shoulder, he told Tess, "We will be in my library. Send Henri there when he comes in. And make a pot of tea."

He walked away, arm in arm with Jeanette, leaving Tess to stare after them, her puzzlement giving way to irritation. He was talking to her as if she were a servant.

"And make a pot of tea," she muttered, mimicking him in disgust. "Of all the nerve . . ."

She strode to the kitchen. Slamming the kettle of water onto the stove, she seized a poker and began to stoke the fire savagely. "If he thinks he's going to treat me like a parlor maid, he's out of his head," she told Augustus, who was curled in the corner, watching her with mild interest. "Of all the brass-faced gall—"

"I think the fire is well-stoked, madame," an amused voice from the doorway pointed out. "You can cease demolishing it with your poker."

Tess whirled around to find Henri watching her from the doorway. She set the poker aside, unamused by the teasing gleam in his blue eyes. She jerked her thumb toward the other door. "They're in the library," she said, knowing she sounded grumpy and rude and not caring one whit.

Turning back to the stove, she pulled down the tin of tea leaves from the shelf to her right. The fading tap of the man's boots on the wood floor told her when he had left the room. She shoved the tin back on the shelf, yanked the kettle off the fire, and grabbed her hat.

"Let them make their own tea," she muttered, shoving the hat down on her head and slamming the door behind her as she left the house.

* * *

"What is this all about, Alexandre?" Jeanette leaned back against the sofa, facing the man who sat in the chair opposite. "When did you acquire a housekeeper?"

Alexandre didn't quite know how to begin. What he had told Jeanette had been true—he hadn't expected them to arrive for at least a few more days. He'd thought to have more time to rehearse explanations. "Perhaps we should wait until Henri comes in. There is much I have to tell you."

"I should say so!" Jeanette removed her hat and tossed it to the other end of the sofa. "We haven't heard from you for months," she reminded, pulling off her gloves and reaching up to smooth her chignon of dark brown hair. "You could write more often, you know."

"Is my wife lecturing again?" Henri strode into the room.

Alexandre rose to his feet and walked across the library to meet him. They embraced.

"You're looking well," Alexandre said. "It's been a long time."

"Too long," Henri agreed, stepping back to study him. "And you are looking better than I expected, although I see you still haven't managed to get your hair properly cut. Last time I saw you, you hadn't shaved for a month. You hadn't a clean shirt to your name and—"

"Now who is lecturing me?" He smiled. "It's good to see you, Henri."

The other man removed his wife's hat from the sofa and sat down. Alexandre resumed his seat. All of them were silent for several moments, none of them knowing quite what to say. Jeanette, as usual, spoke first.

"Enough of this beating around the bush, Alexandre. Henri and I are thrilled that you've invited us for a visit, but I confess your letter did come as a surprise to both of us." She leaned forward and reached out her hand for his. Squeezing his fingers, she looked at him with hungry affection. "It has been much too long, *mon cher*. But I have the feeling that there is more to this than a desire to see us, *n'est-ce pas?*"

Alexandre sighed and answered her question with a brief nod. Pulling his hand from hers, he rested his forearms on his knees and clasped his hands together, staring down at them for a moment before he spoke. "I asked both of you to come here, but it was really Jeanette I needed to see."

He looked at her and saw her eyes widen. "I? Alexandre, if you don't tell me, and quickly, what this is all about, I'm—"

"It's about Tess," he interrupted, receiving a blank look from both Jeanette and her husband.

"Your housekeeper?" Jeanette suddenly gave him a hard stare.

"Yes. You see—"

"Your *pregnant* housekeeper?"

The acidity in her voice told him exactly what she was thinking. "The babe isn't mine!"

Jeanette sniffed, unconvinced.

He looked at Henri, who was smiling with some amusement. "It isn't!" he repeated. They said nothing. He leaned back in his chair and sighed again. "I can see I shall have to begin at the beginning."

Tess stood in the stable, holding a bucket of oats under Flower's nose. She patted the donkey's neck and talked softly to her. "I don't understand this at all, Flower. Who are those people?"

Flower, her nose in the bucket, continued to munch on oats, oblivious to her mistress's questions.

Tess shook her head. "It doesn't make sense. He

doesn't like having people around. He doesn't even want me around half the time. Yet, he invited them here. I wonder who they are."

Flower snorted and lifted her head, indicating that the bucket was empty. Tess set it aside and gave the donkey a final pat. She turned around and stared at the pair of grays that belonged to the strangers. They were fine-looking horses, an expensive, well-matched pair. The carriage was also of fine quality. Whoever they were, they were not poor.

Tess left the stable and went out into the yard. After she had guided the chickens into their coop and securely locked the door against foxes, she wandered over to the pen where the goose was now kept. "Good evening, Mathilda," she greeted, resting her elbows on top of the fence. The bird strutted over to her and honked in reply.

"How's your wing today?" she asked, leaning over the fence to look at the splint. The binding still seemed secure.

She rested her cheek in the palm of her hand, staring into space. She didn't have anything more to do out here and it was growing dark. But she didn't want to go back inside and face the strangers, with Alexandre treating her like a servant.

Still, she was forced to admit, she *was* a servant. She wasn't mistress here. She wasn't Alexandre's wife. No, she was just the housekeeper. And that was what bothered her the most. She wanted to be more, so much more.

She stepped inside the pen and led the goose inside the tiny shed that served as a coop, latching the door. She then turned and walked back to the château, realizing with a sinking feeling that housekeeper was all she would ever be.

*　　　*　　　*

"You mean, you want me to deliver the girl's baby?" Jeanette spoke slowly as if unable to believe what he was asking. "You want me to be the midwife?"

"Your mother was the midwife in Fréjus," he pointed out. "You assisted her many times."

"Yes, but that was years ago!" She shook her head. "Alexandre, it would be best if old Françoise—"

"No!" His answer was vehement. "I will not ask her to do it."

"I could ask her for you."

"And have her look at me as she did at Anne-Marie's funeral? Have her say again what she said to me that day? No!"

Jeanette spoke very softly. "That was three years ago. And it was very difficult for her. She loved Anne-Marie—"

"And I didn't?" Alexandre rose and began to pace before the fireplace. He raked a hand through his hair and his ribbon fell away unnoticed. "No, I will not ask her. Françoise was right when she spoke to me at the funeral. Don't you understand? She was *right*." He stopped and looked at Jeanette, who was watching him with an expression that conveyed she did indeed understand, all too well.

"We could get a midwife elsewhere," Henri interjected. "Fréjus, perhaps."

But Alexandre shook his head. "It's too far from here." He turned back to Jeanette. "A woman should have another woman close by at a time like this. Please. Do this for me, *chérie*."

She rose to her feet and came to stand before him. She took his hands in hers and looked up into his eyes. "Of course I will. We're family, aren't we?"

His lips tightened slightly. "Yes," he agreed. "We're family."

"Now that we've settled that business, isn't it time we had dinner?" Henri suggested, standing up. "Jeanette and I were in such a hurry to arrive, we stopped for only a brief meal in Sainte-Maxime, and that was many hours ago."

"Excellent idea," Jeanette agreed. "But first, I would like the two of you to bring in the trunks, and I will unpack." She cast an inquiring glance at Alexandre. "Did you say the girl doesn't know why we're here?"

"No, she doesn't. I thought it best if you told her." He paused, then added, "But not every detail, Jeanette."

She made an exclamation of irritation. "Of course not! I will simply say that you thought she needed female companionship and that I have done midwifery before. Will that do?"

"Very well." He looked at Henri. "Shall we bring in those trunks?"

The other man grinned. "If we must. But if you had servants—"

Alexandre held up his hands to stop Henri's flow of words. "Don't even think such a thing. The one I have has caused me enough trouble already."

14

Tess hesitated in the doorway, a pile of linens in her arms, watching Jeanette. The other woman was looking out the window of the bedchamber at the vineyards beyond. She heard her sigh deeply and watched her turn away from the window with a shake of her head. Catching sight of Tess, she smiled, beckoning her to enter with a wave of her hand. "Come in, come in."

Tess put the linens on a chair and pulled a sheet out of the pile. "Alexandre told me to bring these up. If I had known you were coming, I would have had a room ready for you."

"Pray do not worry about it." Jeanette grasped one end of the sheet Tess opened over the bare mattress. As the two women tucked in the edges, she said, "I am Alexandre's sister-in-law."

Tess paused for a moment. "Oh." She couldn't think of anything else to say. She began to smooth the sheet over the mattress.

"My husband," the other woman continued, "is Alexandre's brother by adoption. Henri's father, Lucien, adopted Alexandre after his parents were killed during the Revolution."

"He told me about his parents," Tess answered and turned to reach for the top sheet. *He also told me he killed his wife. Is that true?* She snapped the sheet open over the bed with a flick of her wrists.

They had finished making up the bed by the time Alexandre and Henri brought up the trunks. As the two men laid the trunks at the foot of the bed and departed, Tess moved to follow them, but Jeanette laid a hand on her arm. "Tess, please wait."

She walked over to the door and closed it. Turning, she leaned her back against the door and met Tess's inquiring glance. "I wanted to talk with you for a moment, if I may."

"Of course."

Jeanette moved to the bed and sat down. Patting the mattress, she indicated for Tess to sit as well. After Tess had done so, Jeanette said, "Alexandre has told me about your situation."

Tess felt the color drain from her face. Alexandre couldn't know, she thought frantically. She hadn't told him anything. "What did he tell you?"

Jeanette must have heard the panic in her voice. She smiled and touched her hand to Tess's shoulder in reassurance. "I'm sorry if you think he shouldn't have. But he felt that it was necessary, given your condition, and the fact that you are living in his home, with no one else in the house."

Their eyes met and Tess flushed, realizing what she meant.

Jeanette said, "Tess, there is no reason to be ashamed. It's the man who should be ashamed, refusing to accept his responsibilities and do the honorable thing, forcing you to go off on your own."

She gave Jeanette a blank stare. Is that what they

thought? Is that what Alexandre had told them? That she was having an illegitimate child? Beginning to put it all together, Tess realized that Alexandre's conclusion was a logical one, given her circumstances and the fact that she hadn't told him the truth. She murmured, "That doesn't really matter now, though, does it?"

"No, it doesn't. What matters now is your welfare and that of the child. That's why I'm here."

"I don't understand."

"Alexandre asked me to come here because he felt that you needed another woman around. My mother was a midwife, and I have done midwifery in the past. I have also borne four children of my own. He thought I might be able to help." She paused and their eyes met. "He felt that you needed a friend."

Tess stared at the pretty woman she had met for the first time only a few hours before and didn't know what to say. It had been so long since she'd had a friend, a female companion with whom to share confidences. "I think I'd like that," she confessed shyly.

Jeanette smiled. "Excellent! Let's unpack these things and go down for dinner. I'm certain that Henri has already persuaded Alexandre to concoct a delightful meal for us. He's a wonderful chef, you know."

Tess made a face and sighed. "Yes, I know. He's a much better cook than I am."

"I wouldn't worry about that." Jeanette rose to her feet and gave Tess a mischievous grin. "After all, a man should be good for something."

After the evening meal, which was as excellent as Jeanette had predicted, the four of them sat in the salon. Tess had made tea for herself and Jeanette while the men opened a bottle of very old cognac.

Henri lifted his glass to his lips, then paused without

drinking, his eyes fixed on Augustus, who had announced his entrance into the room with a loud meow. He and Jeanette both watched in astonishment as the kitten walked over to Alexandre's chair and continued to meow, rubbing his head against the man's leg.

"When did you get a cat?" Jeanette asked, looking bewildered. "I thought you hated cats."

Alexandre glanced down at the kitten ruefully. Setting his glass on the table, he reached down and picked up Augustus, placing the animal in his lap. "This cat has developed an incomprehensible affection for me. He follows me everywhere."

Tess added, "His name is Augustus. He's a stray I found in the barn when he was only a tiny baby. I think the foxes got his mother and siblings. I adopted him, but he seems to have a greater fondness for Alexandre, as you can see."

Jeanette and Henri watched as Alexandre gazed down at the cat on his lap with an expression that bordered on affection. "Well," Jeanette murmured, "I can hardly believe it."

"Speaking of animals," Henri said, "I noticed a donkey in the stable when I put away the horses. I hope you didn't pay much for her. She's a pathetic creature."

Alexandre's face took on a wry expression. "I paid far too much for her, Henri. I admit it."

Tess choked back a laugh, and Henri and Jeanette turned toward her inquiringly. She said, "I found the donkey in the vineyard. Its former master had abused it shamefully, and Alexandre let me keep her. Her name is Flower."

She smiled at Alexandre, but he was looking down at Augustus. She added, "We have a goose, too. Named Mathilda."

Henri laughed aloud. "Quite a menagerie. I do believe you're becoming a farmer, *mon cher*."

"Not until Tess brings home a stray cow and a few sheep," Alexandre answered, lifting his head to grin at his brother. "But enough about me. Tell me about the children. How are they?"

She listened as Henri and Jeanette told Alexandre the latest news about his nieces and nephew. She noticed how avidly he listened as Jeanette related the woes of parenthood.

"So, Heloise has finally discovered that boys are more important than climbing trees?" He sipped his cognac and glanced at Henri. "You should take care. Soon she'll be wanting to marry."

Henri groaned. "I don't even want to think about it. She's only fourteen, but she's already a beauty. Half the fathers in Marseilles have approached me this summer on behalf of their sons."

"And what of Georges?" Alexandre asked. "Will he go into the business with you?"

Henri shrugged. "He has little interest in being a wine merchant. But he's still quite young. Who can tell?"

"Alexandre, you must come to Marseilles." Jeanette set down her teacup and leaned forward. "Mercedes is out of short coats and wearing dresses now. She's becoming quite the little lady. And you haven't even seen Chantal, who is nearly three."

Tess watched Alexandre frown down into his glass. Did she really see the yearning in his face, or was it only her imagination? More than ever, she sensed how much he loved children, what a good father he would be. She wished he was the father of her child and knew it would never be that way.

To stop the depressing direction her thoughts were taking, Tess excused herself from the group and went upstairs to fetch her sewing basket. Bringing it down-stairs, she placed it on the sofa between herself and Jeanette and pulled out the tiny shirt she was working on.

Jeanette noticed what she was doing and turned away from the two men, who were now discussing the wine trade. She leaned over the basket to take a look at Tess's sewing. "A shirt for the baby?"

Tess nodded and held up the tiny piece of cambric. "It's nearly finished. I'm just sewing the lace to the cuffs."

"May I see it?"

Tess handed the shirt to her and Jeanette examined it. "What exquisite stitching. I enjoy sewing, but I don't stitch as well as this. It's lovely."

"Thank you." Tess took back the shirt, noticing Jeanette looking at the garments in the basket with curiosity. "Would you like to see what else I have? Perhaps you can give me some suggestions. I'm sure I've forgotten something."

Jeanette nodded, and the two women began sorting through the baby clothes Tess had made.

"This year's harvest is expected to be bad." Henri shook his head. "There won't be much brandy to market this winter, I'm afraid."

Alexandre nodded absently, but he was not really listening. His eyes were on Tess as she held up a pair of absurdly small knitted boots. He observed the animation in her face as she and Jeanette talked about babies and baby things. Could a woman really want a baby so much?

Anne-Marie hadn't wanted babies. Her fear of childbearing had overshadowed any joy she might have felt.

As he watched Tess and Jeanette, he saw his sister-in-law glance his way. He quickly dropped his gaze to his cognac. But he could feel her watching him. He wondered if she, too, was thinking of Anne-Marie.

"Well?"

Henri paused in the act of unbuttoning his shirt and looked at his wife. "Well what?"

Jeanette turned from the dressing table where she was brushing her long, dark hair. "What do you think of all this?"

He shrugged out of his shirt and tossed it onto a chair. "I don't know what to think. It's rather odd, to say the least."

"Henri, there are hooks in the wardrobe on which to hang your shirts," she pointed out, then returned to her former subject. "I think having the girl here might be the best thing that could happen to Alexandre."

Emerging from the wardrobe where he had obligingly hung his shirt, Henri said, "I'm surprised he allowed her to stay. I couldn't believe it when he told us she'd been here nearly three months."

"I know. When Anne-Marie died and he dismissed all the servants, I was certain it wouldn't last. I thought he'd eventually get over it and resume a normal life again. But after three years, Henri, I had begun to give up hope."

Henri paused, his trousers half-unbuttoned. "You did? But whenever we've talked about it, you've always been the one to reassure me he would be all right."

"I know. I was beginning to worry about him, but I didn't want you to be worried, too." Jeanette set down the brush and walked over to the bed. Pulling down the counterpane, she slid between the sheets and continued, "When you came home after your last visit here and told me how distant he was, I really began to worry. But when he wrote and asked us to come, I never expected anything like this."

"Neither did I." Henri put his trousers in the wardrobe then walked naked to the opposite side of the bed.

Jeanette took a moment to admire her husband's muscular physique before her thoughts returned to Tess. She said, "That poor girl. Abandoned, having to travel across France the way she did, alone."

"Whoever the man is, he ought to be shot." Henri slid into the bed beside his wife. With a yawn, he added, "It's a pity. She seems a sweet girl. If she traveled across France alone, on foot, she has courage. She's quite pretty, too."

He ducked when she hit him with the pillow.

She said, "I don't think it's a pity. I think it's wonderful."

"What?" Henri sat up in bed and stared at her. "You think what happened to that poor girl is wonderful?"

"Not that. Of course, she's been through a great deal. But I think it's wonderful that fate led her here. It could be the best possible thing for Alexandre."

"You said that before. What do you mean?"

She fingered the low neckline of her thin silk nightgown thoughtfully. "Why do you suppose he's letting her stay?"

"He feels sorry for the girl, obviously."

She shook her head. "No. I think he's lonely."

"Jeanette, if he wanted female companionship, I'm sure he could find it easily enough. Besides, she's pregnant. And knowing Alexandre, I doubt anything of that sort is going on. He would never take advantage of the girl."

"Of course not! That isn't what I meant!" Exasperated, she reached back and plumped up her pillow. Leaning against it, she explained, "I simply meant what I said. He's lonely. I don't think he realized how lonely he was until Tess came here."

"Don't you think you're being a bit too romantic?"

Jeanette shook her head. "No, I don't. He painted her portrait. Did you see it?"

"I saw it. But he's painted portraits of many women. He didn't fall in love with any of them. Once this girl has her baby, he'll send her on her way and go back to the solitary life he's been leading for three years now."

"You're wrong." She turned on to her side. Leaning her weight on her elbow and resting her cheek in her hand, she asked, "Do you want to know what else I think?"

Henri sighed. "Does it matter? I'm sure you'll tell me anyway."

She ignored that. "I think he's trying to atone for what happened to Anne-Marie. You know he feels he's to blame for what happened. He'll let Tess and her baby stay as long as they want. I think he feels responsible for them."

He turned toward her. "Perhaps. But now I'll tell you what I think."

"What?"

He leaned closer. "I think it's time you stopped talking about Alexandre and his housekeeper and used your lips for something far more important."

Jeanette was happy to oblige.

Alexandre looked up from the watercolor he was working on as Henri entered the studio. "*Bonjour,*" he greeted his brother. "You're awake early. After your journey, I thought you'd sleep late this morning."

Henri laughed. "I wanted to, but Jeanette wouldn't let me. She was eager to begin helping Tess make preparations for the baby, and she insisted that I rise as well. She seemed to think I should come up here and keep you company."

"I'm glad she did, *mon cher.* I have paintings for you to take to Marseilles with you when you return home, and I wanted you to have a look at them. I hope they fetch a good price."

"Your paintings always fetch a good price." Henri walked over to the table to study the watercolor Alexandre was working on. "This is the Meadow of the Fairies," he said in surprise.

Alexandre looked down at the half-finished painting. He closed his eyes briefly, remembering the day he had kissed Tess beneath the plane tree, remembering the day that had followed. "Yes."

"You once said that was the one place you'd never paint. It was too magical to capture on canvas, you said. Yet, you've painted it twice now. First Tess's portrait, and now this."

Alexandre turned away from the table, not wanting to discuss the damned painting, not wanting to think about why he was painting it. But he knew the reason. Because he couldn't keep the events of that day out of his mind, and the meadow had been beckoning him to paint it again ever since that day. "I know what I said," he muttered. "I changed my mind."

"I received another invitation for you to do an exhibition at the Royal Academy in London," Henri said, changing the subject. "I wish you would consider it."

"I have no desire to go to London."

"What about Paris, then? I have also received invitations from several of the galleries there, asking you to exhibit paintings. The English would pay more, but Paris is closer to home."

"I am finished with exhibitions." Alexandre turned to his brother with an irritated frown. "I don't show my work like wares in a shop window any longer."

"It isn't the exhibitions that bother you," Henri pointed out, "and we both know it. Leaving here, even for a short time, is what makes you refuse."

"I don't want to discuss it," Alexandre said coldly. "My reasons are my own."

Henri raised his hands in a gesture of exasperation. "I don't understand this attitude of yours. Why not go to London or Paris? What could possibly be holding you here?"

"I am here because I *choose* to be here."

"You're here because this place is filled with reminders of Anne-Marie. You won't leave, because if you left, you might start to forget what happened. You might begin to forgive yourself and that—"

Alexandre slammed his fist down on the table. "I have said no! And that is the end of it, Henri. I will not discuss it any further!"

The two men faced each other, their gazes locked, each determined to make the other see and accept his point of view.

A soft cough from the stairs caused both men to turn in that direction. Tess stood there, a tray in her hands. "Pardon me," she apologized. "I thought the two of you might like some morning tea."

Alexandre watched her intently, wondering how much she had heard. But her face was impassive as she brought the tray over to the table. He swept an impatient glance over the tray. On it rested two cups, the teapot, milk, sugar, and a plate of blackberry tarts.

He looked at Tess, but she was busily straightening the items on the tray. When she finished, she turned toward the stairs. "I will leave the two of you to continue your argument now." She gave Henri a smile as she passed him and went down the stairs.

Henri looked at the tray, then he began to chuckle. "I can see she wasn't concerned about whether or not I was hungry. Jeanette would have told her I detest blackberry tarts. But," he added, looking at Alexandre, "I don't suppose she made them for me."

Alexandre picked up one of the flaky morsels. "Well, she is *my* housekeeper."

"After you've finished eating all the tarts on the tray—and I know you *will* eat them all—why don't we go down and do some fencing? I am sorely in need of practice with you, *mon frère*. I lost to a left-handed opponent only a week ago."

Alexandre grinned. "So you want to defeat me and soothe your wounded pride?"

"Of course."

"It will never happen." Alexandre took another bite of tart, shaking his head.

"We'll see."

After taking the tray for the men up to the studio, Tess returned to the kitchen, where Jeanette was making a fresh pot of tea for the two of them. After a light breakfast of toast and tea, Tess showed her new friend the nursery. Leading her into the wardrobe room adjoining her bedchamber, Tess said, "It's very small, I know, but it will do. I imagine a lady's maid once slept here."

Jeanette nodded, but did not reply. Her gaze was fixed on the cradle that sat in one corner. Stepping forward, she leaned down and studied it. It was the same one. The same cradle Alexandre had ordered from a local carpenter when Anne-Marie was pregnant. Alexandre had painted the flowers on that cradle himself. "Where did you get this?"

She glanced at Tess, who was also gazing at the cradle, a tender expression on her face.

"Alexandre gave it to me for the baby. He didn't say anything about it. I just found it in here one day." Tess turned to her. "It was meant for his own baby, wasn't it?"

Jeanette met her eyes. "Yes."

"What happened?"

Jeanette wasn't certain how much to reveal. She knew Alexandre would not be happy to learn she had told Tess anything about the baby or about Anne-Marie. "The baby died."

"So did his wife. Isn't that right?"

Jeanette nodded and turned to walk out of the room, hoping that would end any discussion of the subject, but

Tess reached out and touched her shoulder. "Please tell me."

Jeanette looked into Tess's pleading face. "Has Alexandre told you anything about his wife?"

"Yes." Tess lowered her hand from Jeanette's shoulder and clasped her hands together, resting them on her abdomen. "He told me that he killed her."

Jeanette expelled her breath in a sharp sigh. Even now, after three years, he was still blaming himself. "He didn't do anything of the sort."

"What happened?"

Jeanette knew she didn't have the right to answer Tess's question. "I don't think that is something I should be telling you. If Alexandre wanted you to know, he would tell you himself."

Tess nodded reluctantly, but she asked, "Could you at least tell me something about his wife? Who was she? What was she like?"

Jeanette could tell that Tess was not simply curious. There was more to it than that. "Anne-Marie was Henri's sister," she said reluctantly. "Alexandre, my husband, and Anne-Marie all grew up together. When Alexandre was twenty-one, he wanted to go to Italy to paint. But Lucien would not allow his daughter to marry Alexandre because she was only sixteen and he thought her too young. They eloped and went to Italy together. They did not return until six years later, when Napoleon fell."

"She was very beautiful," Tess said. When Jeanette shot her a questioning glance, she added, "I saw the portrait Alexandre did of her."

"It is an excellent likeness. Anne-Marie was full of life. Always laughing, always wanting a new adventure. She was a passionate girl. She was also a capricious girl. A flirt. She . . . she liked to tease, and she could never see the consequences. She and Alexandre had a . . . tempestuous marriage. She quite often led him a merry chase." Jeanette closed her eyes. It was painful to talk about Anne-Marie.

"Alexandre loved her very much, didn't he?"

Tess's wistful tone caused Jeanette's eyes to open in surprise. "Yes, he did. She was carrying a child and when she died, the child died as well." Jeanette added sadly, "When they died, Alexandre dismissed all the servants, closed the winery, and began living the life of a recluse. That was three years ago."

"He didn't kill her." Tess shook her head and looked at Jeanette. "Alexandre could never do such a thing. But, somehow, he blames himself for what happened, doesn't he? Is it because she died having his baby?"

"It's more complicated than that, I'm afraid." Jeanette glanced once more at the cradle and said, "I don't have the right to tell you anything more. As I said, if Alexandre wanted you to know, he would have told you himself."

She walked out of the nursery. Tess watched her go, wanting to find out more, knowing the subject was closed. She glanced down at the cradle, wishing that Alexandre loved her, wishing that her baby could take the place of the one he had lost. Perhaps, in time, her wishes would come true. Tess tucked in a fold of the blanket that lay in the cradle and left the nursery to follow Jeanette.

As she descended the stairs, she noticed Jeanette standing on the first landing, staring down into the hall below. She heard a noisy clatter and the sound of shouting male voices. Looking past Jeanette, she saw Alexandre in the center of the wide hall, thrusting the rapier in his hand at Henri, who was parrying and retreating. Both men wore masks, but Alexandre's large frame and the long hair streaming down his back gave him away. She moved to stand beside Jeanette, watching the men practice.

"You will hit the wall in a few more steps," Alexandre informed his opponent, taking another lunge at him. "Would you like to yield now?"

"Never," Henri shouted back, parrying the lunge and striking out for Alexandre's exposed flank with a lunge of his own.

Alexandre blocked that thrust, but it was his turn to retreat as Henri became the aggressor. Tess watched as the two men, both skilled duelists, moved across the floor, their weapons clashing to send echoes through the hall. She leaned forward against the stair rail beside Jeanette, her gaze fixed on Alexandre, admiring his skill and speed, loving the strength and natural grace in his movements.

The match continued for some moments more, until with a feint and a quick thrust, Alexandre pointed his sword at Henri's chest.

"I yield, I yield!" Henri laughed, lowering his weapon and reaching back to pull off his mask. "Damn you left-handed fencers. You always have the advantage."

Alexandre set down his rapier and pulled off his own mask. Shaking back his hair, he gave his opponent a triumphant grin. "You were right, Henri. You are definitely in need of practice."

"Does this mean we'll be asked to visit you more often?" Jeanette asked from the stairs, her voice teasing.

Alexandre glanced up at the two women. His gaze moved from his sister-in-law to Tess and lingered there. "Perhaps," he allowed, with a slow nod of his head. "Perhaps."

15

Over the next several days, while Alexandre gave Henri the opportunity to practice his fencing, Tess and Jeanette spent much of their time making plans for the baby and getting to know each other. Though they talked about many things, the subject of Anne-Marie was not mentioned. Tess didn't ask any more questions, but she couldn't help wondering about the things Jeanette had told her that day in the nursery.

Tess thought of Jeanette's comment about things being complicated. "I wonder what she meant by that," she murmured aloud.

Sophie stirred restlessly and turned her head to nudge Tess's shoulder.

"Hold still," she told the goat. "I'm almost finished."

After a few more moments, the milking was done. Tess pulled the bucket out from under Sophie and rose awkwardly to her feet. After putting away the stool and setting the milk in the shade, she led Sophie out of the pen to take her to the pasture. As she closed the gate of the pen, she saw Jeanette walking down the path toward her.

"Good morning," she greeted the other woman.

Jeanette looked down at Sophie. "I see Alexandre still has the goat."

Tess patted the animal's head. "This is Sophie. I'm just taking her out to the pasture. Would you like to walk with me?"

Jeanette fell in step beside her. "Do you milk the goat every morning?"

Tess nodded. Opening the gate, she waited until Sophie had ambled into the pasture, then she closed the gate again. "I never milked a goat in my life until I came here. We had cows at the vicarage where I grew up, but we also had a servant to milk them, so I never learned how. Alexandre taught me."

Jeanette laughed. "That doesn't surprise me. He hates milking that goat."

Tess smiled. "Really? I didn't know that." She started back toward the barn, and Jeanette walked with her. "I take care of all the animals. I enjoy it, and I seem to have a way with them."

Jeanette watched as Tess went about her morning chores. As Tess gave the donkey water, she told Jeanette the story of how Alexandre had acquired the animal.

"And he ended up paying fifty francs for her," Tess concluded, setting aside the empty water bucket and giving Flower a pat. "He didn't want the donkey, but he felt sorry for her." She turned to Jeanette. "He's a good man."

Before Jeanette could reply, Tess turned back to Flower and began to lead the donkey out of the stable. Jeanette followed, watching Tess thoughtfully as she led the donkey to the pasture.

After Tess had gathered the eggs, the two women returned to the house. As they entered the courtyard, Tess paused. She bent to pick up something from the ground, and as she straightened, Jeanette realized it was a long ribbon of black silk.

Tess smiled down at the strip of silk and shook her head. "Another one," she murmured. Glancing up, she met Jeanette's curious gaze, and her smile widened. "It's one of Alexandre's ribbons. He's always losing them. When he gets frustrated or worried or angry, he rakes his hand through his hair and his ribbon comes loose. He never seems to notice."

"Men do have their quirks, don't they?" Jeanette responded. "At night, Henri starts undressing the moment he's in the bedchamber, and he leaves a trail of clothes from the door to the bed. As a young man, he never had a valet, and he refuses to get one, even though we can afford it. We do have a cantankerous chambermaid who has been with us for years, but she refuses to pick up after him. If I don't remind him to put his clothes in the laundry basket or back in the wardrobe, he finds himself without any clean shirts. When he does, he's always puzzled how such a thing could happen."

The two women laughed together. Tess's eyes twinkled with merry indulgence. "I find these ribbons everywhere. But I never say anything. I just press them and return them to the drawer where they belong."

Jeanette watched as Tess looked down at the ribbon, rubbing the silk between her fingers. She listened as Tess added in a soft voice, "I don't mind."

Jeanette stared, suddenly realizing the truth. Tess was in love with Alexandre. The tender expression on her face and the loving nuance of her voice whenever she talked about him gave her away.

But Jeanette wondered if Tess's love could ever be returned. She knew Alexandre was capable of the deepest passions, but he was also a man who now avoided any possible intimacy. She followed Tess up the stairs and into the château, wondering if it would be possible for Alexandre to find love again.

*   *   *

Late the following afternoon, while Tess was taking a nap, Jeanette decided it was time to make good on her promise to help with the making of baby clothes. She took the sewing basket out into the courtyard to enjoy the sunshine as she worked.

She was absorbed in fitting a tiny shirt sleeve into an armhole, and didn't hear the sound of footsteps. A shadow fell across her, and she looked up to find Alexandre standing before her.

"*Bonjour, mon cher,*" she greeted him and gestured to the seat beside her. "Have you finished your fencing practice with Henri?"

He nodded and sat down beside her. He was silent, watching as she pinned fabric together.

He was silent so long, she paused in her task to look at him. She gave him a teasing smile. "I don't suppose you'd like to help?"

He did not return her smile. "I wanted to talk to you about something."

His voice was so serious, she set aside her sewing to give him her full attention. "What is it?"

"I asked you to come here to deliver Tess's baby. I'm very grateful that you came, *chérie.* But I have another favor to ask of you."

"Anything. You know that."

He reached out and ran his hand along the edge of the sewing basket. "I want you to find some servants for me."

"What?" Jeanette stared at him in astonishment.

"*Oui.*" He reached into the basket, fingering a piece of soft white flannel. His brows drew together in a thoughtful frown. "Tess has been working too hard, and I don't like it."

She heard the worry in his voice. "I've tried to tell her not to do so much."

"I know. I, too, have told her, but she doesn't listen. She became my housekeeper in exchange for room and board, and she feels she is obligated to earn her keep. For the sake of her pride, I have allowed it, but that cannot continue." His frown deepened.

She smiled, knowing his concern was a good sign. A very good sign indeed. "So, you want me to find servants for you. How many?"

"I don't know. What do you think?"

She did not reply. She knew that Alexandre would be uncomfortable with having local people in the house, although he was willing to do so for Tess's sake. She also knew that it would be difficult to find local people who would be willing to come here. She was fully aware of the hideous rumors that surrounded her brother-in-law. She thought for a few moments, then she gave an exclamation. "I have an idea. Henri and I have more servants than we can use, but Henri is much too soft-hearted to turn any of them out."

"Henri?" he asked, giving her a teasing glance.

She blushed. "Well, I must confess, I'm rather the same way. But that's neither here nor there. I will write home and ask if Paul and his wife, Leonie, would be willing to come and assist with things here."

She gestured to the crumbling courtyard. "There are many things that Paul could do. And Leonie would be able to help with the housework. Although she is nursing her second child, I'm sure she would be willing to come. She would also be able to assist me with the birth."

"Do it."

"I'll write a letter tomorrow. When do you want them to come?"

He rose to his feet. "As soon as possible. I don't want Tess taking any risks with her health. She's too close to having the baby."

Jeanette smiled as he walked away. This was a momentous step forward for her reclusive brother-in-law. More than that, it was a miracle.

Nigel stared at the innkeeper with distaste, careful to remain at least half a dozen strides away. The man reeked of garlic and rancid grease and bad wine. The inn, located on the road from Paris to Lyon, was dark and empty and smelled as bad as the man who owned it.

Nigel held a perfumed lace handkerchief to his nose for a moment, breathing deeply, then tucked the handkerchief back in the pocket of his cream silk waistcoat. "You're certain?"

The man nodded, glancing once again at the painted miniature in his hand. "*Mais oui.* She was here. Two days, perhaps three, she stayed here, but that was months ago."

"If it was months ago, how can you remember so well?" Martin Trevalyn stepped closer to the man, unmindful of the smell, and retrieved the miniature.

"She was dressed like a man. *Tout de même*, she did not fool me." He gave a coarse laugh and shrugged. "But what will you? My wife, she watches me like a hawk. Ah, *les femmes . . .*" He sighed at the temptations of the flesh that had been denied him.

Nigel also stepped forward, furious at the man's implication, but Martin placed a warning hand on his arm. His look told Nigel plainly that the man was not worth a fight and pleaded for patience. Nigel let out an angry hiss between his teeth, but once again stepped back.

Martin asked, "Did she say where she was going?"

"*Non.* She did not say."

Nigel tossed a handful of coins that scattered on the floor at the innkeeper's feet. The two men departed, leaving the innkeeper to scramble for the coins rolling across the greasy floor.

"Splendid idea. The girl works much too hard." Henri nodded with approval, holding up his glass to down the last swallow of brandy. "I'm glad you've finally come to your senses about servants." He started to take another sip of brandy, realized the glass was empty, and declared, "I'd like another." He held out his glass, and Alexandre poured.

But only a few drops trickled from the crystal decanter. Alexandre frowned down into the bottle. "It's empty."

Henri sighed, leaning forward to rest his elbows on the table between them. "We've finished it? How many is that? Two or three?"

"Just two, I think."

Henri sighed again. "Well, there has to be more here somewhere."

"I'll see what I can find." Alexandre rose unsteadily to his feet, walking across the library to the cabinet in one corner. Opening it, he let out a triumphant, if rather loud, exclamation. "Ah-hah! More brandy!"

"Knew you'd find some," Henri said with the complacence of a truly drunken man. He held up his glass. "Pour. Try not to miss this time."

Alexandre tried to give his brother his most intimidating stare as he pulled the top from the decanter. He poured, but as much brandy ended up on the floor as in the glass. He refilled his own tumbler, spilling more of the fiery brown liquid in the process. He set the decanter on the table and fell back into his seat. Lifting his glass, he said, "Let's drink to . . ." Pausing, he frowned. "What shall we drink to?"

"Do we need a reason?"

"No."

Both men laughed, thinking themselves quite witty, and drank their brandy.

A loud meow sounded, and Augustus rose from where he had been sleeping in the corner, indignant at being roused from his nap by a pair of drunken fools. He walked over to the table, and Alexandre lifted the kitten onto his lap.

"Hello, *mon ami.*"

Henri shook his head in disbelief. "Never thought you'd have a cat. I think you actually like the animal."

"*C'est possible,*" Alexandre admitted, rubbing Augustus between the ears. The kitten responded with loud purring. "But I'm glad Tess didn't bring home any more."

Henri grinned. "No, she came home with a donkey instead. And what a donkey!"

Alexandre picked up the bottle, and with a frown of complete concentration, refilled his glass once more, only spilling a few drops on the table. He took a hefty swallow and grimaced. "Never should've bought the damn thing. But she wanted to keep it."

"She seems to love animals."

"She didn't want its owner to hurt it anymore, but I was going to give it back. Then I saw her eyes." He leaned back in his chair, staring up at the ceiling. "She wasn't even there, but I saw her eyes . . . knew she'd be hurt if I gave the thing back. I couldn't do it . . . paid fifty francs for that pathetic creature."

Henri shook his head, trying to clear his mind of the alcoholic haze and listen to his brother. Alexandre had paid fifty francs for a donkey he didn't want just so his housekeeper wouldn't be hurt? He thought of Tess. Lovely girl, with eyes that could persuade a man to do a great many things he didn't want to do.

He glanced again across the table to where Alexandre stared moodily into his glass, and recalled Jeanette's words of the other night. Alexandre *was* lonely. But it was more than that, Henri realized. His hard shell was crumbling, and the girl was responsible for it.

But Henri was not as romantic as his wife. Alexandre obviously cared for the girl, but they knew nothing about her. If she ever hurt him, he might withdraw into himself again, possibly so far that he would never come out of it. Henri hoped, for Alexandre's sake, the girl was as charming as she seemed.

Augustus meowed, bringing both men out of their pensive mood.

Alexandre looked down at the kitten, who was rubbing affectionately against his chest. "We are the only males in the house, are we not?" he asked Augustus. "There is Tess, and Flower the donkey, and Sophie the goat. We are surrounded by females. And there's the goose, Mathilda. I'd forgotten Mathilda." He glanced at Henri and said with a scowl, "I hate that goose."

Henri laughed. Downing the last swallow of brandy in his glass, he refilled it from the decanter between them. "You hated cats once, too, *mon cher*. On my next visit, I expect you and the goose will be fast friends."

"Never," Alexandre vowed, setting Augustus on the floor. "Every time I go near that goose, she tries to attack me. She is a *femme formidable,* that one. But Augustus understands me."

Both men looked down at the kitten, who was happily lapping up the brandy that had spilled on the floor.

"I see he also understands the value of an excellent brandy," Henri commented.

"So do we," Alexandre answered, picking up the decanter. "But this is the last bottle."

"Shame, you know." Henri leaned forward again, elbows on the table, glass in hand, staring at his brother through bleary eyes. "Vintners should never run out of drink."

Alexandre leaned forward as well. "We aren't vintners anymore," he reminded.

"But when we were, we made excellent wine. And our brandy . . ." His voice trailed off, and he lifted his glass. "It was better than this stuff."

"This *is* our brandy."

"I knew it was good." Henri emptied his glass and promptly refilled it with an unsteady hand. "We should make wine again."

Alexandre shook his head. "Won't make wine again. No more wine."

Drunk as he was, Henri heard the pain in Alexandre's voice. He, too, had felt the pain when Anne-Marie died. But he had not had to deal with the guilt that Alexandre carried. "She didn't die because of the winery," he said softly. "You know that."

"I know. She died because of me."

"She did not!" Henri sat up straight in his chair, trying to gather his sodden wits. "It was an accident."

"No. She didn't want a baby. I wanted it." His words were slurred, but filled with the anguish of guilt. "She didn't want to sleep with me anymore. But I didn't listen."

"But . . ." Henri started to speak, then stopped himself. This was the first time Alexandre had talked about Anne-Marie since her death. He let him talk.

"And then she was so scared. She thought she'd die." He paused long enough to take a swallow of brandy. "I said things to her. I was angry. I wanted the baby, but she didn't. She didn't want it."

Henri felt the anguish of Alexandre's words, and memories of their childhood came before him. Alexandre had always loved Anne-Marie. Henri remembered how his sister always wanted to tag along with them, and how Alexandre would always allow it. Henri was her brother, but Alexandre had always been her protector. And Henri knew that when his sister had died, Alexandre had felt that he had failed. "It wasn't your fault."

"I told her she was selfish. That she only cared about herself." He leaned forward, resting his head in his hands. "I called her a coward."

"When we're angry, we all say things we don't mean."

Alexandre's laugh was bitter and humorless as he lifted his head and leaned back in his chair. "But I did mean it. I meant every word. I thought she was a coward. But look at me, Henri. *Mon Dieu!* Who is the coward now?"

Henri tried to think of something to say, but he couldn't. He stared at Alexandre, his heart aching for his brother.

16

Tess stood in the library doorway, staring at the sight before her. The morning sunlight pouring through the window revealed Alexandre and Henri exactly where she and Jeanette had bid them goodnight over eight hours before.

Alexandre was sprawled back in his chair, his long hair loose and tangled, and a dark shadow of beard on his jaw. Augustus was lying across his lap. Henri was seated in the opposite chair, leaning forward over the table between them with his head resting in his folded arms. The table held three empty decanters and two empty glasses. The kitten and both men were sound asleep.

Tess placed hands on hips, watching them in disbelief. She heard footsteps behind her and turned as Jeanette came down the corridor toward her. "I found them," she told the other woman.

"You mean they're still in there?" Jeanette stopped in the doorway, peering over Tess's shoulder.

Augustus heard the voices of the two women and lifted his head, giving a rather pathetic-sounding meow.

Tess stepped into the room and walked over to the table. Shaking her head at the three empty bottles, she lifted Augustus from Alexandre's lap, cradling him in her arms as he meowed again, a bit louder this time.

The sound awakened Alexandre, who lifted his head slightly and opened his eyes. Wincing at the bright sunlight and giving a groan of pain, he fell forward to rest his elbows on the table, cradling his head in his hands.

Henri stirred, lifting his head long enough to answer with a commiserating moan, before letting it fall again to rest in his folded arms.

"Really!" Tess looked from one man to the other as they slowly sat up. "Of all the childish, immature things to do!"

Alexandre held up one hand to stop her flow of chiding words. "Don't talk so loud," he croaked in a low voice. His face was pale beneath his tan, and when he glanced at her, she noticed his eyes were bloodshot.

Jeanette entered the room, coming over to the table to stand beside Tess and add her own opinion. "Henri, three bottles! Couldn't you have exercised a bit of common sense?"

"It seemed a marvelous idea at the time," Henri muttered in reply, shielding his eyes from the bright sunlight with one hand.

Jeanette and Tess exchanged amused, exasperated glances.

Alexandre lifted his head and rubbed his eyes with the tips of his fingers. "Henri, I think we had a cup too much," he told his drinking partner. "I feel awful."

"Feeling a bit down-pin are you?" Tess inquired with false sympathy. She set Augustus down on the floor, and watched the kitten amble on shaky legs over to a corner. She frowned suspiciously. Turning back to the table, she glared down at the two men. "Alexandre! You didn't give the cat any drink, did you?"

He rubbed the back of his neck with one hand. "We may have," he admitted.

"You got the kitten drunk?" She turned to Jeanette and repeated with disbelief, "They got the kitten drunk!"

Jeanette shook her head. "Absolutely disgraceful, the pair of you."

"Don't say any more," Henri pleaded. "We feel bad enough as it is."

"It's no more than you deserve!" Tess told them. She walked over to the corner and lifted Augustus gently into her arms, cuddling him as he let out a thin wail. "Poor baby," she murmured. Glancing at Jeanette, she asked, "Do you know any remedies for the after effects of too much drink?"

The other woman nodded. "I know a recipe guaranteed to work."

"Good." Tess walked toward the door, followed by Jeanette. "We'll make some for Augustus."

"Augustus?" Alexandre lifted his head again to stare after them. "What about us?"

Tess paused in the doorway, glancing over her shoulder at the two men. "Alexandre, you're an excellent chef. Jeanette would be happy to give you her recipe, wouldn't you Jeanette?"

"Certainly."

The two women departed, leaving the two astonished men to fend for themselves.

It was two weeks after Alexandre's conversation with Jeanette that the servants arrived. She had wasted no time, but had written immediately to Marseilles. Paul and Leonie Renault had agreed to come to Saint-Raphael for as long as necessary.

Tess anticipated their arrival with mixed feelings. She was, of course, grateful to have the help, and she knew she couldn't continue to do as much work as she had been doing. She knew Jeanette had sent for the servants out of concern for her welfare. Yet, she hated being idle, and she did not want to spend the next several weeks doing nothing.

She estimated that she was about two or three weeks from delivery, and her mood seemed to change by the hour. Sometimes, she was filled with restless, uncontrollable energy; other times, she felt so fatigued, she didn't want to do anything but sleep. She frequently felt small contractions in her abdomen, but Jeanette assured her that was quite normal. Jeanette had also told her the baby had descended and birth could happen any time.

Tess was glad. With each passing day, she was becoming more irritable, more awkward, and more uncomfortable. She wished it was over.

She and Jeanette had prepared rooms in the servants quarters on the third floor of the château, and all was in readiness when Paul and Leonie arrived with their two children.

As they stood in the hall, Jeanette performed the introductions, while Henri drove the carriage around to the stable and unhitched the horses. Alexandre was introduced first, as master of the house. Tess came next, introduced as the housekeeper.

Paul was a tall, extremely thin young man with brown hair and a shy manner. Leonie was a sharp contrast to her husband, being short and plump, with dark hair and merry black eyes. Their son Claude took after his mother in both looks and temperament. But it was their baby daughter, Elise, that captured Tess's immediate interest.

"Oh," she said breathlessly, stepping forward to eye the dark-haired baby with admiration and a touch of envy. "She's lovely!"

Leonie smiled. "*Merci*, mademoiselle." She glanced down at Tess's swollen abdomen, and her eyes widened in horror. "I mean madame—I mean—"

Tess waved a hand to stop Leonie's embarrassed flow

of words. "Please call me Tess," she said with a smile. Reaching out her arms, she asked, "May I hold her?"

"Of course." Leonie put the baby in Tess's waiting arms.

Tess gazed down at the infant, looking into round eyes as black as twin coals. "What a beautiful baby," she murmured, feeling a tightness in her throat. Soon, very soon, she'd be able to hold her own child in her arms.

The voices of the others receded from her ears as she lifted Elise to rest the baby's head on her shoulder. She closed her eyes and tried to imagine what her own baby would look like. Would her baby's face be round as a dumpling, like Elise? Would her baby's skin be as soft?

Tess suddenly felt someone watching her, and she opened her eyes. Standing out of the circle of people in the hall, Alexandre studied her from a shadowy corner several feet away. Their eyes met.

His gaze was serious and speculative, and she wondered what he was thinking. She smiled at him over Elise's dark head. His expression did not change, but she thought there was a momentary flicker of an answering smile in his eyes.

Tess set aside the currycomb and gave Flower an affectionate pat. "There," she said, "you look much better."

Flower did, indeed, look considerably better than the day Tess had found her in the vineyards. Her wounds had healed, though the scars would always be clearly visible. She had gained weight and looked almost healthy. She also, Tess decided, looked happy.

She glanced over her shoulder to the open door at one end of the stable, expecting Jeanette or Leonie to catch her any minute. Both of them were so overprotective, it was becoming quite tiresome. They wouldn't be pleased she was out here working, she supposed.

In the one week since Paul and Leonie's arrival from Marseilles, Leonie had taken over all the indoor household chores, and Paul had assumed responsibility for the garden and the animals. Tess was relegated to "lying-in," which in her opinion meant doing nothing but listening to the clock chime away each quarter-hour. She simply couldn't stand it anymore.

As if Jeanette fussing over her wasn't bad enough, now Leonie and Paul fussed over her, too. Henri was just as bad, behaving like an overprotective brother. The only one who paid no attention to her at all was Alexandre.

They had scarcely exchanged more than a few dozen words since Henri and Jeanette's arrival. He had been withdrawn and silent ever since that day in Anne-Marie's bedchamber. Now, with servants in the house to look after her, he was gone most of the time, painting or sketching. Sometimes Henri accompanied him, but often he went alone. It was almost as if he now felt he'd passed the responsibility for her welfare onto others, and that hurt Tess deeply.

She sighed and closed her eyes, remembering with longing the days when it had been Alexandre who fussed over her, lecturing her for working in the garden, helping her with the laundry, teaching her to cook, carrying her about after she'd sprained her ankle. It was almost as if she'd imagined it all.

Had she imagined that he cared? Was her love for him only a foolish, wistful dream?

The sound of Mathilda honking loudly intruded on her melancholy thoughts, closely followed by a series of passionate French curses. Tess walked out of the stable and around the corner to the goose's pen, wondering what was going on to cause such a fracas.

She soon found out. Alexandre was standing in one corner of the pen, a strip of linen binding in his hand. Mathilda was standing in front of him, emitting loud, belligerent honks. Every time Alexandre tried to move, the goose nipped at him or beat at his legs with her good wing.

Tess couldn't help it. She burst into gales of laughter at the sight of Alexandre cornered by the goose. She grasped the fence post for support, doubling over as far as her belly would allow, unable to control her laughter.

"You think this is amusing?" Alexandre demanded. "Tess, if you don't get this goose away from me, I'm going to wring its neck and cook it for dinner!"

Wiping the tears of laughter from her eyes, Tess stepped into the pen. She paused several feet away, another laugh quivering on her lips, but she suppressed it. Alexandre obviously didn't find anything in the situation to laugh about. She came closer, and Mathilda quieted.

"What are you doing in here?" she asked him.

He glared at her. "I was trying to have a look at the goose's wing to make certain it was still securely bound. Suddenly, it attacked me!"

Tess sighed and shook her head. "I don't think she likes you. I can't understand it."

"It hates me," he answered. "I don't know why, and I don't care. Put it back inside."

Tess shooed the goose toward the small coop and closed the door once the animal was inside. She turned back to Alexandre, still smiling at the picture he'd made.

He scowled. "It bit me." He held out his hand, where a tiny trickle of blood on his wrist stained the cuff of his white linen shirt.

Her smile disappeared, and she stepped closer. "Let me see it."

She reached out, barely touching him before he pulled his hand back. "It's only a scratch," he said and started to move past her.

She felt the wall come between them. She couldn't let him walk away. Not this time. Suddenly desperate to break down the wall, she reached again for his hand. "Let me see it."

She grasped his hand firmly in both of hers, turning it palm up to examine the cut on his wrist. "It is just a scratch, but we should put some of that ointment on it," she said. Slowly, she slid her palm over his to entwine their fingers. She looked up into his face.

He jerked his hand away as if her touch burned him. He looked left, then right, seeking some way to escape.

Hurting, she impulsively reached up to put her hands on his shoulders, as if by sheer strength she could somehow hold him there. "Why are you doing this?" she whispered.

His mouth tightened to a thin line and he moved to leave.

Her grip on his shoulders tightened. "Don't," she said. "Don't avoid me."

His voice was barely above a whisper. "You don't understand."

"No, Alexandre," she contradicted softly, "it is you who does not understand. I need you."

"There are servants to do the work. Jeanette is here to look after you." He still would not look at her. "My presence is not necessary."

"Look at me."

He didn't.

Her hands left his shoulders to cup his face, turning it towards her. "Your presence is necessary to me," she said. "I need you to be what you have been from the beginning. My friend, my companion, my protector."

He shook his head violently. "No. You don't know about me. You don't know—"

"It doesn't matter. I need you."

He shook off her touch and stepped around her before she could reach for him again. As he strode away, he muttered something under his breath. The words floated back to her on the breeze. He said, "Then God help you."

The tide was going out, and the ocean swirled gently over the pools formed by the rugged coastline, depositing in its wake a treasure of mussels and other shellfish. Crabs crawled amid the kelp festooned over the rocks of the sea before him as the sun set beyond the hills of the *Massif des Maures* behind him. It was a cloudy, late September evening, and with the sun's slow descent, it was becoming chilly.

Alexandre sat on a rock high above the water, his arms resting on his bent knees, his gaze fixed unseeingly on a pair of bickering crabs in the tide pool below.

He didn't believe her. It was as simple as that. She'd said it didn't matter, but it mattered more than she could possibly know.

He was willing to acknowledge that she had needed him at one time, but that time was past. There were others here to take care of her now. She wouldn't have to depend on him anymore.

That thought did not make him happy. It didn't even bring a sense of relief. All it brought was the painful reminder that he could never be what she wanted him to be.

It would be best if he sent her to Marseilles with Jeanette and Henri after her baby was born. They already had a housekeeper, but he was sure Jeanette would willingly provide her with some sort of employment. She couldn't stay here with him much longer. She needed a stable life, he told himself, and she deserved a man she could truly depend upon. Perhaps in Marseilles she would find them.

He didn't want to think about what it would be like when she left. He didn't want to think about what it would be like to fetch water in the mornings only for himself. He didn't want to think about how quiet the château would sound without her humming, or how lonely he would feel, or how empty his life would be.

He closed his eyes, wishing he could see himself the way she saw him. But he was afraid, why not admit it? He was afraid to believe in love, afraid to believe in himself.

A startled cry broke into his thoughts, and Alexandre opened his eyes. Scanning the rocky coast below, he could see someone flailing in the water some distance from shore. Without further thought, he jumped to his feet and scrambled down the hill, pausing only long enough to pull off his knee-high boots before plunging into the water.

He could see the figure more clearly now. It was a child. He began swimming in that direction with the powerful strokes he'd learned from a lifetime spent on the coast.

He paused, treading water, and glanced around. He felt a moment of panic, thinking the child had gone under. But he saw the boy's dark head bob above the water once again only a few yards away. He reached the child just as he saw him disappear once again beneath the surface.

Alexandre lunged forward, grabbing for the boy and pulling him up by the shirt. The child let out a terrified cry and flailed at him in a panic, but Alexandre held him fast. "It's all right. I have you!"

It was then that he realized this boy looked familiar. It was Jean-Paul, one of the two boys who had invaded his courtyard six weeks before.

At this moment, Jean-Paul seemed more terrified of the water than of him and wrapped his arms around Alexandre so tightly, he thought he'd choke. "Hold on, *mon enfant,*" he ordered, "but not so tight. I have you. I'm taking you back to shore."

He felt the pull of the undertow and fought it with every ounce of strength as he swam back toward the shore, with a very scared Jean-Paul clinging to him like a barnacle. The boy didn't loosen his grip until after Alexandre had pulled them up onto the rocky peninsula.

Jean-Paul was sobbing with panic and coughing with the water he'd swallowed. Alexandre rose to stand behind the boy and locked his arms around his waist, holding him suspended in the air like a sack of potatoes. Jean-Paul's head and shoulders hung toward the ground, a position that forced the water from his lungs as he made choking, gagging sounds.

Satisfied that all the water was gone from the boy's lungs, Alexandre lowered him to the ground. Dropping wearily beside Jean-Paul, he raked back his hair, pulling the long, wet strands away from his face.

Both of them sat silent for a few moments, catching their breath. Finally, Alexandre said, "Are you all right?"

The boy hiccupped and nodded, staring up at Alexandre with astonished eyes. "You're the man in the castle."

"I am."

"You don't look like a monster."

Another man might have laughed at such a comment, but Alexandre found nothing amusing about it. His lips tightened slightly. "You think not?"

"Monsters don't save people, do they?"

"*Non,* perhaps they don't." He gave the boy a stern look. "You shouldn't be out in the sea if you don't know how to swim, *jeune homme.*"

The boy looked sheepish and hung his head. "I know." He looked up and pointed to the chain of rocks that led out into the sea. "I was fishing, over there. I slipped and fell in. Then the water just carried me away."

"The undertow is very strong here. You won't go out there again, will you?"

"No, monsieur. I won't. But I wish I knew how to swim." His tone was wistful.

Alexandre looked at him thoughtfully. "Every child

who lives near the sea should learn to swim. I learned
when I was a boy much younger than you."

"You did?"

"*Mais oui.* My father taught me when I was very
young."

Jean-Paul sighed. "My father doesn't know how to
swim. That's why Pierre and I don't know how."

"Pierre is the boy who was with you when you tres-
passed in my courtyard? He is your brother, *n'est-ce
pas?*" Receiving an affirmative nod, Alexandre went on,
"You should both learn." He added in a indifferent tone,
"I could teach you."

Jean-Paul eyed him for a moment with skepticism.

Reading his hesitation as fear, Alexandre said, "You
do not have to be afraid of me."

"Everybody says you're mean. My *maman* wouldn't
like it if you taught us how to swim."

Alexandre tried not to let the boy's words bother him.
He ought to be used to what the villagers thought by now.
But he wasn't. He said, "What if we don't tell your
maman? We'll keep it a secret, just between us. Agreed?"

Jean-Paul hesitated a moment longer, studying the
man beside him thoughtfully. Then he nodded.
"Agreed."

Alexandre rose and reached out a hand to pull Jean-
Paul to his feet. "Come to my château on the next sunny
day, and we will go." He stared down at the thin boy
before him. "You don't have to trespass anymore. You
and your brother may come and go on my land as you
please, if you promise you won't go down to the sea until
you know how to swim."

Jean-Paul nodded once again, his gaze still thoughtful,
but no longer wary.

Alexandre added, "And you don't have to be afraid.
I'm not as mean as they say."

17

Tess went into labor the following night. As if to announce the impending birth, the mistral began, sending dry, bitterly cold winds down from the north to whistle eerily through the château.

Tess had felt a constant backache all day, and by sunset her water had broken. She was having pains, and Jeanette had sent her to her room.

Alexandre and Henri had been in the village most of the day. By the time they returned, night had fallen, the cold winds of the mistral were rattling the windows, and Tess was having contractions every quarter-hour.

The two men entered the kitchen just as Leonie was preparing to take a pile of clean linens and a kettle of hot water up to Tess's room. Jeanette was giving orders. "Paul, take Claude and the baby up to your room and put them to bed. Stay with them. Leonie, take the water up to Tess's room. Start a fire in the grate so her room is warm."

She glanced at Alexandre and Henri, explaining before either man could ask, "Tess's labor has begun."

Jeanette's words were like a physical blow to Alexandre. "Now?" Panic seized him, sending chills as cold as the mistral through his body. "But I thought you said it would be at least another week."

Jeanette spared a moment to give him a wry glance. "A woman's body isn't a clock, Alexandre. It happens when it happens, and it's happening now." She turned to her husband. "Henri, I need you to fetch wood. Pile it in the corridor outside Tess's room, beyond the door so it's out of the way. We need to keep her room warm, so fetch plenty. With the mistral coming, it's going to be cold tonight."

As Henri went off to get the wood, Alexandre swallowed his waves of panic and asked, "What can I do?"

"You can go into the salon and pour yourself a brandy. Unless, of course, you and Henri drank it all."

Drink brandy? He stared at her, unable to believe she was serious. But she brushed past him without another word, carrying two empty basins. Idiotically, he wondered what they were for as he followed her up the stairs to Tess's room.

"But Jeanette, I want to help. I can't just . . ."

He stopped in the doorway of the bedchamber, completely forgetting what he was about to say at the sight of Tess walking calmly back and forth across the room. "What are you doing out of bed?" he demanded and looked at Jeanette. "What is she doing out of bed? Shouldn't she be lying down?"

"Alexandre, I told you to go have a drink." She turned to Leonie, who was laying linens on the floor at the foot of the bed. "That's enough sheets, I think."

Leonie nodded, straightening and stepping to the wall to stoke the fire.

Jeanette looked at Tess. "Are the pains getting closer together?"

"I think so," Tess replied, "but I can't tell how close."

How can she look so calm? Alexandre wondered. He sucked in a deep breath, his eyes worriedly scanning her face.

She smiled as if she could read his thoughts. "I'm fine," she told him. "Don't worry."

She might just as well have told him to stop breathing. He opened his mouth to ask her what he could do to help her, but just then Henri stuck his head in the room.

"Is this enough wood?" he asked his wife. She looked out into the corridor and nodded. "For now. If it's a long birth, we might need more."

"A long birth?" Alexandre asked. "How long?"

Jeanette frowned at him. "Are you still here?" She turned to her husband. "Henri, take Alexandre downstairs and keep him occupied. Play cards, get drunk, sing songs. I don't care, but keep him out of my way."

Alexandre allowed himself to be led away under protest. His last glimpse of Tess was a grimace of pain as she grasped the bedpost and cried, "I'm having another one!" The door slammed in his face.

The clock on the mantel in the library chimed again. The mistral answered, whistling through every crack in the ancient château.

Alexandre glanced at the clock. Had it only been fifteen minutes since the clock had chimed last? It seemed like a month. He glanced at Henri, who sat in the opposite chair. Their eyes met, but neither man spoke.

Five hours, now. Alexandre jumped to his feet and began to pace the room. He had long since lost the ribbon from his hair, and he once again raked back the black strands with a restless hand. Fear lay like a stone in his gut.

He had been through this once before. Waiting hour after hour, frustrated by his own helplessness. This was the time when the women told the men what to do, when women ruled the house, and bewildered men were relegated to the library. They were expected to get beastly drunk, boast of their male prowess, and celebrate.

Celebrate. *Mon Dieu!*

Alexandre paused before the fire, staring into the flames, drowning in memories. There had been no celebrating three years ago. There had been guilt and pain. There had been screams, followed by a cold, deadly silence. There had been accusations and blame, followed by a funeral.

His hands began to shake. He gripped the edges of the mantel above the fireplace, bowing his head until his forehead touched the smooth wooden surface. He closed his eyes, but the visions that came before his mind were not of Anne-Marie's death.

Images of Tess flashed before him, one after the other, as if he were flipping the pages in his sketchbook. Her pale face streaked with the mud of his garden. Her delighted expression the first time she'd milked that goat. Her soft smile as she'd talked about the baby. Her hair shining like copper in the sun of the meadow. Her hips swaying as she walked, the wind whipping the hem of her dress. Her eyes telling him how much she needed him.

He remembered her cries of fear and whimpers of delirium. He heard her soft humming and her conversations with the animals. He heard her laughter.

She'd brought laughter to his house and purpose to his life. *I need you . . . my friend, my companion, my protector.*

A loud cry of pain echoed through the house, eclipsing the wail of the wind, and Alexandre's head shot up as his insides clenched with dread. She needed him, but he wasn't there for her. He was down here, pacing and helpless, watching the clock tick.

He straightened, turning away from the fireplace, striding out of the room and down the corridor. He shook off Henri's restraining hand with a violent curse and mounted the stairs.

When he yanked open the door, his gaze immediately went to Tess. She was sitting in bed, leaning back against the pillows. Jeanette sat in a chair near the foot of the bed. Leonie was seated beside Tess, holding her hand.

Tess's white chemise clung to her, damp with sweat. In the lamplight, he could see the bulk of her belly outlined beneath the light sheet that covered her lower body. She didn't look much closer to giving birth than she had when he had seen her last, and that was many hours before. He looked into her face, and his heart twisted with pain. She looked tired, vulnerable, and completely overwhelmed.

"Tess?"

She opened her eyes and smiled at him, but it was a wan smile that did not reach her eyes. "I'm all right," she said. Suddenly, she grimaced, one hand moving to her abdomen, the other gripping Leonie's. "Another one's coming," she gasped, clinging to Leonie's hand like a lifeline.

Jeanette rose from her chair and lifted the sheet to look beneath. Alexandre's view was blocked by Jeanette's back, but he did see Tess's body arch and twist, and he heard her cry of pain. Frantic questions raced through his mind. What was happening? How much longer would she have to go through this? What the hell could he do for her?

Jeanette's voice rang out sharply. "Don't push! Tess, don't push. It isn't time yet."

Alexandre circled the bed to the other side, reaching for Tess's free hand. She wrapped her fingers around his, squeezing his hand with a strength he hadn't known she possessed. The seconds ticked by with agonizing slowness, until finally the pain ebbed away, and Tess fell back against the pillows with a relieved gasp, letting go of his hand. He opened and closed his numb fingers, trying to bring some life back into them.

"How much longer?" Tess's voice was a hoarse whisper.

"Soon," Jeanette answered, lowering the sheet. "The pains are very close together. A few more of those and you'll be ready." She looked at Alexandre. "There's nothing you can do," she told him. "Go back downstairs."

"No."

"Alexandre, don't argue with me. This is no place for a man. Go."

"I'm not leaving." Their gazes locked. Three years ago, he had been ordered to stay away. He had obeyed, and Anne-Marie had died. "Not this time."

Jeanette scowled at him, but he didn't move. "Very well," she finally agreed, "but stay out of the way."

Another pain hit Tess, and there was no further discussion. Alexandre held her hand, bathed her face with cool water, and tried not to think about what might happen.

It seemed an eternity before Jeanette finally lowered the sheet with the words, "It's time."

Leonie jumped to her feet, and Alexandre was pushed aside as the two women moved Tess to the foot of the bed, spread her bare legs apart, and put her feet on the sheet-covered floor. Jeanette moved her chair directly in front of Tess, while Leonie stood nearby with a pile of clean linens.

Alexandre watched as Tess leaned back on her elbows, her tired face flushed with exertion as Jeanette told her, "Push when you hit the peak of the pain. Not before, not before!"

Tess cried out, her head flung back, her face contorted with concentration and agony. The vision swam

before his eyes, and Alexandre violently shook his head
to clear it.

For the next hour, Alexandre took on each pain as if it
were his own, wishing it were. He mumbled frantic,
whispered prayers. He sat on the edge of the bed, holding her hand when she fell back exhausted on the bed
between pains. He'd never felt more helpless in his life,
watching Tess grow more and more weary with each
pain.

When Jeanette told her once again to push, he felt as
frustrated as she when she mumbled, "I can't, I can't do
it anymore."

"Tess, you have to."

Tess shook her head and refused to sit up. "Can't . . .
too tired."

Jeanette shot Alexandre a worried glance, and said,
"She can't stop now. She has to keep trying."

Alexandre didn't pause to worry about what might
happen if she didn't. He lifted Tess back into her half-sit-
ting position, supporting her with an arm behind her
back. "Tess, you must finish this," he told her.

She shook her head again. "I don't want to do this
anymore. It hurts too much."

"I know it hurts, but you must have courage."

"I'm tired. I can't."

"You have to, *petite.*" Tenderly, he wiped the sweat
from her brow with one sleeve. "Push," he told her as
she cried out with the pain of another contraction.

She tried to lie back down, but he held her firmly.
"Push," he ordered.

"I can't."

He had to urge her to try again, and he said the first
thing that came into his head. "Tess, if you don't start
pushing, I'm going to go outside, get that donkey, and
give her back to that peasant."

"You wouldn't do that."

"*Mais oui,* I would."

She stared up into his face, disbelief mingled with exhaustion in her expression. Another pain came and she grunted, making a halfhearted attempt to bear down.

"And then," he continued, unimpressed by her paltry efforts, "I'm going to wring that goose's neck, pluck it and roast it."

"I don't believe you," she gasped frantically.

"I'll do it, Tess. I swear I will. And then I'll give Augustus to Jeanette and Henri. They can take him to little Chantal. She'd love a kitten."

Her head shot back and she glared at him. "No!" she choked, "you can't give my animals away."

"If you don't want me to do it, then push."

Her jaw tightened as the pain hit again, and she groaned through clenched teeth, pushing with all her strength.

"Push," he told her. "Damn it, Tess, push!"

"I am pushing!" she shouted back at him in fury and redoubled her efforts.

"The baby's coming," Jeanette said. "I see the head. Just a bit longer, Tess. You're doing fine."

It was with a final, heart-wrenching scream that Tess pushed one last time. Alexandre glanced up as a bloody, squirming bundle was lifted in Jeanette's hands. He heard a loud wail of protest.

"It's a girl," Jeanette pronounced. "A beautiful, healthy girl."

He studied the wet, slippery, grayish-pink thing that now rested on Tess's belly with worry and skepticism. It didn't look healthy at all. It looked quite sick. But it sounded healthy—and loud.

He watched as Jeanette grasped a scissors and thread. After cutting the cord, she handed the child to Leonie.

He glanced at Tess's flushed, tired face. She wore an expression of both relief and exultation, but when she met his eyes, she frowned at him. "Don't you dare do anything to my animals."

"I won't," he promised, reaching out to brush a sweat-soaked lock of hair back from her face. "How do you feel?"

"Better."

At that moment, Jeanette came to the opposite side of the bed, holding a squirming, linen-wrapped bundle. She placed the bundle in Tess's outstretched arms.

Tess looked down at her daughter, feeling such a powerful combination of happiness and pride, she thought her heart would burst with it. Exhaustion and pain were forgotten. *There can be no greater accomplishment,* she thought, *and no greater joy than this.*

She picked up one of her daughter's tiny hands, trembling with awe as she felt the tiny fingers wrap around her own. "She's beautiful," Tess whispered. "Oh, Alexandre, isn't she beautiful?"

Studying her happy, flushed face, he was glad that her features were no longer contorted with pain. He'd never witnessed anything like this, and he was filled with a profound sense of relief. He was glad that it was over, and that she was all right, and that the baby was alive and healthy. He covered her hand and the baby's with his own. "Yes," he answered, "she is beautiful. Just like her mother."

18

She was a beautiful baby. Tess didn't care that her skin was blotchy, or that she didn't have any hair, or that her head was such an odd shape. To Tess, she was the loveliest baby in the world.

She tucked a fold of the flannel blanket around the sleeping baby's shoulder, then leaned back against the pillows, cradling the infant in her arms, wishing she was able to nurse. She had tried several times following the baby's birth, but her milk was not coming in fast enough, and the baby had become impatient with the lack of adequate nourishment, crying and fussing, leaving Tess unable to get any rest. At Jeanette's suggestion, she had reluctantly agreed to let Leonie act as wet nurse, and Jeanette had moved the nursery upstairs to give Tess the peace and quiet she needed.

But now, three days after the birth, she'd had enough peace and quiet. She was ready to get out of bed, but Jeanette had insisted she rest another day or two. Boredom, she decided, was much more tiring that a little hard work.

A soft knock sounded at the door. "Come in," she called out, and as the door swung wide, she saw Alexandre's large frame fill the doorway. He smiled at her, and she ran a self-conscious hand through her hair. "Good morning."

He noticed the feminine gesture, but he could have told her it wasn't necessary. Her hair was lovely, copper caught in the light of the morning sun. "*Bonjour*. I wanted to see how you were feeling today."

"Bored." Her answer was swift and sure.

His gaze moved to the baby in her arms and he shifted his weight from one foot to the other, feeling suddenly uncomfortable. He had been the one to insist on moving the nursery so that Tess could rest. He had ordered Jeanette to make sure Tess stayed in bed. He'd waited three days before coming to see her. Now that he was here, he could only stare at her with yearning, wanting to come in and see the baby, wanting to tell her he would be glad to keep her company, but unable to say the words.

Sensing his hesitation, Tess raised her hand and beckoned him forward. "Come see her. She's sleeping, of course. New babies don't do anything but sleep."

Alexandre walked slowly toward the bed, surprised by the powerful pounding of his heart. He sat on the edge of the bed, gazing with wonder at the tiny round face nestled against her mother's breast. His breath caught. She was so small. It was odd, but three days ago, when he'd seen her for the first time, he hadn't really noticed how tiny she was. He reached out as if to touch her, then pulled his hand back, not wanting to wake her.

He glanced up at Tess, who was watching him, a gentle smile on her face. He smiled back. "She's real," he said, shaking his head as he rose to his feet. "Until I saw her being born, she didn't seem real to me, somehow. She was . . ." He paused, trying to find words to say what he meant. "She was part of you."

Tess patted the bed. "Sit back down and talk to me. If I lie here doing nothing for much longer, I'll go mad."

"You should rest."

"I feel fine," she assured him. "Truly. I don't need rest. I need company."

He eased himself onto the edge of the bed. "Have you thought of a name for her?"

Tess nodded, her gaze falling to the baby. "I'm going to call her Beatrice."

"Beatrice? Bah!" That exclamation clearly conveyed his distaste. "What a hideous name!"

Tess looked up, setting her jaw stubbornly. "Her name is Beatrice Elizabeth, after my mother."

He didn't care if her mother's name was Beatrice, it was still a hideous name. It was so *English*. He said, "It is not a pretty name, *non,* not at all. She is a beautiful baby, she should have a beautiful name."

"I like Beatrice."

"Well, I don't." He gestured skyward. "*Sacré tonnerre!* She would scare the angels in heaven with such a name."

Tess gave an exasperated sigh. "What would you suggest then?"

He glanced at the baby, who was still sleeping, oblivious to their raised voices. "Madelaine?"

She shook her head. "No, everyone would call her Maddie." Her brows knitted thoughtfully. "Victoria?"

He shuddered. He could not imagine having a daughter named Victoria. "Vivienne?"

Tess wrinkled her nose. "Too sophisticated."

"Renata?"

Her only response to that was a grimace of distaste. "Eleanor?"

He thought about that name for a moment, then he shook his head. "No, that doesn't suit her at all."

Both of them fell silent, trying to come up with just the right name. Alexandre stood up and walked over to the window, looking at the shimmering blue of the sea in the distance. She had to have a name that spoke of sunshine and poetry and beauty, all the things she would become.

He would paint her. There, on the cliff, overlooking the sea, with the wind in her hair. He and Tess would take her to the Meadow of the Fairies for picnics. He would teach her to paint, Tess would teach her to sew. In the evenings, he and Tess would talk about her, sometimes with pride, sometimes with concern, always with love.

He thought about the days ahead, watching her grow into a woman as beautiful as her mother. Would she have Tess's expressive eyes, her smile, her glorious copper hair? He could imagine the two of them in a few years, walking along the rocky coast below, hand in hand. Tess would stop and kneel beside her daughter, an arm around her waist, pointing out the birds flying overhead, the crabs crawling along the shore, and the fishing boats in the distance.

He thought about coming home to the light burning in the window. The child would be asleep, but Tess would be there, waiting for him as she always did. She would be there.

He could see it in his mind as a starving man imagines a tantalizing meal. He felt a hunger just as strong. He wanted it, all of it, for the rest of his life. He wanted Tess beside him as they watched their daughter grow up. He wanted to wake every morning seeing happiness in her eyes. He wanted to hear her humming, he wanted wildflowers in the hall, he wanted stray animals. He wanted Tess. He loved her.

Shaken by visions of a future he'd never thought possible, Alexandre stiffened. Fantasy. He closed his eyes and swallowed hard. It was nothing but fantasy. He opened his eyes again. Turning away from the window, he walked across the room, unable to look at Tess and the baby.

"Suzanne," he said as he opened the door. "We'll

name her Suzanne." Not wanting to leave, unable to remain, he hesitated in the doorway for a moment, then walked out of the room without looking back.

But later, as he sat on the shore looking out to the fishing boats on the sea, he wondered if fantasies ever came true.

Shortly after Alexandre left the room, the baby awakened and began to cry. Tess held her child in her arms, rocking her and humming softly. "Suzanne," she said the name aloud. "I like it." She smiled down at the crying baby. "I know you're hungry, darling. I haven't tried to feed you since yesterday. Let's see if I can do it this time."

She untied the ribbons at the neckline of her night dress, pulling it down her shoulders to expose her breast. She cradled Suzanne close, but the baby refused to suckle. Pushing her tiny fist against her mother's breast, she turned her head away, and wailed even louder.

It was a rejection and it hurt. Tess sighed with disappointment and lifted her head to find Leonie standing in the doorway, watching her.

The other woman must have seen something of what she felt in her expression. She said, "You mustn't think ill of yourself because you haven't been able to nurse the baby. That happens sometimes. It doesn't make you a bad mother."

"I know." Tess found no comfort in that.

Leonie came to her side, and Tess handed the crying baby over to her. Leonie sat in the chair near the bed and opened her dress to feed Suzanne. Tess watched the baby seek Leonie's offered breast and accept it, sucking greedily, and she tried not to feel envy.

Leonie looked over at her and smiled. "I know how you feel. I had a fever for four days after Claude was born, and I wasn't able to nurse. When I was well, the baby refused to take milk from me. He was accustomed to the wet nurse, you see."

Tess nodded, but it didn't make her feel any better. She sighed, leaning back against the headboard. If she had something to do, something else to think about, she might not feel so bad about not being able to feed Suzanne.

When Jeanette came in a few moments later, Tess frowned at her friend and spoke before the other woman could say a word. "Jeanette, I am getting out of this bed right now. I feel fine, and I refuse to lie here another minute."

To her surprise, Jeanette nodded. "Very well," she agreed. "If you're well enough to scowl at me like that, I suppose you're well enough to get up. But don't overdo it," she added as Tess threw aside the blanket and jumped out of bed.

"I am going to take a walk," Tess declared, pulling a dress from the armoire.

"I said, don't overdo it," Jeanette pointed out, reaching out to fasten the hooks of Tess's dress.

"Jeanette, I feel fine. Truly. I can't stand to be confined to this room any longer. I must get some fresh air. Please don't tell me to stay in the house."

Leonie rose from her chair. "The fresh air will do you good," she said, setting the baby on the bed and reaching up to button her dress. Raised in the country, Leonie firmly believed that fresh country air would cure anything, from a cold in the head to a new mother's depression.

Jeanette looked from Tess to Leonie and back again. She lifted her hands in a gesture of acquiescence. "All right. All right. Go."

Tess went for her walk, after assuring Jeanette she would not go far. It was a beautiful October afternoon. The mistral had gone, and the sun was warm. She walked around the château toward the meadow.

As she crossed the meadow and entered the forest,

she suddenly heard Alexandre's voice. Moving through the trees, she came to the pond and her eyes widened in surprise at what she saw.

Alexandre was facing her, standing in hip-high water. His bare torso gleamed like well-polished leather, the sun reflecting off his brown skin. Sunshine and shadow defined every muscle of his wide chest and strong arms.

In front of him, a child lay face-down, naked in the water, turning his head to the side occasionally to breathe and kicking with his feet. Alexandre had one hand beneath the child and one hand on his back to hold him in place. He was talking as two other boys standing nearby listened.

Tess could tell, even though their faces were in profile, that one of the two boys listening to Alexandre was Claude. But who were the other two? She moved closer and gave a gasp of surprise. It was Pierre, one of the two boys who had been in Alexandre's courtyard. Then the boy floating in the water must be—what was his name? Jean-Paul.

Alexandre was teaching these boys to swim? Stupefied, she stared at them through the trees, wondering how these swimming lessons had come about.

She watched Alexandre help Jean-Paul regain his feet. As the boy moved to stand aside, she heard another voice, and she glanced at the shore of the pond where Henri was seated. He was leaning back against a rock, lounging in the sun, watching the swimming lessons. "This is going to take all day," he commented. "The four of you are going come out looking like prunes."

"This wouldn't take so long if you'd stop being lazy and help me," Alexandre called back and beckoned to Pierre, who came to stand before him, only his head and shoulders visible above the surface.

"Oh no, *mon cher*," Henri answered with a chuckle. "This is your project."

Alexandre ignored his brother's amused laughter and

did not reply. He lifted Pierre to lie on his back in the water and began talking to him.

"Relax. Don't worry, I've got you. Close your eyes and feel how the water holds you up."

Pierre's body dipped slightly and the water washed over him. He gave a cry and began to panic. "It's all right," Alexandre told him, but the boy was thrashing about, and Alexandre lifted him to a standing position again. He said, "It is very important that you relax. If you do, the water will hold you up. Watch me."

He moved to lie on his back in the water, and Tess watched, feeling tingles of warmth radiate through every part of her. He was completely naked and the ripples of water caressed his bare skin.

Running suddenly sweaty palms down the sides of her dress, Tess knew she should look away, but she couldn't. She couldn't see a great deal from her vantage point some distance away, but just the realization that he was naked brought that odd, fluttery quiver. She took a deep breath.

He was speaking to the boys, but Tess didn't hear a word he said. Her own heart was pounding too loudly for that. She watched him stand again, and she gazed at him with love and longing, remembering the day he had kissed her in the meadow only a few yards away.

She raised a trembling hand to her lips, feeling her insides tighten with the memory. She watched him explain something to the boys, gesturing with his arms, and she remembered how those arms had held her with such gentle strength. He had made her feel like a precious treasure to be cherished, a feeling she had never experienced before.

But all that had changed the very next day. Alexandre had made it clear that any future with her was impossible.

But she wanted the impossible. She wanted him to forget Anne-Marie. She wanted him to forgive himself for whatever he thought he had done. She didn't care what action lay at the heart of his guilt. That was in the past. She could see that only the future mattered. She was determined that someday he would see it, too.

Her eyes focused once again on the scene before her. Alexandre was still talking to the boys who now stood before him in the water, but he was staring over their heads, looking directly at her.

With a gasp, she realized he'd caught her watching. Mortified, she turned and walked away, her cheeks burning, her pace quickening with every step, wondering what he must think of her.

Alexandre thought she was incredibly lovely, her body dappled with the light of the sun and the shadow of the trees. He watched her disappear into the forest, fading from view like a wood nymph, out of his sight, always out of his reach.

He wanted to call out to her. He wanted to go after her. He didn't move until he felt a tug on his arm. He looked down at Pierre.

"What are you looking at?" the boy asked.

He glanced back to the trees. She was gone. "A wood nymph, *mon ami,*" he answered, "just a wood nymph."

"I still don't believe it." Jeanette settled back against the pillows and glanced at her husband. "I almost died of shock when you told me. Alexandre teaching village boys how to swim."

"If I hadn't been there and seen it for myself, I wouldn't believe it either." Henri yawned, snuggling down into the sheets. "It was good to see."

"Good? It's marvelous. And if you ask me, I think it's all because of Tess. She's brought him out of his shell."

"I know."

Having been married to Henri for fifteen years, Jeanette knew when her husband was troubled. "What bothers you?"

He shook his head, frowning. "I don't know. I just hope it all works out for the best. Alexandre deserves to be happy."

"She's in love with him, you know."

"Is she? She told you that?"

"She didn't have to. It's in her voice whenever she talks about him. It's in her face whenever she looks at him."

"I hope you're right."

Both of them fell silent. Jeanette thought of Tess holding a silk ribbon and talking about Alexandre. She was right, she knew she was. All Tess and Alexandre needed was time to bring them together. Time and privacy.

"Henri?"

"Hmm?"

"I think it's time for us to go home."

Nigel looked up as his valet entered the sitting room of his hotel suite in Lyon. "Yes, Sullivan, what is it?"

"Sir, Martin Trevalyn is here. He has brought with him a . . ." There was a pause. "A man, sir."

Nigel's eyebrows rose. Sullivan was very particular about his descriptions of people and their station in life. The man Martin had brought with him was obviously a peasant. "Show them in, Sullivan."

"Yes, sir." The valet's tone conveyed clear disapproval. Peasants, in his opinion, had no business talking to peers of the realm. He departed, returning moments later to announce, "Mr. Martin Trevalyn and Jacques Beauchard."

Nigel rose as the two men entered the room. He wasted no time on unnecessary preliminaries. Giving Martin an interrogatory glance, he asked, "Well?"

Martin gestured to the man beside him. "This man has seen her."

Nigel studied the man. His blue gaze moved from the

man's mud-encrusted boots to his weary face, noting with disdain the linsey-woolsey trousers and sweat-stained cotton shirt. Definitely a peasant.

After a few moments of silence, Nigel gestured impatiently. "Well, speak up, man. You've seen her? Where? When?"

The man twisted the wool cap in his hands nervously. "I own a small farm outside of Valence. Five months ago, I caught the girl stealing eggs from my hen house."

"And?" Nigel prompted when the man paused.

"I agreed to let her do some work for my wife in exchange for food. We barely have enough for ourselves, monsieur, but my wife and I felt sorry for her."

Nigel's anger flared at the man's words. The idea of his wife, his countess, doing peasant labor in exchange for food was appalling. The knowledge that this peasant had felt sorry for her was degrading. When he found Teresa, he would lock her in her room for the rest of her life.

He reached for his money purse and removed a napoleon. He held it up for the man to see. "How long did she stay with you and your wife? Where did she go when she left?"

"She stayed five days, monsieur. She did not say where she was going, but I saw her walking toward the road to Marseilles."

Nigel tossed the napoleon to the man, who dropped his cap to catch it. "You may go," Nigel told him.

The man bent to retrieve his cap and departed.

When the door had closed behind the peasant, Nigel turned to Martin. "We will both proceed to Marseilles. We'll leave in the morning."

Martin nodded and left the suite, noting that Nigel had given him no words of praise for finding the peasant. But then, Martin hadn't expected any.

19

Alexandre set aside the brush. He'd been trying to paint all morning, but he couldn't concentrate. Henri had told him that morning that he and Jeanette would be leaving for home the following day. Paul and Leonie were willing to stay, but Alexandre felt they would not be needed.

He knew the time had come to give Tess the option of going with them. She would go, and there would be no reason for Paul and Leonie to remain.

Tess was only here because she had nowhere else to go. But if she were given the chance to make a life for herself and Suzanne in Marseilles, she would take it. He was certain Jeanette and Henri would willingly make a place for her in their household, perhaps as governess to their children. She would have friends to care for her. She might even find a man to marry in Marseilles. She would have a future there. She had none with him.

He wished he could make her life as comfortable here as it would be in Marseilles, but he had nothing to offer her and the baby. Nothing but a crumbling château and an abandoned winery. And himself. They added up to very little.

When Tess went with Henri and Jeanette to Marseilles, he would have the solitude he had once craved. The solitude he now dreaded.

He turned away from the easel and left the studio. Downstairs, he found Leonie in the kitchen making tea. "Where is Tess?" he asked.

"She and Jeanette took little Suzanne for a walk." Leonie gestured toward the back door. "They said they were going to the rose garden."

He started for the door, but Leonie's voice halted him. "Monsieur, if you're going down there, would you tell them their tea is ready?"

He nodded and went down the back stairs out of the château, taking the path that led toward what had once been the rose garden. He found the two women seated on a stone bench, surrounded on three sides by a tangle of overgrown rose bushes. Tess's head was bent as she gazed down at little Suzanne, who was wrapped in flannel and cradled in the crook of her arm. She'd forgotten her hat, and the October sunshine turned her hair to burnished copper. She was singing to the baby, and Alexandre paused several feet away to listen. His eyes were on Tess, and he forgot that Jeanette was even there.

"For my fair lady, Greensleeves . . ." Her voice softened as she ended the song and brushed a kiss across Suzanne's forehead. "I think we should sing another one," he heard her say. "Something French this time."

His throat tightened at the smile that lit her face. He thought of her standing amid the trees watching him swim with the boys the day before, and his body tensed with the ache of wanting.

She began to sing. "*Frère Jacques, Frère Jacques, dormez-vous . . .*"

He tried to be content with just being near her, listening

to the sound of her lovely voice and watching her hold the baby. He was afraid this was the only time he would enjoy such a sight.

He stared, concealed from view by the shadow of trees, knowing it would be best for her if she left. But he loved her, and he knew how empty his life would be without her.

". . . Ding dang dong, ding dang dong." He joined in for the last few words of the song, stepping from the shadows as both women looked up.

Tess gave him a smile that was warm and welcoming. "Good afternoon. We've been taking the air. It's a beautiful day."

He looked down at her and watched her cheeks blush a rosy pink as she ducked her head self-consciously and busied herself with wrapping the flannel blanket more securely around the baby. Aware that he was staring, he turned his gaze to his sister-in-law. "Leonie told me to tell you that your tea is nearly ready."

Jeanette rose. "Shall I have Leonie bring your tea here?" she asked Tess.

"Oh, yes, thank you. That would be lovely."

The other woman nodded and moved to leave them, but Alexandre's voice stopped her. "Jeanette, take Suzanne with you, *s'il vous plaît.*"

He felt Tess's questioning gaze on him, but she handed the baby over to the other woman. He sat down on the bench beside her, waiting until Jeanette had left the garden before he spoke. Still not looking at her, he said, "Henri and Jeanette are leaving in a few days."

"Yes, I know. Jeanette told me."

Careful to keep his tone indifferent, he said, "You could take the baby and go with them."

He heard her sharp intake of breath. "Why would I want to do that?"

"I'm sure Jeanette would be willing to make a place

for you in their household. Governess to the children, perhaps. You could make a new life."

He felt her hand on his arm, and he reluctantly faced her. That look was in her eyes again, that look that he dreaded. But all she said was, "If you don't mind, I'd rather stay here."

He turned away, staring at the wild tangle of rose bushes straight ahead. "There is nothing for you here. No future for Suzanne. In Marseilles, you could—"

"Marseilles is a wonderful place, I'm sure," she interrupted him. "It probably has a great deal to offer. But there is one thing Marseilles does not have, one thing that is very important to me."

He glanced at her. "What?"

"You."

He shook his head slowly, not wanting to hear this. He'd suspected all along that she saw him as some kind of hero. He didn't want to be a hero. Did she think that what he'd told her about Anne-Marie wasn't true? "Tess, you don't understand. I tried to tell you . . ."

He jumped to his feet and started to walk away, but her voice stopped him.

"Don't go."

He stiffened, his back to her. He turned around to find her standing with hands outstretched, beckoning him back. He felt like a moth blundering in the light, flying into the candle flame, knowing his fate and unable to resist it. He took one step toward her, then another.

The wind teased a dark red curl that had fallen over her brow, and he reached out to brush it back. His fingertips trailed down her cheek and lingered there too long for common sense. Before he could think, before he could reason, his arms wrapped around her, he bent his head and kissed her.

The taste of her lips went to his head like strong wine, making him dizzy. Dormant for so long, desire now pounded through his body, and he lost whatever thin grasp he had on restraint. He pulled her closer, plunging his tongue into her mouth, savoring the sweet taste of her.

Her body pressed against him and her hands caressed his back, sending delicious shivers through his body. He tore his lips from hers and muffled a groan against her throat. But her silky skin proved to be an even greater temptation, and he nibbled at the base of her throat, feeling her pulse race as fast as his own.

Lost in the maelstrom, he didn't feel the sudden resistance at first. But her hands came up between them to push him away and her frantic whispered words finally penetrated his drugged senses.

"Stop, Alexandre, you must stop!"

Confused by this sudden rejection, he pulled back, dismayed by the resistance in her eyes and the tenseness of her body. When she stepped back, his arms fell to his sides.

"Leonie's coming," she whispered between gasps for breath.

"What?" He shook his head, trying to clear it.

"Leonie's coming up the path, bringing tea."

Damn the tea. He reached for her, but she stepped back again. Out of his reach.

She smiled and waved as Leonie approached, looking much more at ease than he felt. He whirled away, sitting down heavily on the bench. He raked a hand through his hair, knowing he had lost all control. It was a bitter realization.

He looked up as Leonie handed Tess the tray and walked back toward the house. Tess sat on the bench, placing the tea tray between them. She picked up the pot and started to pour, but his words stilled her movements. "I think you should go with Henri and Jeanette."

She placed the teapot back on the tray. "Why?"

He looked away, staring at the overgrown rose bushes. "After what happened just now, do you have to ask?"

"I don't want to go."

"If you knew the whole story about Anne-Marie, you'd go quickly enough."

"I'm not leaving."

"Damn it, Tess! I told you—"

"I know what you told me," her soft voice interrupted him. "It doesn't matter."

He gave a choked sound. "Doesn't matter? *Mon Dieu!* I killed my own wife."

She didn't answer, and he rushed on, "It was all my fault to begin with. I wanted a baby. I knew she was afraid, and I didn't care. We moved into separate rooms . . . we'd never had separate rooms . . . and I tried to understand, tried to be patient, but one night she locked her door against me, and I couldn't take it any more. I broke the door down."

He turned to her. "Do you understand? I forced her."

Tess felt her cheeks flush at hearing the intimacies between a husband and wife, but she knew all about being forced, and she knew Alexandre. She also knew what Jeanette had told her about Anne-Marie. "I think," she said softly, "that I understand very well. I think you had never tried to do such a thing before. I think that you both lost your heads in"—she paused, blushing furiously—"in the heat of the moment. And I would wager that she never said no, but that she held it against you afterwards. Didn't she?"

"It doesn't matter. She became pregnant, she was scared, and it wouldn't have happened if I hadn't ignored her wishes."

His voice was filled with self-loathing, and her heart ached for him. "Why was she so afraid of having a baby?"

He leaned forward to rest his forearms on his knees. "We were married for seven years. She'd had two miscarriages when we lived in Italy and both were very painful for her. Shortly after we came back here, she witnessed a very difficult birth. One of the maids. The baby was born dead, and the girl died. After that, she wouldn't even discuss having children. She asked me to move my things into the adjoining chamber and I did. That was eighteen months before she died."

"Is that why you think you killed her? Because she died in childbirth?"

He lifted his head to look at the blue sky over their heads. "God, no! There was more to it than that."

"What happened?"

"She wouldn't take care of herself. She didn't want the baby, she didn't even want to admit she was going to have one. She loved the winery and had always helped with the winemaking. I didn't want her working in the winery after she became pregnant, but she refused to give it up. We fought about it constantly."

He lowered his head, cradling it in his hands, still refusing to look at Tess. "One day, when she was about seven months along, I found her coming up the stairs from the wine cellars, and I saw her stumble. I was furious, and I'd had enough. I ordered her to stay out of the winery. She said I had no right to tell her what to do."

He was speaking rapidly, the words flowing out of him. Tess listened, remembering all the times he had told her not to work so hard, how angry he'd been that day in the garden. She realized now how scared he'd been.

He went on, "We stood on the stairs, shouting at each other. We both said things, terrible things. I said I wouldn't have her taking any risks with my child. She said she'd never wanted the baby. I told her a cat would be a better mother than she. She said I loved the baby more than her, that the baby was all I cared about. I asked her why, if she hated the baby so much, she didn't pay Babette to get rid of it. She said . . ." His voice broke. "She said she had. Babette had refused."

Tess felt sick. She looked down at his dark head, bent in anguish, her heart breaking for him. "What happened?"

"I was so angry. I wanted to hit her. God help me, I almost did." He lifted his head, staring straight ahead as if it were all happening before his eyes. "She dared me to do it. I grabbed her arms, I shook her. She called me a pig, I called her a coward. And she . . ."

"What?"

"She yanked away from me. We were on the stairs. I was so angry, I never thought . . . I watched her fall . . . couldn't catch her. She tumbled all the way down, over and over. She died three days later. So did the baby. My fault."

There was a long silence. Then he said, "Now you can see why it would be best if you left."

Tess rose and moved to stand before him, waiting until he lifted his head to look at her. She dropped to her knees and reached out to hold his face in her hands. "All I see," she whispered, "is what I have always seen. I love you."

His head jerked to the side, and he slid along the bench until he could get past her. "No, you don't," he muttered. "You can't. You should go with Henri and Jeanette. It would be best."

He walked away. She rose to her feet and turned, calling out to him, "I'm not leaving."

At her words, he paused, but only for a moment.

She watched him disappear through the shrubbery. "I'm not going anywhere, Alexandre," she murmured.

*   *   *

He walked, paying no attention to where he was going. She couldn't love him. Hadn't she heard a word he'd said? Didn't she understand that he was no good at being a husband and father?

He stopped abruptly, realizing he was walking down a path he hadn't taken for three years, his footsteps carrying him to a place he had vowed he would never go again. He found himself in the vineyards.

Now that he was here, he was seized by an overwhelming need to go on. He kept walking until he reached the winery. His footsteps faltered and he came to a halt, eyeing the stone buildings with something akin to fear. His heart began to pound as he walked toward the first building. When he turned the door handle, his hand was slick with sweat. The door creaked loudly as he pushed it open.

A rat scurried past him. Cobwebs tickled his face as he walked between huge empty vats toward the other end of the windowless room. He stared down the stone steps leading into the wine cellars, the light from the door fading into the inky blackness below. Echoes from the past.

His own words came back to him. *A cat would be a better mother than you. You don't give a damn about this baby.*

Anne-Marie's voice answered him. *The baby, the baby. That's all you care about. I hate this baby! Do you hear me? I hate it, hate it, hate it!*

He closed his eyes, breathing deeply, inhaling dust and memories. *Why didn't you go to Babette? For enough money, even she might have helped you rid yourself of it!*

I did. She refused.

He could still feel the impact of those words like a punch in the stomach. The anguish, the anger. He rocked on his feet and reached out for the edge of the wine vat beside him. He stood there for a long time, taking slow deep breaths, thinking of Tess.

He thought of her arms wrapped around him, he remembered the taste of her lips, heard her whispered words. *I love you.* Tess took away the loneliness and replaced it with love.

Opening his eyes, he stepped forward, staring down into the darkness of the cellar. He spoke to Anne-Marie. "You were so afraid of dying. I know I am to blame and there is no way I can atone for that."

Leaning one shoulder against the wall, he went on, "When you died, I wanted to go with you. I wanted to die, too. Then, after a little while, I realized my penance was to go on living. I have been alone for so long, *chérie.* I don't want to be alone any more."

He turned away from the steps into the cellar and sat down on the dirt floor. He closed his eyes and thought again of Tess.

Tess, with eyes the color of wet leaves and hair as bright as a Provence sunset. Tess, with courage enough to have a dozen children and a heart big enough to love them all. Tess, with a heart generous enough to love even him.

I love you.

He didn't deserve her love. He knew that, and yet, he wanted it. He loved her. It would be best for her if she left, and yet, he was selfish. He wanted her to stay. He wanted her words to be true, he wanted to believe she really meant them.

But, if she and the baby stayed, how would he take care of them? What legacy could he leave Suzanne? He had nothing but a crumbling castle and a broken-down winery. Tess deserved better.

The winery.

Opening his eyes, he looked around him. He rose to his feet and began to examine the winemaking equipment, wondering if he were truly crazy. The idea in his head certainly was.

The equipment seemed to be in fairly sound condition. Several of the oak vats had been gnawed through by the rats and would have to be replaced.

He ran his hand over one of the heavy wooden beams of the wine press, knowing he'd have to find the money to buy a new one. This one had been horribly out-of-date and inefficient three years ago, and he knew better presses were available.

He left the first building and entered the second one. Shelves of empty bottles lined the walls, covered with a thick film of dust. Crates of more empty bottles were stacked in the center of the room, still waiting for the wine that had never filled them.

At his feet were many tiny piles of debris. The rats had been busy in here as well. He knelt and examined an open crate of wine corks, realizing immediately that none of them could be used. Many of them had the teeth marks of the rats that had chewed on them.

He tossed down the cork in his hand and rose. The bottles would need to be washed, but they could still be used. He moved on to the third building.

The brandy distillery was in very poor shape. Both stills were gone, stolen, he guessed. All the bottles had been smashed by the vandals. All the coal used to heat the fires was gone.

Doubt assailed him. He didn't know if he could do it. He knew there was a very strong possibility he would fail. But Tess had told him she and the baby would stay. If so, he had to be able to take care of them. They were his responsibility now.

If he were going to reopen the winery, he had to have cash. He would need to purchase new equipment and supplies. Workers would have to be hired to prune the vines and replace any that were diseased, as well as tend the vines through the summer.

He had some money, enough to maintain his present way of life permanently. But what he had was not even close to what he would need to make the winery a going concern.

He could probably raise the capital he needed by painting. Henri had said he was still receiving invitations to do exhibitions, which would bring in some money. But the real profit would be in the portrait commissions that would come from those exhibitions. At the height of his fame in Florence, he had done as many as three portraits a week.

If Henri could arrange it, he would go to Paris in the early spring, then perhaps journey to London around Easter. He could go to Florence as well. Improvements to the winery could be made as the money came in, and they might even manage a decent harvest in the autumn.

He left the distillery and went to examine the vineyards. The vines, though tangled from three years of neglect and laden with unpicked fruit, showed no sign of disease. Many of the vines had powdery mildew, but that was nothing serious. He knelt, pushing aside the debris of fallen leaves and rotted fruit, digging around the base of a plant to examine the shallow roots. He was relieved to see no galls.

Rising to his feet, Alexandre brushed the dirt from his hands and pulled a few grapes from the nearest bunch. He popped one into his mouth. Not bad, he decided, chewing the grape and analyzing the taste. All things considered, it would have made a fair vintage.

He headed back toward the château in search of Henri, suppressing every doubt that came into his mind, discounting everything that could go wrong, refusing to listen to the pessimist in himself.

He found his brother playing cards with Jeanette. "Could I speak with you a moment, *mon frère?* There is something I want to discuss with you."

Henri set down his cards, answering Jeanette's inquiring look with a shrug, and followed his brother out of the library, through the kitchen, and out of the house. It was not until they reached the path leading to the vineyards that Henri stopped Alexandre by laying a hand on his arm. "What is this all about?"

Alexandre turned to his brother. "I want to reopen the winery."

Henri's brows lifted in surprise. "What?"

He nodded emphatically. "I need your opinion on the condition of the vines and the winery and what it will take to begin making wine again. I want a harvest by next autumn."

"Is that all?" Henri inquired in a joking tone to cover his surprise.

"No. I have a great favor to ask of you." He took a deep breath and raked a hand through his hair. "I want you to become a vintner again."

Henri's jaw dropped as he stared at his brother for a long moment. Finally, he closed his mouth, swallowed hard, and said slowly, "You mean, you want me to move back here and help supervise the winery?"

"No, this time, I want you to be a partner. I know you are a very successful wine merchant now, but I would like to have your help and expertise." He met his brother's eyes and added, "I wouldn't blame you if you refused. I know I have no right to ask you to do this after I closed the winery and sent you packing. If you refuse—"

"I accept," Henri interrupted with an impatient waving of his hands.

"You do?" It was Alexandre's turn to be surprised. He'd expected a flat refusal. "Are you certain? Being a vintner is risky at best."

"I've never been more certain of anything in my life," Henri assured him, and could no longer contain his joy. With a whoop of delight, he jumped high in the air and spun around, making it perfectly clear how he felt about the idea. His eyes shining, he grasped Alexandre by the arms. "I never wanted to be a merchant. You know making wine is what I love. I have never wanted to do anything else."

"I also know that I treated you badly after Anne-Marie died," Alexandre replied. "I dismissed you from your position as head vintner. I—"

"Forget about that," his brother interrupted again. "I have."

"But—"

"Alexandre, I forgave you a long time ago. I was angry, yes, and I was hurt. But after a time, I understood your reasons. Besides, we're family. And you're making me a partner!" He let out a jubilant laugh.

"What will Jeanette say?"

"She hates Marseilles and she loves it here. She always has. Her father was a vintner, too, remember. Making wine is in our blood, all of us." He started down the path toward the winery. Alexandre did not move to follow, and Henri gestured impatiently. "C'mon. If you want a harvest by next autumn, we'd better get started."

"Wait." He laid a restraining hand on Henri's arm. "There's more I have to tell you. I've been down to the winery, and I know I'm going to need a great deal of money to make it run again. I don't have enough to do it."

"I do. I'll provide the capital."

"No."

"But—"

"No." Alexandre shook his head in the face of Henri's protests. "You may invest up to half, if you wish, but I will provide the rest."

"How?"

"Do you think you can arrange for those exhibitions we were discussing a few weeks ago?"

Astonished, Henri stared. "This is certainly a day for surprises," he murmured.

"Can you do it?"

"Of course. I get invitations for you all the time."

"Good. When you return to Marseilles, begin making the necessary arrangements. Now, let's go have a look at the winery."

"With pleasure."

As the two men walked down the path, it finally occurred to Henri to ask what had brought about this decision.

Alexandre proceeded to give his younger brother a lecture on a man's responsibilities in life.

Henri and Jeanette left for Marseilles the following day as planned. Tess, firm in her decision, did not accompany them. At Alexandre's request, neither Henri nor Jeanette mentioned the plans for the winery to her. He wanted to do that himself at the right time.

As the days passed, Tess noticed that Alexandre was spending a great deal of time painting in his studio or taking long walks. That was nothing unusual, but she sensed a definite change. It didn't seem that he was doing it to avoid her. But she couldn't pinpoint the specific cause of his long absences from the house.

There were other changes in his behavior. He kept Paul busy with tasks such as repairing fences, replacing flagstones, and cleaning out the unused outbuildings. One day, she found the two men rebuilding the walls around the courtyard with mortar. Alexandre had never taken much interest in the appearance of the château, and his sudden preoccupation with making these repairs was very odd indeed.

One morning in early December, after many days of rain, the weather was fine, and she decided to take

Suzanne for a walk. But Leonie informed her that Suzanne was with Alexandre. He had left the house a short time before, taking the baby with him. When she asked where they had gone, Leonie's answer astonished her. He had said he was going down to the winery.

Tess couldn't believe it. She knew Alexandre well enough to know he never went near the vineyards. When asked about the winery, he had always refused to discuss it. What was he up to?

She walked down to the winery, bewildered and curious. She found the door to one of the buildings standing open and as she approached the doorway, she heard Alexandre's voice.

"Now, *mon enfant,* this is the wine press. We use it to squeeze all the juice out of the grapes. When my father was young, the villagers would take off their shoes and stomp the grapes, but we don't do it that way anymore."

He was standing beside a large machine. He was turned away from her, but she could see that he held Suzanne in his arms and was pointing out to her all the advantages of having a wine press.

Choking back a laugh, Tess watched from the doorway, unobserved.

He went on, "I will have to buy a new press. This one is much too old. With a new press, Henri and I will be able to make the best wine in the Midi."

He was going to make wine again? Tess was amazed by this unexpected turn of events. But his next words amazed her further.

"It is very important that we make the best wine and that our winery has an excellent reputation. I have to make sure you and your mother have a secure future."

Tess pressed a trembling hand to her lips. So that was why he was planning to make wine again and why he was making all the improvements to the château. He wanted to take care of Suzanne. He wanted to take care of her.

She was overcome by a myriad of emotions. Joy, relief, love. Love, most of all. She stared at him hungrily, loving him so much she couldn't hold back a tiny cry of joy.

He turned at the sound, looking into her eyes with all the same hunger she felt. He walked toward her and put Suzanne in her arms. Then he reached out, cupping her face in his palm.

"You truly want to take care of us?" Her voice was a husky whisper.

"Yes. I probably won't do a very good job of it, but I'll do my best."

"Suzanne and I will do our best to take care of you, too."

He smiled at that. "You think I need taking care of?"

"Definitely."

He leaned forward and touched his lips to her left cheek. "Do I get blackberry tarts?"

"Every summer," she promised.

He kissed her right cheek. "And you won't put my paintbrushes away without telling me where?"

"I'll put them in the studio."

He kissed her mouth. Against her lips, he asked, "And you'll make certain I always have plenty of ribbons?"

She laughed. "Yes, yes, yes! I promise."

"Good." He straightened and his gaze traveled down the length of her and back up again. "Have Paul take you into the village today. I want you to buy some things."

"What things?" Tess swallowed hard, her joy fading at the prospect of going into town. "Why?"

He reached out and grasped a fold of the lavender muslin dress she wore. "I want you to get some fabric. For dresses of your own."

Tess looked down at Anne-Marie's dress. It was important to him that she not wear his dead wife's clothes. He obviously wanted her to have her own things.

Tess struggled with the idea of going to town. She didn't want to go, but if she and Alexandre were going to have a future together, she couldn't hide in the château forever. If the British authorities wanted to find her, surely they would have done so by now. Perhaps they weren't searching for her any longer. Perhaps they never had been. She nodded agreement. "All right. I'll go."

She stood on tiptoe and pressed her lips to his in a quick kiss. Then she took Suzanne and went back up to the house, hoping she was doing the right thing.

20

"*This is a* very fine silk, mademoiselle. It would make a lovely evening gown." Claudette Giraud unrolled the bolt of azure blue silk for her customer to see.

Tess fingered the delicate material, enjoying the fine texture, but after a moment, she shook her head. "It's lovely, but I've no use for it. What I need are good, sturdy cottons."

"Ah!" Claudette set aside the silk and turned to the shelves behind her, pulling down several bolts of printed fabrics and laying them across the wooden counter.

Tess knew Paul was waiting outside with the carriage, but she lingered over the materials before her, wanting to choose those Alexandre would like best. She'd been apprehensive when she had first entered the draper's, not knowing what to expect. But the proprietress had a manner that was natural and friendly, and she soon put Tess at ease.

Not wanting to be extravagant, she chose enough fabric for three dresses, several petticoats and chemises, and some soft wool for a pelisse, with buttons and trims to match.

She also bought two sets of stays, half a dozen pairs of
stockings, several pairs of gloves, and two straw bonnets.

As she paid for her purchases with the money Alexandre had given her, Tess dodged a series of questions with
tactful, but vague replies. Asked if she would like the
materials delivered, she answered, "No, I've a carriage
outside." Asked if she would need a dressmaker, she
replied that she had one.

By this time, she was certain the woman's questions
were borne of curiosity and nothing more. She was a
stranger in this small village, after all. But she stopped
lingering over her purchases and departed, asking Paul
to put the materials in the carriage before walking to the
shoemaker's shop next door.

At the shoemaker's, she was fitted for a pair of halfboots
and two pairs of slippers. Upon being told the shoes would
be ready within the week, Tess returned to the carriage.

As Paul drove her home, Tess leaned back in her seat
with a contented sigh. No one had recognized her. No
one was searching for her in Saint-Raphael. She must be
safe. She didn't dwell on the reasons why, she simply
breathed a prayer of thanks.

While Tess was in the village with Paul, Alexandre
was busy with work of his own. He had brought two
dozen wooden crates up to the château from the winery.
By the time he finished his task, the crates were full and
standing in the front hall. Tomorrow, he would have
Paul load them into the carriage and take them to the
church in Saint-Raphael.

He looked around the room. Other than the bare fur-
niture, only one item remained. He picked up Anne-
Marie's carved ivory jewel case and removed the few
Dumond jewels that had not been confiscated during the
Revolution, then he dusted the case carefully.

Opening it one last time, he stared at the blue velvet interior for a long moment. "Good-bye, *chérie*," he murmured. Closing the case, he packed it in a box to send to Marseilles. The jewel case had been a gift to her from Henri. He would want to have it.

Downstairs, Alexandre put the jewels in the safe in his library. Then he went to the kitchen where Leonie was preparing the evening meal and instructed her to go upstairs and clean both rooms. He also told her to make up the bed in the master's chamber and move his things in there. When Leonie finished these tasks and returned to the kitchen, she found that Alexandre had turned her simple country dinner into a seven-course meal.

Tess set aside her dinner napkin with a contented sigh and cast a glance down the long length of the table at her companion. "Either you've spent your afternoon in the kitchen," she teased, "or you've been giving Leonie cooking lessons."

Alexandre looked up from his dessert of chestnut meringue. "I couldn't stand the thought of one more meal of fried fish and boiled potatoes," he confessed in a low, teasing voice that wouldn't carry to the kitchen, where Leonie was serving the plainer courses Alexandre had made to her husband and son.

Tess rose to her feet and began to collect the plates, intending to carry the dishes to the kitchen, but Alexandre's voice stopped her.

"Let Leonie do that."

"But Leonie has been working hard all day, and I've done nothing."

He shook his head. "I pay her very well to do the work she does." Tess started to protest once again, but he interrupted her. "I am giving my housekeeper the evening off so she can play chess with me. No arguments."

She laughed. "You are an impossible man!" Setting down the plates, she added, "If I'm going to leave the dishes to poor Leonie, the least I can do is put the babies to bed for her."

Alexandre nodded and rose, picking up his glass of wine. "I'll be in the library. Join me there."

She went to the kitchen and relieved Leonie of the two babies, carrying them upstairs to change them and tuck them into bed. She lingered a bit longer with Suzanne, taking extra care with folding the blankets over her.

Her daughter, she decided, was becoming an extremely pretty baby. Her eyes had turned from the common slate blue to deep green, and her hair was a lovely fusion of blond and red. She was also as round as a ball of butter, obviously happy with Leonie's frequent feedings.

Tess sang her daughter to sleep with a lullaby, then returned downstairs to join Alexandre in the library. He had the pieces already laid out on the board and soon the two of them were engaged in a competitive game of chess.

Alexandre still won the game, but Tess was happy to note that she was improving. "Shall we play again?" she asked, hands poised over the board to arrange the pieces for a rematch.

"No. You're becoming much too good at this. You might win."

She made a face at him. "I doubt it."

After he had taken a sip of wine, he asked, "Why don't you show me what you bought in the village today?"

"You really want to see?" She set down a carved wooden chess piece and shot him an inquiring glance. Getting an affirmative nod, she asked softly, "What if you don't like what I bought?"

He settled back comfortably in his chair. "I'm not the one who has to wear it."

She watched him put his feet up on the table, loving him with all her heart. He would never know how much that answer meant to her. Nonetheless, she said, "Alexandre, take your feet off the table."

"Yes, madame." He straightened, trying to assume a properly chastised expression and failing completely.

She laughed. "I knew it." She rose to her feet and headed for the door. "An impossible man."

She returned a few moments later with an armful of parcels. One at a time, she displayed the three dress fabrics she'd bought. As she brought out each one, he would frown thoughtfully as if seriously considering the purchase.

But as she folded the third length of fabric to set it aside, she saw him sigh and slowly shake his head. "What is it?" she asked, feeling suddenly anxious.

He leaned back in his chair, tilting his head to one side. "Well, none of them were quite what I had in mind."

Tess's anxiety tripled in the full five seconds it took her to respond. She lowered her chin and stared at the floor. "What," she asked in a choked voice, "did you have in mind?"

"A wedding dress."

Her head shot up. She hadn't heard him right. Or he was teasing her. But his grave expression told her he wasn't teasing at all. She took a step forward and faltered. "Really?"

He closed the distance between them. "You must admit, it is a sound idea," he said. He pulled the swath of fabric from her fingers and tossed it aside. "Suzanne would have a name and a father."

He bent his head and kissed her. "I would take care of you."

His arms wrapped around her, and he pulled her close. "And, as you pointed out only this morning, you would take care of me."

He bent his head again, this time trailing kisses from her lips to her chin to the ruffled collar at her throat. "And, perhaps," he added, moving his lips to the lobe of her ear, "Paul and Leonie will stop thinking dreadful things about me if I do the honorable thing and marry you."

The thought flashed through her mind that now was the time to tell him about her past. But the idea of telling Alexandre about Nigel, talking aloud about the things her husband had done, filled her with dread. She couldn't do it, she couldn't relive those horrible days. Not now, not yet. Later, she promised herself as Alexandre began to nibble on her earlobe, she would tell him about Nigel later.

"Your reasons seem to be very good ones," she said breathlessly.

"There is one other reason." He pulled back to gaze down into her face. "I happen to love you very much."

Before she could reply, his lips captured hers. Reasons, sound or otherwise, were swept aside as his tongue teased her lips, parting them for a deeper kiss.

All the strength seemed to drain from her, and she clung to him, molding her body against his. She felt the fire in him, and it wrought sparks of apprehension and desire within her. Past experience had been a brutal teacher, but instinct and love guided her now. She was not afraid.

She slid her arms between them and ran her hands up his broad chest to his collar. Her hands shook as she undid the three buttons one by one. Pulling back white linen, she pressed her mouth to his tawny skin and felt a tremor run through his body at her soft kisses.

"Tess . . ." Her name was a groan on his lips. His fingers

caught in the tangle of her hair, encouraging her to explore further.

She did, savoring a power she'd never known as she moved her lips across his skin, enjoying the raspy softness of the hair on his chest and the rise and fall of his rapid breathing.

He groaned again and his hand left her hair. Suddenly, she felt herself lifted into his arms, carried out of the library and up the stairs. She saw the raw sensuality in his black eyes, and knowing it for what it was, felt her apprehension return. "Alexandre?"

He paused on the landing. Looking down into her face, he must have sensed her uncertainty, for he bent his head and brushed a kiss across her lips that banished all her doubts.

It wasn't until he paused before a door and asked her to open it that she realized where he was taking her. She shot him a questioning glance, but opened the door without a word. He carried her into the master's chamber and closed the door behind them with the heel of his boot.

Setting her down on the edge of the bed, he ran his hands through her hair, tilting her head back to look down into her face. Her silent answer to his silent question must have satisfied him, for his hands left her hair and he dropped to his knees in front of her.

She watched as he lifted the hem of her gown over her knees. One at a time, he removed her slippers, tossing them carelessly toward a corner of the room. He pulled at the tie of one garter, the bow came loose, and the garter fell away. Tess couldn't stop the gasp of pleasure that escaped her as his fingertips caressed the back of her knee. Slowly, he pulled the silky wisp of stocking down her calf and over her ankle.

Her passion-drugged senses came to the startling realization that he was actually undressing her. Such a thing was so unexpected, so beyond her experience, that she couldn't move. This tender patience, this consideration, was like soft rain on her dry, parched soul. Through a sensuous haze, she watched him remove her other stocking and toss it aside.

His hands grasped hers. He pulled her to her feet and turned her around. Beginning at the top, he undid the hooks down her back, then pulled the gown from her shoulders, down over her hips, to fall in a pool of muslin at her feet. She closed her eyes, feeling the soft cotton petticoat slide down her bare legs to join the gown on the floor.

He pulled the lacing through the holes of her stays, his knuckles brushing against her back. The corset fell away, and he drew up her chemise, pulling it over her head. The cool air teased her hot skin, and his fingertips teased her spine, causing her to shiver. He pushed aside short wisps of hair and kissed the nape of her neck.

Every remaining ounce of strength she possessed deserted her and her knees buckled. His arms came up to encircle her waist, holding her against him, as his lips trailed kisses over her bare shoulder.

She felt a strange heat building inside of her and, restless, she tried to turn around, but he held her prisoner against his hard length. She felt his hands move up to cup her breasts.

She moaned as his thumbs caressed, and only his arms around her kept her from falling. "Alexandre," she gasped, suddenly afraid of the unfamiliar and turbulent feelings he was arousing within her. "I feel so strange."

His laughter was low and warm against her ear. Loosening his embrace, he allowed her to face him, before gently guiding her backward. The edge of the bed hit her knees, and she fell back into the soft mattress.

In the lamplight, she could see reflections of her own passion burning within the black depths of his eyes. Slowly, his eyes never leaving hers, he began to undress.

His boots hit the floor. His shirt flew somewhere behind him. Their gazes remained locked until he slid his trousers off his hips. The realization of what was to come suddenly hit Tess. Memories intruded, and she froze. With a cry of alarm, she turned her face away.

He was beside her on the bed in an instant, wrapping his arms around her, soothing her fears with softly murmured words in French and English, fanning her fires with caresses until he had gained a series of pleasurable cries from her lips.

Tess was stunned by the feelings he was arousing in her with his hands and his lips and his words. She'd never dreamed a man's touch could make her feel this way. Her entire body tingled with sensation and a longing for something more. She opened her eyes and looked at him. "I love you," she whispered. Reaching out to touch him, she hesitated and started to draw back.

But he grasped her hand and pulled it toward him. "Yes," he said hoarsely, rolling onto his back and pressing her hand to his chest. "Touch me. Touch me."

Experimentally, she ran her hand over the hard muscles of his chest, to his shoulders, to his face. Her fingertips brushed back and forth across his mouth, lingering there a long moment before descending once again.

Her hand moved lower and Alexandre tilted his head back, letting out a groan of pleasure. Her hand moved lower still, and he grasped her wrist to stop her.

He turned, pushing her onto her back once again, rolling with her. His weight pinned her to the mattress, his knee parted her legs. She bit her lip and allowed it, fighting another wave of fear, but when his fingers caressed her, every painful memory shattered with his touch. She cried out, needing release and not knowing why, her body arching upwards against his hand.

He settled his weight between her thighs, murmured

one more endearment, and entered her with one swift thrust.

Soft. God, she was soft. He held himself motionless for a moment, savoring the warmth of her all around him. Willing himself to go slowly, he began to move, but her body was pulling him deeper and deeper.

He couldn't hold back. The softness and warmth of her were too much for his starved body, and he quickened the pace. She clung to him, her hands caressing his back. She matched him thrust for thrust, but it wasn't until he heard her cry his name and felt her body shudder in a climax beneath him that he allowed his own release. With a shout of triumph, he plunged deep inside her one last time and the confession was torn from his lips. "Tess, Tess, I love you so!"

His body jerked convulsively, then stilled. He fell against her, drinking in great gulps of air and the floral fragrance of her skin.

It was a long time before he had the strength to stir. He started to roll away, but she made a sound of protest, her arms tight around him. He lifted his head, resting his weight on his arms, his gaze roaming possessively over her.

She reached up to touch his face, running her fingers down his lean cheek. Then she weaved her fingers through his hair. Black as a raven's wing, thick as a horse's mane, it was as soft as silk. She wrapped the long strands around her hand and gently pulled his head down to hers. "Don't ever cut your hair," she ordered, her mouth an inch from his.

"I won't." Touching his lips to hers, he vowed, "I'll let it grow until it reaches my ankles."

She laughed softly. "That will probably take a long time."

"Mm-hmm. The rest of our lives."

21

Nigel stepped out of the carriage and took a quick, disdainful look around. Saint-Raphael was a backward little fishing village, without the excitement of Nice or the convenient amenities of Menton.

"Wait here," he told the driver. "You, too, Sullivan," he added, as his valet prepared to step down and accompany him. "I probably won't be long."

Nigel began his inquiries at one end of the main street, but no one he spoke with recognized the miniature of Teresa.

He crossed the street and retraced his steps on the opposite side, wondering if perhaps Martin was having better luck. The two men had separated at Orange, with Martin taking the road through the Languedoc region to Spain, and Nigel taking the road along the Côte d'Azur to Italy. They were scheduled to rendezvous in Marseilles five days from now.

He stepped inside the draper's shop and waited with barely concealed impatience as the proprietress behind the counter assisted a very stout woman with her purchases. Tapping the end of his gilt-edged walking stick against the wooden floor, he waited.

The proprietress glanced at him. "I will be with you in a moment, monsieur."

But it was quite a few moments before she finally escorted the stout lady to the door and turned to him. "Yes, monsieur?"

He held out the miniature of his wife in one gloved hand. "I wish to know if you have seen this lady."

The woman took the tiny portrait and glanced at it. Her dark brows lifted in surprise, and her gaze lifted to Nigel. "*Oui,* monsieur. Only yesterday."

A flash of triumph shot through him. "She means a great deal to me, and I have been searching for her for a long time." Digging in the pocket of his waistcoat, he pulled out a napoleon, twirling it in his fingers before the woman's eyes. "Tell me everything you can."

She related every detail she could remember of the lady's visit. Nigel listened, a slow, deep anger building within him. He wondered where she had gotten the money to buy clothes.

"She did not tell you where she was staying?"

"*Non,* monsieur. I have told you everything she said."

He put the coin in her hand. "I will be staying at the inn. If she returns, come and fetch me at once. If you do, there are three more gold coins for you."

The proprietress nodded in amazement as he left the shop. But she did not question why the wealthy Englishman wanted to find the girl. She put the napoleon in her pocket with a grateful prayer to heaven and a hope that the girl came back.

The shoemaker was able to tell him that Teresa had been there as well. She had ordered two pairs of slippers and a pair of half-boots and would be returning for them in a few days. Nigel made the shoemaker the same promise he had made the draper and left the shop.

Returning to the carriage, he instructed the driver to take them to the inn, where he spent the remainder of the morning deciding exactly how he would punish his wife for all that she had put him through.

The sun was in his eyes. Alexandre blinked and turned his face from the sunlight pouring through the window to the woman in bed beside him. Turning onto his side, he rested his weight on one elbow and studied her just for the sheer pleasure of doing so. She was asleep, her expression soft from lovemaking and slumber. There was a crease on her cheek from the pillow, and he reached out, tracing it lovingly with his finger.

She stirred and her eyes opened.

"*Bonjour.*" He leaned forward, pressing his lips to her bare shoulder above the sheet. Her body moved, radiating warmth and arousing him. Pulling away the sheet, he traced a path of kisses from her shoulder to her breasts and back again. He captured her lips with his and lingered there, rolling on top of her and ignoring the embarrassed, whispered protest she uttered against his mouth.

He watched her face as he entered her. Her lips parted, her body arched, and he came in a rush of pleasure. Burying his face in the tangle of her hair, he smiled, feeling the small shudders she gave beneath him. It was a long time before he moved again.

Finally, he kissed her hard and rolled away, swinging his legs over the side of the bed. Knowing she was watching him, he dressed slowly with no regard for modesty.

He was beautiful. She sat up, wrapping the sheet around herself, and watched the sunlight play across the powerful muscles of his body, appreciating how beautiful a man's strength could be. When he sat on the edge of the bed to pull on his boots, she leaned toward him, pressing her breasts against his back and wrapping her arms around him, loving him.

He turned his head. With a smile and a kiss, he said, "Are you planning to lie abed all day, my love?"

Emboldened, she kissed his ear and whispered, "Only if you do the same."

He made a sound that was half laugh, half groan, but he shook his head. "A very tempting offer, *petite,* but we both have things to do today." Turning around, he kissed her nose. "You have to go to town and buy fabric for a wedding dress. Or had you forgotten?"

"No," she answered, caressing his cheek. "I hadn't forgotten. But what is it that you have to do?"

"I am going to paint today." He rose, rolling back the cuffs of his shirt. "I think it is time I did a portrait of Suzanne."

She laughed, falling back against the pillows. "You are going to spoil her."

"I certainly hope so." He bent down for one last kiss then walked to the door. Pausing in the doorway, he turned to her. "Tess?"

"Hmm?"

"Je t'aime."

"I love you, too," she said, watching him disappear through the doorway.

Paul halted the carriage in front of the draper's shop. "This may take some time," Tess told him as he assisted her down.

"Very well, mademoiselle." He gave a shy bow and added, "I will return for you in an hour?"

"That will be fine." Tess smiled and turned toward the shop as Paul made for the tavern across the street.

He stepped into the dim interior and took a seat on one of the wooden benches, indicating to the pretty brunette serving girl that he wanted a glass of wine.

The tavern was crowded with men. Many were travelers, seeking a quick midday meal, but the men seated nearest him were evidently locals for they were discussing the local gossip with avid interest.

"He's an *aristo*," one man was saying. "English. Got pots of money, by the look of him."

Another man spoke. "Looking for a girl, you say?"

Taking a sip of wine, the first man nodded and continued, "He's been showing her picture all around. She'd be his mistress, I'd guess."

The serving girl set Paul's glass of wine before him and added her knowledge of the man to the conversation. "He said they had a quarrel and off she went. He's been trying to find her for a long time." With a dreamy sigh, she added, "He's a handsome fellow."

The first man scowled up at her. "You women, always wanting the handsome ones. He's English." The man spat out the word with obvious contempt. "Don't you go getting any ideas, Lise, my girl."

She huffed indignantly. "And who are you, Gaspard Leclare, to tell me what to do?" Sweeping a pile of coins off the table and into her apron, she stormed off.

Paul frowned thoughtfully into his wine. The mademoiselle was English. He wondered if the woman they were discussing could be her.

Tess fingered the length of luxurious white silk. "Yes, I'll take it."

"*Oui*, madame." Claudette measured off the yardage, cut the fabric and set it aside. "You will want trims and laces, *n'est-ce pas?*"

When Tess replied in the affirmative, the woman indicated the shelves containing all manner of trim and said,

"Please take your time, madame. I must go out for a moment."

Absorbed in making her selections, Tess nodded absently and the woman departed from the shop. When she heard the door open again and the bell above the door ring some moments later, she said without looking up, "I'd like eight yards of this Mechlin lace, I think."

"I think not."

Tess froze at the sound of that familiar voice. Slowly, she turned around, her heart pounding with dread.

There he was, standing with his back against the closed door of the shop, an impassive expression on his handsome face. The room began to spin and Tess fell back against the wooden counter, gripping the edges for support.

"You seem surprised to see me," Nigel commented, studying the ivory and gold walking stick in his hand.

"You're dead," she stated, staring at him in a daze. "I shot you."

He reached up and caressed the scar at his temple. "So you did." He smiled, but there was no humor in his eyes. "Forgive me for saying so, my dear, but you are not a very good shot. I survived."

She closed her eyes, trying to tell herself it was only a nightmare. But she knew it wasn't, and when she opened her eyes, he was still there. "Oh, God," she moaned, pressing her clenched fist against her lips.

Nigel shook his head and sighed. "Teresa, did you really think you could hide from me forever?"

"I wasn't hiding." She glanced around desperately, but there was no one to help her. "I thought you were dead."

Three quick strides and he was in front of her, preventing any attempt at escape. She shrank back against the counter, lowering her gaze to the gold buttons of his silk waistcoat.

The tip of his walking stick caught her under the chin, lifting her face. "No kiss of greeting for your husband?" he inquired. "Ah, well, we will remedy that later, when we have more privacy."

The door opened and Nigel's valet entered the shop. "The innkeeper has been paid, sir, and the carriage is outside."

"Excellent. We will join you in a moment, Sullivan."

"Very good, sir." The valet departed.

Nigel held out his gloved hand to her. "My dear?"

She stared at the hand offered to her. She knew what Nigel's hands could do to her. She knew how futile it was to fight, how much worse it would be if she did. She didn't care. "No!" she choked, pushing his arm aside and darting past him.

But he caught her in an instant. She felt as if her arm was being wrenched from its socket as he pulled her around and slammed her against the nearest wall. His grip on her arms was bruising, but his voice was deceptively soft. "There is nowhere to run, my dear."

She lifted her chin. "I'm not going anywhere with you. You cannot force me."

It was a lie and they both knew it. He could force her to do anything he wanted. "You are my wife and you will do as I say."

"I'll divorce you."

"You have no grounds."

"I'll run away again."

"Teresa, it will do you no good to defy me." He reached out to caress her trembling chin. "Any place you go, I will always find you. Don't you know that by now?"

She jerked away, fighting the sobs of panic that rose in her throat. What he said was true, of course. She'd always known there was no escape from hell.

Her thoughts whirled round and round. She could take the baby and run.

But if she did manage to get away, he would still find her. He would find Suzanne. He would take her anyway and the baby, too.

She thought of her tiny baby and Nigel's brutality. He would hurt Suzanne, and she would not be able to stop him. He didn't know about the baby, and she could not let him find out. No, at all costs, she had to protect Suzanne.

She knew the baby would be safe with Alexandre. He would take care of her. He would be such a good father. The idea of leaving him was agony, and she wavered, desperately seeking another option and finding none. She pushed aside the pain. She could not think about Alexandre now. Not now.

The baby. Focusing all her thoughts on Suzanne, she made the only choice she had. Sagging against the door, she went limp in Nigel's grip. "You are right, my lord, of course. I have nowhere to go, except with you."

He did not loosen his hold for some moments, searching her face for any sign of deception. Finally, he relaxed his grip somewhat. Keeping one of her arms firmly in his grasp, he said, "Since the carriage is outside, we will depart immediately. When we walk out, I expect my wife to behave with the decorum of her station. If you try to run again, Teresa, I will be very displeased."

She shuddered, remembering how painful Nigel's displeasure could be. She followed him obediently out to the carriage, her head high, ignoring the curious stares and whispers of the villagers who had gathered outside the shop. Only pride and thoughts of Suzanne's safety kept her from wild panic.

When Nigel assisted her into the carriage, her hand trembled only slightly in his as she meekly accepted his assistance and stepped inside.

The carriage lurched and began to move. Tess stared out the open window, too numb to think, too numb to feel. She watched the shops of Saint-Raphael disappear, replaced by a view of the sea, as they traveled the coast road toward Marseilles.

She turned away from the window and cast a sideways glance at her husband. He was watching her, and when she met his gaze, she felt another surge of panic. She saw the anger raging within him, and fear forced explanations from her lips. "I thought you were dead. I was terrified of what might happen. That's why I ran away."

Lowering her head, she stared at her shaking hands and steeled herself to stay calm as she desperately sought a plausible lie. "I've been living with a family near Saint-Raphael for the past six months. A w . . .wine merchant and his family. I've been their . . . um . . . nursery governess."

Governess sounded good, she thought. Better than housekeeper or maid. "They have four children," she added, thinking of Jeanette and Henri. "One son and three daughters . . ."

Her voice trailed off as Nigel reached out and lifted her hand. He pulled off her glove, then turned her palm upward. She felt his thumb caress the callouses there. "Really, my dear?" he drawled. "A fascinating story."

His hand closed over her wrist and he yanked her toward him. "We will not discuss this again until we are at home. In the meantime, perhaps you will be able to think of a more beleivable explanation, and I will decide what punishment you deserve."

He pushed her away, and she fell back against the side of the carriage. Drawing a deep breath of relief, she straightened and once again turned to stare out the window.

Foolish, she thought. She should know by now that her explanations never made any difference. He wouldn't believe her, and he would still punish her. But he wouldn't do anything to her here and now. No, he would wait until they were home, until he had complete privacy. She thought about the other two times she had run away from him, and how he had waited then, too. His goal was to frighten her and force her to imagine what he would do to her. It was all part of the game, but this time she wasn't going to play. She wasn't going to torture herself with speculation. She closed her eyes, and another man immediately replaced Nigel in her thoughts.

Alexandre would wonder what had happened to her. He would go to the village looking for her. He would believe that she had left him. A crack of pain fractured her heart and the first tear fell. She didn't care if Nigel saw it.

The window was open and she moved to put her head through. Perhaps she could see . . .

Nigel's hand on her knee gave her a moment's pause. "Careful, my dear. I wouldn't want you to fall out."

"It's stuffy in here, Nigel," she answered. "I wanted some air."

Turning back, she put her head through the window, twisting to stare at the peninsula in the distance, where Château Dumond stood high on the rocky cliffs. She could see the tower. Alexandre was probably there right now, painting that portrait of Suzanne.

"Good-bye, Alexandre," she whispered silently, staring at the château through a blur of tears. "Please take care of my baby."

The carriage followed a bend in the road and the château disappeared from her view, tearing a sob of complete desolation from her throat.

22

Alexandre laughed, looking down at the baby in the cradle. "You are not a good subject, Suzanne," he chided and pointed his paint brush in her direction. "You refuse to keep still."

The baby made a gurgling sound and waved her plump hands in the air.

"Don't be impertinent," he told her. "This is very serious work. I—"

"Monsieur, monsieur!" An agitated male voice and the clatter of hurried footsteps on the stairs interrupted him. Alexandre turned to see Paul take the last two steps at a jump and come flying into the studio.

The young man skidded to a halt, knocking over a table in the process. Out of breath, he grasped the edge of the table, righted it, and gasped, "Monsieur, the mademoiselle is gone!"

Alexandre frowned, puzzled by Paul's vague statement and obvious agitation. "Gone where?"

"I don't know. I came out of the tavern and saw her getting in a carriage with the English fellow. I tried to run after the carriage, but I couldn't catch it. I'm sorry, sir. I tried. I didn't know . . ."

Alexandre tried to make sense of this chaotic jumble of nonsense, and failed. "*Sacré tonnerre!* Speak slowly, Paul. I can't understand a word."

The young man waited a moment, taking several deep breaths, then began again. "I took the mademoiselle to the village and left her at the draper's shop. She said she would be awhile, so I went to the tavern for a glass of wine. I didn't mean any harm, monsieur," he hastened to add, seeing the frown darkening his master's face. "I was only gone a little while. When I came out, I saw the mademoiselle walk over to a carriage with the Englishman and get inside. The carriage drove away, taking the road to Marseilles. As I said, I tried to run after it, but I was too late."

A sick feeling of the inevitable began to spread through Alexandre. He fought it, refusing to believe what instinct and fear were whispering to him. "What Englishman? What carriage?"

"The Englishman, monsieur. Everybody's talking about him. Arrived only this morning, looking for the mademoiselle. Talk was that she was his mistress. He was showing her portrait to everybody, asking if they'd seen her. Rich *aristo*, by the look of him."

The paintbrush snapped in his hand, and Alexandre looked down at the broken pieces in bewilderment. Tess was gone? She'd just gotten into a carriage with some rich Englishman and driven off? He tossed aside the pieces of the broken paintbrush and headed for the stairs, his heart hammering with dread. "Take the baby down to Leonie," he told Paul. "I'm going to find her."

He was in the carriage and on the road within moments. Horseback would have been faster, but he didn't own a saddle. The day had started sunny and beautiful, but a storm was moving in and ominous clouds of gun metal gray gathered above his head, a perfect com-

266 LAURA LEE GUHRKE

plement to his dark mood. He arrived in Saint-Raphael with no conscious thought of the journey. All he could think of was finding Tess. Paul was mistaken. She'd just gone for a ride. She'd been kidnapped. Desperately, his mind sought sane reasons for an insane thing.

He yanked on the reins and halted the carriage in front of the draper's shop. Tossing aside the reins, he jumped down. But the shop was closed, and Alexandre realized that it was now evening. Not to be thwarted, he pounded on the door, knowing the widowed proprietress lived above the shop.

Claudette Giraud, finally hearing the loud, insistent pounding, came and opened the door. Though knowing Alexandre's reputation and frightened by the intensity of his manner, she answered his questions readily enough.

She confirmed that the Englishman had been looking for a petite, red-haired English girl. She also verified Paul's statement that the girl had gotten into a carriage with the man and driven off. When asked if the girl had seemed unwilling to go with the man, a surprised Claudette denied it. Indeed, the girl had walked to the carriage arm in arm with the Englishman.

Refusing to believe it, Alexandre went to the inn. The innkeeper confirmed that the Englishman and his servant had arrived that morning. He also repeated the gossip Paul had heard in the tavern, that the girl was the Englishman's mistress, and he'd spent months trying to find her.

Still refusing to believe, Alexandre returned to the carriage, determined to follow Tess and the Englishman. Without stopping to think about the fact that he had no money and no clothes with him, he headed the carriage in the direction of Marseilles.

When it was dark, he pulled off the road and tried to rest. But the rain falling on the roof of the carriage, the persistent wind that chilled his bones, and his own turbulent thoughts prevented sleep. She wouldn't go away with a stranger. Was the man her lover? Was he Suzanne's father? Agony and uncertainty were Alexandre's companions that night, and before dawn, he was on the road again.

He made inquiries at every inn he passed, eventually locating the one where Tess and her Englishman had spent the night. He continued on, panic and desperation driving him. He reached Marseilles by late afternoon.

The rain had turned into a raging storm by the time Alexandre found the address he was seeking in the fashionable Rue de Madelaine. Halting the exhausted horses in the circular cobblestone drive, he jumped down from the carriage and mounted the wide steps leading to the house. He pounded on the door, and when it was opened, he wasted no time on polite introductions to the butler. He shoved his way in, striding toward the sound of laughter emanating from the salon.

"Monsieur! You cannot barge in this way! Madame has guests for tea this afternoon. You cannot—"

Alexandre pushed open the glass doors leading into the salon. The sounds of laughter and conversation gradually ceased as the people in the room stared at the dark stranger in the doorway who was dripping water all over the expensive carpets. A brunette in rose pink silk noticed the stares and the sudden silence and turned around in her chair. What she saw made her gasp in astonishment. She rose and took a tentative step toward the door. "Alexandre?"

"She's gone, Jeanette," he said, his voice choked with all the despair and desperation he was feeling. "She's gone."

"This would be much easier if you had learned the man's name," Henri told Alexandre as the two men walked through the doors of the Hotel d'Arterre, one of

Marseilles' most fashionable hotels and a favorite with wealthy English tourists.

"I wish you'd stop saying that," Alexandre muttered, following Henri across the richly appointed lobby to the desk of the concierge. As they approached, the distinguished-looking man behind the desk glanced up inquiringly. "Messieurs? May I help you?"

As Henri explained their search and gave a description of Tess, Alexandre examined the lobby. He saw many people strolling in and out, but there was no sign of the woman he sought. This was the fifth hotel at which they had made inquiries, and so far they'd had no luck.

He pulled restlessly at the silk cravat he'd borrowed from Henri, and continued to look about, only half listening to what Henri was saying.

"They would have arrived today."

"A petite English lady with short red hair, you say?" The concierge paused as if pondering the matter. "I seem to recall such a lady arriving this afternoon, though I cannot for the moment recall her name. She was wearing a blue dress."

Henri and Alexandre exchanged glances.

"Yes," Alexandre confirmed the concierge's last statement. "It was blue."

The man sniffed. "Several years out of fashion. The English ladies really have no sense of style. And she wore no cloak. Can you imagine? In this weather?" He sniffed again.

Alexandre leaned forward, placing his palms on the desk. Through clenched teeth, he asked, "Where would the lady be now?"

"I haven't any idea," the concierge replied in an offended tone. "However, since it is the dinner hour, she might be in the dining room." He pointed to a set of glass doors. "I believe an English couple staying here have arranged a dinner party. She may be with that group."

Alexandre headed in that direction, Henri close behind him. He paused in the doorway, scanning the crowded room.

He saw her almost immediately. She was seated with a large group of people at a long table near the opposite end of the room. Diamonds glittered at her ears and throat and the light of the chandeliers above made her fiery hair glow. The "unfashionable" blue dress had been discarded in favor of bronze silk and the neckline plunged low, revealing a generous expanse of her creamy skin.

The man seated beside her, a blond, typically English dandy, leaned closer to her and whispered something in her ear. The corners of her beautiful mouth lifted in a smile, and raw pain ripped through Alexandre's chest.

Unable to bear the truth staring him in the face, he turned away and left the hotel, oblivious to the rain pouring over his borrowed clothes, or Henri's voice calling his name.

Alexandre arrived home two days later. Paul and Leonie asked no questions, and he was grateful. He wouldn't have known what answers to give them.

He could have told Paul and Leonie the truth. Tess had lied to him. She had told him she loved him, and he had believed her. What a fool he had been. A lonely, foolish man. Now he knew she had used him, she'd told him she loved him only so that he would let her stay, only so that he would take care of her and the baby.

Her lover had obviously not wanted that privilege. When the opportunity to return to her lover had presented itself, she'd abandoned Suzanne to go with him. Every time Alexandre thought of her sweet deception, of how he'd been used, it filled him with a bitter, corrosive anger.

He tried to paint, but even inspiration had deserted him.

He stared at the mess he had made of his latest painting and tossed down the brush with a curse. Leaving the studio, he walked downstairs and stared at the painting he'd done of Tess in the meadow. She looked so happy . . . had his eyes deceived him? He stared at the portrait, wondering if she had, even then, been thinking of her lover, wishing he were the man with her. Had she really been such a good actress? Had he really been such a fool?

Alexandre took the painting down from its hook on the wall. He carried it up to his studio and wrapped it in a swath of linen sheeting. He folded the white cloth across the canvas, refusing to look at her face again, and put the painting against the wall with the others.

He left the studio and went into the nursery. Suzanne was crying. It seemed almost as if she, too, knew her mother had deserted her. Alexandre's lips tightened in a thin line. He would not think about Tess again, he vowed. He would not torture himself with questions. Suzanne was his daughter now. She was his responsibility, and his alone. He would never abandon her as her mother had done.

Leonie was holding Suzanne and pacing the floor, trying to soothe the wailing baby. He walked over to her and took Suzanne from her arms. "You should take Elise out for a walk," he told her, "else you'll have two crying babies."

"Yes, monsieur." Leonie started to turn away, but paused. "Monsieur?"

He looked into her black eyes and saw the sympathy there. He glanced away. "Yes?"

"Paul and I would like to stay with you permanently. If you wish it?"

"*Merci,* Leonie. Yes, please stay. I will need your help."

"That is what we thought, monsieur." She bent and lifted Elise from her cradle, then left the nursery, closing the door behind her.

Alexandre sat down in the nearest chair and cradled the crying Suzanne against his chest. He felt his heart breaking with each sob she gave. He watched her grasp his finger in her tiny hand as if she were clinging to a lifeline, and a fierce wave of protectiveness washed over him. "Hush," he murmured, placing a kiss on her forehead. "You are my daughter, and I will take care of you, *mon enfant.* I will always take care of you. I swear it."

As the sun set and the room faded into twilight, he heard the church bells of Saint-Raphael announce the evening mass, each toll a melancholy echo of Suzanne's sobs. Alexandre continued to hold her, never certain if the tears that stained her cheeks fell from her eyes or from his.

Tess watched the trunks filled with beautiful new dresses being carried up the sweeping marble staircase of Aubry Park. Nigel, of course, had chosen them during their five-day stop in Paris, and had paid handsomely to have them made in so short a time. But then Nigel was always able to pay for what he wanted.

She pulled off the luxurious merino traveling cloak she wore and handed it wordlessly to her maid. Sally smiled and murmured shyly, "It's good to have you home, my lady," but Tess only nodded and moved toward the stairs, feeling like a marionette in a children's puppet show.

Nigel insisted she dress for dinner. There was, of course, no discussion, no argument. She wore the new ecru silk he liked, not out of a wish to please, but because he told her to. She ate, she smiled when she was told to smile, she went through the motions of making polite dinner conversation, but she did it all as if in a dream. She thought nothing, she felt nothing.

After dinner, she was allowed to go to her room. She stood in the center of her richly furnished bedchamber, staring at the polished parquet floor. No bloodstains, she noticed.

The shivers began in her belly, radiating through her until her entire body was shaking so badly she couldn't stand. Falling into a chair, she sat, not knowing how much time passed. And she waited.

Gradually, the trembling in her body stopped, and a cold, calm fear took its place. She knew what would happen tonight. He would demand explanations, and she would repeat her story of being a nursery governess. She remembered how he'd examined her hands in the carriage. He'd seen callouses on her hands. She'd have to think of a way to explain those. He probably wouldn't believe her explanations, but even if he did, he would still punish her.

The door opened, and she stiffened in her chair. Lamplight spilled into the room and she heard his footsteps behind her. She didn't turn, but stared straight ahead of her, seeing his reflection against the window glass. She watched him, and she waited.

He set the lamp on her dressing table. Then he walked around to stand in front of her. She lowered her head, staring at his boots, not wanting to look at him. And she waited.

He bent over her, lifting her chin with one finger to look into her face. His smile was benign, and if she had cared, it would have frightened her more than any angry words. But she didn't care. Her gaze was steady as she looked into his angel-blue eyes.

"Welcome home, my dear," Nigel said and slapped her across the face.

Part II

Part II.

23

April 1819

Alexandre went to Paris as he and Henri had planned, and his exhibitions there proved both successful and profitable. When he returned home, the first thing he did was take a tour through the vineyards. He followed Henri down the hillside, making observations of the work that had been done in his absence. The vines had been expertly pruned, there wasn't a weed in sight, and the soil had already been aerated. His examination of the vineyards was thorough, but he found no fault with any of the work that had been done.

They passed two men who were replacing diseased vines with new cuttings, and he paused to watch them. They did their work methodically and well, and he was pleased.

"*Bonjour,*" he said as both men noticed him and looked up from their work.

The two men scrambled to their feet, looking uncertain and apprehensive.

He gestured to the newly planted vines around them. "Well done, messieurs," he complimented. "We should have a good vintage from these in five or six years."

Henri, who had paused beside him, said, "This is Monsieur Armand Calvet. He will be in charge of the cuttings nursery when it is finished." He beckoned to the man on their left, who stepped forward with a slight bow.

Alexandre studied the younger man for a moment. "You look familiar to me, monsieur. Have we met before?"

"My father was in charge of the nursery under Monsieur Lucien Caillaux."

Alexandre nodded. "I remember your father from when I was a boy. He was a fine nurseryman."

"Comte de Junot," Armand spoke, using Alexandre's formal title, "my sons told me about their swimming lessons with you and how that came about. My thanks, seigneur."

"Monsieur, your sons are fine young men. They do you honor."

"*Merci.*"

The two men stared at each other for a moment, each taking the other's measure, and a feeling of mutual respect was born. Alexandre said, "Monsieur Calvet, I am interested in your opinions for the building of the nursery. Come with us to the winery and share your views."

"Gladly, monsieur." Armand put aside his shovel and, after giving his companion instructions for what to do in his absence, accompanied Alexandre and Henri.

The three men spent the afternoon debating which new varieties to cultivate, and the discussion was a long one. When evening came, Armand accepted an invitation to stay for dinner and the discussion continued.

It was well into the evening before the nurseryman departed. But it was not too late for Armand to stop at the tavern for a few glasses of wine. The other men listened as

Armand related his observations about the Comte de Junot, some shaking their heads in disbelief.

There had been plenty of speculation in the village about him during the last few months. Everyone knew of his plans to reopen the winery, a move that meant more work and prosperity for everyone.

They knew of how the Comte had saved Armand's son from drowning. Armand had related that tale months earlier, when he'd discovered the Comte was giving his sons swimming lessons.

They knew of the English girl who'd been his house-keeper and who'd gone off with the rich Englishman, leaving behind a baby. Since he'd adopted the child, it was obvious that the child must be his. But Armand's tale of how he'd sat at table with the Comte and he'd seen with his own eyes how the man adored the child astonished everyone.

"But what about his wife?" Gaspard Leclare's voice rose above the din of speculative voices. "We all knew Anne-Marie Dumond. She died after he pushed her down the stairs."

"If that's true, why would her brother come back here and become a partner in the winery? Would you live in the same house with the man who killed your sister?" Armand took a sip of wine and added, "I think Françoise was mistaken. I don't think she saw the Comte push his wife down the stairs, even though she says she did. She's old, you know. Her eyes are bad, and the light in the winery is not good. I think it was an accident."

Many nodded, willing to consider for the first time the possibility that old Françoise might have been wrong about Alexandre Dumond.

"You have done wonders in my absence," Alexandre told his brother as he poured a brandy for each of them.

"I should hope so," Jeanette interjected from her seat on the sofa, pouring a cup of tea for herself. "He's been working so hard, I've seen less of him than you have."

"She exaggerates," Henri assured when Alexandre gave him a questioning glance. "And what about you?" he asked, accepting his snifter of brandy and taking one of the two chairs before the fireplace. "Tell me about Paris."

"It was quite profitable." Alexandre sat in the opposite chair and gave Henri and Jeanette a summary of the past three months. "We will have enough cash to continue as planned. Just barely enough."

"I see." Henri grinned and turned to his wife. "No lavish parties for you, Jeanette."

She made a face at her husband. "As if I care! Tell me, Alexandre, how long will you be home?"

"Not long. A few days, perhaps." He looked at Henri. "Have the arrangements been made for London?"

"London!" Jeanette's tea cup clattered against the saucer as she put it down, interrupting any reply Henri might have made. "I thought you were going to Florence."

"I'll go to Florence later in the summer." Alexandre stared at the glass in his hand, suddenly seeming to find it a fascinating study. "I want to go to London first. It will be the Season there, and that is the time to make contacts. The annual exhibitions are held at the Royal Academy in May."

"I see." Jeanette's dark brows knitted in a worried frown. "Are you certain you want to go to London?" she asked gently.

He gave a start and rose to his feet, turning to stand before the fire. "I have no choice. If I don't go now, it will be too late."

"The arrangements have been made," Henri added. "He was invited to apply, they accepted him. If he cancels now, the Academy will never invite him again."

"Is this trip really necessary?" Jeanette stood and walked to Alexandre's side.

He stared into the fire, not looking at her. "London will be full of rich, important men who will want portraits done. It would be stupid not to go."

"Would it?" Jeanette placed a hand on his arm. "You might see her, you know."

He shook off her touch. "It doesn't signify. I have to go." He knew what Jeanette said was true. She moved in circles where women wore diamonds and bronze silk dresses. It was quite possible they would meet. He closed his eyes, not wanting to think about how much it would hurt him if they did.

"You might want to consider not taking Suzanne with you." Jeanette's voice was soft as she made the suggestion.

"No!" Alexandre seized the poker and began to stoke the fire with savage stabs. "I will not leave her behind."

"It's only for a few months."

"I don't care. She is my daughter now. I will not abandon her, not even for a day. And we will not discuss it any further," he added through clenched teeth.

Jeanette sighed and turned away. "Very well." But under her breath, she added, "I hope you know what you're doing."

May

Tess sat at her dressing table, watching as Sally packed her things for the journey to Town. There was still a great deal to do before they could depart, but she felt no inclination to stir. Lethargy and apathy were her best friends now.

She turned her head and stared dispassionately at the stunning emerald bracelet that lay in a velvet-lined box on her dressing table. Idly, she pushed up the sleeve of her dressing gown and observed that the bruises were fading. Soon they would be gone, and there would be no more excuses for remaining at Aubry Park.

He always gave her gifts afterwards, as if that could make up for the bruises. She had hoped he would go to London without her, but of course, he hadn't. He had insisted on remaining by her side until she was fully recovered from her latest "illness."

Sally bustled to and fro, setting aside some items to be packed and putting others back in their place, but Tess paid no attention when the abigail asked her preferences. She simply shrugged and said, "Pack whatever you think best."

Sally, it seemed, never left her alone for a moment. On those rare occasions when she managed to escape the abigail's vigilant supervision, a footman would appear within moments to take Sally's place at her side. She knew why, and she could not blame them. They were only following orders.

Only at night could Tess be alone. But even then there was no escape. The door was always securely locked from the outside.

Every time she ran away, every time he dragged her back, he always made sure that she was carefully watched and well guarded. But she knew that when they went to London, he would give her more freedom, if she behaved herself. Not so much because he trusted her, but because it was more difficult to confine her, given the social demands they both would face. If she were lucky, she could manage to keep a measure of that freedom when they returned to Aubry Park in July.

The door opened and a maid appeared with a tray. Tess did not glance up as the maid cleared a space on the table and placed the breakfast tray before her. It contained a pot of tea, hot buttered toast, and jam. Blackberry jam. Almost violently, she pushed at the tray. "Take it away, Nan. Please take it away!"

"Yes, my lady." The maid took the tray and departed, shaking her head sadly at Sally, who frowned with worry and disapproval at the mistress's constant lack of appetite.

"You must eat, my lady." Sally came to stand beside her chair.

"I'm not hungry." Tess put her elbows on the table and lowered her face into her trembling hands. Dark purple blackberries. Azure blue skies and brick red hills. Her daughter's green eyes. Lavender in bloom and orange kittens. Hair black as a raven's wing. All the vivid colors of Provence.

"My lady," Sally's voice pleaded with her, "you must have something to eat. The master said—"

"All right, Sally." Tess lifted her head. "Have Nan get me some fresh tea and toast, please. But no jam."

The abigail left the room to find the maid. Tess rose and walked to the window, watching the rain fall. It seemed as if the rain never stopped falling. In the distance, she could see the flowers of her newly planted garden blooming. Nigel had torn out the shrubs that had been there, allowing her to put a garden of her own design in that spot. But had taken no joy in the project. The garden was a gift from Nigel. She couldn't get excited about a gift that resulted from her husband's violence, a gift she knew would be taken away from her the next time he was angry.

She leaned closer to the window and looked down, watching the rain spatter against the flagstones below. Far, far below.

With a trembling hand, she opened the window. A damp draught of wind and a shower of rain hit her face, but she put her head through the window and studied the distance to the hard surface below. It was a long way down. If she should fall, she might be killed.

Irresistibly drawn, she leaned a little farther out the window.

You must have courage. Alexandre's words came back to her, and she froze, poised on the edge. She stared down at the ground below, thinking of Alexandre, of all he had suffered. But he had courage, the courage to endure. She bit her lip, uncertain, and the will to pitch herself forward deserted her. She yanked herself back from the window, hating herself for not having the will to die and for not having the courage to live.

"My lady!" Sally's astonished voice intruded.

She watched the abigail walk past her to the window and close it. Sally turned the latch, and Tess turned away.

She endured the remaining days at Aubry Park as she had endured all the other days before. She got through them one at a time. In the mornings, she practiced at the pianoforte or did embroidery. In the afternoons, she gave instructions to the gardeners about modifications to her garden. But late at night, when the heavy English rain drummed against her window and she was alone, Tess would close her eyes and remember the colors of Provence.

The drawing room was crowded with people. It seemed as if all the rich and fashionable of London were gathered in this one room. Although it was a flattering tribute to his success, Alexandre felt the need for some air.

He shouldered his way through the crowd, oblivious to the many pairs of speculative feminine eyes watching him, and made his way out of the room. The foyer, he was relieved to discover, was empty.

He leaned back against the wall, enjoying the solitude and the silence. Even after spending two months in Paris and nearly a month in London, he still wasn't comfortable with the constant social whirl required of him. But making agreeable conversation with rich patrons, making flattering comments to their wives, and partnering their daughters for waltzes and minuets, was tedious work. He had forgotten how grueling it could be.

But his success spoke for itself. Tonight's soiree was in his honor, the crowning achievement to his success at the Royal Academy exhibition. Even the Prince Regent, who always made an appearance at the annual event, had complimented his work. Immediately afterward, he had been inundated with commissions.

Now he worked at a breakneck pace, painting portraits of anyone who could afford him. He continually raised his fees, but each time he did, his commissions doubled. He had, he realized, become a fashion.

Alexandre was amazed at his own rapid rise to the top, but the irony of it did not escape him. His social and commercial success seemed to be fate's compensation for private failure.

"There you are."

The rich, languorous voice and the smell of subtle, expensive perfume broke into his thoughts. Alexandre opened his eyes to find his hostess before him.

Though she'd buried two husbands and was no longer in the blush of youth, Camilla Robinson was no man's idea of a dried-up widow. Beauty, style, and charm clung to her as effectively as the scarlet silk dress she wore. She could discuss the latest fashion or the latest political intrigue with equal knowledge. She and Alexandre had become great friends, and her connections made her one of his most powerful allies. "With all of London at your feet, why are you hiding in here?" she asked, laying a hand on his arm.

"I wanted some air."

"You realize it ruins my reputation as a hostess when the guest of honor feels the need for some air?" Her voice was teasing, but he sensed the concern behind it.

He straightened and gave her his arm. "My apologies, madame. We should go back before people begin to wonder exactly where we have gone. I might ruin your reputation."

Her warm laughter filled the foyer as they walked back toward the drawing room. "You're too late, I'm afraid. I've been considered a scandal for years. And you're an artist, so of course everyone makes assumptions. Still . . ." She halted and eyed the man who stopped beside her. "Since everyone already thinks we're lovers, we could live up to our reputation, you know."

The words were lightly spoken, but Alexandre knew they were not so lightly meant. He turned to her, taking her gloved hands in his. "Camilla—"

"Would it be so difficult?" Her dark eyes searched his face, and she sighed. "You could tell me about her, you know."

Startled, he dropped her hands. "Who?"

"Suzanne's mother. I'm not blind, Alexandre. You adore that child, and it doesn't take much to guess how you must have adored her mother. You were married for many years, and I can appreciate how difficult it must have been for you when she died."

He wondered now if he should have told Camilla the truth about Suzanne. Everyone had assumed that he was a widower, and that his wife's death had occurred in childbirth eight months, not three years, before. But his private life was not for public display, and he had allowed everyone to think what they liked. Given the isolated life he had led for so long, it hadn't been a difficult secret to keep. But, for a brief moment, as he looked in Camilla's eyes and felt the genuine warmth of her concern, he was tempted to reveal his secret just for the sheer relief of confiding in someone who cared. He pushed aside the impulse.

Recapturing her hands in his, he said, "Your concern touches me deeply, *mon amie.*"

"But?"

He shook his head regretfully. "I cannot."

She let go of his hands and slipped her arm through his once again. "Then we should definitely return to the party. We are neglecting our guests."

Camilla asked no more questions, and the party was declared a smashing success, but Alexandre left before it was over, returning to his rented townhouse in Curzon Street. Though the hour was late, Alexandre lit a lamp and walked down the hallway toward the nursery to look in on Suzanne. He moved quietly so as not to awaken Paul and Leonie, who had accompanied him to London.

As he entered the room, he glanced at the bed where Claude slept, but the boy did not awaken. He moved to the other side of the room. Two cribs stood there, each holding a sleeping baby. He passed Elise's crib with a quick glance and stopped before Suzanne's, staring down at the sleeping child with the fierce, protective love he always felt whenever he looked at her.

Camilla had been right. Alexandre adored his daughter. He knew, with all the objectivity a proud papa could manage, that eight-month-old Suzanne was going to become a great beauty. He reached out and tucked a fold of blanket more securely around the sleeping baby, knowing all his hard work was worth it for her sake. He was determined that she would have the best of everything life could offer, including love.

He touched a delicate wisp of golden-red hair, and a picture of hair a darker shade entered his mind. Most of the time, he refused to think of Tess, but there were frequent moments when she stole into his thoughts unexpectedly, and it took every ounce of discipline he possessed to drive her out again. Even tonight, he had found himself searching the room for a glimpse of her.

Perhaps he should have taken Camilla up on her offer. Perhaps the warmth of another woman's body would banish Tess from his mind for good. But deep down in his heart, he knew that wasn't so. Only time and work would effect a cure for what ailed him, and Alexandre suspected that a great deal of both would be required.

June

Tess pasted a smile on her face as the butler announced her name. Walking across the salon, she held out a pair of gloved hands to the stout, gray-haired Lady Wentworth.

"Tess, my dear! How good to see you." Lady Wentworth squeezed her hands briefly, then released them. "I heard you had finally arrived in Town."

"Yes, Aubry and I arrived only a few days ago. Lovely weather, isn't it?"

"Indeed, it is." Lady Wentworth indicated the other two women seated in her salon. "I believe you already know Lady Ashford."

The tall brunette in yellow silk bobbed her head slightly in acknowledgment. "Lady Aubry, how delightful to see you again."

Liar. Tess smiled, feeling the animosity from Lady Ashford's side of the room and not caring one whit. She turned as Lady Wentworth introduced the other young lady. "This is Miss Felicia Colebridge. You know, of the Shropshire Colebridges."

"Of course. How delightful to meet you." Tess gave the pretty blond a smile and accepted a cup of tea from her hostess. She took a chair.

"Miss Colebridge is a cousin of Lady Grenville," Lady Wentworth went on. "She has already been presented at

Court. Like you, Felicia was delayed in coming to London and has not yet made her debut." She gave the girl an affectionate smile. "But that will soon be remedied. Felicia will be making her debut at the Grenville ball tomorrow night."

"Really?" Tess murmured. She took a sip of tea and glanced at the girl. "It must be exciting for you."

Felicia smiled shyly and confessed, "It's not exciting. It's terrifying."

"I can imagine." Tess's responding smile to the girl was genuine.

"Really?" Lady Ashford's voice dripped sweetness. "Can you?"

Tess met the other woman's eyes. It was on the tip of her tongue to tell Lady Ashford that if she wanted to warm Nigel's bed, she was welcome to do so. But she turned her attention back to Felicia Colebridge instead. "No, actually, I can't imagine it," she confessed. "I was never presented."

"Three years ago, Lady Aubry managed to catch the most eligible bachelor of the Season without even coming to London." Lady Wentworth supplied the information to her young friend between sips of tea. "He met her when he visited his mother in Northumberland that spring. They were married a month later."

"How romantic!" Felicia exclaimed.

Tess's smile faltered. She knew it was nothing of the sort. But most people believed she and Nigel had a match made in heaven. She didn't dare imply otherwise. It had been hard enough for a mere vicar's daughter to be accepted by the *ton*. If they knew Nigel's treatment of her, they would say it was only to be expected when a man married out of his class. She didn't care what the *ton* thought, but Nigel did, and he would punish her for any scandal that came out. Nigel's punishments were extremely unpleasant. A shiver ran down her spine.

"Tess, my dear," Lady Wentworth's voice interrupted her thoughts. "We were so distressed to hear of your long illness. More tea?"

"Yes, thank you." Tess held out her cup, and gave a noncommittal reply, knowing that whatever she said would be common knowledge by the next day. "How sweet of you to be concerned."

"But are you well now? Forgive me, but you look quite pale."

"I'm fine, thank you. My time away did me a world of good."

"We heard you'd gone to France. Menton, I assume. Or Nice, perhaps?"

"Neither, actually." Tess's mind searched desperately for a change of subject. "I spent most of my time there in a small, quiet village on the coast. But enough about me. Having missed all of last Season and half of this one, I'm just dying to hear all the gossip."

That was all the encouragement Lady Wentworth needed.

By the time Tess arrived home, her head ached from the effort of making trivial conversation, and her mouth ached from smiling. Calls were a dreaded necessity. She hated them, she hated making idle chitchat, she hated the effort it took to keep up the pretense of a blissful life. What she wanted and desperately needed was a true friend in whom she could confide. But there was no one she could trust with her secrets. No one at all.

Lady Melanie Dewhurst was at the harp, a situation that demanded everyone's full attention. Alexandre listened politely, but his mind was on the girl, not the music she played. He leaned back in his chair, his glass of wine in one hand, and studied her with an artist's practiced eye, appreciating her beauty as well as noting her flaws. A careful study of her now would help enormously when he began painting her portrait on the morrow.

She was considered to be a beauty. But Alexandre had known within moments of meeting her that her lovely complexion owed more to art than to nature, her sky-blue eyes perceived little of consequence, and the words that came from her rosebud mouth were limited to three subjects: clothes, jewels, and gossip.

He cast a sideways glance at Lady Melanie's father, the Earl of Grenville. A wealthy man, George Dewhurst was also extremely influential, and had taken a fancy to Alexandre's work during the Paris exhibition several months before. He was a patron of the Royal Academy and had proved to be an important contact for Alexandre since his arrival in London.

Unaware of Alexandre's ruthless dissection of his daughter's attributes, Lord Grenville was smiling proudly at the girl. The earl would expect a flawless portrait of his daughter, and Alexandre intended to deliver exactly that. Personal taste and honest opinions had no place in portrait painting for the wealthy.

A polite smattering of applause greeted the conclusion of Melanie's performance, and most people rose from their seats to mingle about the large drawing room. Alexandre's gaze scanned the crowd, searching for one particular face. But, of course, she wasn't there.

"Comte de Junot!" Lady Grenville swept up to him, her vacuous daughter beside her. "I wanted to personally invite you to the ball my husband and I are giving tomorrow night."

"Harriet!" Grenville uttered his wife's name with a weary sigh. "Must you continually bore him with these balls and parties?"

Lady Grenville frowned at her husband. "George, we all know you prefer staying in the country with your dogs and your horses, but there are some people who enjoy those balls and parties, you know."

"You'll be bored stiff," the earl advised Alexandre.

Alexandre gave Lady Grenville his deepest bow, but his eyes were on Lady Melanie. He gave her a long, lingering glance as he straightened and didn't miss the hint of a blush that crept into her cheeks. "On the contrary," he told Lady Grenville, "I would be delighted."

Tess wore Nigel's gift to the Grenville's ball. She allowed Sally to fasten the emerald bracelet over her wrist, but she didn't give it a second glance.

She wore a ball gown of emerald green silk that was gathered just beneath her breasts to form the high waistline, but the skirt was set smoothly to flare at the hem, where a leaf design of padded silk held the skirt in a perfect bell shape. The low, square neckline and tiny, puffed sleeves displayed a generous amount of her creamy skin, but the tinges of black and blue were gone. Sally had dressed her hair quite simply, leaving it to tumble in a riot of curls to her shoulders, with an emerald clip as its only ornament.

She held out her arms, and Sally draped a long scarf of delicate lace over her wrists as the final touch.

She knew Nigel would see any flaw immediately, but she doubted even he would find anything in her appearance to criticize. She was wearing his favorite gown, his family's jewels, and the exclusive perfume he'd bought her in Paris. But she took another careful look, knowing from experience she could never assume anything with Nigel.

The door opened, and the object of her thoughts entered the room. He held it wide, a clear indication for Sally to depart, and the abigail scooted past him. He closed the door behind her.

Tess watched him in the mirror as he approached,

careful to keep her face expressionless. He placed his
hands on her shoulders and their gazes met in the glass.
"You look lovely, my dear."

The words were perfunctory, but his approval was
clear. Tess felt his gloved hands slide over her bare arms,
and she suppressed a shudder. She lowered her head,
afraid he might see her distaste in her eyes, and pulled
on her white gloves. "Thank you, my lord."

He slid one arm around her waist and reached up to
push aside the hair tumbling over her shoulder with his
free hand. The tips of his fingers caressed the curve of
her neck before he pressed a kiss there, and Tess stiffened in his embrace.

She realized her mistake immediately. Nigel lifted his
golden head from her shoulder, and his arm tightened
around her waist. A spark of anger blazed for a moment
in his eyes, hinting at the violence that always simmered
beneath his polished veneer. She held her breath, waiting to see which way his feelings would turn.

He stepped back, releasing her, and she slowly
expelled the breath she'd been holding.

He turned away. "Fix your hair. I will wait for you
downstairs."

Tess waited until the door had closed behind him
before seizing the handkerchief that lay on her dressing
table. She scrubbed her shoulder where his lips had
touched her, but she couldn't scrub away her revulsion
and fear.

She dropped the handkerchief and raised trembling
fingers to the skin that was now flushed red from the
ruthless rubbing, and a tiny sob escaped her. She closed
her eyes, remembering how different, how glorious, it
had felt when another man's lips had kissed her shoulder.

She had to stop this, she knew. Thinking of Alexandre, remembering his touch, made her come alive. She
didn't want to be alive. It hurt too much. She hadn't had

the will to jump out of the window that day at Aubry
Park, but she was dead just the same. Dead in her soul.
And that was her only protection against the pain.

24

The ballroom was ablaze with candlelight. Music and laughter filled the room as couples whirled to the rhythm of a waltz beneath the crystal chandeliers. Lord and Lady Grenville were standing near the double doors, greeting their guests as the lord of the chambers announced them.

Tess's restless gaze roamed about the room. Nigel was beside her, engaged in conversation with several of the people surrounding them, but Tess had no interest in their discussion of Queen's Race Day or the latest fashion in cravats.

She took a sip from the glass of punch in her hand. She saw Felicia Colebridge several yards away, looking both angelic and terrified, and she gave the girl an encouraging smile. Making one's come-out, she decided, must be a terrible ordeal. Trying to find a husband, always being on one's best behavior . . .

"The Comte de Junot!"

Tess was jolted out of her musings by the booming voice of the lord of the chambers. Her stomach plummeted at the sound of that name. *No.* Desperately, she tried to deny what her own ears had heard. *It can't be him. It can't.*

Thunderstruck, Tess slowly turned around, feeling the ballroom floor tilt beneath her feet as she fixed her gaze on the huge double doors located at the opposite end of the room. But her eyes only confirmed what her ears had heard.

She stared at the tall figure in the doorway, feeling both horror and hunger at the sight of him. His hair, still well past his shoulders in length, hung loose. His ruffled shirt, plain silk waistcoat, gloves, and perfectly tied cravat were snowy white, a stark contrast to the black coat and trousers he wore. The coat needed no padding to complement his wide shoulders, the tight-fitting trousers clearly outlined the powerful muscles of his legs, and the shoes needed no heels to give him height. He moved into the room with languorous grace, seemingly unaware of the stares and feminine whispers that began to filter through the room.

Tess swallowed hard, watching him greet Lord and Lady Grenville and their daughter. A scream rose in her throat, but she made no sound. She watched him bow over Lady Melanie's hand, and the image before her eyes began to swirl and fade out of focus as Alexandre took the blond girl's hand and led her to the floor where an allemande was beginning.

Tess had tried so hard to put her days in Provence behind her, she had tried so hard to forget. Fate had a cruel sense of humor to play such a joke on her.

"My dear?"

Nigel's voice cut into her thoughts, and Tess jumped. She tore her gaze from the couple on the dance floor and glanced down at the glass of punch in her trembling hand, watching the liquid slosh over the sides, staining her glove. She was coming apart, she decided, she was losing her mind. She had to get control of herself. "I feel quite ill, all of a sudden," she whispered. It was no lie, she felt sick.

She set her glass on the nearest table and moved toward the withdrawing room, desperate to be alone before she revealed her secret thoughts to the entire *ton*. Finding the withdrawing room deserted, she fell into a chair.

Her thoughts swirled in chaotic directions. What was he doing in London? He looked even more handsome than she remembered. Had he brought Suzanne with him?

Suzanne. *Dear God in heaven.* She buried her face in her hands with a helpless moan of despair.

Her one thought in leaving France had been to protect Suzanne. If Alexandre had indeed brought the baby here, and Nigel found out the truth, her efforts would be for naught. If Nigel had even the tiniest suspicion of Suzanne's true identity, he would use all his considerable influence and power to get her back. He would have Suzanne as another of his possessions.

Tess had no idea how long she remained sitting there, but the opening of the door and the sound of a voice startled her out of her reverie. "Lady Aubry?"

Tess dragged her hands from her face and looked up at the maid standing before her. "Yes?"

"Lord Aubry asked me to tell you he wishes you to return to the ballroom."

It was a command, and she knew it. Fighting down the sick feeling of dread, she rose and retraced her steps to the ballroom, pausing at the entrance to glance about.

She saw Alexandre almost immediately. He was standing amid a group of people, but it was hard not to spot him, for he stood several inches taller than most of the other men in the room.

She turned her head away and continued to search for Nigel. She located her husband standing near the refreshment table, talking to Anthony Montrose, the young Duke of Rathburn. They were surrounded by a large group of acquaintances.

Tess pressed a hand to her stomach, trying to control her quivers of trepidation as she saw Nigel glance her way and beckon to her. Resisting the impulse to scurry back into the withdrawing room and wondering how she could persuade Nigel to let her leave the ball, she squared her shoulders and lifted her chin. Schooling her features into an inscrutable mask, she made her way to Nigel's side, keeping her eyes averted from the tall, black-clad figure across the room.

Nigel took her arm, placed it over his own, and studied her face. "Are you all right, my dear? You're not ill?"

Tess knew her husband so well. She'd made him angry again. She could hear the warning beneath his solicitous words, an unspoken message that if she was ill, she'd better recover quickly. With a sinking feeling, she knew he'd never let her leave the ball early. She forced a smile to her lips. "I'm fine, my lord. It's just that this ball is such a crush, and I was feeling overwhelmed."

He nodded and turned to the handsome young gentleman beside him. "Your grace, I believe you already know my wife?"

"Indeed, I do," the duke answered, bowing over her hand. "Lady Aubry, it is a pleasure to see you again."

She gave a deep curtsy. "Your grace."

The two men resumed their conversation, and Tess turned her head, her gaze inevitably straying across the room. Between the couples that swirled across the dance floor, she could see him standing directly opposite her, leaning down to whisper something to the pretty blond girl at his side. Melanie must have answered him, for he smiled down at the young woman, and Tess's heart twisted. There had been moments when he'd smiled at her that way, moments when she'd even made him laugh, but now it seemed like a lifetime ago.

The music stopped, and as the dancing couples left the floor, fate decided to make Tess's life much worse than it already was. Alexandre chose to look up at that moment.

She could see his features harden into an expressionless mask at the sight of her. His gaze still locked with hers, he said something to Melanie.

Even from this distance, she could feel the coldness emanating from him, but she was powerless to turn away. Instead, it was he who broke their eye contact, and it took a moment for Tess to realize he was making his way around the dance floor in her direction, Melanie clinging to his arm.

Tess turned away, desperation forcing words to her lips. "Gentlemen, forgive me for interrupting this fascinating discussion." She gave her husband and the duke a melting smile. "But I feel compelled to point out that a waltz is beginning, and my husband has not yet danced with me."

Nigel stiffened, but the duke laughed. "Dance with your wife, Aubry. If I had a wife as lovely as yours, I would certainly be dancing with her, rather than discussing politics with other men."

Nigel led her to the floor. As they danced, she caught occasional glimpses of Alexandre. He and Melanie were talking to the duke, and she knew her avoidance of him would only be temporary. If so, she had paid a high price for her reprieve. She could feel the tenseness emanating from Nigel, and she knew her request for a dance had angered him.

But it probably didn't matter, she acknowledged wearily. No matter what she had done this evening, it was just an excuse for his anger. He would let the tension build and build, whether for weeks or months, until he exploded in a rage. Nigel's explosions were sporadic, and she never knew what trivial transgression would set him off. But one thing she did know. He would blame her for any punishment he might inflict. He always did.

Alexandre felt smothered by the group of people surrounding him. He listened politely as many of them complimented his work, but his gaze strayed continually to the dance floor, and he couldn't keep his mind on what they were saying. His startled senses were still trying to assimilate that Tess was here. He had known, of course, there was a chance they would meet. But he wasn't prepared for what the sight of her would do to him. He wasn't prepared for the violent combination of rage and desire that stormed within him whenever he looked at her.

The gentleman standing next to Alexandre spoke. "I understand your exhibition at the Royal Academy was quite successful. Does this mean you are doing commissions?"

"Yes." Deliberately, he turned away from the dance floor and gave all his attention to the group surrounding him.

"Comte de Junot has already received a number of commissions," Melanie informed them, touching his sleeve in a possessive manner that set his teeth on edge. "Papa has requested several portraits. So has Lord Ashford."

"Indeed?" The Duke of Rathburn eyed Alexandre thoughtfully. "I must say, it's time I had a portrait done. I've seen your work and I like it. If you promise not to make me stand in a ridiculous pose, leaning against a marble column with a laurel wreath on my head, I'll have you paint me."

Everyone laughed, aware that the current style in portrait painting demanded that the subject be made to look like a Greek god or goddess.

"I would be honored, your grace." Alexandre gave Anthony a smile, but he caught a glimpse of swirling emerald silk out of the corner of his eye and had to stop himself from turning to stare at Tess. "There will be no laurel wreaths," he told the duke. "I promise you."

Several more people came up to their group, shifting the conversation away from Alexandre for the moment. He couldn't resist the opportunity and stole another look at the dance floor, his gaze roaming over Tess. His head warned him of her deceit, even as his heart tried to deny it.

She was so thin. Her cheeks were hollow, her face was ashen beneath the layer of rouge, reminding him of the girl he'd first pulled from the weeds of his garden. She seemed to be wasting away.

His gaze moved to the blond man who held her in his arms, the same man who had been beside her at the hotel in Marseilles. Anger at her treachery and concern for her well-being warred within him, until he thought of how she had abandoned Suzanne. He savagely cast aside any feelings of concern for her welfare and turned his back on the dance floor. Being a rich Englishman's mistress must be hard work, he told himself.

The waltz ended, and Alexandre steeled himself for their meeting as the pair approached the group.

"Aubry," the duke called out, beckoning to the couple, "I know you'll want to meet this gentleman."

Disentangling himself from Melanie's grasp on his arm, Alexandre turned toward Tess and her escort. He couldn't look at her. Instead, he focused on the blond dandy in dark blue superfine beside her as Anthony performed introductions.

"Aubry, this is the Comte de Junot. You'd probably know him better by his surname of Dumond than by his title. Comte, this is the Earl of Aubry, Nigel Ridgeway."

Fighting down his emotions, Alexandre bowed smoothly. "Lord Aubry."

"Dumond!" Nigel exclaimed. "Of course! I say, it's a pleasure to meet you, sir. I admire your work enormously."

"*Merci*," he replied for perhaps the hundredth time that night.

"And this beautiful lady," the duke continued his introduction, "is Nigel's wife, Lady Aubry."

Wife? She curtseyed to him. He bowed, taking the hand she held out to him and pressing his lips to the white glove, noting how her hand shook in his grasp. He straightened slowly, striving to keep his anger and frustration in check. He succeeded, but when he looked into her eyes, he was nearly undone. Acute anguish was clear in their dark-green depths.

What did she have to agonize over? He was the one who had been left behind. He and Suzanne. He would do well to remember that.

He dropped her hand and turned away. After only a few moments, Melanie led him from Tess's group and began introducing him to members of her own set. Talk swirled around him, but all he heard was the duke's introduction ringing in his ears, over and over again. *Nigel's wife, Lady Aubry.*

As the evening wore on, Alexandre's anger became a blessed numbness. He conversed with the men on the important topics of the day. He charmed the married women and flirted carefully with the unmarried ones. He made many contacts, and he soon had enough portrait commissions for the entire Season.

He was able to get through the next several hours by always knowing exactly where she was and avoiding whatever corner of the room she happened to be in.

But he couldn't manage to avoid her for the entire evening. When he and Melanie ran into Anthony again and he asked the young duke where in London a man might practice his swordplay, a languid male voice behind him said, "Angelo's, of course."

Turning, he found himself face-to-face with the Earl of Aubry. Tess was beside her husband, looking more wan and weary than she had earlier. Concern for her once again began to gnaw at him.

"I practice at Angelo's every week," the earl told him. "It's first rate."

"Excellent." Alexandre watched as Nigel drew his wife closer to his side, and the possessive gesture brought all his anger flaring back, smashing down the barricade of numbness he'd fought so hard to build. When a waltz began to play, and Anthony offered his arm to Melanie for a turn about the floor, Alexandre seized the opportunity and bowed to Tess. "Lady Aubry, would you honor me?"

Her pale face went even whiter and he took a bitter satisfaction in that. After a moment of hesitation, she turned to her husband. "My lord?"

Nigel hesitated only a moment before he nodded and released his possessive hold on her arm. "Of course, my dear. Go ahead."

Alexandre escorted her to the floor and they began the waltz. Catching a glimpse of Nigel observing them through his quizzing glass, he felt the pain twist his insides. "So, you've become a countess, have you?" he asked through teeth clenched in a smile. "And you didn't even invite me to the wedding."

She refused to look at him, but kept her gaze fixed on the knot of his cravat. "I don't know what you mean."

"Don't you? When were the happy nuptials?"

"My . . . my husband and I have been married for three years."

"Three years?" The anger within him warred with the pain, and the battle threatened to tear him apart. "Do you mean to tell me that you were married when you came to me? You were married when I asked you to be my wife? When I took you to my bed?"

He felt her draw back, and he tightened his grip on her hand to prevent her from pulling away. "You'd best be careful, *Countess*. Leaving me in the midst of a dance would be a serious breach of etiquette, don't you think?"

"Why are you doing this?" she asked, her voice a whisper. "Please, just go away."

"Go away? When I'm having such a marvelous time?" He gazed down into her face, but she still refused to look at him. "Tell me, Lady Aubry, how does it feel to have your husband and your former lover at the same ball?" He felt her stiffen in his arms and added, "Doesn't it give you a glorious sense of power?"

She didn't answer.

Her silence and her downcast face made him even angrier. He glanced at her husband as they waltzed past him and noticed that the other man was still watching them through his quizzing glass. "Look up at me and smile. If you don't wipe that martyred expression off your face, your *husband* is definitely going to think there is something between us."

He saw her chin quiver. But his anger and his pain were in control of him now, and he couldn't regret his cruel words. He wanted her to feel something akin to what he was feeling, even though he knew it wasn't possible. "But then," he continued ruthlessly, "perhaps that's what you want. A duel at dawn. If I kill him, you become a rich widow and can have as many lovers as you please. If he kills me—"

"Don't!" she cried, still not looking at him. "Please don't do this."

"You don't want to discuss your husband? Very well. I will change the subject. Let me tell you about *my* daughter."

A tiny sound that sounded too much like a sob escaped her lips, and he felt a twinge of guilt.

Tess spoke, her voice so low, he had to bend down to catch her words. "How is Suzanne?"

The question was so hypocritical, his guilt disappeared instantly. "Why should you care?" he countered.

She lifted her chin. Her eyes were dark with such pain and fear, he almost stumbled. Her eyes again. His nemesis.

"I care," she whispered.

He tore his gaze from hers before he could become lost in it. The realization that he was so vulnerable to her expressive eyes fueled his anger. "*Mais oui!* Of course you do." He nodded in mock understanding. "Your actions over the last six months make that perfectly clear."

"Damn you!" The sudden savagery of her voice caught him up short. Her face tilted up again, but this time her eyes blazed with anger. "I had my reasons."

He had wanted her to feel what he was feeling. He had finally succeeded. It was a hollow victory. The music stopped, and he led her back to her husband's side without another word.

He remained at the ball for another hour, careful to avoid any contact with Tess or her husband. He danced with several more beautiful women, made several more contacts, and hoped he wasn't wearing his heart on his sleeve. By the time he claimed his carriage and returned to his townhouse, it was nearly four o'clock in the morning. But he had no desire for sleep. What he wanted was oblivion.

He went into the study. He stripped off his evening coat and gloves and tossed them carelessly into a corner. Not bothering to light a lamp, he poured himself a brandy by the moonlight shining through the window and sank into one of the leather chairs.

Tess was married. Tess was a countess. Tess didn't give a damn about him. She didn't even care about her own daughter, despite her words to the contrary.

For the first time since he'd danced with her, he allowed himself to think about their conversation. If

Tess had been married to Aubry for three years, why had she run away to France? Probably because her popinjay of a husband would have known he wasn't the father of her child. She must have taken a lover behind her husband's back.

He took a swallow of brandy. The liquid burned his throat, and he remembered the way Tess's touch had burned his skin. Even now, he could still recall every detail of their night together, try as he might to forget. He could still smell the fragrance of her skin, like wildflowers in bloom. He could still taste her lips, like ambrosia on his tongue. He could still feel the softness of her body beneath him, like sinking into a bed of feathers.

He drank off the rest of his brandy in one draught and poured himself another glass. Then another. He drank until visions of her disappeared from his mind and his heart was numb again. By the time he succeeded in finding the oblivion he sought, the bottle was empty.

25

The day was warm, the carriage top was down, and Hyde Park was crowded, but Tess was too preoccupied with her thoughts to take much notice. Alexandre was in London.

Every time she repeated that knowledge to herself, a cold shudder of fear ran through her. Their conversation replayed itself in her head again and again, but repetition of his words couldn't lessen the pain she'd felt at hearing them.

During her months in Provence, she'd seen many sides of Alexandre, but she'd never have imagined he could be deliberately cruel. Last night, he had shown her that he could. The fact that she was the victim of it wasn't nearly as hard to bear as the knowledge that she was also the cause.

She'd hurt him, wounded him deeply, and that realization was the worst of all.

"It's a lovely day."

Felicia's words registered somewhere in her mind, but Tess paid no attention. "Mm-hmm," she answered absently, not turning her head to the girl seated beside her in the carriage.

"I think everyone in London is in the park today."

Tess continued to stare with unseeing eyes at the other carriages clogging Rotten Row. "Mm-hmm," she said again.

"Lady Aubry?"

It wasn't until Felicia put a hand on her shoulder that Tess came back to the present. She turned to her companion with an inquiring glance.

"I don't know why you invited me to come with you today." Felicia's voice was teasing. "Something tells me your mind is elsewhere."

"What makes you think so?"

"Lady Aubry—"

"Call me Tess, please."

"Tess, we've been in this carriage for over an hour. During that time, your participation in our conversation has consisted of three mm-hmms, two oh reallys, and five or six indeeds."

Tess felt a guilty flush creep into her cheeks. "How rude of me! I'm so sorry."

Felicia's hazel eyes danced with amusement. "It's all right, really. My papa says I'm a chatterbox, and he's right. I've been talking enough for both of us."

Tess smiled. She opened her mouth to reply, but another voice interrupted as an open carriage holding four young ladies drew up beside them.

"Felicia, darling! I thought that was you." Melanie Dewhurst nodded to Tess. "Good afternoon, Lady Aubry."

"Good afternoon." Tess gave a returning nod to Melanie and her companions.

"What a crush your papa's ball was last night." Felicia leaned forward in her seat to better view the girls in the other carriage.

Melanie laughed. "Don't call it Papa's ball in front of him. He hates balls and parties and things. But Mama wanted you to have a proper debut."

"It was lovely. Aunt Caroline went to a great deal of trouble for me."

"Trouble? Rubbish! Mama simply *lives* for that sort of thing. Besides, you're her favorite niece." Melanie leaned forward over the side of the carriage. Eager curiosity was in her voice as she asked, "How many gentlemen have asked to call on you, cousin? Do tell!"

Felicia began mentioning names, and as the girls discussed the possibilities for Felicia's matrimonial future, Tess leaned back in her seat, listening with genuine interest and a hint of envy. These girls were all bosom bows and their camaraderie was something Tess had not experienced since her girlhood in Northumberland. She hadn't developed a close friendship with any woman since her marriage. Nigel didn't like it.

"Speaking of gentlemen . . ." Felicia eyed Melanie with speculative mischief. "It's your turn to confess. I demand to hear all about the Comte de Junot!"

Tess stiffened, all her senses alert.

Melanie fell back in her seat, a gloved hand to her bosom, and gave a sigh of exaggerated rapture. "Simply divine, isn't he? He's painting my portrait, you know."

"I didn't know! How could I? I haven't seen you for days and days. If Mama had allowed me to stay with you for the Season, I would know these things."

The look of pity the other girls exchanged was not lost on Tess. It was well known that Felicia's own parents didn't have the blunt to sponsor her for the Season, but they had plenty of pride and had scraped together the money for a rented town house.

"Yes," Melanie continued, smoothly covering the sudden silence. "He's doing a portrait of me. I'm dying to take a peek at it, but he won't let me. He says he never

308 LAURA LEE GUHRKE

lets anyone see a portrait until it's finished. Papa was quite upset about that."

Tess closed her eyes. She hadn't been allowed to see her portrait either until it was done. How long ago it seemed.

"I was amazed when I saw him," Felicia confessed. "He looks so . . . so formidable. Handsome, too, in a devilish sort of way."

"He's very mysterious." Melanie's small mouth curved in a secretive smile. "But I happen to know he owns a great deal of land on the southern French coast. Vineyards, I believe. He's quite wealthy, I hear."

Tess's lips twitched with a secretive smile of her own as she thought of Alexandre's crumbling castle and deserted vineyards.

"So, if he's titled and wealthy, why won't your father consider him as a match for you?" one of the other girls asked.

Melanie's eyes widened with horror. "Darling! A Frenchman? And a painter besides? Papa wouldn't hear of it!"

"I heard his painting is only a hobby," another girl commented. "But, still, he is French."

"Isn't he though?" Melanie sighed again. "When he speaks to me with that lovely accent, I simply want to die."

Tess found herself feeling that same emotion at this moment. Hearing these girls talk about Alexandre as if he were some sort of god made her want to scream.

"He's quite tall," Felicia commented. "I noticed it when I danced with him."

"He waltzes divinely," Melanie told them. "When he holds you in his arms and moves you across the floor, it feels as if you're floating on air."

All the girls, with the exception of Tess, sighed in unison at this poetic description.

"Is that really how it felt?" another girl asked.

"Definitely," Melanie assured them, adding, "Wouldn't you agree, Lady Aubry?"

All eyes turned eagerly to Tess, as if she was expected to relate in detail exactly how it had felt to be held in Alexandre Dumond's arms. She felt a moment of panic, but merely said, "He dances quite well," in a voice she was proud to note was indifferent.

All the girls looked disappointed, but Felicia said, "Tess is married to one of the handsomest men in England." All the other girls nodded in understanding agreement at that well-known fact.

Yes, Tess decided, she definitely wanted to scream.

A collective set of gasps, followed by giggles, diverted Tess from that impulse.

"There he is!" one of the girls exclaimed. "What a magnificent horse he's riding! He's coming this way. Melanie, I'm sure he's coming over to speak with you!"

Melanie did not turn around to look, but her eyes widened expectantly. "Is he? How lovely!"

"He doesn't have his daughter with him today," one of the other girls commented. "I was out riding with my mother a few days ago and saw him in his carriage. He had his daughter with him then, sitting in his lap. Can you imagine?"

Tess could imagine it. She could imagine Alexandre taking Suzanne for rides, rocking her to sleep, telling her stories. The visions filled her with a mixture of emotions. Relief, knowing she had made the right decision. Jealousy, knowing she would never have those moments with her baby. Sadness, knowing she would never see her daughter grow to womanhood.

"He adores his daughter," Melanie told them. "He takes that baby with him nearly everywhere. It's not quite the thing, you know, but it is rather quaint."

Tess longed to disappear as she turned her head and

watched Alexandre, astride a big, black stallion, approaching the carriages. Hatless, dressed in black riding costume, he truly looked the part of a centaur, seeming to blend with the stallion so man and animal were one. She looked away and plucked nervously at the reticule in her lap. She took a deep breath, steadying herself for what was to come.

"*Bonjour,* mesdemoiselles." He halted his horse on the opposite side of Melanie's carriage. One thick lock of his long ebony hair fell forward over his shoulder as he bowed his head to them in greeting. He tossed it back with a careless gesture.

"Comte de Junot!" Melanie greeted him with a pleased smile. "How delightful to see you."

"The pleasure is mine, Lady Melanie." He glanced toward Tess's carriage. "Good afternoon, Lady Felicia. Lady Aubry." His black eyes bored into her for only a moment before he turned back to the blond girl in the other carriage.

"Have you come to eavesdrop on our gossip, Comte?" Melanie inquired, coquettishly peeping up at him from beneath her lashes.

He wrapped the reins in one hand to lift the other in a gesture of regret. "Alas, *non,* although it is a tempting idea." He gave them a wicked grin and added, "Although, perhaps it is not so tempting. You might be talking about me, and eavesdroppers never hear good of themselves, *n'est-ce pas?*"

The girls laughed at that. Tess did not.

An irate male voice behind them suddenly overrode the laughter. "My dear ladies, can you please move forward? You are blocking the path!"

"Oh, what a bother!" Melanie exclaimed and rose to cast a glance at the carriage behind them.

"Ladies, my regrets, but I must be on my way. *Au revoir.*" Alexandre gave them a final wave and turned his horse around.

"Isn't he handsome!" Melanie sighed as she watched him lead the horse away at a rapid canter.

"What extraordinary hair!" one of the other girls exclaimed. "It's so out of fashion, but it suits him, does it not?"

All the other girls agreed it suited him well indeed. Tess expressed no opinion, but she wrapped her hand around the silk ribbons of her reticule, remembering the extraordinary feel of Alexandre's hair tangled within her grasp.

"Ladies, please!" the man behind them spoke again, causing both Tess and Melanie to give their drivers instructions to move forward.

"Felicia, come calling with me tomorrow," Melanie called to her cousin as her carriage began to move ahead in front of Tess's. "You too, Lady Aubry, if you like," she added.

The thought of making calls was bad enough, but the idea of running into Alexandre again was worse. She didn't think she'd be accepting Melanie Dewhurst's invitation.

Although she did not go calling with Melanie and Felicia, Tess did see Alexandre again. Over the next fortnight, she seemed to encounter him at every ball or party she attended. She managed to avoid him on each occasion, and they exchanged no words. But it seemed that every time she looked at him, he was watching her thoughtfully. From across a crowded drawing room, or separated by dancers on a ballroom floor, she could see him staring at her, she could see the questions in his eyes. They were questions she hoped he would never have the opportunity to ask her.

But Tess was afraid she would not be able to avoid him for the entire Season. Her worst fears were confirmed when an invitation arrived by post from Alexandre, requesting the honor of Lord and Lady Aubry's presence at a *conversazione* to be held at his home seven days hence. The seven days dragged by as Tess tried to find a way out of going, but Nigel would accept no excuse. He wanted to see Dumond's gallery, and he refused to go without her.

She cast a rebellious glance at her husband as the two of them entered Alexandre's luxurious townhouse in Curzon Street. It was bad enough that she'd had to hear his praises being sung by debutantes and dukes alike and that she had seen him at nearly every rout or ball she went to. It was bad enough to hear everyone talk of how the Prince Regent had lavishly praised Alexandre's work. But to be forced into attending one of his parties passed all bounds.

She knew Nigel was angry with her again. After all her indirect attempts to avoid going had failed, she had unwisely told Nigel she did not want to attend the party. His response had been a simple, "You will do what you are told." But the glitter in his eyes and the tight clench of his jaw told her that she had angered him a great deal.

The room was packed with people, but one corner of the room was more crowded than any other, and her quick glance in that direction confirmed that Alexandre was standing there, surrounded by a group of admirers. She closed her eyes and drew a deep breath. It was going to be a long and tedious evening.

Alexandre's gaze wandered over his crowded drawing room, searching for a glimpse of Tess. He hadn't really expected her to attend, but the fact that she wasn't here bothered him more than he cared to admit.

Taking a swallow from the glass of wine in his hand, he took another look about the room and stiffened. Tess and her husband were standing in the doorway.

Just the sight of Nigel Ridgeway made Alexandre angry. A vision of the man making love to Tess plagued his mind constantly, and the knowledge that Tess had married the fellow turned his blood cold.

Camilla, who stood beside him, also noticed the couple. "I see Lord and Lady Aubry have finally arrived." She leaned closer to him and murmured, "It's such a shame, you know."

"What?" Alexandre asked, his gaze moving to Tess.

"Lady Aubry. She's quite often ill. Why, last year, she was in such a decline, Aubry sent her to France for treatments of some kind. She missed all of last Season and most of this one."

He could have told Camilla that Lady Aubry had been in the pink of health last summer. He could have told her that Tess hadn't left England for anything more serious than an unwanted baby. He said nothing.

Camilla went on, "She's quite delicate, the poor dear."

Tess wasn't delicate. No, he knew the gossip Camilla had just related to him wasn't true. Tess had probably circulated that rumor herself to explain her absence. But what had she told her husband?

"You're looking quite thoughtful," Camilla commented.

"Aubry . . . interests me."

"Does he? Well, he's certainly rich enough to afford a portrait, but don't waste your time. I know he had his portrait done by Turner less than a year ago. Paid an incredible price, I understand, since Turner does so few portraits these days."

"What about his wife?"

"Lady Aubry?" Camilla paused to take a sip from her wine glass. "No, she was in France at the time."

He studied her as she stood beside Nigel, listening to the conversation going on around her. He was struck

again by how pale and thin she looked. No, she hadn't
been ill last summer, but she certainly looked it now.
There was no light in her eyes, and no life in her face.
She was an empty shell of the woman he had known.
Something was very wrong, and Alexandre wanted des-
perately to know what it was.

Excusing himself from Camilla, he moved across the
room to greet the latest arrivals.

"Comte de Junot!" Nigel exclaimed. "It is a pleasure
to see you again."

"The pleasure is mine. Lady Aubry," he greeted Tess,
lifting the hand she offered him to his lips. "I'm
delighted the two of you could come this evening."

"Wouldn't miss it," Nigel assured him, taking a glass
of wine from the tray a maid carried past. Gesturing to
the crowded room, he added, "It seems half of London
feels the same. Quite a squeeze."

Tess said nothing, but it was clear she did not share
her husband's enthusiasm.

"I understand your exhibition was a smashing success," Nigel continued. "Sorry my wife and I were unable
to attend."

"Since you missed the exhibition, would you care to
see my gallery?"

"Yes, indeed."

"Follow me." Alexandre led the way into the room on
the opposite side of the foyer.

"Did you exhibit any of these?" Nigel asked, gesturing
to the paintings that lined the walls.

"*Non,* all three of the exhibits have been retained by
the Academy."

"Indeed?" Nigel raised an eyebrow. "That's quite an
achievement, but understandable. You are quite talented."

"*Merci.*"

"I have always admired your work," Nigel told him. "I
have several of your early landscapes at my country estate

in Sussex." He gestured to a watercolor hanging on the wall. "This is extraordinary. Is this place in England?"

"No, it is a meadow near my home in Provence."

Tess had been listening to the polite conversation and compliments with gritted teeth, but mention of a Provence meadow caused her to give a start of surprise.

She stepped up beside her husband, her gaze following his to the watercolor landscape he was studying, and she stared at the painting in shock. It was the Meadow of the Fairies, the meadow where Alexandre had painted her, where he had kissed her for the first time. Her mind flew back to that hot August afternoon where they had argued over the fate of a wounded goose. She could still smell the fragrance of pine trees, she could still feel the warmth of the sun and the strength of Alexandre's arms around her.

She studied the painting closely, searching. But though her gaze raked over every inch of the painting, she couldn't find what she was looking for. There were no fairies in the meadow now.

Nigel glanced back at Alexandre, who stood several feet behind them. "I would love to add this landscape to my collection."

Tess knew she couldn't bear to have that painting in her home, to have a tangible reminder of Alexandre's kisses mocking her for the remaining days of life. Panic filled her, and she rushed into speech. "Nigel, it's a lovely painting, but I don't think it would match the decor of your library."

"Teresa, I do not recall asking for your opinion on the decor of my library." Nigel's voice was deceptively gentle, and Tess felt sick with fear. Her gaze flew to Alexandre, who was watching her thoughtfully.

He met her eyes for a moment, then he turned back to her husband. "I'm afraid this particular painting is not for sale."

"Pity." Nigel cast a covetous eye at the watercolor. "It's a fine work. I'd pay handsomely for it."

Alexandre tilted his head to one side and glanced from the painting to her. Realizing he was actually considering it, Tess drew a sharp breath, her eyes pleading with him as she waited for him to give her husband an answer.

"I'm afraid I cannot bear to part with that one," he told Nigel with a shake of his head, and Tess breathed a silent prayer of relief. "I have several others, however, that might appeal to you."

The two men began to stroll about the room, discussing the other works displayed in Alexandre's gallery. Tess did not follow. She moved a few feet, pretending vast interest in a still life of wild lavender, but her gaze continually strayed to the landscape of the meadow. Why had Alexandre refused to sell it?

Nigel continued to roam about the gallery, making favorable comments about many of the works in Alexandre's collection.

When Lord and Lady Ashford strolled into the gallery, Nigel turned to greet the pair. Tess moved back to the watercolor. When Alexandre stepped up beside her, she didn't look at him. "Why wouldn't you sell the painting to Nigel?" she asked in a low voice.

"It would be a bit inappropriate, don't you think?"

"I don't see the fairies," she whispered.

"No. They went away."

She did look at him then. He was staring at the painting, and she burned his hard, lean profile into her memory, wishing she could soften the bitter lines she saw there.

He moved to greet Lord and Lady Ashford. She watched his rigid back as he walked away, realizing again how deeply she had wounded him and knowing there was nothing she could do to change that.

*   *   *

"How dare you contradict me in public!" Nigel's backhand caught her across the cheek, and Tess reeled from the force of the blow. Her face tingled with tiny needles of pain and she saw stars. Dizzy, she clutched at the back of the upholstered chair beside her, trying to stay on her feet.

He was getting worse, she realized through the haze of pain. He never used to hit her in the face.

"How many times do I have to tell you not to contradict me?"

His fist caught her in the ribs, and she doubled over, trying to catch her breath. She should have known better than to express an opinion on that watercolor. She had seen his anger building for weeks now, and she should have been more careful this evening.

His hand locked over her arm in a bruising grip. He twisted her arm behind her, pulling it up until a cry tumbled from her lips.

"I won't stand for it, I tell you!" He hit her in the ribs once more, then shoved her away from him. She staggered, tripping over the hem of her skirt, and felt herself falling backward. Her head hit the marble fender of the fireplace, and darkness wiped out all the pain.

26

Nigel paced up and down in the drawing room of his town house, wondering what could be taking so long. When the door opened and the doctor entered the room, he whirled around to face the other man. "Well?" he demanded.

Doctor MacGregor gestured to the chairs at the opposite end of the room. "Let's sit down and discuss this."

"I don't want to discuss anything. I want to know how my wife is."

MacGregor gave him a long, level look from beneath his bushy eyebrows. Nigel bristled at the speculative accusation in the Scot's eyes. "If you don't know, doctor, simply say so, and I will find another physician."

"Your wife has a concussion." MacGregor stroked his thick beard for a moment, then asked, "Any idea how she got it?"

"She fell," Nigel answered shortly and turned to pour himself a whiskey.

"If that's Scotch whiskey you're pourin', make it two."

Nigel obliged, filling a second tumbler from the decanter in his hand.

As MacGregor took the tumbler of whiskey, he said, "She fell, hmm? There's blood on the fender of the fireplace. Hit her head there?"

Nigel drew a deep breath and took a deep swallow of whiskey. "Yes."

"There are severe bruises on her ribs. Any idea where she got those?"

Nigel ground his teeth. He wished his usual physician had been available. Dawson understood Teresa's disobedient behavior and the discipline required to keep her in line. MacGregor, obviously, did not. But Dawson was in Sussex, not in London. "I told you," he replied, meeting MacGregor's eyes again, "she fell."

"I see." The doctor set down his whiskey untouched. "Lord Aubry, your wife has a very bad concussion. She's going to need rest for the next sennight, preferably longer. But make sure she doesn't sleep too long at one time. I've given instructions to her maid."

"She will receive the best possible care."

"Good. I'll be on my way." The doctor turned toward the door, but Nigel's voice stopped him.

"May I see my wife now?"

"Yes, she's conscious. But make it brief. She needs to rest."

The two men headed for the door, but before they left the room, the doctor gripped his arm. "There must not be any husbandly visits of another nature for at least a month, if you take my meaning."

Nigel flushed beneath the doctor's hard, accusing scrutiny. "I am not a monster, sir."

"I hope not, Lord Aubry. For the sake of your wife, I hope not."

Nigel took the stairs up to his wife's room, and the doctor watched him go, worried about the woman upstairs, and helpless to do anything about it.

Tess heard the door of her bedchamber open and saw

a fuzzy blur she knew to be Nigel step into the room. Sally departed, and Nigel closed the door behind her.

Tess felt no apprehension as she watched him approach the bed. She knew that right now she had nothing to fear from him. His anger had spent itself.

Nigel sat down beside the bed and took her hand. She allowed her hand to remain limp in his, too tired to pull away. But she made no effort to conceal her expression, and she knew all the contempt she felt was in her eyes for him to see, if he would look at her. But he refused to meet her gaze.

"How are you?" he asked, staring down at her hand in his.

"I'm tired, Nigel," she mumbled, turning her face away and pulling her hand from his grasp. "I want to rest."

"I know, darling. I'll go." He stood up and moved to the door. He paused, his hand on the knob, and said, "I'm sorry."

"Of course you are. You're always sorry afterward." She made no effort to conceal the bitterness she felt.

"My dear, you bring it on yourself, you know," he chided in a gentle voice. "It wouldn't happen if you didn't make me so angry."

She knew he truly believed what he was saying. His belief that she was to blame was genuine. The first time he'd hit her, she had been too shocked to do anything but deny what had happened. The second time, she had believed his vow that it would never happen again. The third time, she'd blamed herself as much as he had.

But she didn't blame herself anymore. She knew that what he did to her was not her fault. She no longer believed his apologies and promises that it wouldn't happen again. She knew that they were only words, hollow and meaningless.

For now, he would be kind, charming, and even indulgent. He would buy her expensive gifts. But that phase would end, and the tension would begin building again until he reached the breaking point. Then tonight's episode would be repeated. It was the cycle she could expect for as long as she lived, and it was as predictable and inevitable as the tides.

It was no use. He couldn't concentrate. Alexandre tossed down the brush and left the attic room he was using as a studio. Downstairs, he ordered Paul to have the carriage brought around. If all he could think about was Tess, perhaps it was time he called upon her.

He wanted to know why she looked so different from the woman he had known. He wanted to know what caused her to seem so weary and unhappy. Why had she abandoned Suzanne? All he had were questions, and he wanted some answers. Most of all, he wanted reassurance that she was all right.

But when he handed his card to the butler at Lord Aubry's home in Grosvenor Square, he was informed that Lady Aubry was not receiving.

"I was given leave to call on her today," Alexandre lied.

The butler bowed in deference to this statement, but repeated, "I'm sorry, sir, but Lady Aubry is not receiving today."

"Why? Is she ill?"

The butler raised an eyebrow at the abrupt and indelicate question. "It is not my place to say, sir."

Alexandre took his leave, more concerned than before. Perhaps she was very ill, and Aubry simply didn't want anyone to know it. That thought increased his worry tenfold. He knew that if he was to have any peace of mind, he had get the answers to his questions. He had to talk with Tess alone. If she were ill, that would not be easy, but there had to be a way, and he was going to find it.

But during the week that followed his *conversazione*, Alexandre was kept very busy. His schedule for portraits was full for the remainder of the Season, and he was in such demand that he had been forced to hire a secretary to handle his affairs. He was no longer surprised by his artistic success. What did surprise him was the realization that he seemed to be the toast of London.

Black for daytime wear and going about without a hat were becoming popular among the young gentlemen. Tonics guaranteed to make the hair grow quickly were being sold everywhere. Young men of fashion became daring, calling young ladies they hardly knew *"chérie."* Poor Paul, who was now his valet, was harassed nightly in the pubs by other valets, who demanded to know how to tie the "Dumond cravat." There were even classes in "the Dumond style of painting" being offered at the Royal Academy. Alexandre still had a hard time figuring out how anyone could be *taught* to paint left-handed. If he stayed in London long enough, having a daughter might even become fashionable. He found it all quite amusing, but it was also ironic. A year ago, no man in his own village would cross the street to speak to him.

Despite his hectic schedule, he managed to find at least a few hours each day to spend with Suzanne. Thoughts of her mother only made his time with the baby all the more precious to him.

His evenings were spent participating in the relentless social whirl. He found himself searching the crowd for a glimpse of Tess at every party he attended, but though he encountered her husband several times, he never saw her. As the days went by, he became more and more worried. Gossip confirmed that she was ill, but Tess's "delicate constitution" seemed to be taken for a fact, and no one seemed to find her absence out of the ordinary. She wasn't his wife, and he had no right nor reason to be concerned about her. But he was, and that knowledge both frustrated and angered him.

At the Ashford rout, he realized he'd been spending the entire hour he'd been there looking for her amid the crowd. Frustrated by the entire situation, he bade goodbye to his hostess and started for home. But there was such a crush, he had to spend another hour waiting for his carriage, and there he ran into the Duke of Rathburn.

Somehow, the two men ended up at White's for cards and port and quiet, three things Alexandre had become extremely fond of lately. While waiting for a table, they encountered Lord Aubry and Lord Grenville. The four men decided to play together as soon as a table became available.

"Aubry, I heard your wife has been ill again," the duke commented. "Damned shame."

Alexandre shot Nigel a glance, searching for any worry in the other man's expression, but he saw none. Nigel merely shrugged and said, "She will recover, but I've sent her home to Aubry Park. She needs rest and quiet."

Alexandre frowned, knowing that if Nigel had sent her home, he wouldn't see her again. Just how ill was she?

"I say, Junot," Grenville spoke, intruding on his thoughts, "it's quite a coincidence seeing you tonight." He took a sip of port and gestured to his companion. "Aubry and I have just been talking about you. I've just been telling him of the splendid portrait you did of Melanie."

"It wasn't difficult," he replied. "When a woman is as beautiful as Lady Melanie, the canvas comes to life." Alexandre gave the other three men a wry smile. "Painting ugly women is much more difficult. And much less enjoyable."

The other men laughed. The duke told Nigel, "Alexandre just completed a portrait of me. Did an excellent job of it, too."

"Indeed?" Nigel nodded. "It doesn't surprise me. I have always admired your work."

"So does everyone else, it seems." Anthony's face took on an expression of long-suffering. "You wouldn't believe the ungodly hour I have to get out of bed so that we can have our daily practice at Angelo's. He's too busy painting portraits to fence at a decent hour."

The conversation shifted to fencing and other sport, but Alexandre paid little attention. Nigel's admiration of his work had given him an idea. If he wanted to talk to Tess, if he truly wanted to find out the truth, he had to go to Aubry Park, and Nigel had just handed him the perfect opportunity.

When a lull occurred in the conversation, Alexandre turned to Nigel. "Lord Aubry, I believe you once mentioned that your estate is in Sussex?"

"Yes. Near the South Downs."

"I've heard that's beautiful country. I'm interested in doing some landscapes of the English countryside, and I'm considering taking a journey down that way. Since you're familiar with that part of England and you have a fine appreciation of art, would you perhaps be willing to give me some guidance?"

Nigel's pleased smiled confirmed Alexandre's opinion of him. The man was highly susceptible to flattery. "Of course," the earl replied. "What would you like to know?"

"In your opinion, what parts of Sussex would be best for landscape painting?"

"There are several areas that are quite splendid." Nigel straightened proudly in his chair. "But, I must say, my own estate has much to recommend it."

"Sussex? Bah!" Grenville made a gesture of distaste.

"My estate at Dartmoor is much more interesting."

"That gloomy place?" Nigel grimaced. "I assure you, Junot, Aubry Park is an excellent example of the English countryside and perfect for your plans. Aubry Park would make for some fine landscapes."

This was going to be even easier than he'd first thought. "Would you mind if I did some paintings of your estate?"

"Mind? Of course not. I'd simply love it."

"Splendid. What inns thereabouts would you recommend?"

"Inns? Nonsense, my dear fellow. Stay at Aubry Park as my guest."

Alexandre suppressed a smile of triumph. "I would be delighted. But I would not want to impose upon your kindness."

"But—"

Alexandre held up his hands to stop the earl's protest. "In exchange, you must allow me to do something for you. A portrait of yourself, perhaps?"

"That isn't necessary. Besides, I just had my portrait done a year ago."

Alexandre mentally thanked Camilla Robinson for giving him that bit of information. "I must insist on repaying you in some way," he said to Nigel, then added smoothly, "A portrait of Lady Aubry, perhaps?"

Grenville spoke again. "I say, Aubry, that's a splendid idea. You must be the only fellow in London who doesn't have a Dumond of his wife. I know that when I told Caroline I'd asked him to paint her, she was delighted."

"Your wife is an acknowledged beauty," Anthony commented. "A Dumond portrait of her would be splendid."

Nigel tilted his head to one side, considering the idea. "It would be a wonderful addition to my collection," he said. "And my wife should have a new portrait done. But she has been ill." He looked at Alexandre. "When were you planning to journey to Sussex?"

"I still have several commissions here in London. One week, perhaps two."

"I'm certain Teresa will be fully recovered by then. I accept your generous gift, Junot. And may I say I am anticipating your visit to my home with tremendous pleasure."

Alexandre wished he could say the same. Despite everything that had happened, he was still in love with Tess. He wanted to see her, he wanted to talk with her, he wanted to be near her. He had the feeling what he had just arranged was the most idiotic thing he had ever done, but given the chance, he'd do it again.

27

Tess wished she could enjoy the days of freedom at Aubry Park before Nigel returned, but she found her thoughts continually straying to London and Alexandre. Soon he would leave England, and she doubted he would ever return. He would take Suzanne away, and she would never have the chance to see her daughter. Thinking of Alexandre and Suzanne only made her more unhappy, but she couldn't stop herself. Memories of them were all she had left.

Nigel's mother arrived shortly after Tess's return to Aubry Park, providing a welcome diversion. Tess was in her special garden, giving instructions to the gardeners, when a maid appeared to inform her of Margaret's arrival.

The dowager countess was sitting at one end of the sofa sipping a cup of tea when her daughter-in-law entered the drawing room. Tess's gaze roamed over the other woman with concern. Margaret always looked tired, and older than her fifty-three years.

Tess greeted her mother-in-law with affection. She

liked Margaret, even though she knew the dowager's visit would make Nigel's mood more violent when he arrived home. "Margaret, it's good to see you."

"Tess, my dear." Margaret clasped her daughter-in-law's hands warmly. "You look lovely. How was Town?"

Tess took a seat on the sofa. "Exhausting, of course. Lady Wentworth sends her regards."

"How is Caroline? I haven't seen her for years!"

Tess assured her that Caroline was fine, and proceeded to relay as much Town gossip as she could remember. When that topic was exhausted, Margaret found another. "When I arrived, Chilton told me you were out in the gardens. Something about a new flower bed. Have you taken up gardening again?"

"No, not really." Tess met her mother-in-law's gaze. "I was giving instructions to the gardeners. Nigel allowed me to put a garden of my own design near the maze, with the stipulation, of course, that I do none of the work myself. You know how he feels about that." Her smile was slightly bitter. "A countess should not be found on her knees in a flower bed. Her lily-white hands might get dirty."

Margaret set down her teacup and gave Tess a gentle smile. "Why don't we go down and walk through it?"

The two women left the drawing room, passing through the adjoining conservatory to the doors leading outside. They strolled the path down to Tess's garden in silence. Nigel's strict rules regarding his wife's conduct was a subject the two women never discussed.

When the Season ended, Nigel returned to Aubry Park, not pleased that his mother had arrived for her obligatory annual visit. He wished the dowager countess would stop feeling that it was necessary to give a yearly display of her motherly affection when they both knew it was a sham. But for the sake of appearances, he tolerated it.

He found his mother and his wife taking tea in the drawing room, and he joined them there. "Mother," he greeted and bent to place a dutiful kiss on her cheek before taking a chair on the opposite side of the room.

The two women resumed the topic they'd been discussing before his arrival, and he found that quite irritating. They were talking as if he wasn't even there. He endured this for exactly seven minutes, long enough for one cup of tea, before jumping to his feet with a scowl. "Zounds!" he shouted. "This is a warm welcome indeed! I can see that the two of you are overjoyed by my arrival."

He threw the teacup across the room. It hit the wall and shattered as he turned and left.

Tess and Margaret exchanged glances, and a look of understanding passed between them. But Nigel's violent temper was another subject the two women never discussed.

Although he had arranged to stay at Aubry Park to do the portrait of Tess, Alexandre refused to take any risks where Suzanne was concerned. He intended to spend no more than a week at Nigel's estate, just long enough to confront her and get some answers, but he could not bear to leave his daughter in London. He found an inn only a short distance from Aubry Park, and there he left the baby in Leonie and Paul's care.

When the hired carriage pulled into the wide circular drive of Nigel and Tess's country estate, Alexandre felt all his bitterness return. He'd tried to bury the hurt deep down in the unreachable recesses of his soul, but one look at Aubry Park brought it all back. The house and grounds displayed the gracious perfection only the very wealthy could maintain. He thought of the crumbling stones and dilapidated condition of his château, knowing he could have provided Tess with none of the luxuries she had here. He probably shouldn't blame her for choosing this life over the one he could have given her, but he did.

The butler took his name and showed him to the library with the assurance that the earl was expecting him. Alexandre walked down the long room, observing that there were several fine portraits on the wall. A portrait of Tess was not among them, although there was a blank space beside the fireplace where her portrait would probably be placed when he completed it. He paused to admire the fine rapiers that hung above the mantel.

He stared absently at the swords, his mind still occupied with the task ahead of him. The ramifications of his decision hit him with full force for the first time. How would he manage to paint her again without remembering the first time he'd painted her in the meadow? How would he be able to look into her expressive eyes without drowning there? But he was determined to find out the truth. He wanted Tess to face him and answer his questions. Only then would he have any peace of mind. Only then would he be able to put her behind him.

The door opened, and Alexandre turned away from the window. The sight of the earl coming toward him brought up all Alexandre's defenses, reminding him of Tess's treachery and protecting him against the hurt.

"Junot," Nigel greeted him, "it is a pleasure to see you again. A room has been prepared for you, and Chilton will have your things put there. Have you not brought your valet with you?"

"No, he is attending to some other matters for me. I will do for myself."

"As you wish." Nigel pulled out his watch and noted the time. "I have asked my wife to join us here."

"Have you decided where you would like the portrait done?" Alexandre asked, deliberately steering the conversation away from Tess.

"I think the conservatory will do nicely."

It was the middle of summer, all the gardens were in bloom, and he wanted his wife to be painted in the conservatory? Alexandre stifled the artistic protest that came to his lips. "Very well. My paints and supplies are in the carriage. Would you arrange for them to be brought in?"

"Certainly."

The door opened again, and Tess came into the room. Her steps carried her only a few feet before she caught sight of Alexandre and came to an abrupt halt, her eyes widening in horror.

He realized instantly that his arrival was a complete surprise to her. She clutched at the folds of her cream-colored skirt, looking so alarmed he felt a stab of pity. She looked so beautiful and weary it made him ache. He watched as she struggled silently for composure, and within a moment, her face was set in an expressionless mask.

"Lady Aubry." He bowed.

"Comte de Junot, this is indeed a surprise."

Nigel came to her side and took her hand in his, an action that set Alexandre's teeth on edge. "Teresa, my dear, Comte de Junot has come to Sussex to paint. He'll be staying with us for awhile."

There was a long pause before Tess finally spoke.

"How delightful." Her voice told Alexandre it was nothing of the sort, and the smile was automatic.

Alexandre studied her as Nigel continued, "He was going to stay at an inn, but I insisted he stay here as our guest. I've also arranged for him to paint your portrait while he's here."

Tess said nothing, but her eyes were dark and luminous in her pale face. He saw the pain there, and he knew it was going to be the longest week of his life.

*   *   *

Tess dressed for dinner as if in a dream. The moment Sally had finished fastening the hooks of her gown, Tess sent the abigail away so as to complete her toilette in solitude. Her hands shook as she tried to fasten the clasp of a sapphire necklace around her throat, and she wondered why Alexandre had really come here. To torment her, she was certain.

For all the months since her return to England, he had haunted her dreams. In London, she'd had to see him, she'd had to hear about him. Now, she would have to face him as he painted her. She couldn't endure it, and she was terrified that she would be unable to conceal her feelings. Nigel would find out that she and Alexandre had been lovers. She thought of what her husband would do to Alexandre, and a violent shudder rocked her body. "Go away, Alexandre. Please go away from here," she whispered to the empty room as the necklace slipped from her fingers.

The door opened. She turned and watched her husband enter the room. She had tried to act pleased by his surprise, but she'd failed. One look at his face as he crossed the room told her he was not happy with her lukewarm response. The charming, indulgent phase was over.

Hoping to distract him, she turned back to the dressing table and picked up the necklace. She pasted a smile on her face. "Nigel, I can't seem to fasten this and I've sent Sally on an errand. Would you do it for me?"

His handsome features hardened, and she knew her ploy hadn't worked. He took the necklace from her hand and tossed it onto the table. Then his hands grabbed her shoulders, and he turned her around to face him.

"I went to a great deal of trouble to persuade Junot to do this portrait. I'd have expected you to display a bit more gratitude." He shoved her back against the table. "I think you should miss dinner this evening," he told her as he walked to the door. "Perhaps an evening alone in your room will improve your peevish disposition."

The moment he was gone, she let out a sigh of relief. Nigel thought that forcing her to remain in her room was a punishment. Tess knew it was a blessing.

Alexandre ate the lavish meal before him without tasting any of it. Tess had a headache, he had been told, and would not be joining them for dinner. The dowager countess, to whom he'd been introduced earlier, ate her meal in silence, staring at her plate. Conversation between the two men was limited to Nigel talking and Alexandre making the appropriate replies.

After dinner, Nigel showed him the conservatory. Since the room was located at the southeast corner, Alexandre told the other man he would like to have the portrait sessions with Tess in the mornings when the light would be best. The time of ten o'clock was decided upon, then the two men adjourned to Nigel's library for cheroots and cognac. "I apologize for my wife," Nigel said, handing him a glass. "She wanted to join us for dinner, but I'm afraid her headaches are often quite painful."

In the six months Tess had stayed with him, he couldn't recall her having a single headache. "Pray don't worry about it," he answered. "You mentioned your wife's delicate health to me once before."

"It is unfortunate," Nigel said, taking a draw on his cheroot and leaning back in his chair to blow the smoke toward the ceiling. "It is a source of considerable inconvenience to me."

Alexandre didn't fail to notice that Tess's pain was obviously less important to her husband than his own convenience.

"You're a widower, I believe?" Nigel asked.

"Yes." Alexandre took a much-needed swallow of cognac. "I have a daughter."

"So I heard. Damned shame about your wife. Pity she couldn't give you a son."

Alexandre tightened his grip on the glass in his hand. For the rest of the evening, he had to fight back the overwhelming desire to put his fist through Nigel Ridgeway's handsome face.

When Tess entered the conservatory the following morning, the clock was just striking ten, but Alexandre was already there, waiting for her. She halted in the doorway, and he gave her a brief glance, then pointed to the opposite corner of the room.

He had chosen a trellis of potted clematis vines as the backdrop for her portrait, and Tess moved to sit in the chair he had placed there for her. She arranged the folds of her lemon-yellow silk gown around her, then clasped her hands together in her lap. Staring down at her hands, she waited with tense apprehension for him to begin.

"Look at me."

The sharp words broke the silence and caused her to lift her chin. He stood with pencil and sketchbook in hand, studying her. Their eyes met and the seconds ticked by until Tess couldn't hold his intense gaze any longer and turned her face away.

She heard his impatient sigh and the tapping of his boots on the tiled floor as he came over to her chair. He grasped her chin in his fingers and turned her head towards him, then dropped his hand and walked away. "Don't move," he said.

He studied her a moment longer, then he once again picked up his sketchbook and began to draw. She watched him, remembering all the other times she'd seen him sketch, remembering the Meadow of the Fairies and the delicious scent of meadowsweets.

She wanted to ask him about Suzanne. There were so many things she wanted to know. All the questions she longed to ask whirled around in her mind. When had Suzanne gotten her first tooth? When had she started crawling? Was she walking yet? Will you tell her about me someday? She continued to watch him draw, but the questions hovered on her lips, unspoken.

As he sketched, Alexandre didn't take time to ponder tactful ways to find out what he wanted to know. "I heard you've been ill. What's wrong?"

Startled, she held his gaze for a moment before she lowered it to stare at her hands. "I . . ." She swallowed. "I'm fine."

"Fine?" He barked out the word and saw her give a start of surprise. He tossed down his pencil and sketch-book and came to stand before her. She didn't look up. He lifted her chin and looked down into her pale, weary face. "Fine? You're thin as a stick. You jump at the slightest sound. You go to London for the Season, but after only two weeks you take to your bed. Your butler says you're not receiving but won't say why. And you tell me you're fine?"

Her eyes widened. "You paid a call on me? You came to see me?"

"Yes. I left my card. Didn't your butler tell you?"

"No." She pulled her face away. "Why did you call on me?"

"I kept hearing rumors of your 'delicate condition' and everyone in the *ton* seemed to find your illness a common occurrence. So, have you been ill? Have you seen a physician?"

"My health is not your concern," she whispered.

"Not my concern?" he repeated, his voice rising. "I—"

"Ssh!" she cut him off, glancing toward the open door

336 LAURA LEE GUHRKE

of the room with a look of alarm. "I told you, I'm fine
now," she said in a low voice, her gaze fixed on the doorway. "I'm not ill any longer. I . . . recovered."

He waited, but she said nothing more. He wanted the
truth. He gripped her chin and again forced her to look
at him. "What illness did you have? I want to know."

"Why?" she asked in a desperate whisper. "What difference would it make to you?" She raised her hands in a
gesture of despair. "Oh, why did you come here?"

He took a deep breath. "I came here because you owe
me some explanations, countess, and I want them. I
want to know why you pretended to love—"

"Don't!" she implored softly with another apprehensive glance at the door. "Please, don't. Someone will
hear."

"Who?" he asked in a low, tight voice. "Your husband? Afraid he'll find out about us? Afraid he'll find
out where you spent those months in France? How did
you explain it all to him, I wonder. I'll wager—"

"Stop!" She pressed her hands to her ears. "Oh,
please stop!" She waited a few moments and when he
remained silent, she dropped her hands and looked at
him. "Just go away," she mumbled. "Go away."

"I'm not going anywhere until I get some answers."
He looked into her eyes, and felt a twist of pain. She was
doing it again. Giving him that look that pleaded for
understanding. He couldn't handle it. With an impatient
sigh, he turned away and walked to the door. "We're finished for today."

"Alexandre?"

He halted at the sound of her voice but did not turn
around. "What?"

"How . . ." He heard a whisper of silk and saw her out
of the corner of his eye when she came to stand beside
him. She glanced out into the drawing room, then turned
to him and laid a hand on his arm. "How . . ." She

paused and he knew she was struggling with what she wanted to say to him. He waited, unmoving, not daring to look at her, and she finally spoke again. "How is Suzanne?"

He didn't answer.

"Please tell me," she whispered. "Please."

He sucked in a deep breath, the pain in her voice tearing at his heart. "Suzanne is fine."

"I know you brought her to London. Is she still there?"

"No." He closed his eyes and fought against the pull of her pain. "She is staying nearby."

"And Jeanette and Henri are well?"

"Yes." He moved to step through the doorway, wanting only to escape, but her voice stopped him again.

"And the animals? Mathilda's wing is healed?"

"Yes, she's fine. The animals are fine." Not wanting to hear any more, he left the room without a backward glance.

28

Tess was only half dressed when the first gong sounded, announcing that dinner was thirty minutes away. "Is it half-past four already? Sally, hurry. You know how Aubry hates it when I'm late."

Sally fastened the complicated tapes of Tess's willow green evening gown as quickly as she could, but it was still seven minutes later when Tess rushed down the stairs to the drawing room.

Her husband was a stickler for punctuality, and Tess was expected to be in the drawing room no later than three minutes after the first gong. But when she entered the room, Alexandre and her husband had already enjoyed their first glass of madeira, and Margaret was sipping a sherry.

"I'm sorry I'm late," she said, trying to keep her voice dignified when her protesting lungs wanted to gasp for air from her rapid dash down three flights of stairs. She walked to the table where a glass of ratafia had been poured for her, glancing at her husband as she passed. As expected, Nigel was not pleased.

"We have been waiting for you, Teresa." Nigel pulled his watch from his waistcoat pocket and opened it. He noted the time then gave her a pointed glance.

"I'm sorry, Nigel. I was unavoidably delayed."

"Your abigail again? That girl is very irresponsible. I fear we shall have to find you a new maid."

Tess bit her lip, knowing he'd sack Sally on the morrow. The girl's wages helped to support her entire family. Hoping to pacify Nigel, she said, "It wasn't Sally's fault. She'd laid out a lovely gown for me, but I decided to change." Though it galled her to say it, she added, "I wanted to wear this gown because I know how much you like it."

Nigel gave her a hard stare and did not reply. But she knew he was considering her words and deciding whether or not to let the transgression pass.

Alexandre's smooth voice broke the tense silence. "It is well worth the wait, madame, when the gown's as lovely as that one." He gave her a gallant bow and gave the other man a smile. "Your wife's beauty does you credit, Aubry."

Nigel took a sip of wine and seemed pleased by the compliment. Tess shot Alexandre a look of gratitude before turning to pick up her glass. After she had taken a seat beside Margaret on the sofa, the two men also resumed their seats.

"How is the portrait progressing, Junot?" Nigel asked.

"Very well. I should be done in a few days."

"Excellent. Perhaps tomorrow or the day after, I'll wander in and have a look at it."

"Forgive me, Lord Aubry, but I would prefer that you did not."

"What?" Nigel set down his glass and eyed Alexandre askance. "Why not?"

Alexandre gave an apologetic cough. "I never allow anyone to see a portrait until it is finished. Call it an eccentricity of mine."

Tess remembered how he had locked her portrait away in his studio so that she wouldn't be able to take a look at it. She glanced at Nigel, noticing the irritation that marred his handsome features, and she smiled. For once, Nigel was not going to have things all his own way. It was a petty revenge, but she enjoyed his irritation immensely.

Nigel let out a petulant sigh. "Very well," he conceded with a nod of agreement. "I suppose I'll simply have to wait until it's finished. Tomorrow after your session with my wife, perhaps you'd like to see the estate?"

"I should like that very much."

"Teresa." Nigel turned to her. "I believe you should make calls tomorrow. You have not done so since returning home. Mother will accompany you."

Her smile disappeared when her husband looked at her. "Certainly," she murmured, her soft voice giving no hint of the flash of rebellion she felt. Rebellion was dangerous where Nigel was concerned. She looked at Margaret, but her mother-in-law's face was devoid of expression, and no emotion flared in the faded blue eyes that met hers. Tess suddenly felt as if she were looking into a mirror, seeing an older reflection of herself. It was a disturbing realization.

The second gong sounded, announcing that dinner was served. According to custom, Alexandre gave Tess his arm to escort her into the dining room, and Nigel followed with his mother.

Alexandre cast a puzzled sideways glance at Tess as they entered the dining room. He didn't understand the mild way she acquiesced to Nigel's every whim. Instinct told him her mild behavior wasn't to please her husband, but he couldn't understand what her reasons were. He could read nothing in her expression to give him any clues. Did she love her husband or hate him?

"I think you'll enjoy our tour tomorrow," Nigel told

him as the first course of Mulligatawny soup was placed on the table.

"It's a beautiful estate," he answered politely, picking up his spoon. "I might paint some of your gardens. They're lovely."

"Thank you." Nigel looked at his wife, who was seated at the opposite end of the table. "Speaking of gardens, my dear, I took a walk through the new flower garden you had put in. I'm not certain I like the design."

Out of the corner of his eye, Alexandre saw Tess's body stiffen, and he heard her sharp intake of breath.

"What is it that you don't like about it, my lord?" Her voice was soft, but wary.

"Well, it's a bit too chaotic, don't you think?" Nigel reached for a slice of bread and the butter knife. "I mean, it's too many different kinds of flowers all thrown together with no plan or design. Really, Teresa, it looks like a peasant's cottage garden. I would prefer something more formal, more elegant."

"But—" Tess bit back whatever she was going to say, and Alexandre knew she was struggling not to disagree with her husband. "What flowers would you like?" she asked instead.

Nigel spread a thick layer of butter on his bread. "You don't need to worry about it, my dear. I've already given instructions to the gardeners, and they will take care of everything. I should never have allowed you to take on such an ambitious project. You do far too much as it is."

Alexandre looked at Tess, and his jaw tightened. Her expression was still unreadable, but there was something terrible in the rigid stillness of her form. He sensed within her a deep ache of disappointment and resignation. But more than that, he sensed her anger because he felt it, too. He was furious.

Nigel treated his wife with cold disapproval if she was a few minutes late to dinner. He belittled her ability to design a garden, or choose a picture for their library. Even if she was standing beside him, he talked to others as if she wasn't even there.

It made Alexandre angry to see her treated this way. But what made him angrier was the way she meekly sat back and tolerated it, without so much as a word of protest.

When dinner was over, he excused himself and went for a walk. He'd only been in this house for twenty-four hours and already he found the atmosphere stifling. He felt as if the tension would suffocate him.

As the sun set behind the rolling green hills, he strolled through precisely laid-out beds of Michaelmas daisies, roses, and neatly trimmed boxwood. His artist's eye took in the perfection of their symmetry, but his mind was elsewhere.

There was something very wrong about Tess's relationship with her husband. Why had she ever married that passionless dandy? Was it only for the position, the jewels, the gowns? He could hardly credit Tess with such mercenary motives.

On the other hand, he had experienced firsthand her ability to deceive. She had told him that she loved him, she had agreed to marry him. But all the while she'd already been married to another man.

He crossed the lawn toward the maze. His gaze caught the huge flower bed directly ahead, and it was so different from everything else he'd seen that he stopped walking and stared.

Tall spikes of delphinium and foxglove, fat bunches of white daisies, and graceful spires of pink yarrow were mixed with herbs and other flowers, creating a riot of color and shape. This had to be Tess's special garden.

Nigel was right about one thing. It was chaotic. But as an artist, Alexandre could see the forethought that had gone into its design. The colors and shapes blended into each other so naturally, it looked as if this garden had come about on its own, through the work of nature rather than man. It was wild, almost primitive, and he found it much more beautiful than all the precise and perfect gardens on the estate.

But Nigel was going to have it taken out. He was going to tear up Tess's special garden. Alexandre thought of the way she'd reacted to Nigel's pronouncement. She hadn't made a single protest and her face had betrayed no emotion, but he knew that beneath her surface calm, she'd been angry and upset. Yet, she had not been surprised. It was almost as if she'd known her husband wouldn't like her garden.

Did she really love that selfish prig? He could hardly believe it. She didn't look like a woman in love. She didn't even look happy.

No, every instinct he possessed told him she was not content in her marriage, but he also knew there was more to it than that. Had she run away from her husband because she was carrying another man's child, as he'd first thought? Or was it simply desperate unhappiness that had sent her running away?

She had said she'd had reasons for leaving Suzanne behind. He hadn't believed that at first. But now he was beginning to see things from a different point of view, and this new vantage point made him more worried and more angry than before. And, if he were honest with himself, he'd have to admit that the empty, lifeless look of hers scared the hell out of him.

What had been her reasons for leaving Suzanne behind? Was she ill? Why had she deceived him? He felt as if he were trying to solve a riddle and the answer was right before his eyes, but he just couldn't see it.

*　　　*　　　*

When Tess entered the conservatory the following morning, Alexandre was already there, standing by one of the windows, pencil in hand. Knowing he hadn't heard her come in, she paused in the doorway to study him. This moment of freedom to watch him unobserved was an irresistible temptation, and her hungry gaze took in every detail.

His hair was loose, and she wondered where he'd left his ribbon this time. His white shirt was immaculate, with no tears or smears of paint, and she knew that someone else was mending and ironing them now. He was sketching in the book, and she wondered how many drawings he'd added since she'd looked through that book in the meadow nearly a year ago. She watched his hand move the pencil, and she remembered how his hands had touched her with a tenderness she had never known before and would never know again. Never again would he hold her in his arms. Never again would she have the luxury of being cherished. Silently, she wrapped her arms around her ribs, as if to keep her heart from breaking. She loved him so much, and he could never be hers. She could never be his.

Sensing her presence, he turned to see her standing in the doorway. Walking away from the window, he dropped his sketchbook on the table and pointed to her chair. "Let's begin."

Tess sat in the chair, positioning her body in the same pose as the day before. But as Alexandre lifted his pencil to the canvas, he looked at her and shook his head. Walking over to her chair, he bent down and pulled at the folds of her yellow silk gown, rearranging them. Straightening, he looked down into her face.

Tess met his dark gaze, wishing she could hide what she felt. But memories of what they had once shared were impossible to forget, and having him stand so close to her was becoming impossible to ignore.

She tensed as he suddenly reached out his hand toward her.

Don't touch me, Alexandre. Don't. I can't bear it.

His fingertips brushed her cheek and lingered there. He knew he should walk away, but her skin was so soft. He ran one finger along the hollow dent of her cheek, and when she opened her mouth to protest, he brushed his finger across her lips to silence her. *Don't say it. Don't say anything.* His fingertip traced a path across the line of her jaw, and he felt the tremor that ran through her.

He had to ask his questions. But he looked into her face, and he couldn't ask them. He wanted to ask if she loved her husband, but he was afraid to hear her answer. He tilted her chin up and a bit to the side, then dropped his hand and walked away.

He continued to sketch, blocking out her shape on the canvas. "I took a walk in your garden last night," he found himself saying. "I thought it was beautiful."

"Thank you." A tiny, humorless smile touched her mouth. "Nigel obviously does not agree with you."

The bitterness in her voice tore at his heart. With an effort at concentration, he continued to sketch. "Nigel," he said with deliberate contempt, "is a fool."

He waited for her to defend her husband. But she said nothing, and her silence told him more than any words she could have spoken.

That afternoon, Nigel was forced to cancel his plan to take Alexandre on a tour of the countryside. He had to meet with his steward about estate matters. Alexandre made other plans and left the house. Tess learned from one of the grooms that he had gone riding. He'd said Suzanne was nearby, and she wondered if he'd gone to see her.

Both men returned to the house in time for dinner. It was a tense affair for her and she said very little, but neither her husband nor Alexandre seemed to notice. They discussed political issues and agriculture as if she wasn't even there. When Nigel asked Alexandre about the possibilities of wine-making in England, Alexandre seemed willing to discuss the issue, and that subject carried on through the evening meal. Tess left the two men to brandy, cigars, and grape growing and escaped to her room, where she spent the rest of the evening thinking about Alexandre and wondering about Suzanne.

The following morning, Alexandre continued to work on the sketch for her portrait. Neither of them said more than a few words, and for all the notice he took of her, he might have been sketching a bowl of fruit. Alexandre asked her no questions, and she was afraid to ask him about Suzanne.

That afternoon, she dressed in riding habit and took her mare out, grateful that Nigel no longer deemed it necessary to keep a footman or maid at her heels. She stayed close to the house, and when she saw Alexandre ride past, she followed him, careful to remain a good distance behind.

She followed him to the Bells & Motley, an inn located on the road to London, and when he went inside, she halted in the grove of trees across the road. Dismounting, she tethered her mare to a tree and sat down to wait, her gaze fixed on the inn in the distance.

By the time Alexandre reappeared, several hours had gone by. She rose to her feet, watching as he rode his horse back toward Aubry Park. Certain that this inn was where he'd left Suzanne, she longed to go inside, but she didn't dare. Someone would be sure to recognize her, and she couldn't run the risk of Nigel finding out she'd gone to an inn.

Reluctantly, she untied her horse's reins from the

branch and started to follow Alexandre back to the estate. But as she prepared to swing herself up into the saddle, she caught sight of a dark-haired woman emerging from the inn, a bundle in her arms. She knew the woman was Leonie, and the bundle she carried was either Suzanne or Elise. She once again tethered her mare. Emerging from the cover of trees and underbrush, she glanced about to make sure no one saw her and headed in the direction Leonie had taken. She followed the other woman behind the inn and through the forest to the meadow beyond.

Desperate to see her daughter, Tess quickened her steps until she was close enough to call the other woman's name. Leonie turned around and froze, a stunned expression on her face as she watched Tess approach.

Tess stared at the baby Leonie held against her shoulder. It was Suzanne. Her heart pounding, she took a step closer.

"Tess?"

Tess was still looking at her daughter. "Yes, Leonie, it's me." She watched Suzanne's head turn at the sound of her voice, and she found herself staring into a pair of round eyes as green as her own. She smiled and Suzanne smiled back before gurgling something unintelligible and jamming her tiny fist into her mouth.

But Tess's smile faded when Leonie began to step back from her, clutching the baby closer to her breast.

The two women stared at each other for a long moment. Tess watched the astonishment in Leonie's expression become hostile. She knew she wouldn't be able to get any closer to Suzanne unless she was able to soothe the other woman. "I know it must be a great shock to see me," she said in a gentle voice. "But I also know that Alexandre must have told you he was here to paint a portrait of me."

Leonie nodded. "*Oui*. The monsieur told me." She turned her head aside as Suzanne began pulling at her hair, and she shifted the baby to her opposite shoulder.

Tess reached out her hand as if to touch Suzanne, and Leonie took another step back, holding the child more tightly than before.

"I wanted to see her," Tess explained, letting her hand fall to her side. "I know you think I don't care about her, but I do."

"I don't believe you. What sort of mother are you to abandon your own baby? How could you do such a thing?"

Tess's throat clogged at Leonie's accusing words, and tears stung her eyes. For a moment, she couldn't find her voice, but she finally choked back the tears and said, "I had reasons for leaving. I don't expect you to understand, or to forgive me."

"I will not let you take Suzanne back." Leonie's black eyes snapped with determination and scorn.

"I don't want to take her back. I can't keep her, and I know that Alexandre loves her very much."

Leonie's frown deepened. "I will never forget the look on the monsieur's face when he came back from Marseilles. My Paul told him you had gone off with an Englishman in a carriage. He followed you and your lover to Marseilles. When he came back, he looked so heartbroken, I cried for him." She scowled at Tess. "Go away. Haven't you done enough to hurt him?"

Leonie tried to step around her, but she blocked the other woman's path. "Leonie, please listen to me. That man who took me away is not my lover, but my husband. I had to go with him. I had no choice."

"How could you leave Suzanne behind?"

"I had to." Tess hesitated, not wanting to say more. "I had reasons."

Leonie scowled again, unimpressed.

"I don't want to take Suzanne away from Alexandre," she said again, looking at her baby with love and longing. "I only wanted to see her."

Leonie's hostility faded somewhat, and when she spoke, her voice was gentler. "She is fine. You have seen her, and you can see there is no reason to worry about her. Now, please go away, and don't come again."

As Leonie walked past her, Tess was no longer able to hold back the pain. "I only wanted to see her," she said chokingly, watching through a blur of tears as Leonie carried Suzanne away and disappeared among the trees. Sobs racked her body as she brokenly repeated her plea to the empty air. "I only wanted to see my baby."

29

Alexandre snapped the reins across the horse's neck, quickening the stallion's pace from a canter to a gallop. The morning breeze stung his cheeks and sent his long hair flying behind him as he raced the horse through a meadow. He cleared a high shrubbery and made for the elegant estate beyond. He'd been to the inn to see Suzanne, and Leonie had told him of Tess's visit. He was angry that she'd tried to see the baby. He was bewildered by her motives. He was scared.

Maybe she was having second thoughts about having given up Suzanne. Maybe she wanted the child back. He wouldn't let her take Suzanne from him. She had no claim on the baby, he told himself as he dismounted by the stables and handed the reins to a groom. She couldn't prove anything.

By the time he had changed out of his riding costume and arrived at the conservatory to begin their session, his anger had cooled, leaving only confusion.

When he walked into the room, she was already seated, waiting for him. When he closed the door behind him, her eyes widened, but she said nothing.

"You went to see Suzanne."

"Yes."

"Don't do it again." He walked past her to the easel and picked up his pencil.

Silence reigned for the next hour, but Alexandre didn't do much sketching. He couldn't seem to look at her. He couldn't bear the unhappiness in her eyes.

"Alexandre?"

He frowned at the canvas. "What?"

"I only wanted to see her."

He tossed down the pencil. "Why?" he demanded. "Why should you want to see her? If you have any idea of trying to take her back, think again. I will not give her up."

Tess shook her head, and her body seemed to wilt. "I don't want her back."

"That doesn't surprise me."

Her chin shot up. "I know you won't believe this, but I love my daughter."

He walked over to her. Leaning down, he placed a hand on each arm of her chair. "You have a very odd way of showing it."

Tess blanched at his words and pulled back as far as the confines of the chair would allow. "Alexandre, I'm so sorry. I know I hurt you, but—"

"Who is Suzanne's real father?"

The words were so calmly voiced that for a moment she did not take in their meaning. When she did, she was so astonished, she could only stare up at him. When could finally speak, she could say only one word. "W . . . what?"

"I believe you heard my question."

"I . . ." She took a deep breath. "I heard you. But I don't know what answer you are expecting."

"The truth would be good."

"Nigel, of course," she answered, puzzled. "How could you ask me such a question?"

"I was wondering why a woman who was married and who was going to have a child would run away from her husband. And I was wondering why that woman would journey all the way to southern France to escape. It seems to me there's only one reason."

"You think I had a lover," she said slowly. "You think I left my husband because I was having another man's child and my husband would realize it?" She began to tremble, and a hysterical bubble of laughter escaped her. It was too absurd, it really was. "During the last few months, I have often wondered what you must think of me," she managed to choke out the words. "Now I know, don't I? The strange thing is, I don't blame you for thinking it."

"Why did you leave Suzanne behind, if Nigel is her father?"

"Nigel would not . . ." She paused and took another deep breath. "Nigel would not have wanted a daughter. He would not have been good to her."

"That," Alexandre answered dryly, "does not surprise me." He hunkered down in front of her. "So, you didn't take a lover?" His voice was harsh, revealing the strain he was under, and she hated herself for all the pain she'd caused him.

"Yes, I did," she admitted, turning her head away. "I did have a lover, once. B . . . but he's French, you see. And he has . . ." She swallowed hard, fighting back the tears that always seemed ready to fall. "He has the blackest eyes I've ever seen. And the m . . . most glorious hair. And he was so good to me, and I betrayed him. I . . ."

His arms came around her, and she fell off the chair into his embrace. Her hands moved up to encircle his neck as she buried her face against his ruffled shirt front. "Alexandre, I'm so sorry. I thought I was doing the right thing. I thought—"

"Hush," he murmured, brushing his lips across her temple, tightening his arms around her. "Don't say any more."

She felt so safe in his embrace. But she knew there was no safety for either of them if Nigel found out the truth. She pushed him away and rose to her feet. "I have to go." She choked out the words and moved past him to the door.

Tess left the room without another word, and he didn't try to stop her. When the door closed behind her, he breathed a deep sigh and raked a hand through his hair, knowing he would have to leave her and hoping that when the time came he would have the strength to do it.

He spent the afternoon with Nigel, touring the estate and wishing the other man would disappear so that he might enjoy it. But when they had finished, it was still quite early in the day, and he decided to spend the time with Suzanne.

He ordered a picnic from the innkeeper's wife, and when she handed it to him, he put his sketchbook and pencils inside. Cradling Suzanne in one arm and the basket in the other, he started for the back door leading out of the kitchen, when the woman's voice stopped him. "Sir?"

He turned around inquiringly. "Yes, madame?"

"If you be takin' the wee one on a picnic, you'll be needin' a blanket for her."

"*Merci.*" He straightened his arm that held the basket, and she draped the soft flannel blanket over it. "I will return it to you this afternoon."

He left the inn and made for a particularly pretty spot he'd noticed earlier in the day. He set down the basket, then unfolded the blanket with one hand and spread it

out on the grass. He laid Suzanne on the blanket, then
sat down on the ground beside her. He watched as she
immediately turned over and began crawling away. But
in her long skirts, she couldn't crawl very fast. Laughing,
he seized her before she could move out of reach, lifting
her in his arms and swinging her around.

The baby gave a squeal of delight as he tossed her
into the air and caught her again. She reached out,
catching a handful of his hair in her chubby fist and
shoving it toward her mouth.

"Ah!" he cried, disentangling his hair from her hand.
"Are you hungry, *mon enfant?*" He shook his head from
side to side, leaning his face closer to hers. "But hair is
not good to eat. *Non,* it is not good at all."

Holding the baby against his chest with one arm, he
reached into the basket and pulled out the loaf of bread
the innkeeper's wife had put there. Tearing apart the
hard crust as best he could with only one hand, he pulled
out a piece of the soft white middle. He held it out to
Suzanne, who snatched it from him, jamming it into her
mouth.

"Don't be so greedy," he admonished. "A lady would
never eat her food in such a fashion."

Unrepentant, Suzanne gurgled something to him, her
mouth still full of bread.

"What?" he asked, pretending he knew exactly what
she'd said. "You're too young to be a lady? *Parbleu!*
That's true enough." He held her away from him, making faces and watching her laugh. He tried not to see her
mother in her, but Suzanne's eyes were a deep, clear
green, and her hair was turning auburn. The resemblance was too clear for him to ignore.

He set the baby on her feet, still holding her. "I saw
you standing up just yesterday, *petite.* Why don't you try
to take a few steps?"

He held her until he felt that she no longer needed his

support, then slowly pulled his hands away. She wobbled a bit, but stayed on her feet. He moved back, watching her carefully, his hands outstretched and ready to catch her if she fell. His voice coaxed her to walk toward him. "It's only two or three steps, Suzanne. You can do this. One foot, then the other."

He watched as the baby's left foot moved clumsily forward and she took her first step. Then she took another. But the grassy ground was uneven and on her third step, she stumbled, pitching forward into his waiting hands. "*Epatant!*" he praised her. "That was splendid!"

He lifted her against his chest, patting her bottom, but an unexpected sound stilled his hand. Slowly, he turned his head in the direction of the sound.

Standing at the edge of the meadow, only about twenty yards away, was Tess. She had one fist pressed against her mouth, but he heard the second sob that escaped her. Before he could speak, or even react to her presence, he saw her brush her hand across her cheeks and whirl away to run into the shelter of the forest.

He started to rise, but she disappeared amid the trees, and he remained where he was. She'd followed them here, she'd been watching Suzanne take her first steps, and she'd been crying. He hadn't imagined the look of agony on her face or the way she'd wiped away her tears. She'd told him she loved Suzanne, but in his anger and hurt, he hadn't wanted to believe her. He believed her now.

He remembered all the cruel things he'd said to her, and he felt guilt tug at his heart. Her words came back to him. *Nigel would not have wanted a daughter. He would not have been good to her.*

He thought of Nigel's careless disregard for Tess. He thought of how unhappy she was. He could well imagine what a horrible father Nigel would be. Had that been her only reason for leaving Suzanne behind? Did she really love her husband so much that she would abandon her daughter to return to him?

Alexandre thought of how she had professed to love him. He couldn't believe she was that good a liar. And yet, he found it equally difficult to believe she would go back to a man she did not love.

Suzanne squirmed in his arms, and he put her down. He watched her protectively, but his mind was on Tess as he wondered what to do next. There was one more thing he had to know, and what she told him would determine the action he would take. Her answer would decide his destiny.

Tess had dinner in her room. She'd told Nigel she wasn't feeling well, and he hadn't insisted on her presence at the table, much to her relief. She hadn't lied to Nigel. She was sick, sick at heart, and the sight of Alexandre right now was more than she could bear.

He was such a good father. It had been both beautiful and painful to see the way he'd coaxed Suzanne to take her first steps, the way he'd been there, ready to catch her if she should fall. But she knew Alexandre would always be there for Suzanne, just as she knew she would never be.

The next morning, she went to the conservatory for their session, but she dreaded it. He had ordered her not to try to see Suzanne, and he would probably be angry with her for following him and Suzanne to the meadow. But she had seen him ride away from the house, and the temptation to follow had been irresistible.

But when she walked into the conservatory, he didn't notice her arrival. His back was to her as he mixed paint on his palette. She cleared her throat softly, alerting him to her presence, and watched as he straightened, glancing over his shoulder at her. He didn't look angry. Encouraged, she gave him a tentative smile and walked over to stand beside him. "How do you know which colors to mix if I'm not here?" she asked, curious. "Don't you need to see me in order to do that?"

Alexandre could have told her that the exact combinations of paints needed to duplicate the deep fire of her hair and the dark forests of her eyes were burned in his memory. He said nothing.

As he worked, he tried not to look at her. He didn't want to see how eight months in England had turned her creamy skin to ashen white. He didn't want to see how the insipid English weather had faded the impudent freckles on her nose. He mixed the colors from memory, knowing he couldn't paint her as she was now, as a ghost of the woman he'd once known.

"Go and sit down," he said. "We're ready to begin."

As she walked over to the chair, he picked up his palette, placing it in the crook of his right arm, then pulled a brush from the packet of them that stood on the table.

He turned to the canvas and raised the brush to lay on the first stroke. But then he glanced at her and paused, his hand poised before the canvas. What he saw filled him with dread. He was seeing her eyes as he remembered them, filled with love and desire. His mind was playing cruel tricks on him, his eyes were seeing what they wanted to see. He lowered his hand but could not turn his gaze away from hers. "Why?" he asked softly, throwing all his pride away. "Why did you leave me?"

After a long pause, she answered him. "I had to. Nigel came for me, and I had to go. He's my husband. I had no choice."

"And if you'd had a choice?"

She turned her face away. "Don't," she whispered. "Don't make me imagine choices that I never had."

"Was not telling me about your husband another choice?" He couldn't keep the angry edge out of his voice. "Or did you just happen to forget about him for those six months?"

Tess's head shot up, and she took a frantic look around. "Please, don't. Someone will hear."

He turned, setting the palette and brush on the table, then he walked toward her. "Do you love him?"

She met his questioning gaze squarely. "No. I did once." Her voice faltered, her chin lowered, and she swallowed hard before adding, "I was a stupid, foolish girl. I loved the man I thought he was."

He lifted her chin. "You don't love him," he said, feeling a sweet mixture of relief, tenderness, and triumph. "What are you going to do about it?"

"Do?" She stared up at him, her eyes filled with misery. "There's nothing I can do."

"Yes, there is. You could leave with me now, this minute."

She shook her head. "No, I can't. You know that isn't possible."

"It is possible." He knelt before her and grasped her shoulders. "We could go somewhere he'll never find us."

"No, no, no!" she cried, pulling away from his touch. She pushed back the chair and rose to her feet. "Don't you understand? He will find us. It wouldn't matter how far we went, he'd find us. He'd take me back, and I would have to go. I'm his wife."

"Petition for divorce."

"On what grounds? The courts would never grant me a divorce!"

"A separation, then."

"Nigel would have to agree, and he won't. I'm trapped. Don't you see?" Her voice broke. "I'm trapped."

"Tess, I love you. I have never stopped loving you. You don't love him. Come with me."

"I can't." She stepped back as he reached for her. "Go away, Alexandre. Take Suzanne and go. Please."

Whirling around, she raced for the door. Her voice caught on a sob as she paused in the doorway. Then she stepped out into the drawing room and disappeared.

He could have caught her, but he let her go. He knew she was right about divorce or separation. He couldn't imagine that pompous English ass granting his wife either option.

Yet, he couldn't leave as she had asked him to do. He couldn't leave her here, knowing she was trapped in a loveless marriage and miserable.

So what was left for them? A clandestine affair, carried on until they were caught? Alexandre picked up his palette and brush. He continued to work, trying to find comfort in painting the woman he loved, trying not to give in to the despair that threatened to tear him apart.

Margaret knew she was the sort of woman who faded into the background. People often forgot her presence. As a result, she had become a keen observer of life, rather than a participant. She had also developed the ability to eavesdrop on conversations without feeling guilty and without being caught.

When she heard Tess's footsteps, she slipped noiselessly out of the drawing room and into the library across the hall. She listened as the sound of Tess's footsteps on the tiled floor faded away.

With a sigh of relief, Margaret crossed the long length of the library and sank into a chair. It was inevitable, she supposed, that Tess should take a lover. Her son was not an easy man to love. He was so much like his father.

A vision of her husband came before her eyes, and Margaret shivered. He had been dead for over ten years now, but he refused to die in her memory. Even now, he had the power to make her afraid.

Father and son. So much alike. Both handsome and charming on the surface, but with the same rage seething beneath. When Nigel was a boy, she had already been able to see what he was learning from his father's example. The years had passed, she had hoped she was wrong. She had known that Nigel had fallen in love with Tess, she had hoped their marriage would change her son. None of her hopes had come to pass.

She knew that Tess was suffering the same fate she had suffered. Guilt weighed heavily on Margaret's shoulders. She should have spoken to Tess about it, tried to warn her. But she had kept silent, and Tess had been the one to suffer.

She hadn't been able to watch her own life being replayed and had withdrawn permanently to her home in Northumberland, only returning to Sussex for a dutiful visit once a year.

She buried her face in her hands, very disturbed by the conversation she had overheard and what she knew was going on between Tess and the Frenchman. Tess had evidently met him when she'd run away to France. Margaret knew her son had tried to beat Tess and that she'd shot him. Nigel thought he'd kept that a secret, but Margaret knew the truth. The truth was easy to pry out of servants if one knew how to go about it.

Tess and the Frenchman were in love. Margaret knew what would happen if Nigel found out. She had to do something before it was too late.

30

Tess was alone in her room, preparing for bed, when a soft knock sounded on her door. She glanced up as Margaret stepped into the room and closed the door behind her. "Margaret?" She stared at her mother-in-law with surprise and concern. "It's very late. Is something wrong?"

The older woman came to stand beside her. "I overheard your conversation with Comte de Junot in the conservatory," she said. "I know he wants you to go away with him."

Tess felt her face grow hot with embarrassment. She didn't know what to say.

"Go with him, Tess."

Astonished, she sank onto the edge of the bed. "What?"

"This may be your last opportunity to escape. Go now, while you have the chance."

"Go where?" Tess's question was bitter.

The older woman gave her an understanding smile and patted her cheek. "My dear, I know better than anyone in the world how you feel."

"How could you know? How could *anyone* know?"

"I know." The words were soft but spoken with conviction. "Tess, I've known you since you were a little girl. I've watched you grow up. You were such a happy child, and you grew into a lovely young woman. But I know that you are no longer happy."

Margaret sighed and sat down beside her daughter-in-law on the edge of the bed. "I have done you a great disservice," she confessed sadly. "I knew a long time ago what my son's character was. I suspected what would happen when he married, and I dreaded it. But I said nothing. I did nothing. I told myself that Nigel would change his ways when he married you. I convinced myself that he would not do to you what his father did to me."

"His father?"

The older woman nodded. "Yes, Nigel learned at his father's knee how to handle women." Tess could see Margaret's lined face grow even older and sadder as she spoke. "Nigel remembers the day his father shot my lover in a duel. So you see, my dear girl, I know exactly what you are feeling right now.

"Do you remember the first time you ran away from him?" she continued. "You came to me for help, and I had no help to give you. When Nigel came for you, I sent you back with him. God help me, I sent you back."

Her voice was filled with regret, and Tess's heart twisted with pity. "There was nothing you could have done," she whispered.

"But I can do something now." Margaret squared her shoulders, and for the first time since Tess had known her, the other woman sat straight and proud. "Go with your Frenchman," she urged, laying a hand on Tess's arm. "Have him take you as far away as you can go."

"But what about you?"

"My life was over the day Nigel's father killed my beloved John. I don't want the same fate to befall you. I

will be all right. Not even Nigel would dare to hurt me."
Her voice turned a shade bitter. "A man may beat his
wife, but no one would tolerate it if he beat his mother. I
made it clear to my son long ago that if he ever laid a
hand on me, the entire *ton* would hear of it. My own
form of protection."

"But I can't leave." Tess shook her head. "If Nigel
found out I went with Alexandre, he'd follow us. He'd
kill Alexandre. I can't let that happen."

"That is a possibility," Margaret allowed, "but if you
don't leave, Nigel will eventually kill you." Her voice was
filled with pain as she made the admission about her
son. "You know that as well as I do, Tess. If you don't
leave now, you may never have another chance. I know I
never did." The older woman rose to her feet. "Go with
Junot while you still can."

Tess lifted her hands in a gesture of despair. "I can't
risk Alexandre's life. I can't."

Margaret sighed and shook her head. Turning away,
she left the room, closing the door behind her.

The following morning, Alexandre was waiting for
Tess in the conservatory, but when the clock struck ten,
it wasn't Tess who entered the room. It was Margaret.

"Madame?" He watched, puzzled, as the woman
glanced around to make certain they were alone before
closing the door behind her. "Where is Tess?"

Margaret walked over to him. "Tess will not be coming down this morning," she said in a very low voice.
"She asked me to tell you to go away and forget her."
Taking another fearful glance about the room, Margaret
whispered, "I happened to overhear the suggestions you
made to my daughter-in-law yesterday." Alexandre
started to interrupt, but she held up one hand to halt his
words. "I urged her to go with you, but she refused.

She's afraid that if Nigel found out, he would follow. She's afraid my son would kill you."

She studied him thoughtfully for a moment. "What sort of man are you, Junot? Do you have courage?"

Alexandre frowned at the odd question. But she seemed to want an answer, and he nodded.

"Good," she said. "Because if you take Tess with you, you will need it. My daughter-in-law could very well be right. Nigel *will* follow you, and he might kill you. Are you willing to take that risk?"

"Yes," he said without hesitation.

"Very well. There's a deserted gamekeeper's cottage about two miles east of here, in the forest just beyond the meadow. The road to London is just past it and there's an inn there. Do you know the place I mean?"

That meadow was where he had taken Suzanne on a picnic. He nodded again.

"Be there at two o'clock this afternoon. Nigel has an appointment then. I will get Tess to the cottage. It is up to you to persuade her to go with you."

Alexandre studied the woman's face carefully, but he saw no deception there. Nonetheless, he was wary. "Why are you doing this? Aubry is your son."

Margaret sighed. "I know," she whispered in a voice filled with pain. "God help me, I know."

Alexandre found the cottage, a tiny structure of stone nestled within a grove of trees. He saw a horse tethered to a tree nearby and knew Tess had already arrived. He tied his horse beside hers and entered the cottage.

The one room of the tiny house was thick with dust and contained only a cot, two rickety chairs and a footstool. At the sight of him, Tess jumped up from one of the chairs. "Alexandre!" she gasped, staring at him in astonishment. "What are you doing here?"

He closed the door behind him. "Margaret told me to come here."

"What?" Tess rocked back on her heels, her expression one of alarm and dismay. "Oh, no! She told me to meet her here. She arranged this?"

"Yes." He studied her face tenderly, and he saw fear in her eyes.

She glanced at the cottage's one window. "Did anyone see you? Follow you?"

He shook his head. "I don't think so."

She sank back into the chair. He saw her clasp her hands together in her lap to stop their trembling. Head bent, she stared at her hands. "Why? Why did you come here? Did she tell you to meet her here as she told me?"

"No." He walked over to the cottage's one window and stared out at the trees. She looked up, gazing at his profile as he stared out the window, loving him so much, yet knowing she had to make him leave. Knowing that when he was gone, she would have nothing left but memories.

He turned from the window and looked at her. "She wants me to take you away from here."

"I can't," Tess whispered. "I can't go with you. He'll find us. He'll kill you."

Alexandre walked over to her. He reached out and grasped her trembling hands then pulled her to her feet. "*Non, petite,*" he said, cupping her face in his palm. He brushed his thumb against her cheek. "He will not kill me. I have too much to live for."

She shook her head violently. "You don't understand!" she cried. "He'll hunt us down, no matter where we run, he'll find us. And when he does, he'll kill you. I can't let that happen." She gave a sob of despair and buried her face against his chest as he pulled her close. "I can't let that happen to you."

He wrapped his arms around her and held her until

the trembling in her body stopped. Then he pulled back and looked into her eyes. "Just tell me one thing," he said. "Do you love me?"

She didn't answer but turned her face away.

He grasped her chin, lifting her face. He bent his head and kissed her cheek, capturing a solitary tear. "Do you love me?" he repeated his question, moving his lips to brush them lightly over hers as his arms tightened around her once again.

The heat of his body against hers began the slow thaw of her frozen spirit. Her lips parted against his and he deepened the kiss as another sob escaped her. She clung to him fiercely, afraid he would disappear like the image of him that haunted her dreams.

He tore his lips from hers and trailed kisses along her jaw to her ear. He slid his hands down her spine, caressing her with the same gentle strength she remembered, arousing all the need and desire that had lain dormant within her for so long.

He nibbled her earlobe. "You love me," he murmured, his warm breath against her ear sending shivers through her. "Say it."

She opened her mouth, but the only sound that escaped her was a soft moan. His hands moved across her ribcage and upward to caress her breasts. Through the layers of her clothing, she could feel the heat of his hands burning her.

"Say it, Tess. Admit it. You love me."

This was madness, but she was powerless to stop it. When she felt his hands undoing the front closures of her riding habit, she reached up and pulled at ends of his silk cravat, untying the knot. Both of them sank to their knees. Their movements were frantic, hurried, as clothes and barriers were stripped away.

He pulled her chemise over her head and tossed it aside. Then she felt him ease her backward until she was stretched out on the dusty floor. He cupped her breasts in his hands and her back arched as she offered herself to him. When he lowered his head to kiss her there, she cried out his name, her hands tangling in his hair, pulling him closer.

When he entered her, she couldn't stop herself from giving him the words he wanted. They tumbled out between her soft cries. "I love you, I love you. Yes, I love you!"

"My solicitor will have the agreements drawn up and sent to you within the week." Nigel rose to his feet, and the man seated across the desk from him also stood up. The two men shook hands, and Nigel escorted his new business partner to the door of the library, where Chilton was waiting to show him out.

Nigel let out a triumphant laugh the moment the other man was gone. This new venture was going to be quite profitable, and he was very pleased.

Checking his watch, he realized the appointment had ended much earlier than he had anticipated, and he decided he would spend the time until dinner with Teresa. Perhaps he would make another attempt to teach her how to play chess. He'd tried once about two years before and she'd been hopeless at the game, but perhaps he simply needed to have more patience with her. She was a woman, after all.

"Chilton?" he called through the open door of the library, and within moments the butler appeared.

"Yes, my lord?"

"Where is Lady Aubry this afternoon?"

"She took her mare out for a ride about an hour ago, sir. She said she would return by four o'clock."

He frowned, but dismissed the butler with a nod. He knew how much Teresa loved riding, and he'd been willing to indulge her in that regard. He knew she went riding nearly every afternoon. But now, when he had some free time and was willing to spend it with her, she was unavailable. He would have to have a talk with her about that. He really didn't like her spending so much time away from the house.

He glanced at the empty space on the wall where Dumond's portrait of his wife would soon be placed. He was certain the portrait would be an excellent one, and he wished he could have a look at it, but he had promised the Frenchman that he wouldn't look at the work until it was finished.

Nigel frowned again. He wanted to see that painting. Well, why shouldn't he have a look at it? It was his wife, after all, and this was his house. He had the right to see how the portrait was progressing.

He left the library and walked through the drawing room to the conservatory. Crossing the room, he stepped in front of the easel by the window where the portrait stood.

He stared at the canvas in complete astonishment. Her cheeks were flushed a delicate pink, her lips were curved in a dreamy smile, and her eyes sparkled with life and fire. Her expression was familiar to him, though he hadn't seen her look at him that way since their wedding. She looked as beautiful in this painting as she had looked that day.

She looked like a woman in love.

The realization hit him like a bolt of lightning, and his body burned with the raging fire of jealousy. That look on her face was not meant for him, but for another man, and he knew who the man was. Dumond.

He'd come here to paint her portrait, and he had become her lover. That was why Teresa had gone riding this afternoon and why Dumond was also away from the house. They were probably together at this very minute, making love and laughing at him for being the cuckolded husband. Here, at Aubry Park!

But had their trysts begun here?

Another thought struck him, and Nigel staggered back as if from a physical blow. Dumond came from the south of France.

Turning away from the easel, he caught sight of a sketchbook on the table. Seizing it, he began to flip through the pages. His hand stilled at a sketch midway through the book, and he stared at it in shock. It was a drawing of Tess's face. The date penciled into the top right corner was July, 1818. One year ago. It was true.

When she'd told him about how she had been living in France, he had reluctantly believed her tale of being a governess. He had wanted to believe her. Now he knew her explanations were a pack of lies. She hadn't been a nursery governess at all. She'd been living in sin with that damned French painter when he'd found her in that village on the Côte d'Azur. Dumond had been the one to give her the clothes on her back and the money to buy more.

Visions of his wife making love with the Frenchman in some remote Provence villa flashed through his mind, and the fire inside him burned out of control. With a savage cry of pain and rage, he threw the book across the room and struck out at other evidence of his wife's infidelity. Painting and easel crashed to the floor. That unfaithful, lying bitch!

Bending down, he seized the easel and began ripping the frame apart, throwing the long wooden pieces in all directions. One hit the wall. Another hit a priceless Oriental vase, sending it to the tiled floor with a crash. The third he used to smash anything within reach.

He vented his rage until the conservatory was in shambles. He paused, drawing in great gulps of air, and he looked about him, but there was nothing left to destroy, nothing left to feel his wrath.

Tossing the battered piece of Alexandre's easel aside, Nigel left the conservatory. The servants who were gathered outside the door parted like the waters of the Red Sea to let him through, their faces full of fear and dismay. He ignored them and passed through the drawing room without a word. He crossed the hall into the library and went to his desk. Opening a drawer, he removed a pistol and loaded it. But he wasn't planning to fight a duel. He put the pistol in his coat pocket, then left the house and went to the stables.

A groom confirmed that Lady Aubry had gone riding and indicated the direction she had taken. When he asked the groom if the Comte de Junot had also taken a horse out, the boy replied in the affirmative. He had gone the same way as Lady Aubry but had left about twenty minutes later.

"Of course," Nigel muttered, swinging up onto the horse the groom had brought out for him. "They wouldn't dare be seen riding out together."

As he rode away from the house, he began to plan his wife's punishment.

Tess sighed contentedly and ran her hands lovingly up and down Alexandre's back. His skin felt warm and smooth beneath her fingers, and the weight of his body covering hers felt so safe, so right. She turned her head, pressing a kiss into his shoulder.

He pulled back, resting his weight on his arms as he looked down into her face. "I love you," he said, and leaned down until his lips were an inch from hers. "I have never stopped loving you."

His mouth moved over hers for a quick kiss before he rolled away from her.

The interior of the stone cottage was cool, and she shivered suddenly. Without the warmth of Alexandre's body to shield her, sanity returned like a shower of icy water. Dear God, what had they done?

She sat up. Alexandre saw her movement out of the corner of his eye and rolled onto his side, watching her reach for her chemise.

She was so lovely. He lifted his free hand to touch her soft skin, but he noticed something odd, and his hand stilled in midair. There were two large marks on her ribs. He frowned and reached out to touch them lightly with his fingertips. "What happened?" he asked her. "These look like bruises."

She froze for an instant then pushed his hand away and pulled her chemise over her head. "I fell," she mumbled, covering the marks with white linen.

She was lying. He looked into her face, and he knew. Disbelief filled him at the thought that entered his mind. He yanked the chemise back up, ignoring her protesting hand, and he studied the purple and yellow marks against her skin. These weren't the result of a fall. He'd been in enough fights to know these bruises had come from a fist.

"He hit you." Even as he said it, he could hardly believe it. And yet, he knew it was true. The way she jumped at an unexpected sound, the way she flinched at an angry voice, the protective way she'd held up her arm that day in his garden, her unexplained "illnesses," all confirmed where her bruises had come from.

Rage swept through him, consumed him, threatened to burn him alive. Nigel had hit her, he had beaten her, and Alexandre knew this wasn't the first time. He looked into her downcast face. "He did this, didn't he?"

"Yes."

The admission was a whisper, a soft sigh of pain and despair. Never before had Alexandre felt the urge to kill. He felt it now. He pulled down the chemise to cover her, his hand shaking with the fury he felt. He lifted her chin and looked into her eyes. "He never will again."

Alexandre reached for his trousers and rose to his feet. "I want you to get dressed. Then I want you to take your horse and go to the inn. Wait for me there."

"What are you going to do?"

He didn't answer. He yanked on his trousers and bent down to retrieve his shirt.

"Alexandre?" Her voice rose with fear.

He pulled on his shirt and fastened the buttons. "You told me you love me. Do you?"

"Yes."

"Then trust me."

He gave her a gentle smile, and she knew what he was planning. "No!" she cried out and jumped to her feet. "You don't know him as I do! Even if you challenged him to a duel, it wouldn't be a fair fight because he'd do anything to win. He'd kill you." She gave a soft sob and held out her arms in a pleading gesture. "Oh, Alexandre, I couldn't bear it if anything happened to you!"

"Nothing is going to happen to me." He pulled her to him and gave her a quick hard kiss. "Trust me, *petite.*"

Nigel saw the cottage at the edge of the meadow and the horses tied to a nearby tree. So this was their little meeting place. As if to confirm that thought, the door of the cottage opened. Tess emerged first, followed by the Frenchman. Jealous rage coursed through him. He pulled the pistol from his pocket and quickened the stallion's pace to a gallop. Gun in hand, he raced across the meadow as he watched the pair mount their horses.

By the time he was close enough to fire a shot, his wife and the Frenchman had taken off in separate directions. He halted his horse, and lifted his arm, aiming for Junot. He cocked the pistol and fired.

Tess heard the shot and glanced over her shoulder in time to see Alexandre's horse rear up, tossing him.

"Alexandre!" she cried and yanked hard on the reins to turn her mare around.

Alexandre lay on the ground, unmoving, as his frightened horse galloped away. Her heart in her throat, she stared at Alexandre's motionless body through a haze of shock, even as Nigel turned his roan stallion in her direction. She heard the pounding of horse's hooves and turned her head to see her husband toss aside the pistol in his hand as he rode toward her.

Sick with fear, she kicked her mare into motion. She had to get to Alexandre. But Nigel's stallion was faster than her mare. He came parallel with her when she was still some distance from the cottage. Reaching out, he grabbed her horse's reins close to the bit and brought both their horses to a stop. He yanked her reins from her hands.

She started to dismount, but Nigel was too quick. He leaned toward her, wrapped an arm around her waist, and pulled her from her horse. She landed hard across the front of his saddle.

"Out for a ride, my dear?" he asked, his breath hot in her ear.

She struggled, but his arm was like a steel band around her. She glanced at Alexandre, who still lay unmoving where he had fallen some thirty yards away. "You shot him."

"Your lover was trespassing on my land. At least, that is what I will tell the authorities when they come for his body." He loosened his hold on her, but when she began to struggle, trying to get down, his arm tightened, squeezing her until she couldn't breathe. "If you move an inch, I'll break your neck. Is that clear?"

She turned her head. Looking into his eyes, she saw the danger. He meant what he said. Resistance was futile.

She glanced again at Alexandre's body. He was so white, so still. He must be dead. Her shoulders slumped in defeat. Nothing mattered anymore.

"Teresa, you and I are going back to the estate." Keeping his arm tight around her, Nigel used his free hand to fasten the reins of her horse to his saddle. "There is no point in trying to escape me. So, try for once to be an obedient wife."

He turned his stallion in the direction of the estate, leading her mare behind him. As they rode back across the meadow, she cast a desperate glance back at Alexandre's motionless body, and she was too heartsick to care that Nigel was probably going to kill her, too.

31

When they came to the stable and dismounted, Nigel grabbed her arm. He dragged her toward the house.

He paused in the front hall and released his hold. But she didn't try to run. She turned and faced him calmly. "What are you going to do, Nigel?" she asked. "Punish me? Beat me?"

"Don't you think you deserve it?" he shouted. "You lying, unfaithful bitch! How many lovers have there been, Teresa?"

She said nothing.

"How many? One? Two? A dozen?" She remained silent, and he lifted his hand to strike her. But a voice from the doorway into the library stopped him.

"Nigel, no!" Margaret stepped forward.

"Stay out of this, Mother. This is not your concern."

He glanced toward the stairs, where several servants had come down in response to his raised voice. "What are you looking at?" he snarled at them. "Get out!"

Chilton and the two maids on the stairs scurried back up like frightened mice.

376 LAURA LEE GUHRKE

He turned back to Tess. "How long did you think you could carry on your love affair with that Frog before I found out?" he demanded. "Or were you planning to run away with him?"

"Yes," she confessed. "I was leaving you."

His smile was a sneer. "Really, Teresa, don't you ever tire of this little game we play? You run away, I bring you back. How often do we have to play it before you understand? I will not let you leave me. Not now, not ever. You are my wife."

Tess took a deep, steadying breath. What he said was true, of course. But it didn't matter anymore. "Then you might just as well kill me."

He laughed, a harsh sound in the quiet hall. "Kill you?" He walked toward her, and she squared her shoulders. He came to a halt in front of her and cupped her chin in his hand. He shook his head slowly. "Oh, no. I will not even let you leave me that way. You are mine. And I never relinquish what is mine."

She felt his hand move across her jaw in a caress of possession and she jerked her chin away. She took two steps back. "Then I will kill myself."

She turned as if to go, but with a cry of rage, he caught her wrist. "No! I will not let you do this to me!" He tightened his grip and dragged her toward the library.

"Nigel, stop!" Margaret cried, trying to block his path. "Don't do this."

But Nigel struck out at her with his free hand, pushing his mother aside. "This is not your affair," he told her. "Don't interfere, or by God, you'll regret it."

He yanked Tess hard, pulling her toward the library. "I will never let you cuckold me again," he raged. "I shot your French lover, and if you ever take a lover again, I'll kill him, too!"

At the mention of Alexandre, the shield of shock surrounding Tess fell away. She struggled, she struck out at

Nigel with her fist, she tried to free herself from his grasp. But he did not loosen his hold until they were in the library. He threw her from him and as she tried to regain her balance, he slammed the doors behind them. He slid the bolt across, and it locked into place with a click.

"Are you going to beat me again, Nigel?" Tess asked him in a low, tight voice as he turned to face her. His eyes were blazing with rage, and she took a step backward, but she wasn't afraid. "You say you love me, but all you do is hurt me." He advanced and she retreated down the long length of the room. "Your so-called love for me is sick, Nigel, sick and twisted. It always was."

"You bitch!" he shouted at her. "If I beat you, it's no more than you deserve. Taking a lover behind my back!"

"Yes, that is the lowest blow of all, isn't it Nigel?" she taunted. "I took a lover. It will haunt you forever. Always, you'll picture me in another man's arms, and you'll wonder if he was a better lover than you." She retreated another step, watching him move forward. "But you don't need to wonder about it. I'll tell you the truth. He was."

Nigel lunged for her, but she was out of reach. "I love him, and he wanted to take me away," she said, her words coming faster now. "I wasn't going to go with him because I was afraid you would follow us. I was afraid you would hurt him. And you did. He was unarmed, and you shot him. You wouldn't have fought him in an honorable way because you are afraid of him, aren't you, Nigel? It's easier to fight me. You can overpower me."

She smiled at him as she took another step back, taunting him, daring him to do what she knew he was going to do anyway. "Do you know what you are, Nigel?" She hit the desk and came to a stop. "You're a coward."

With a cry of pure rage, he struck out at her. She closed her eyes and tried to remember the colors of Provence.

*   *   *

Alexandre sat up with a groan, pressing his hands to his throbbing head. He tried to stand, but it took him a few moments before the waves of dizziness passed and he could get to his feet. He blinked until his vision focused and his mind cleared.

He'd heard a shot, and his horse had reared, throwing him. He glanced at the ground and saw a smear of red on the rock near his feet. He touched the back of his head and winced. His fingers came away sticky with a bit of blood. He must have hit his head, and the blow knocked him unconscious. He wondered how long he'd been out and looked about him. Tess. Where was Tess?

Nigel must have taken her. He must have found out about the two of them. He'd fired that shot. The coward had not had the courage to face him, but had shot him when he was unarmed. Only *le bon Dieu* knew what Nigel was doing to Tess at this minute.

He shook his head, but the dizziness was gone. Taking a deep breath, he broke into a run and headed across the meadow toward Aubry Park.

What if he were too late? The question haunted him as he ran, quickening him to an even faster pace. He remembered how terrified Tess had been when she'd first come to live in his home. He had thought she was afraid of him. But that assumption had been wrong. She was afraid of her husband.

When he reached Aubry Park, he gave himself only a few moments to catch his breath before he entered the house.

As he came into the entrance hall, he heard a woman's frantic voice and a man's enraged one. He raced across the hall in the direction of the voices. Turning a corner, he could see Margaret outside the double doors of the library, pounding on the wood, screaming, "Stop, stop! Nigel, don't do this. Please!"

Through the doors, he could hear Nigel raging and cursing. He couldn't hear Tess's voice, and he went cold. His fear for her safety and his wrath at her husband fused within him to an icy calm. He stepped up to the door.

Margaret turned, sagging with relief at the sight of him. "Comte de Junot! You've got to stop him. He's going to kill her!"

"Stand away," he ordered, and when Margaret stepped aside, he slammed the heel of his boot against the lock. The bolt splintered from the wood and the doors gave way, swinging wide and hitting the walls on either side.

At the other end of the long room, Nigel whirled about at the sound of the doors crashing open, revealing Tess to Alexandre's gaze. She was on her knees, her arms curved protectively over her head to ward off her husband's blows. Alexandre looked back at Nigel. He was, he decided, going to destroy this English bastard.

Nigel's face was twisted with rage. "Get out, Junot! This is not your affair."

Alexandre strode forward.

"Leave at once!" Nigel shouted. "You have no right to interfere in how I discipline my wife."

Alexandre spoke to Tess. "Move out of the way, *petite.*"

Nigel reached for his wife as she struggled to her feet. But Alexandre was prepared for that, and he lunged forward, catching a handful of the other man's ruffled shirt and yanking him away from Tess before he could use her as a shield. Bending his arm back, he did what he'd been itching to do ever since he'd met the man. He slammed his fist into Nigel's face. He followed it with a blow to the ribs, and Nigel doubled over with a scream of pain and fury.

"How does it feel, Aubry?" he taunted, landing another blow to Nigel's ribs, savoring the way the other man's body jerked in response. "How does it feel to get a taste of your own *discipline?*"

Nigel straightened and lashed out. The blow caught Alexandre square under the chin. He staggered back a step, allowing Nigel to dart past him. But the pain in his jaw only doubled his fury. This was how Tess had felt, this was what she had suffered.

He whirled around as Nigel started to run for the door. Catching him by the coat, he spun the other man around, prepared to tear him into pieces.

"Chilton!" the earl screamed, struggling against Alexandre's hold. "Chilton, by God, get in here!"

Alexandre shoved Nigel back, releasing him, and he did not miss the fear in the other man's face. He did not miss the furtive glance Nigel cast about the room. "There's no one to help you, Aubry. You will have to fight your own battle."

With another scream, Nigel flung himself at Alexandre, knocking both men against the desk. "I'll kill you, you French dog," he shouted, pummeling Alexandre's face and body with his fists. "I'll kill you."

Nigel was lean and wiry, but he was strong, and he was quick. Several of the blows found their mark before Alexandre managed to shove the other man away.

The earl staggered, tripping over a book that lay on the floor, but he regained his footing and began moving backward, retreating toward the door at the opposite end of the room. Alexandre followed, closing the distance between them. He cast a quick glance at the doorway.

Tess was standing there, Margaret hovering behind her. The dazed look was gone from her face, and she stood ready to try and block any attempt Nigel might make to escape. Alexandre knew that Nigel could easily overpower her, but he admired her courage. After all she'd been through, she was prepared to come to his aid.

He knew he had to get between Tess and her husband so that the other man could not use her as a shield. And if he managed to do that, Nigel would be trapped. He feinted left, and when the earl moved to seize him, he darted to the right.

Whirling around, he faced the other man, their positions reversed.

Nigel realized what he had done, and when Alexandre began moving toward him, he once again began to retreat, glancing about him for any way to escape.

Alexandre could see that the other man was beginning to panic. He could see the sweat on Nigel's brow, he could smell the fear, he could feel the desperate rage of a cornered animal.

When Nigel stopped moving backward, and halted in the center of the long room, Alexandre also paused, waiting for him to make a run for it.

But Nigel did not. He turned toward the fireplace, reaching above the mantel for one of the dueling rapiers that hung there. Seizing it, he whirled around to face Alexandre, his desperate expression changing to one of triumph.

Flourishing the sword in a mocking salute, Nigel laughed. "Well, well. Now we'll see who wins this battle, Junot." His features hardened. "I'm going to cut you to ribbons."

Nigel slashed at him with the rapier, and Alexandre jumped back, but the point of the weapon caught his shirt, slicing open the white linen. He took another step back as he heard Tess give a cry of fear behind him.

"Did you really think you could kill me, Junot?" Nigel lunged at him, and Alexandre was forced to retreat another step. "My wife knows I am very difficult to kill. She shot me with a pistol once." He must have seen Alexandre's surprised look, for he nodded. "Oh, yes, my sweet, mild little wife tried to murder me. Astonishing, isn't it? I hadn't thought she possessed the courage. She's such a mouse."

He lunged again, and there was no time to think. Alexandre kicked out with his foot, aiming for the other man's hand. The unexpected movement freed the rapier from Nigel's grasp, and it went flying out of his hand.

Alexandre followed the kick with a blow to Nigel's jaw. As the other man staggered from the impact, Alexandre turned to the fireplace. Reaching up, he grabbed the remaining sword from its place above the mantel and whirled around. A quick glance at the floor told him where the other rapier lay, and he moved toward it. Getting the toe of his boot beneath it, he kicked the sword in the other man's direction. "Pick it up, Aubry, and fight like a man."

Nigel bent to pick up the weapon that had landed at his feet. "Foolish, Junot," he said, hefting the rapier in his right hand. "Very foolish. I am the best swordsman in England." As if to prove it, he lunged, aiming for Alexandre's chest.

Alexandre parried the blow and retreated a step. They faced each other in fencing stance. Each stood tense and ready, waiting for the other to make the first move. Alexandre studied his opponent, knowing that if caught unaware, Nigel would panic. Men who panicked made mistakes.

He retained the sword in his right hand, and when Nigel began advancing, he retreated, allowing the other man to be the aggressor for the moment.

Nigel had not been merely bragging. He was very skilled with the rapier and very quick.

But Alexandre was able to parry each lunge. He knew his movements were slower right-handed and it showed. When Nigel caught him open and jabbed the sword at his flank, Alexandre wasn't able to completely parry the thrust, and the point of the sword pricked his thigh, drawing blood.

He heard Nigel's laugh of triumph. He knew the moment was right, and he made his move.

He deliberately left himself open again, and when Nigel thrust as expected, he parried and took a long step back. Before Nigel could recover, step forward, and thrust again, Alexandre switched the sword from his right hand to his left and feinted toward Nigel's thigh.

Caught off guard, Nigel automatically tried to parry the blow as if his opponent was right-handed, twisting the rapier out and down.

With a flick of his wrist, Alexandre lifted his sword over the top of his opponent's and lunged to the vulnerable area of Nigel's torso. The rapier sank into the shorter man's midsection like a knife into butter.

Alexandre pulled out the sword and recovered backward, watching as Nigel sank to his knees, emitting a gurgling sound of surprise and terror at the sight of his own crimson blood spilling from his body onto the pale blue carpet.

Nigel's astonished gaze lifted to his face. "You Frog bastard," he mumbled. "You've killed me."

Alexandre watched as Nigel fell forward to sprawl at his feet. But he thought of Nigel's brutality to Tess, and he felt no pity. Perhaps *le bon Dieu* would have mercy on him. Alexandre had none.

He stared down at the man's motionless body for a long moment. Taking a deep breath, he bent and grasped Nigel by the forearm. He felt for a pulse, but there was none. He straightened, releasing the earl's limp, lifeless wrist.

A sob from behind him caused Alexandre to turn. Tess was still standing in the doorway, as if rooted to the spot. But sometime during the fight, she must have moved, for in her hands was a pistol. She was as pale and motionless as a marble statue, but the hands that held the pistol trembled.

Alexandre threw down the rapier. "It's over, my love. He is dead."

"Nigel shot you," she said.

"He missed." Alexandre began to walk toward her. She tossed aside the pistol and took a step forward. She faltered, then took another. Then she broke into a run.

He opened his arms, and she ran into them. "I would have shot him," she choked out, "but you kept getting in the way."

He enfolded her in his arms. "Sorry to spoil your aim."

She buried her face against his shirt front. "It was true what he said. I shot him once before. I th . . . thought I'd killed him, and I p . . . panicked. I r . . . ran away."

She raised her head, the words rushing out of her. "I was so afraid they'd find me. I was afraid they'd arrest me for murder. But it was the baby. He would've hurt the b . . . baby."

"Hush," he said, tightening his arms around her. "Everything's all right now."

She pulled back, running her hands over him as if to be certain he was real. She examined his chest where Nigel's sword had sliced open his shirt. But her sigh of relief turned to a gasp of dismay as her gaze caught on the blood caking his thigh. "You're wounded. He hurt you."

The anger in her voice went straight to his heart. "I'm all right. It's only a scratch."

He reached out his hand to touch her face. He pushed back the loose tendrils of her auburn hair and ran his fingertips gently over the dark purple bruises on her face. "Are you all right, *petite*? Perhaps we should fetch a doctor."

She shook her head. "No, I don't need a doctor. I'm all right."

"He'll never hurt you again." Alexandre tenderly wiped away the tears on her cheeks.

"You came back," she whispered, still unable to quite believe it. "You came back for me."

"You should know I cannot seem to stay away from you, *petite*." Gently, he wrapped his arms around her, the safest haven he could provide, and she clung to him, resting her cheek against his chest, feeling the strong, sure beat of his heart. She still found it hard to believe that Alexandre was alive and Nigel was the one who lay lifeless on the floor, hard to believe that the nightmare was finally over. It could so easily have been the other way about. She tightened her arms around his waist, holding him to her and vowing never to let him go.

He rubbed his cheek against her hair, savoring the fierceness of her hug. He held her for a moment longer, then pulled back. He looked over her head to where Margaret stood in the doorway. "Madame," he said to her, "you must send for the local magistrate."

"What?" Tess looked up at him, dismayed. "The magistrate? Why?"

He cupped her face in his hands, and studied her features lovingly. But he told her the truth. "My darling, a man can't kill an earl and just expect to be allowed to go on his way. This fight would not be considered a duel."

"But what if they arrest you? Alexandre, I can't bear to lose you again."

"I'll tell them what happened. Perhaps they will believe me when I explain that it was self-defense."

"No." Margaret's voice rang out, and both of them turned to her. "I shall tell them." Tears stained her cheeks, but her voice was more firm and resolute than Tess had ever heard it before. "I am the daughter of a duke. They may not believe you, but they will believe *me*."

Alexandre nodded and led Tess out of the room. He pulled her back into his arms.

She looked up at him, her bruised face filled with determination. "They will let you go. They must."

"And when they do, my love, what shall we do then?" he asked, smiling down at her.

"We'll go home," she whispered. "It's blackberry time in Provence."

He smiled, remembering the last time they'd had this conversation. "And you'll make me blackberry tarts?"

"Every summer."

"And you won't put my paintbrushes away without telling me where?"

"I'll put them in the studio." She reached up, tangling her hand in his long hair. "And I'll make certain there are always plenty of ribbons for your hair."

"I was thinking of cutting it off, now that I am once again a man of the world."

She scowled at him. "Don't you dare."

He laughed and bent his head. When his lips were an inch from hers, he murmured, "I won't, my love. I promise. I'll let it grow to my ankles."

She smiled and pulled him closer. "How long will that take?"

"A long time," he murmured and kissed her. Against her lips, he added, "The rest of our lives."

Epilogue

It was harvest time in Saint-Raphael. Tess watched from the window of Alexandre's studio as workers in the distance scurried like ants amid the vineyards of Château Dumond, harvesting the grapes. Alexandre had told her that grapes didn't do well if their life was too easy. To produce great wine, grapes had to suffer. Life, she realized, was very much the same for people.

But the suffering was over now.

Margaret had been right about the aftermath of Nigel's death. The magistrate had been sent for, and once the dowager countess had explained the situation, emphasizing that Alexandre had acted in self-defense, he had been allowed to go free. He and Tess had returned to Saint-Raphael for a quick wedding before journeying to Florence for Alexandre's exhibitions there and a month-long honeymoon. But they had returned to Saint-Raphael in time for the harvest, and had arrived to find a letter from Margaret awaiting them.

In her letter, the dowager had reported that she

decided to stop hiding herself away in Northumberland and had gone to London for the Little Season. She added that the *ton* was still reeling from the shocking events at Aubry Park. But that, she had added in a wry postscript, would last only until the next shocking event came along.

The sound of childish laughter behind her caused Tess to turn away from the window, and she smiled at the sight of her daughter toddling awkwardly across the floor, away from Alexandre, who was pretending to chase her. She watched as Suzanne ducked behind the stout stone pedestal of a table, peering around it to search for her father, unaware that he had moved directly behind her.

Tess tried not to laugh and give her husband away as she watched him stealthily approach Suzanne. When he caught her, pulling her away from the table and lifting her into his arms, she shrieked, giggling and squirming as Alexandre began to tickle her.

"If you stop every few minutes to play, you two will never finish the painting," Tess told them.

"They will not be finishing it today," a voice declared from the top of the stairs. Jeanette stood there, smiling at them. "Leonie asked me to come fetch Suzanne. It's time for her nap."

Alexandre laughed, setting his daughter on the floor. He turned her in Jeanette's direction and patted her bottom to send her walking that way. But Suzanne didn't. Instead, she tugged at her father's trouser leg and pointed to the sunny corner where Augustus was curled into a ball, sound asleep. "Gus-gus, Papa. Gus-gus."

"You want Augustus to go with you?" Alexandre leaned down and took his daughter's hand in his. Together they walked across the studio, where Suzanne released her father's hand and tried to pick up the huge, full-grown cat. Augustus meowed a greeting and allowed himself to be half dragged out of his corner before he hopped to his feet and followed his young mistress to the door.

As Jeanette left with the child, taking her to the nursery, Augustus went with them. Tess watched them go, feeling as if she were the richest woman in the world.

Alexandre came to stand behind her. Wrapping his arms securely around her waist, he rubbed his cheek against her hair. "The harvest is an excellent one. The vintage should be superb."

She leaned back against her husband, and the two of them stared out of the window, watching the harvest of the grapes. She thought about how much her life had changed, how quickly the painful memories of life with Nigel had faded from her mind. Alexandre had given her a new life, a life rich in love and laughter.

She had once thought her life to be hell on earth. But now she knew that life with Nigel had only been the prelude to heaven. And heaven was now.

COMING NEXT MONTH

HIGHLAND LOVE SONG by Constance O'Banyon
From the bestselling author of *Forever My Love* comes a sweeping and mesmerizing continuation of the DeWinter legacy begun in *Song of the Nightingale*. In this story, set against the splendor of nineteenth-century Scotland, innocent Lady Arrian DeWinter is abducted by Lord Warrick Glencarin, laird of Clan Drummond—the man of her dreams and the deadly enemy of her fiancé.

MY OWN TRUE LOVE by Susan Sizemore
A captivating time-travel romance from the author of *Wings of the Storm*. When Sara Dayny received a silver ring set with a citrine stone, she had no idea that it was magical. But by some quirk of fate she was transferred to early nineteenth-century London and found a brooding and bitter man who needed her love.

ANOTHER LIFE by Doreen Owens Malek
Award-winning author Doreen Owens Malek takes a steamy look behind the scenes of daytime television in this fast-paced romantic thriller. Budding young attorney Juliet Mason is frustrated with her job and pressured by a boyfriend she doesn't want to marry. Then she gets assigned to defend handsome leading actor Tim Canfield, who may be the most wonderful man she's ever met—or the most dangerous.

SHADOWS IN THE WIND by Carolyn Lampman
The enthralling story of the Cantrell family continues in Book II of the Cheyenne Trilogy. When Stephanie awakened on Cole Cantrell's ranch, she had no idea who she was. The only clues to her identity were a mysterious note and an intricate gold wedding band. Feeling responsible for her, Cole insisted she stay with him until her memory returned. But as love blossomed between them, could they escape the shadows of the past?

DIAMOND by Sharon Sala
Book I of the Gambler's Daughters Trilogy. Diamond Houston has always dreamed of becoming a country and western singer. After her father's death, she follows her heart and her instincts to Nashville with legendary country star, Jesse Eagle. There she learns that even for a life of show biz, she must gamble with her soul.

KILEY'S STORM by Suzanne Elizabeth
Daniella "Dannie" Storm thought she had enough trouble on her hands when her father found gold in the local creek and everyone in Shady Gulch, Colorado began to fight over it. But when Marshal Jake Kiley rode into town to settle the matter, she realized that her problems had only just begun—especially her strong attraction to him.

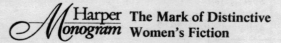 **Harper Monogram** **The Mark of Distinctive Women's Fiction**